Praise for the Dragonfire Novels

Winter Kiss

"A beautiful and emotionally gripping fourth novel, *Winter Kiss* is compelling and will keep readers riveted in their seats and breathing a happy sigh at the love shared between Delaney and Ginger. . . . Sizzling-hot love scenes and explosive emotions make *Winter Kiss* a must read!"
—Romance Junkies

"A terrific novel!" —Romance Reviews Today

"All the *Pyr* and their mates from the previous three books in this exciting series are included in this final confrontation with Magnus and his evil Dragon's Blood Elixir. It's another stellar addition to this dynamic paranormal saga with the promise of more to come."
—Fresh Fiction

Kiss of Fate

"An intense ride. Ms. Cooke has a great talent. . . . If you love paranormal romance in any way, this is a series you should be following."
—Night Owl Romance (reviewer top pick)

"Second chances are a key theme in this latest Dragonfire adventure. Cooke keeps the pace intense and the emotions raging in this powerful new read. She's top-notch, as always." —*Romantic Times*

continued . . .

Kiss of Fury

"Those sexy dragons are back in the second chapter of Cooke's exciting paranormal series. . . . The intriguing characters continue to grow and offer terrific opportunities for story expansion. Balancing a hormone-driven romance with high-stakes action can be difficult, but Cooke manages with ease. Visiting this world is a pleasure."
—*Romantic Times*

"This second book in Deborah Cooke's phenomenal Dragonfire series expertly sets the stage for the next thrilling episode."
—Fresh Fiction

"Entertaining and imaginative . . . a *must read* for paranormal fans."
—BookLoons

"Riveting . . . Deborah Cooke delivers a fiery tale of love and passion. . . . She manages to leave us with just enough new questions to have us awaiting book three with bated breath!"
—Wild on Books

"Epic battles, suspense, ecological concerns, humor, and romance are highlights that readers can expect in this tale. Excellent writing, a smart story, and exceptional characters earn this novel the RRT Perfect 10 Rating. Don't miss the very highly recommended *Kiss of Fury*."
—Romance Reviews Today

"Combustible . . . extremely fascinating. . . . Deborah Cooke has only touched the surface about these wonderful men called the *Pyr* and their battle with the evil dragons. . . . I am dying for more."
—Romance Junkies

Kiss of Fire

"Cooke, aka bestseller Claire Delacroix, dips into the paranormal realm with her sizzling new Dragonfire series. With a self-described loner as a hero, this heroine has to adjust to her new role in the supernatural and establish bonds of trust. Efficient plotting moves the story at a brisk pace and paves the way for more exciting battles to come."   —*Romantic Times*

"Wow, what an innovative and dazzling world Ms. Cooke has built with this new Dragonfire series. Her smooth and precise writing quickly draws the reader in and has you believing it could almost be real. . . . I can't wait for the next two books."   —Fresh Fiction

"Deborah Cooke has definitely made me a fan. I am now lying in wait for the second book in this extremely exciting series."   —Romance Junkies

"Paranormal fans with a soft spot for shape-shifting dragons will definitely enjoy *Kiss of Fire*, a story brimming with sexy heroes; evil villains threatening mayhem, death, and world domination; ancient prophecies; and an engaging love story. . . . An intriguing mythology and various unanswered plot threads set the stage for plenty more adventure to come in future Dragonfire stories."   —BookLoons

The Dragonfire Novels

Kiss of Fire
Kiss of Fury
Kiss of Fate
Winter Kiss

WHISPER KISS

A DRAGONFIRE NOVEL

DEBORAH COOKE

A SIGNET ECLIPSE BOOK

SIGNET ECLIPSE
Published by New American Library, a division of
Penguin Group (USA) Inc., 375 Hudson Street,
New York, New York 10014, USA
Penguin Group (Canada), 90 Eglinton Avenue East, Suite 700, Toronto,
Ontario M4P 2Y3, Canada (a division of Pearson Penguin Canada Inc.)
Penguin Books Ltd., 80 Strand, London WC2R 0RL, England
Penguin Ireland, 25 St. Stephen's Green, Dublin 2,
Ireland (a division of Penguin Books Ltd.)
Penguin Group (Australia), 250 Camberwell Road, Camberwell, Victoria 3124,
Australia (a division of Pearson Australia Group Pty. Ltd.)
Penguin Books India Pvt. Ltd., 11 Community Centre, Panchsheel Park,
New Delhi - 110 017, India
Penguin Group (NZ), 67 Apollo Drive, Rosedale, North Shore 0632,
New Zealand (a division of Pearson New Zealand Ltd.)
Penguin Books (South Africa) (Pty.) Ltd., 24 Sturdee Avenue,
Rosebank, Johannesburg 2196, South Africa

Penguin Books Ltd., Registered Offices:
80 Strand, London WC2R 0RL, England

First published by Signet Eclipse, an imprint of New American Library,
a division of Penguin Group (USA) Inc.

First Printing, August 2010
10   9   8   7   6   5   4   3   2   1

For Kon, as always

Chapter 1

New York City
June 26, 2010

Rox came home, triumphant. She'd finally found the perfect job for her roommate and current "project."

This would work.

Thorolf, who called himself T, was a big bike courier with no direction or ambition. Rox had known from the outset that T could make more of himself, but she'd had a hard time persuading him to try. Every option had been impossible in his view, but Rox hadn't given up. And now her efforts would pay off. True to form, Rox had pulled in a favor and found exactly the right job for T.

Reduce, reuse, and recycle didn't apply to just goods in Rox's world. People could be reinvented, too.

And if there was ever a man who needed reinvention, it was T. She'd never met anyone with such a lack of focus, yet so much potential. Once she'd seen what he could do, Rox had been determined to help him make the most of his innate gift.

T, unfortunately, wasn't inclined to change.

Delivering groceries for the neighborhood organic store would be a perfect step for him. The job would give him a paycheck, enable him to help with the rent, allow him to be outside—which he preferred—and keep him from partying late so that he could get to work early each day. Rox thought it was the perfect combination of responsibility and freedom.

But it would work only if Rox could persuade T to accept the job. He was the obstacle to his own success.

She unlocked her apartment door and heard T rummaging in the bedroom. It was a good sign that he was home. She dropped the bag of groceries on the counter—scored while she finalized the job offer—and strode into his bedroom, only to find T packing his few possessions.

He was still in his black Lycra tights with the khaki shorts over top of them, the mud up his back fresh from a day of being a bicycle courier. He was home early, though—and the fact that he hadn't just grabbed himself a beer from the fridge and crashed on the couch, or gone drinking with his buddies, meant something was up.

Something, Rox would bet, that she wasn't going to like.

The furtive glance T shot over his shoulder in her direction, as if he had been caught, only fed her suspicions.

"What's going on?" she asked.

T dropped his gaze and returned to his packing. If anything, he was moving faster. "I'm, uh, leaving."

Rox folded her arms across her chest. "Leaving as in taking a vacation or leaving as in moving out?"

"Door number two," he mumbled, not looking at her.

Rox feared he was going to move in with one of his friends, whom she considered to be bad influences. "You find a job or just a better offer?"

"Both."

Rox waited, but T said nothing more. He picked up greasy bike parts from the floor in the corner of the room and packed them with a reverence most people would have saved for precious gems. She waited, but he kept packing, gaining speed. She tapped her toe and he ignored her.

Rox's anger flared at his evasiveness. "You've finally found a job, after three years of my bugging you about it, and you can't even look me in the eye to tell me?"

T shuffled his feet. "I know you'll be pissed." In another time and place, Rox might have been amused that this man—who was almost two feet taller than she and weighed easily twice as much, who could use his fists like no one she'd ever known, and who could change into a dragon at will—was afraid of *her*.

As it was, her mouth went dry. What had T gotten himself into?

"It's not a real job, is it?" she guessed. "Are you involved in something illegal? Because you know that has to be the stupidest choice—"

"It's not illegal, Rox. Just weird." He faced her, but still didn't meet her eyes.

This *was* bad news.

"Tell me the truth," Rox demanded. "No matter what you've done, I'll be more mad if you lie to me." She poked him in the shoulder when he didn't immediately reply. "What's going on, T?"

"Not T," he insisted, as had become his habit recently. It was exactly the opposite argument he'd made when she'd first met him—then, he'd insisted that he had to be T.

And they said women changed their minds too much.

"Thorolf," she said deliberately, wondering what the hell had gotten into him. If he needed direction, she had one for him. "I found you a job today. That organic grocery store by the tattoo shop needs a delivery guy. You'd be outside pretty much all day, but you'd get a regular check. . . ."

His lips set stubbornly. "No. I gotta go, Rox. That's all there is to it."

"Where are you going to live?"

"That's taken care of, too."

It wasn't much of an answer, not enough of one to suit Rox, but T turned back to his packing. He began to jam T-shirts and bicycle parts into his backpack in no particular order, obviously in a rush to get away from her. It was incomprehensible that this man who had never shown a spark of initiative or determination, despite her many efforts, had finally developed some resolve.

And it meant he was saying no to her.

After three years of encouraging him, after three years of trying to make something of the mess of a man she'd met in a bar and taken into her protection, Rox was not amused.

She was worried.

"Why?" she demanded.

"There's something I gotta do. Something I gotta learn." He ran a hand over his hair. "A whole lotta stuff I gotta learn and it's not easy."

"You?" Rox was incredulous. "You've never had any ambition to learn anything, no matter how many ideas I shove under your nose. You don't even have the initiative to stock beer in the fridge."

"Well, that's gonna change." His tone was resolute. "I know this guy and he's teaching me things. . . ."

Rox felt her eyes narrow as everything began to make sense. "Guy?"

"Yeah." For perhaps the first time ever, T—*Thorolf*—showed real enthusiasm. "His name's Niall Talbot and he's a bit of a pain—snotty; you know—but he's teaching me this great stuff that I want to know. And now it's time to take the next step."

"What kind of great stuff?"

"I, uh, can't tell you." His nervousness gave Rox a pretty good idea of what was really going on. T was a lousy liar. "I need to go and live there with him, like an apprentice, and learn as much as I can."

"There?"

"He runs an ecotourism travel place, with an office down in Chinatown. I'm gonna stay with him. Erik said so."

Rox's suspicion rose with the introduction of another unfamiliar name. "Who's Erik?"

"He's, um, this other guy." Thorolf rummaged in the pockets of his shorts and came up with a business card that looked the worse for wear. "There! That's Niall." He smiled triumphantly as he handed it to Rox, then began to whistle as he plucked his spare brake parts off the radiator.

He was leaving and he was happy.

Rox found her hand shaking as she stared at the card. Either T had finally gotten a decent job, just the way she'd been bugging him to do for years, or he was lying to her and had found some big trouble.

Rox would have bet her favorite tattoo gun on option number two. She was pretty sure "Niall" was a cover story for a woman. T only showed this much energy when he thought he was going to get lucky.

What was she going to tell Gary about the delivery guy who was no longer around to take the job?

And what would happen to T?

"You found this card," she accused, "or you delivered a parcel there. You don't know this guy."

"Sure I do." He gestured vaguely with one hand. "He's, um, like me." Thorolf slanted Rox a glance that made her heart stop cold.

That admission changed everything. She had seen T shift shape in that bar fight when they had first met; she had seen him become a dragon right before her eyes.

If she hadn't been stone-cold sober, she wouldn't have believed it. If she hadn't already been crazy in love with dragons, she would have been afraid.

As it was, Rox had taken T's nature in stride.

In fact, she'd thought—very, very briefly—that he might have been her dream come to life. One morning had been all it had taken to relieve Rox of that romantic notion.

T was a mess.

He was a project, not a dream date.

Part of the reason she had taken T into her care was to give him an alibi and an endorsement. She didn't doubt there were many people who would take advantage of his odd talent, and T was ridiculously trusting.

But two dragon shape shifters in New York? With a bit more thought, Rox had more doubts. She flicked the corner of the card, not troubling to hide her skepticism. "Have you seen him do it?"

"Well, sure." T shuffled his feet. "He knows stuff, a lot of stuff."

"Like what?"

"I can't tell you."

"No." Rox didn't believe him. "This is a bad idea."

He appeared to be insulted. "Why shouldn't I learn to use my abilities?"

"It would be one thing if you did, but I know you, T." At the flash in his eyes, she corrected herself. "*Thorolf.* You're driven by three things—sex, sex, and beer, in that order. You have no aspirations, no dreams, no desire to learn anything. If you weren't such a big sweetie, I'd have given up on you ages ago."

"That's not why you stick up for me," he said, gesturing toward the living room walls.

Rox wasn't interested in talking about her motivations. She wagged the card at him. "This isn't true. You found this card. You're really moving into some woman's place, aren't you?"

T pushed a hand through his hair and looked discomfited. "Awww, don't make this harder than it is, Rox."

"Why not? I'm worried about you!" It was typical of T to think he could just saunter out of her life without giving a decent explanation, without even realizing that someone gave a crap about him and his survival.

Rox knew that the world could be a tough place, and that an ability to fight wasn't always enough.

"Okay, so maybe it's because of you." T held up a hand when she might have argued. "Maybe because you've been on my ass all these years, I recognized opportunity when I saw it." He appealed to her, apparently sincere. "I'm doing what you've always wanted me to do, Rox. I'm learning about my powers. Be happy for me."

"But . . ."

"But nothing. I gotta go, Rox. Ciao."

As Rox watched, stunned, the hulk of a man who had been the greatest make-work project of her life strode out of her apartment.

Just when she'd been within an inch of making something of him.

The door clicked behind him and she heard T leap down the stairs, as if he'd broken free of a prison.

Whistling, dammit.

Trusting in someone.

Someone other than her. She was perfectly prepared to help her projects find their wings, so to speak, and loved watching them take flight into their own futures.

But this was different.

Something was wrong.

Rox stared at the business card and felt sick with concern. She wondered whether Niall Talbot had ever even heard of Thorolf.

Rox was going to find out.

There was trouble on the wind.

It was late on a Saturday evening and Niall was walking home from the gym. He'd left Thorolf at a café; already he needed a break from spending every moment of the day with the *Pyr*'s newest recruit. The fact that Thorolf was driving Niall nuts within mere hours of Thorolf's having moved in with him wasn't a very good portent for this mentorship.

There had been a partial eclipse in the morning, one that had been mostly visible over the Pacific. Niall hadn't needed to see it to feel his body respond. If nothing else, it reminded him of his self-imposed deadline. In December 2010, the first of three total eclipses would occur. The three firestorms linked to those eclipses had to be key to the *Pyr*, and Niall was determined to ensure that the world was devoid of shadow dragons by then.

He had roughly six more months to destroy all of the shadow dragons. The Dragon's Blood Elixir that had been used to create the shadow dragons was destroyed, and Magnus, the leader of the *Slayers* who had raised dead *Pyr* and *Slayers* with the Elixir, was dead. Niall had volunteered to clean up the details.

He had expected the cleanup to be quick, but it had been an ordeal. The shadow dragons had been unpredictable.

Niall hadn't thought they had it in them. In the past, they had been robotic, mindlessly following the commands of Magnus until they were incapable of doing so. With Magnus gone, they should have attacked in unison, keeping at it until they were dismembered and their ashes scattered.

But they hadn't. Niall couldn't figure out what had changed.

Worse, Erik, the leader of the *Pyr*, had insisted that Niall and Thorolf work together. Niall had eliminated twenty shadow dragons, sometimes with Thorolf's help, including another the night before. But Thorolf was less than reliable, and Niall was sick of having to track down the other *Pyr*. He was fed up with Thorolf's being out partying when he needed him. The shadow dragons tended to appear suddenly, as if conjured from nowhere, always having the element of surprise on their side.

Niall had lost it the night before. Thorolf had arrived so late for the surprise attack that Niall had given up on him. They'd argued after the shadow dragons were destroyed, Niall insisting that Thorolf move in with him or quit. He'd known it wouldn't be easy to live with Thorolf, but he needed eyes at his back.

He needed a fighting partner he could rely on.

He needed some sleep.

And that meant he had to keep a closer eye on Thorolf, whether he liked the prospect or not.

Niall walked quickly, fighting that sense of being watched. He still couldn't get the smell of incinerated shadow dragon out of his nostrils. Maybe it was the scent and the reminder of that near loss that made him feel vulnerable. Maybe it was a lack of sleep that left him feeling stalked.

Maybe he shouldn't have left Thorolf behind.

The streets were oddly quiet, the wind making little gusts that sent the dust scuttling in the gutters. The vegetable stalls and tables of fresh fish that crowded the streets of Chinatown in the daytime had been packed up and towed away, and the evening crowds were surprisingly thin. There was a bit of litter blowing across the pavement and the neon lights seemed to be advertising to no one at all. The wind was a cold one, unseasonable, more like a September wind than one he'd expect in June.

But it was more than the cold. The wind smelled to Niall of decay and death and destruction. The wind was wrong and unsettled, unnatural. The scent of rot riding the wind made him think of *Slayers*, although he couldn't sense any in the vicinity.

Niall caught glimpses of the sky between the buildings and didn't like the way the clouds were dark on their bellies, roiling. The sky was simmering.

He supposed that even humans with their less-sharp senses of smell might find the weather unsettling. Niall found it downright disturbing. He asked the wind for tidings—politely, because its mood was unpredictable—but received no response.

At least, there was no direct response. A swirl of wind ripped down the street immediately after his question. The awning over a Thai restaurant's street-side patio snapped hard, as if it would be ripped free of its support. The metal brace creaked and groaned, and the only couple on the patio stood up with alarm. Their table flipped, and a pair of glasses shattered on the concrete as the wind snatched the tablecloth away.

The cloth sailed down the street, flipping and whipping, wrapping itself around a light standard before it tore free and disappeared. When Niall looked back at the restaurant, a busboy was sweeping up the broken shards of glass and the couple had gone inside.

The power went out; all of the street plunged into sudden darkness. It was odd to see Mott Street without the pulse of neon.

The wind stopped completely, the air turning still.

The hair on the back of Niall's neck prickled and he felt a shiver slide down his spine.

Something had arrived.

Niall began to run toward his studio loft. He didn't need the wind to deliver this omen. He had booked a lot of business this week, and even though his computer had a surge protector, even though he had backed up his files, he had a really bad feeling.

He felt targeted. Niall wasn't going to question that sense—he'd defend himself first and ask questions later.

Could the shadow dragons communicate with one another?

Were they gathering to destroy him before he finished them all off? Had they worn him down with exhaustion just to end the battle when he wasn't at his best?

It was a crummy moment to be alone, and he sent a summons to Thorolf in old-speak.

Of course, Thorolf didn't respond.

Niall ran as fast as he could, down the street and around the corner. His loft was over a store, intended originally as the owner's apartment, but long since sold off as a condo.

There were three condo units in the old redbrick building, two small studios on the second floor, immediately over the Asian furniture store on the street level, then Niall's combined living and work space on the third floor. The furniture store owner used the quieter back studio on the second floor once in a while, whereas the front unit was owned by an artist who traveled frequently. A door to the left of the shop's windows led to a staircase that accessed all three apartments.

Niall turned the corner just in time to see someone enter the door that led to the staircase. It was neither the older shop owner nor the burly artist.

There wasn't a candle or a flashlight shining from the windows of the artist's loft, a reminder that Niall's neighbor was to be in Europe until July.

The door had been locked when Niall left.

Maybe the threat he sensed was human. Maybe it was a simple case of someone intending to rip him off. A thief might know his routine, know that he usually stayed later at the gym.

Niall raced to the door. He caught it just before it closed and he slipped into the darkness of the small foyer without interrupting the door's slow, steady swing.

The lock clicked as the door closed behind him, and the darkness in the stairwell became more pronounced. He glimpsed someone climbing the shadowy

stairs and knew his keen *Pyr* senses were giving him an
advantage.

It was one he would use.

He moved silently, leaving his bag of gear across the
bottom of the stairs. If he spooked the thief, the intruder
would trip, giving Niall another advantage.

He inhaled deeply, surprised by the mingled scents of
leather, body lotion, blood, and a dark undertone.

Ink.

Then he caught the waft of perfume, a floral scent
with the richer base note of a woman's own skin.

His intruder was female.

Niall suddenly felt warm in the stillness of the entry.
He knew it was because he was out of that erratic wind,
because the building was folded protectively around
him. The building had a quiet aura about it that he liked
a lot, maybe because it was so old. He narrowed his eyes,
noting that the intruder was at the top of the stairs.

She had great legs.

Niall frowned at the golden glow between the two of
them, the one that had let him see her legs. She rounded
the corner without looking back, taking the route to
Niall's apartment.

The light disappeared.

Had he imagined it?

He followed the thief silently, his suspicion growing
even as he wiped a bead of perspiration from his lip.

Who was she?

Just as he'd suspected, she continued to the third
floor. She *was* targeting him. He heard the steps creak,
just as they always did, and was surprised at her lack of
hesitation. She moved decisively, quickly, knowing her
destination, and certain she wouldn't be interrupted or
caught.

Maybe she didn't care.

Maybe she was strung out, desperate for money or
alcohol.

Then why break into a flat on the third floor?

No. She was specifically looking for him.

Niall climbed, finding it warmer with every step he took. The heat always rose in the stairwell, wafting up from the hot water radiator just inside the exterior door, but Niall couldn't remember it ever being this hot.

Plus the furnace was turned off in June.

Niall heard her knock once on his door, then try the knob. He smiled at the expectation that anyone would leave a door unlocked in Manhattan. She jiggled the knob then more vehemently and he thought she swore.

"Liar," she muttered. "Liar, liar, liar."

Then she kicked the door. Hard.

Niall frowned, reached the top of the stairs, and eased around the last corner. She was trying to peer through the lock, her skirt rising high in the back.

She was petite, her hair dyed black with fuchsia tips and moussed into spikes. She wore a black leather biker jacket liberally embellished with studs, a black and yellow tartan skirt, biker boots, and black fishnet stockings. He could see tattoos through her stockings and noted her chain-mail gauntlets. On her left hand, on the smallest finger, a silver ring gleamed.

She was tiny, but her legs were lean and muscled—remarkably so. Niall shook his head at his own awareness of her gender, then stepped around the corner.

She was just about to give the door another kick.

"What the hell are you doing?" Niall demanded, and she jumped, pivoting to face him. The spark that leapt between the two of them shocked Niall in more ways than one.

He froze at its sudden brilliance and felt dizzy at the heat it sent rocketing through his body. He understood immediately that he was experiencing his own firestorm.

With a punk chick who was trying to rip him off? Just one look at this woman told Niall she was as unlikely a companion for him as could be imagined. She folded her arms across her chest and glared at him, seeming to share his perspective. Her eyes were lined with black, her lips painted burgundy, and her gaze filled with hostility.

"What the hell was that?" she demanded. Her voice, the low, throaty purr of a jazz singer, was her only asset.

"Who are you?" Niall said at the same time.

"Who are *you*?" She put her hands on her hips, her eyes flashing. He was surprised that she was undaunted—she couldn't have weighed a hundred pounds and he was fully pumped after his workout. "Are you some low-life jerk from the burbs who buys rental buildings and doesn't keep the wiring to code?" It was clear she had an opinion about that, and it was one Niall shared.

But then she cast a disparaging glance over him and shook her head. "You probably think people who live in the city don't deserve to have safe wiring, especially if it cuts into your profits. . . ."

Niall interrupted her. "Who are you and why are you kicking my door?"

"Your door?" She blinked. "So *you're* Niall Talbot?"

How did she know his name? "Who else would I be?"

Her sudden laugh took him completely off guard and transformed her features. She fell against the wall as she laughed. She looked young then, mischievous, and unpredictable. Sexy. Niall checked her legs again, without meaning to do so. He felt something tighten within him, something he wasn't inclined to heed.

He knew the kind of woman who was right for him, and it wasn't this troublemaker. The firestorm could be wrong; it could be misguided, but it was not going to persuade him to make a dumb mistake.

Especially not right now when he had so much else to do.

"You mean you really exist?" She shook her head in rueful amusement. That long silver earring on her left ear sparkled as she moved. Niall couldn't see a mate on her other ear. "Because that would really take it, if that big dope wasn't lying to me, after all."

Then she swore with an earthiness that made him blink.

Niall took a step closer and the firestorm's heat flared between them with unmistakable intensity. "Why wouldn't I exist?" he asked, wondering what she knew about him and his nature.

He noted the curve of her jaw, the soft line of her throat, the fairness of her skin, and he swallowed. She was pretty—prettier than he had initially realized.

As if she wanted to hide her beauty with her heavy makeup and rebellious clothing.

Niall was intrigued.

And that made him angry. The firestorm was not going to mess with his game. He had enough responsibilities, more than enough jobs to get done, without any distraction.

All the same, her perfume teased him, making him keenly aware of her femininity—even if she tried to hide it. She would have been undeniably alluring, dressed conservatively, wearing pearls, her hair flowing loose instead of being sharpened into spikes.

"I just thought T—I mean, Thorolf—was lying to me. Again." He saw her grimace, as if hurt, before her expression turned insouciant once more. It was astonishing to Niall that any woman could care enough about Thorolf to be hurt by anything he said.

That glimpse of her vulnerability, and her struggle to hide it, made Niall wonder what other secrets she had. He was surprised by how much he wanted to know.

"I guess he was telling the truth. There really is a Niall Talbot." She folded her arms across her chest and smiled at him. "Who knew?"

"Who are you and why are you here?" His tone was more challenging than he'd meant it to be, but she didn't appear to be intimidated by him. He found himself arching a brow. "A friend of Thorolf's isn't necessarily a friend of mine."

She laughed. "I hear you. He hangs with some serious losers." She lifted her chin, her gaze sliding over him, and he wondered whether she put him in that company.

"I'm Rox," she said with pride, and another piece of the puzzle slid into place for Niall. Thorolf had mentioned someone named Rox before—in another time and place, Niall might have found it amusing that he'd assumed no person named Rox actually existed. She wrinkled her nose. "Is it true that he's coming to live with you?"

"Yeah." Niall nodded, knowing he looked rueful.

She laughed again, looking so mischievous that Niall took another step closer. A spark flashed between them. It shot to the ceiling, making an arc of brilliant yellow, and cast sparks toward the carpet.

"Holy shit," she whispered as she stared at it. "You ought to do something about the wiring in this place."

"It's not the wiring," Niall said flatly, but she shook her head.

"Bullshit. This place is a firetrap, and T shouldn't be coming to live here. I'm going to tell him so. It's not right or safe. . . ."

"You'll tell him no such thing." Niall hated how much he sounded like his father, stern and unyielding. He had no right to tell Rox what she could do.

And she knew it. Her manner turned hostile again. "What do you want with him, anyway? He says you're going to mentor him, but he won't say in what." It was clear that she had a low view of this plan. She shook a finger at him. "If it's illegal—"

"It's not." Niall declined to tell her about the *Pyr*.

Rox was undaunted, striding closer to him as the firestorm lit the hall with a brilliant yellow glow. "Because, you know, if you're intending to take advantage of him, you're going to have to deal with me first. He might not be the sharpest guy, but he means well, and he trusts people too easily."

Niall shook his head at her fervent defense of Thorolf. There was something particularly bittersweet about the notion of his destined mate being smitten with Thorolf— the bane of Niall's existence—but Niall had no time to express his irritation or defend his own position.

Because the earth heaved.

The building cracked like a walnut.

And Niall shifted shape to defend the human in his company, without a second thought.

Chapter 2

Niall Talbot *was* just like Thorolf.

It was incredible. Rox had taken one glance and assumed he was precisely the kind of straight-and-narrow uptight person she hated most, and exactly the wrong person to teach Thorolf anything. It was annoying, actually, that she found him attractive. She'd been sure Thorolf had lied to her again, not about Niall's existence but about their common abilities.

But this guy, who looked as if he'd just stepped out of an L.L. Bean catalogue, had a hummer of a secret.

When the building shook to its foundations, Rox had half a beat to be afraid. An earthquake? Here and now? And she was trapped in this crappy old building? Then Niall had shifted shape, right before her eyes, becoming a massive amethyst and platinum dragon.

He was even more interesting than he had been a heartbeat before.

Oh.

Niall immediately threw himself over her, protecting her from the falling debris, and Rox was astounded.

Niall Talbot was another dragon shape shifter.

One who defended her.

No one ever protected Rox. Few people ever dared to try. And truly, only a dragon dude could have done it and lived to tell the tale. Rox was self-sufficient. Rox took care of her own.

There was more to Niall than met the eye.

It didn't hurt one bit that Rox had a major thing for dragons. She'd always been intrigued with their power and beauty, their fearlessness and loyalty. She'd always been sure they must exist.

That their flesh-and-blood reality exceeded her imagination was a bonus. Niall's change was almost enough to make Rox forget her precarious situation.

There were sirens going off and the crash of windows breaking. The building tipped and moaned. A long jagged crack opened like a zipper in the opposite wall. That crack rose to the ceiling. A gap yawned in the ceiling, becoming ever wider.

The building shuddered and the roof began to fall in chunks, destroying the ceiling overhead. Plaster and wood and shingles landed on Niall's back and shoulders. Rox saw him thrash his tail and roar, deflecting the falling debris, snarling as the building fell into rubble.

It was Rox's dream come true. She watched him and she marveled. She was awed by Niall's size and power, by the shimmering beauty of his amethyst scales so perfectly edged in platinum. As the building fell around them and Niall kept her safe, Rox's heart pounded with gratitude.

Other parts of her felt a more earthy response. The sight of Niall's chest over her, those scales glimmering as he defended her, made her melt. She ran her hands over him and felt his shudder of surprise at the same time that she felt his muscled bulk. There was a weird golden light between them that Rox couldn't entirely explain, but it made him look magnificent.

Like a lost treasure.

One she was ready to claim.

It didn't hurt that Niall looked good enough to eat in human form, if a bit stern. Thorolf had said he was snotty, but he probably had just been intent on defending his secret.

Plus every word he uttered proved he wasn't another big dope with a big heart and a lack of focus. That worked for Rox in a big way, so she hung on to him and appreciated her good luck. By the time the earthquake was over, Rox knew there was only one way to thank Niall for his decision to defend her.

She was going to kiss him.

She'd been waiting for this moment all her life, and she wasn't going to let it—or him—slip away.

Niall remembered his sense of impending doom and cursed himself for being distracted by Rox and the firestorm. This firestorm wasn't just wrong or inappropriate—it was treacherous. It had distracted him and put them both in danger. It had come at a bad time, when Niall had too much on his plate.

He had to resist it.

Only after he had shifted shape did he worry about the repercussions. He'd been pumped from his workout, shimmering on the cusp of change because of the eclipse, agitated because of his firestorm. The shift was intuitive—but possibly a big mistake. Some humans went insane when they witnessed the change, but it was too late to worry about that.

Niall had heard Rox gasp as he folded himself over top of her, but he could only hope for the best. She was small and delicate and achingly feminine in his embrace. The firestorm flared as he caught her closer, making his blood simmer and giving him other ideas.

Seductive ideas.

Untimely and unwelcome ideas.

Rox curled tightly against him, but she didn't shake and she didn't cry. He heard the quick rhythm of her breathing. She didn't scream, which he liked a lot, but she definitely hung on. Her small hands slid across his chest, launching an array of sparks across his flesh.

Niall's eyes widened with surprise that she was checking him out.

Then he began to feel aroused by her exploration. She flattened her palm and eased it over his scales, her caress coaxing his blood to a boil. She stroked his claws and his belly, traced the outline of his scales with a fingertip, left him dizzy with the firestorm's demand. He felt her catch her breath, heard the pulse of her heart, and felt his own heartbeat synchronize with hers.

This was no drill—it was his firestorm, even though it made no sense. And it was so potent that Niall nearly forgot everything except his mate.

No, he nearly forgot everything except claiming his mate.

The firestorm sizzled and raged, bathing them both in a golden light that teased their bodies to awareness, tormenting Niall with possibilities. He smelled dust and felt the ripping wind; yet he couldn't ignore the sweet scent of Rox's perfume.

Or turn his thoughts from temptation.

In a way, he was oblivious to the chaos around them even as he listened to it. It felt separate from him— irrelevant. He was more aware of Rox, sweetly pressed against him, of the cocoon of the firestorm surrounding them. He felt her breath against his skin. He felt her exploring fingertips. He heard the pounding of her heart and the rhythm of her breathing, then felt dizzy when his matched pace with hers. The firestorm was about union, and Niall had a great many seductive ideas of how the two of them could become one.

That was dangerous, but he couldn't tame his errant thoughts.

He looked down at her and his desire surged. Her burgundy-stained lips were so close, so soft and full; he was tempted to taste them, to take advantage of the opportunity to satisfy his curiosity. He knew what he should do, what he had to do, what obligations he faced, but he couldn't stop wondering how Rox would kiss.

Niall was in deep trouble because his firestorm wasn't inclined to be ignored.

The upheaval lasted less than two minutes, although it felt as if it would go on forever. When the shaking finally stopped, Niall realized Rox was trembling a little. He suspected she might try to hide her fear with bravado.

He shifted quickly. It was a bit too late to worry about her witnessing the change, but he thought it would be better to face the repercussions in human form.

Of course, that was only more distracting. Niall was angled over Rox, his fingers in her hair, the two of them lying in the corridor outside his apartment and office, the floor beneath them tilted at a new angle. Niall cupped her head and held her face against his chest, protecting her small figure from the last of the tumbling debris. He kept his weight braced on his elbows, keenly aware of her small size. He looked down at her cautiously, startled by the knowing gleam in her eyes.

"You *are* the same as him." There was no doubt in her tone. "Who would have believed there could be another one?"

Rox knew what he was.

Niall was shocked. He wasn't sure what to say, but she was watching him, waiting for his agreement. It would have been wrong to lie during his firestorm.

Niall nodded once.

Rox considered him thoughtfully. Niall wondered what she saw, other than a guy in jeans and a T-shirt, a guy anyone would overlook on the street, a guy covered in plaster and fallen wood. He wondered what she was thinking or feeling—he knew what he was feeling.

He knew he should stand up and push her out of

his embrace, but the firestorm's heat tempted him to linger.

This firestorm would get him killed.

Niall stood up abruptly, hoping to regain his sense of purpose with a bit of distance. Rox didn't let go of him. A chunk of plaster fell close at hand and he couldn't stop himself from backing her into the wall and leaning over her protectively.

Her eyes shone, as if she didn't mind.

"So, you are mentoring T, just as he said." Rox's eyes were a vivid blue, snapping with intelligence. "He didn't lie about that."

Niall shook his head. "If that's what he said, it wasn't a lie. I am supposed to be mentoring him."

Her lips quirked and her eyes sparkled. "You don't sound very enthused."

Niall tried to be diplomatic and was pretty sure his tone gave him away. "He's not an attentive student."

To Niall's dismay, he ended up sounding exactly like his father—stuffy, inflexible, judgmental. He could guess what someone like Rox would think of that.

But Rox laughed. "You can say that again. But you know, everyone deserves a second chance." Niall blinked at the change in her. She looked softer when she smiled, less cynical, more alluring.

The firestorm was messing with his clear thinking. He tried to put some distance between them and ignore the firestorm's call, but Rox twined her arms around his neck.

Niall's mouth went dry and he froze.

She met his gaze and wrinkled her nose. "Some people need a hundred second chances to get it right—I'll guess that T is one of them."

Niall had a feeling Thorolf might never get it right, but given that she was fond of the big *Pyr*, it seemed tactless to say as much.

That sounded like his father's thinking, too.

Was he doomed to repeat the errors of his father's firestorm? Niall's father had shifted shape without warning his new bride of his powers, putting a chasm in their marriage before it started. Niall had just done the same thing—despite his determination to do better.

He'd gotten lucky in that Rox hadn't been surprised, but that didn't change his having made a mistake.

The firestorm was treacherous. He tried to step away.

Rox wasn't having any of it.

"Sorry if I came across too strong," she said in that husky tone Niall found so attractive. He froze and looked down into her eyes again. "I was sure someone was taking advantage of him. He's not really good at assessing people's motives, you know." She lifted one dark brow, her eyes shining. "I thought he didn't have the balls to tell me the truth."

Niall smiled despite himself. It was conceivable that the tall *Pyr* would be terrorized by an outspoken little fireball like Rox.

"He thinks he can fight his way out of anything," Niall said, hearing his father in his own tone again.

Rox nodded ruefully. "Fighting's not always the best answer."

"Sometimes avoiding a fight is smarter."

She held his gaze and nodded again, their agreement surprising Niall a bit. "But he needs someone to watch over him."

"And that was you?" At her nod, Niall sighed. "I guess now it's me."

"So, we have something in common, despite appearances," Rox said, that enticing thread of laughter in her tone.

Niall was surprised to hear his own thought on her lips. He saw the glint of awareness in her expression and knew he should let go of Rox. There were things he should do, things he should check, but he couldn't summon the energy to do so.

The firestorm just made it hard to do anything other than hold Rox. He felt her breasts against his chest, her legs against his own, and he wanted something he knew he shouldn't be tempted to take.

"Imagine—I thought you might be a woman," Rox whispered, then laughed again. Niall felt his own lips twitch.

"Not many named Niall."

"Oh, I assumed the whole business card trick was bogus, that he'd found your card and was lying to me."

"And you came after him, even so?"

She grimaced. "Well, I finally found him a job, a job that would keep him out of trouble."

"So, you weren't happy to hear that he had other plans."

"The people I help don't usually say no to me, or to opportunity."

"I can imagine."

Their gazes locked and held, her eyes so filled with stars that Niall couldn't look away. Rox slid her hands across Niall's shoulders and curved her fingers around the muscles there, then cast him an impish smile. Her approval of what she saw was more than clear. She was so direct that Niall didn't quite know what to do.

"I'm pretty sure, though, that you *are* a guy," she whispered.

"Pretty sure?" Niall couldn't help but tease.

He was rewarded by her bright smile. "You can't be faking these biceps." She ran her hands across his chest, his shoulders, his arms again, launching an array of little sparks that made Niall catch his breath. "And the usual suspects are absent and unaccounted for."

"Excuse me?"

Rox's smile turned coy as she arched her back and pressed her breasts against Niall's chest. He glanced down into her cleavage, saw the creamy curves of her breasts, and his mouth went dry. He saw appreciation light her eyes and knew he had to put some distance between them.

Before it was too late.

But Rox caught his neck in her hands. Niall froze, uncertain of what she would do, but wanting to know. The firestorm was sending an insistent message through his body that was impossible to ignore.

"Thanks, Niall," she whispered, her eyes shining. "I would have been squished like a roach without you."

Niall had no chance to answer, because Rox kissed him. It wasn't a sweet kiss or a shy kiss—it was a kiss that knew where it was going and why.

It was going exactly where the firestorm wanted to lead.

That kiss shorted Niall's circuits. It got right to where he lived, eliminated his doubts, and undermined his hesitation. It filled his body and his mind with an urge to consummate the firestorm, with a sense of urgency and demand.

It made him *want*.

It made him need.

It made him forget the merit of duty and logic and deliberate choice. It made him appreciate the call of passion and impulse.

And one cheeky little brunette named Rox.

There was only one thing to do about that kiss—Niall kissed Rox back. He shook debris off his shoulders as he caught Rox even closer. He claimed her mouth, kissing her with a fervor that surprised him more than the firestorm had.

Rox clearly had no issues with his deepening of their kiss. She wrapped her legs around his waist and locked her fingers into his hair, meeting him more than halfway. Her response sent lightning through his body. Niall doubted he'd shake her off soon.

It surprised him that he didn't want to. He liked how direct she was, how honest she was about her desire, and that only made it harder to resist her.

Niall couldn't remember a single reason why he should resist.

The firestorm raged at incendiary levels, blazing like a forest fire and obliterating every thought except Niall's need to possess the woman in his arms. He burned and yearned, his body raged for satisfaction, and he couldn't think of a reason to delay.

Rox slid her tongue between his teeth and made a low growl of pleasure that drove him crazy. He fell against the wall, caught her buttocks in his hands, and pulled her closer. . . .

Then Thorolf cleared his throat from the top of the stairs. "Here I was thinking you might need some help. You did call."

Niall broke their kiss and glanced up as Thorolf ran a hand through his hair.

Thorolf grinned. "But my mistake, dude. It looks like you're doing just fine."

And Niall remembered his objectives and obligations just a little bit too late.

The worst thing he could do was indulge the firestorm, think of his own pleasure, and forget the pledge he'd undertaken to eliminate the shadow dragons. He had a job to do and a duty to his fellow *Pyr* to fulfill it.

Never mind his business and his clients. He had responsibilities.

One of them was a student who was simply not prepared to learn anything.

Niall found his frustration with Thorolf coming to a simmer, aided no doubt by the firestorm's heat. How could Thorolf stand there and razz him—without the distraction of a firestorm, Thorolf should have been aware of the danger to them all.

It was just more proof that Thorolf wasn't really guarding Niall's back.

As soon as Niall moved away from Rox and the firestorm's seductive glow, he could hear the instability of the damaged building. It was a threat not just to the two of them but to the survival of the human in their company.

Thorolf leaned in the doorway, completely at ease.

It was the previous night's surprise attack by the shadow dragons all over again.

Niall was too overextended to put up with laziness and indifference, with the refusal of Thorolf to use his inbred abilities. He caught a whiff of gas, knew Thorolf was completely oblivious, and realized he was finally going to lose his temper.

Right in front of his mate.

So much for the firestorm.

That kiss nearly finished Rox. It was a hot kiss, precisely the kind of kiss a woman could expect from a dragon shape shifter. It lit a torrential heat that left her shaking, set a desire burning within her unlike anything she'd ever felt before. Rox was not unfamiliar with lust or with the pleasure a body would experience, but this one kiss was a revelation.

It left her toes curled.

No, they were singed.

Smoking in her boots.

But it wasn't just a hot kiss—it was a sweet kiss, too. Tender. The kiss was tinged with that protectiveness that made Rox forget everything she knew about who she was. She could be independent and self-reliant later—for the moment, she'd be Niall's willing lover. She couldn't resist Niall's kiss, or the feel of his muscled strength beneath her hands. Knowing what he was, what he could do, just made her burn a little hotter.

Rox liked to keep life simple. When people came

across opportunity, in Rox's world, they should do something about it. Things changed. Chances came and went.
Moments had to be seized when they presented themselves. There was a reason why she had a tattoo that said
carpe diem. This spark might be well beyond the passion
of anything she'd felt before, which only made her philosophy doubly true.

Kissing Niall felt right because it *was* right.

And doing something about his appearance in her
life, about the passion between them, was even more
right.

It was, in many ways, the opportunity she'd been waiting for.

She'd locked her hands into his hair, loving the thick
waves of his blond hair and how luxurious it felt in her
fingers, and wrapped her legs around his waist. She'd
been aware that his response was perfectly in tune with
her own—he was as hard as a rock and holding her so
tightly that there was no doubt their thoughts were as
one. Rox had deepened her kiss and rolled her hips
against him, demanding everything he could give.

No matter what it might be.

She was ready for anything Niall had to share.

Of course, Thorolf had to show up right then. Rox
could have decked him.

Niall quickly put Rox down and averted his gaze.
He seemed to be embarrassed, which didn't make Rox
happy. She would never be embarrassed about a kiss that
was so passionate and potent, regardless of who saw it.

Especially Thorolf.

Thorolf grinned. "Rafferty always says there's nothing like front row seats to a firestorm."

What was a firestorm?

"Very funny," Niall said, and his voice was thrumming
with anger. "Move it—there's stuff to do."

He didn't appear to have the same agenda as Rox.

"Like what?" Thorolf asked.

"I've got to retrieve my backups, then get the hell out of here."

Niall was thinking about work after that kiss? Rox was incredulous, but he turned toward his apartment as if he'd forgotten her. Rox was jangled, her nerves singing, her skin tingling.

Checking backups would not have been the first item of interest on any to-do list she made in that moment.

In fact, she checked out Niall's butt. It was as good as she'd expected, and his jeans were nice and tight across the seat. Baggy jeans, in Rox's opinion, were for men with baggy butts.

Niall didn't have one of those. Every line of his body was taut and trim.

Yum.

Maybe he wasn't so L.L. Bean after all.

"No hurry," Thorolf said, sauntering after Niall.

"Is that right?" Niall demanded, his words low and hot. His eyes were snapping with anger and Rox wondered why.

Niall moved quickly toward his apartment door, the one she'd kicked. He was definitely ignoring her. He put his shoulder to the door and shoved, wincing at the way the door frame had angled. The door was jammed, open only an inch or two. All that could be seen inside was a cloud of swirling dust.

Niall looked upward and Rox followed his gaze, seeing the patches of sky visible through the roof. Then he slammed his shoulder into the door again.

The door creaked and yawned wider as a cell phone rang. Niall didn't wait for Thorolf's help, simply ripping at the door and then kicking it out of its frame. It fell into the apartment, rousing another cloud of dust just as the cell phone rang again.

Rox took a deep breath, certain that the air was full of testosterone. Niall strode into the wreck of what must have been his apartment as he answered his ringing cell phone.

"Talbot," he said tightly, heading straight for a filing cabinet and sorting through his keys with his other hand. He was moving quickly, with purpose, scanning the office for damage as he went. What was the hurry?

She stepped over the threshold, checking out the damaged decor. Niall's was clearly both a work space and home, and she liked the exposed brick on the one wall. The decor had been simple and clean, before it was trashed.

She liked his style—all good.

Niall turned his back on her as he talked, but she sensed he was watching her. "Hey, Brett. I don't know the extent of the damage yet. It just happened. The office is a wreck, though." Niall was shoving broken plaster off a desk, his expression as grim as his tone.

He didn't swear but was so tightly controlled that Rox guessed he was livid. At what? The damage to his apartment and office? It would have ticked her off to have her home trashed by a freak earthquake.

But Rox had a funny feeling it was more than that.

The roof groaned overhead and he cast her a look of disapproval that she had stepped over the threshold. He pointed imperiously to the door. Rox held her ground even though she saw his displeasure. Nobody pitched her out of anyplace she wanted to be.

Niall continued to talk to Brett as he checked the damage. The lights were already out and Rox heard sirens begin to wail in the distance. She'd never heard of an earthquake happening in Manhattan, but she supposed anything was possible.

At least it was over.

Niall unlocked a filing cabinet and removed a laptop with care, blowing off the dust. "I don't know about the airports," he said into the phone, jamming power sup-

plies and CDs into his bag. Why was he packing? Everything seemed stable. The building was a little smashed
up, but still standing.

And why was he in a rush?

Rox had a bad feeling.

"The juice is out here, but I don't know yet how extensive the power failure is. Can I call you back? Or
you call me?" Niall looked at his watch. "Give me an
hour."

"He takes care of his peeps," Thorolf said, his admiration clear. He brushed off one of the office chairs and
sprawled in it happily. Thorolf could never just sit on
furniture—he overwhelmed it, drooped on it, lounged on
it. His casual manner made Rox a bit less concerned.

She perched on the other chair. The pieces didn't
match, as if they'd been bought used. Rox approved of
that. "What people are those?"

"I told you—Niall runs an eco-travel business. There
are tour groups all over the world at any time."

Rox remembered that, and how she'd thought it a lie.
No wonder she hadn't paid much attention.

Thorolf nodded approval, his gaze locked on Niall. "I
think Brett is the tour leader for the group coming back
from Macchu Picchu tomorrow."

The ceiling creaked again and a chunk of wood fell
into the middle of the apartment. Rox noticed that Niall
caught the laptop against his chest with the same protectiveness he'd shown toward her earlier.

Niall frowned as he listened to Brett, zipping the bag
and slinging it over his shoulder. "Yes, if people want
me to check on their families, give me phone numbers
and e-mail addresses. Thorolf can help us get through
the list. Right. I'll get back to you when I find a place to
work. Right."

What was wrong with working here?

"Work?" Thorolf frowned. "He can't work during a
firestorm." He leaned forward and braced his elbows on

his knees, his eyes brightening. "I've got to talk some sense into him."

Rox didn't understand what he was talking about, but to her surprise, Niall had heard Thorolf's soft words. He disconnected, then glared at Thorolf.

"That's not what you've got to do," Niall said angrily.

"What do you mean? We all have to support the firestorm. . . ."

"What you need to do first is use the talents you were born with."

Thorolf looked confused. "I don't think shifting shape is going to solve anything right here and right now."

"That's not everything you can do!" Niall said, his voice rising in frustration. "If you were paying attention, you'd know it's not safe to stay here."

"Huh?" Thorolf straightened.

Niall continued to lecture, his eyes snapping. "You have keen senses, courtesy of your *Pyr* blood, but you never use them. *That's* how we almost got killed last night."

What had happened the night before? Rox got to her feet, concerned.

Niall pointed at Thorolf. "If you're not going to pay attention, then we're both dead meat. We've got to watch each other's backs, which means we both need to use our abilities."

"But . . ."

"But nothing. Now or never."

"But Erik said . . ."

"I don't care. Listen to the building!" Niall shouted, as uninterested in Thorolf's excuses as Rox usually was. His voice dropped low enough to make her shiver, and his eyes glittered a vivid blue. "Smell the extent of the damage," he urged, his words low and compelling. "It's your responsibility to defend humans like Rox, not to sit around yapping when there's danger."

Rox looked between the two of them. "What's he talking about?"

Niall pointed at Thorolf, ignoring Rox. "This is how you get surprised by shadow dragons."

What were shadow dragons?

"So, what should I do?" Thorolf was defensive, as he always was when challenged to change his ways.

"Listen," Niall hissed. He looked dangerous, a predator hungry for lunch, and she was glad he was angry with Thorolf and not with her.

All the same, she found his intense manner really sexy. It was exactly how passionate she thought a dragon should be.

Instead of passive, like Thorolf.

That explained the power of that kiss.

Thorolf narrowed his eyes and breathed deeply, focusing in an uncharacteristic way. Rox was surprised that Niall had gotten through to Thorolf.

Maybe he *was* the perfect mentor for him.

"Well?" Niall demanded, his gaze fixed on Thorolf. He was so intent that Rox felt her heartbeat accelerate. She looked between the two of them, willing Thorolf to get the point.

"Hey! There's a gas leak," Thorolf said with awe.

"You bet there is." Niall was grim. "Where?"

"In the basement." Thorolf's expression turned to one of dismay. "It's leaking fast."

"Right where the boiler is, the one with a pilot light."

"I smell the flame!" Thorolf said with pride.

Rox swore softly. Now she understood why Niall wanted them out of there. She headed quickly for the door.

"Listen to the foundation." Niall was intent, his voice a low murmur as he demanded more of Thorolf. "Push your hearing to the limit. You should be able to hear the bones of the building."

Thorolf closed his eyes, frowned, then nodded.

Rox couldn't hear anything but sirens, and they were

getting louder. "Come on," she said, plucking at Niall's sleeve. "You can mentor him later."

"There's a broken beam in the basement," Thorolf said.

"Three of them," Niall corrected, and Thorolf nodded slowly as he evidently heard them all. "It's going to fall, within the next fifteen minutes."

Niall then suddenly straightened, his eyes wide.

Rox guessed what that meant. She ran for the door.

Thorolf caught his breath. "One beam's breaking!"

Niall leapt after Rox and grabbed her hand. She gasped at the flash of light from the point of contact. "You'll never make it that way," he muttered. Before she could ask questions, Niall ran for the window that overlooked the street, tugging her behind him.

Rox stumbled, but she tried to keep up even as she hoped he had a plan. Running toward big glass windows three stories above the street wasn't part of any scheme Rox might have concocted.

Thorolf was right behind them, urging Rox forward.

Rox heard a rumble like a freight train; then the two of them jumped in the same moment. Thorolf shifted shape first and kicked out the plate glass, sending it scattering. Niall shifted shape a second later, catching Rox against his amethyst and platinum scaled chest. Her heart barely had time to skip in terror before he leapt through the broken window after Thorolf.

There was a groan behind them as the building shifted, then an explosion that sent the pair of dragons flying higher on the plumes of smoke.

Rox saw the emergency crews in the street below, the crowds held back and all of them staring upward in astonishment at the two dragons. She also saw the massive crevasse in the pavement, which seemed to open to its widest point right before the building.

The building held for an instant, then crumpled and fell like a house of cards. Plaster and wood and stone cascaded toward the earth and the emergency crews shouted at onlookers to stand back.

Rox hung on to Niall, even more appreciative of his abilities in this particular moment. She heard the steady beat of his leathery wings and felt his strength beneath her hands. The wind was in her face and her heart was pounding with relief. She also felt that strange warmth and could see sparks dancing between herself and Niall.

It couldn't be the wiring now that the building was trashed. What was going on?

Even in dragon form, Niall looked grim and uncommunicative, and she guessed he wouldn't explain things to her.

At least not by choice.

Rox, however, was used to being persistent.

The pavement rumbled far beneath them and the crack gaped even wider. Rox thought she could see straight into the heart of the earth—there were a lot of pipes beneath the street, some of which broke from the strain. Was it possible to see the subway tunnels? She heard water gushing and the hiss of what might have been gas.

Policemen shouted to the people in the street, trying to keep them from danger, and dust rose on all sides, engulfing the trio in a dark cloud. Rox closed her eyes against the debris and turned her face against Niall's chest.

They were flying over the buildings and it was every bit as wonderful as Rox had always imagined. She said a little prayer of gratitude, knowing that Niall was the reason she'd survived.

He'd protected her again, and for the moment, she didn't care whether it was due to her identity, her gender, or her species.

In fact, she had a really good idea of how to celebrate.

Chapter 3

Niall was livid.

Never mind that there had been an earthquake in Manhattan. Never mind that Niall's building had been the only one destroyed. Never mind that he felt targeted and wasn't sure by whom. Never mind that he was exhausted. Never mind that he was faced with the dangerous distraction of a firestorm at the worst possible moment, or that he seemed doomed to repeat his father's mistakes.

Rox hadn't had any problems witnessing Niall's shift to dragon form. Rox had watched the change—watched *him* change—with no ill effects. That fact was indisputable—but it challenged a basic understanding Niall had about humans in general and mates in particular.

There was a conviction among the *Pyr* that humans couldn't observe the change of man to dragon without going insane. Independent of the *Pyr*'s anecdotal data, Niall knew his own mother had been traumatized by the sight of his father's change on their wedding night. It had taken them years to reconcile. Niall had been prepared to explain the truth early to his own mate when his firestorm came, to avoid making that particular mistake of his father.

He hadn't had a chance.

And it hadn't mattered.

As they flew away from the damage, the firestorm simmering and Rox safely in his grasp, Niall suddenly understood. Rox had been able to see his change because she had already known there were *Pyr* in the world. There'd been no surprise. That was presumably because she knew Thorolf.

But that could only be the case if she had seen Thorolf shift.

Had Thorolf been so careless as to let humans routinely witness his change? The *Pyr* were charged to protect the treasures of the earth, and they counted humans among those treasures. Had Thorolf deliberately—carelessly—risked the mental health of humans?

And that of the woman who was Niall's destined mate?

Thorolf evidently hadn't bothered to beguile Rox afterward, either. That was breathtakingly irresponsible, but perfectly characteristic of Thorolf, who didn't know how to use the bulk of his skill set and didn't seem to care.

The very prospect outraged Niall, especially as it was so plausible and especially as he was a talon shard away from thrashing Thorolf, anyway.

It was time to set his apprentice straight again. Such routine disregard could risk the safety of the *Pyr*, as well as that of the humans they were pledged to protect. If Thorolf needed such basic facts explained to him, Niall was just the *Pyr* for the job.

He didn't care whether Rox overheard him or not.

Niall spun to confront Thorolf, and the larger *Pyr* nearly collided with him in midair.

"*Rox knew*," Niall accused in old-speak as he hovered with his mate in his grasp.

Thorolf immediately looked chagrined, which Niall didn't take as a good sign.

"What's going on?" Rox demanded. "It sounds like trains, but we're nowhere near the tracks."

"*How much does she know?*" Niall demanded of Thorolf. "*How much did she see? Why didn't you beguile her?*"

"*She saw,*" the big *Pyr* admitted, his old-speak slow for lack of experience.

"*How much? When? What?*" Now that Niall was letting his temper loose, he couldn't seem to stop it. This outburst was about as different from his father's total composure as possible, but Niall wasn't happy to be different from his father in this. He shouted in old-speak. "*How could you not take responsibility for what she witnessed?*"

Thorolf exhaled a puff of smoke, glanced down at the city far below them, and grimaced. "I gotta tell you this out loud," he muttered. "It's too complicated."

"What does he mean 'out loud'?" Rox asked. "What's going on?"

Niall was going to have answers himself before he provided any to Rox. "There," he said to Thorolf, pointing to an empty alleyway, one several blocks away from his destroyed home. He glared at the other *Pyr*, who was looking as cooperative as a rebellious teenager. "And don't make me wait for you."

"It's too narrow a space for landing," Thorolf complained.

"*Solve it,*" Niall retorted in old-speak, ignoring Thorolf's grumble of complaint.

It was time to see some progress.

If Thorolf wasn't going to pull his weight, Niall wasn't going to mentor him. Erik could do it, if he thought it so critical.

Niall dove toward his destination of choice, his blood boiling. He had ten thousand things to do—tour coordinators to contact, customers to reassure, databases to cross-check, shadow dragons to destroy—and the last two things he needed were a reluctant student and an inconvenient firestorm.

This clearly wasn't the right time for his firestorm—someone somewhere had messed it up. The last thing Niall needed was a son and a mate when he already had so many duties. He wanted to have a firestorm, wanted to make the most of his destined partnership, and meant to do better than his father had done.

He just couldn't do it, not in this moment. It was too dangerous to add another distraction to his list of responsibilities. Plus one look at Rox proved that they had nothing in common, that after the spark of the firestorm was extinguished, there'd be nothing left to keep them together.

Niall was not going to conceive a child and leave him without a father. His own father had made that mistake, Niall had seen the result, and he wasn't going to repeat the error.

Even if that meant sacrificing the once-in-a-lifetime opportunity of a firestorm.

Rox opened her eyes just as Niall descended into an alleyway. He landed on his feet, instantly back in human form. She respected his grace in making the descent between the buildings, the way he folded his wings and navigated to a safe landing.

He might have just jumped from a porch or fire escape, and the whole dragon bit might have been her imagination, but Rox knew better. The alley, lined with Dumpsters, was otherwise abandoned, and she guessed he had chosen it for that very reason.

She felt the power of his shoulders beneath her hands. He kept his gaze averted from her, but she eyed the firm line of his lips and remembered that kiss. There was a tingling inside her, a yearning impossible to ignore.

She had a feeling that looks were deceiving, that his conservative appearance and manner were intended to keep curious gazes averted. But Rox had seen his dragon side, what she thought was the truth of him, and she wanted to see more of that.

That kiss hadn't been with an uninterested party.

And he had been angry with Thorolf for not appreciating the risks. Rox understood that Niall had defended her again.

Even better, she liked it.

Rox would have kissed Niall again, just to confirm her suspicions about the passionate nature he was trying to hide. Besides, he'd just saved her life and she ought to thank him. It had worked out well before. She slid one hand over his shoulder and up the back of his neck, felt him shiver, and knew she wasn't the only one thinking earthy thoughts.

She had it right. He was just as fired up as she was.

Rox intended to do something about it.

But Niall set Rox on her feet and stepped away from her, putting a distance between them so determinedly that she couldn't fail to understand his meaning.

He didn't want to touch her.

Even though he was as tempted as she was.

"You can't pretend that kiss didn't happen," she said, and he glared at her.

"Watch me." He paced the width of the alley, clearly impatient with Thorolf's delay.

Rox put her hands on her hips, disliking his tone. It was so familiar to her, filled with a disapproval based purely on her appearance. "What changed?"

"Nothing," Niall said tightly. "I haven't got time for this right now." He gave her a hot glance, then turned to watch Thorolf land. His expression turned stony.

Rox's heart clenched. She knew that look. She worked hard on her appearance to ensure that she got that look. The last thing she usually wanted was a man who was truly interested in her, in unwrapping her secrets and discovering her hidden truths. Rox could do without the emotional engagement of a relationship.

Most of the time.

Except that this time, it made her angry. Rox would have thought a man who was more than he appeared to be would be accustomed to looking deeper.

Never mind that she *wanted* Niall's attention.

Thorolf landed then, sending a couple of trash cans toppling as he shifted shape. His arrival certainly lacked Niall's grace, and Niall looked momentarily pained. Thorolf flushed and straightened the trash bins while Niall averted his gaze and sighed.

"I'm trying," Thorolf protested.

"How would I be able to tell?" Niall muttered.

He glanced back at the rubble that was all that remained of the building where he had lived and worked. She followed his glance and thought it strange how Niall's building seemed to be affected the worst. It was crumpled, while the adjacent buildings were damaged much less. Across the street, there were windows broken, but there was less apparent structural damage.

Godzilla might have stepped on Niall's building but left no other footprints in the city. The biggest crack she could see in the pavement came right across the street to the pile of rubble from the building.

As if the earth had tried to eat the building whole, and had pretty much succeeded.

That was rotten luck. Maybe that was contributing to his bad mood. The way Niall frowned made her wonder if he knew more about it all, or had other suspicions.

Thorolf, in contrast to Niall, looked shaken. He eyed the growing crowd and the working emergency crews. "Should we beguile them?" he asked, showing an uncharacteristic anxiety in the way he shifted his weight from foot to foot.

Beguile?

Niall shook his head. "I think there are too many of them, and they'll rationalize that they didn't really see dragons, anyway." Thorolf was visibly relieved, at least until Niall gave him that killer look. "Besides, what do you know about beguiling?"

Thorolf turned as red as a beet.

Whatever beguiling was, it was important.

"Are you seriously telling me that you let Rox witness your shift and didn't beguile her afterward?" Niall demanded.

Rox looked between them in confusion. When had Thorolf told Niall about that? Niall could only be angry because the confession had just been made, but Rox hadn't heard it.

"I didn't know anything about it . . . ," Thorolf began, and Niall snorted with impatience.

"What's beguiling?" Rox asked, taking advantage of the gap.

"Pathetic." Niall hunkered down, pulling his laptop from his bag and cradling it on his lap. He booted it up, his attention focused on the screen. Rox again had the sense that he was angrier than he sounded, angry about more than Thorolf, but keeping his response under control.

She really would like to see him let loose.

"It's a kind of hypnosis," Thorolf explained when Niall didn't. "We can convince humans they didn't see things, or us."

Rox was outraged by the very idea. "It had better be true that you never did that to me!"

Thorolf was clearly embarrassed. "I can't do it very well, actually." His gaze flicked to Niall, whose lips had tightened into a thin line. "That's the problem."

"The problem is that you don't practice," Niall muttered. "The problem is that you never take anything seriously."

He had pretty much nailed it in one.

"Well, what was I supposed to do?" Thorolf demanded. "Rox *saw*. I was in a club and it was late, and this guy took a swing at me. Before I knew it, we were right into it and he was fighting dirty. He slammed my head into the side of the bar and it pissed me off. I shifted shape before I knew what I was doing. . . ."

"Because you had never tried to learn to control the shift," Niall said with disgust. He never looked up from his laptop.

"It's not like I knew anything about it, like I even knew it was possible."

"It's not like you bothered to find out."

"Who was I supposed to ask?"

"I found you," Niall said, his tone challenging. "I just followed my nose. You could have found me."

Thorolf halted, jabbing his finger through the air at Niall. "That's it. *That's it.* I'm sick of you judging me and deciding that I've fallen short of some measure. You're not my father and you're not my judge and jury."

Niall looked up and Rox knew he was furious. His eyes glittered and he had become very still, a strange blue shimmer illuminating the edges of his body. Thorolf took a step back, so she knew her instincts were right. "We nearly got killed last night because of you," Niall said softly.

Rox respected his restraint and appreciated that he was furious. Thorolf could be annoying like that. On the other hand, she thought Niall was getting through to Thorolf in a way she'd never managed. Niall might not realize that he was so close to making a difference. The air was thick and Rox thought the two of them might bail on each other, just a bit too soon.

So she made a teasing comment to diffuse the tension.

"Good plan," she said to Thorolf, who looked startled. "Throw back the one person who's actually trying to teach you something. That'll get you places."

Thorolf nearly snarled at her and Niall glanced at her with surprise.

Before Thorolf could argue, Rox lifted one hand. "You've finally found the mentor you need," she argued, sensing Niall's astonishment. "You've finally hooked up with someone who gets your attention, who maybe could teach you something. You could at least *listen* to him."

Thorolf pointed at Niall. "He could ease up. He could cut me some slack. He could be encouraging."

"Like I was?" Rox laughed at the idea. "That didn't work. I think chewing you out is working a whole lot better."

Thorolf had the grace to blush and avert his gaze.

Rox felt Niall studying her, and she decided not to miss this chance to find out more about dragons. "Either one of you could answer some questions for me." She smiled at Niall. "You know, make it a review for Thorolf."

Niall dropped his gaze to his laptop display.

Rox wasn't daunted—she'd ask questions whether he wanted to hear them or not. "How can you hear a beam in the basement? Or smell a gas leak from so far away?"

"We just can," Niall said flatly.

"Because the *Pyr* have keener senses than humans," Thorolf supplied.

Rox understood then how Thorolf could come back to the apartment in the middle of the night and never trip over anything.

Pyr. Dragon shape shifters called themselves *Pyr*.

"What else can you do? What's the firestorm? What are shadow dragons? How many of you are there?"

Niall shoved his hand through his hair and glared at Thorolf, ignoring Rox's questions. "This isn't a game. We're supposed to back each other up," he said, his tone more temperate. At least she had diffused the tension a bit. "You risked Rox's sanity, and you have consistently failed to be alert to help me. Humans could die. We could die. I can't watch out for both of us all the time. We need to work as a team, and that means you need to lift your game. Now."

Thorolf grimaced. "All right already. I get it."

"I don't think so." Niall frowned. "Erik assigned us to work together, to force you to learn more, but I'm not seeing much improvement."

There was mention of that Erik guy again. Who was he and why did they do what he instructed?

"Not fair," Thorolf insisted. "I'm better at breathing dragonsmoke."

"That's not much of an accomplishment in two and a half years." Niall fixed Thorolf with a look. "Now or never."

Then he dropped his gaze and the silence stretched between them. Niall's eyes narrowed as he considered the display and Rox wondered what kind of messages he'd received. She'd bet there was one that surprised him.

Then she was surprised.

"Okay, you're right," Thorolf admitted. "We nearly got nailed by shadow dragons last night and I missed it. I'm sorry."

Rox was shocked. In her experience, Thorolf never admitted to a failure on his own part. He just brushed off criticism and went out for a beer.

Niall said nothing.

"Are you going to keep mentoring him?" Rox asked Niall.

Niall spoke dispassionately. "You can only mentor someone who tries to learn. Someone who does his homework, maybe a little independent research. Thorolf's research consists of which bar pours the most generous shooters of tequila. I need more than an apology. I need a commitment."

Thorolf shuffled his feet and said nothing.

Niall shut down his computer, then shook his head. "So you've wasted years of Rox's trying to help you," he said to Thorolf. "That's a pretty lousy thing to do. And now you want to waste more of my time. I'm thinking you need to show some appreciation of those who invest their time in you."

"Hey, I do!"

Niall threw out one hand. "You can't land with accuracy, you can't beguile, you don't use old-speak effectively, and you don't pay attention. I'll bet you never paid Rox any rent money, either."

Thorolf blushed more deeply.

Niall showed the same frustration Rox had lived with for three years, and she felt a sense of common purpose with him. She hadn't even been trying to get Thorolf to do anything so difficult as Niall's list. She'd just wanted him to get a steady job.

"He's right," Rox said, and Niall glanced at her with obvious surprise. She gave Thorolf a nudge. "This is your chance to learn what you can do. I don't think you're going to find a better teacher."

"Yeah, but it's hard."

"Everything worth doing is hard," Rox said, earning another surprised look from Niall.

"You have all this inherent ability," Niall said, "yet you refuse to learn to use it."

"We sound like parents," Rox said, thinking it might make Niall smile. Instead, his expression turned more grim, his gaze focused on Thorolf.

"I just need a second chance," Thorolf said. "I'll try."

"Right." Niall was clearly unimpressed by this pledge.

Rox didn't blame him. Thorolf was quick with empty promises.

Niall heaved a sigh, indicative maybe of how annoyed he was. "All right. Maybe you can help with the calls, at least. Let's try that café on Canal."

Thorolf challenged Niall. "Are you taking Rox with you?"

"I've got other obligations," Niall said so impassively that Rox wanted to shake him.

Maybe shake his inner dragon loose.

"It's the firestorm, though," Thorolf protested. "You can't just ignore it. You can't just pretend it isn't happening."

"Watch me," Niall said, and headed for the street.

"But you have to protect Rox!" Thorolf cried.

Rox had never seen him so upset. What *was* the firestorm? No one had answered her question.

But it was clear that Niall was moving on and leaving her behind. Rox didn't need a map—he was a misguided dragon shape shifter, unwilling to take advantage of opportunity. She could understand that he was frustrated with Thorolf, but she also knew that sparks didn't fly like this every day.

She'd give Niall something to think about.

"Nobody needs to protect me," she informed the pair of *Pyr*. "I do just fine on my own, thanks just the same." Niall had turned away, but Rox wasn't done. "You know, Niall, you criticize Thorolf for ignoring the input from his senses." He paused and glanced back at her, curiosity in his expression. "But any guy who can ignore a kiss like that one is either dead or not paying attention."

Niall blinked. Thorolf snickered.

Niall straightened and gave Thorolf a quelling glance. Thorolf shut up. Rox held her ground.

"Is that right?" Niall murmured, his words low and soft.

Rox felt an electrical charge in the air when he turned his attention on her once more, one that crackled enough to make her hair frizz. She had goose pimples and her heart was pounding. She felt alive, as alive as a dancing flame, and she wanted to do something about it. There was that weird golden light between them again, the one that made her mouth go dry and her body tingle.

It gave her ideas.

She could give Niall some ideas, too. She walked toward him, feeling the heat grow with every step. His eyes brightened as he watched her, although he didn't move. If nothing else, she knew her kiss had gotten his attention.

And she was ready for another one.

After a bit of straight talk.

"It is," she retorted. "The funny thing is you don't look dead to me." She put her hand on his chest, and there was a flash of light beneath her palm.

An arousing heat shot through her body. She heard Niall catch his breath, saw his body tense, and knew he wasn't indifferent to her.

Not at all.

She liked the way sparks leapt between them, and how aroused they made her feel. She liked the sense that she was pushing him, maybe nudging him out of some comfort zone. Rox didn't have a lot of use for comfort zones.

Niall's eyes were glittering like blue ice, and he took a step back. As soon as there was distance between them, the light faded in intensity, but the simmer of desire in Rox didn't fade.

Was this the firestorm? Thorolf watched them with awe and Rox wanted to know more.

"Anyone who was paying attention could see we're completely wrong for each other," Niall said quietly.

Rox knew exactly what he meant. "Because real women wear twin sets and pearls?" she scoffed. "I think real dragons should wear studded leather and ride motorcycles, maybe play in rock and roll bands; yet I'm still willing to give you a chance."

His eyes flashed. "This is a distraction, at an inappropriate time." His words fell quickly, as if even he didn't believe them, and his tone was officious. He could have been reading a piece of corporate correspondence. "It's better if we go our separate ways. It's clear that we're not right for each other, that there's no future in this attraction."

Rox didn't believe it.

"Funny," she whispered, "I would have thought a *Pyr* with his keen senses would have looked beyond the surface."

Niall caught his breath and Rox knew she'd provoked him. His nostrils flared and his eyes flashed. He was powerful and a bit dangerous and utterly determined to defend her.

She was unafraid.

Niall leaned toward her and the light brightened. His voice dropped low. "It's more than that and you know it. Your choice of clothing isn't just about self-expression. Punkers endorse anarchy; they want to change the world and overthrow authority."

"I think the world order could use a good shake," Rox retorted. "Don't tell me you're happy with the status quo."

"I don't think rebellion will solve anything."

"I don't think complacency solves much, either," Rox replied, and Niall glared at her.

"Maybe you don't have all the facts," he said quietly. "Maybe you're jumping to conclusions."

Niall looked more like a predator in the golden light that kept getting brighter, but Rox knew he wouldn't hurt her. Niall had already protected her, and even though he was hard on Thorolf, she knew his intentions were good. He might be angry; he might be determined to walk away from her for a whole bunch of reasons, but Rox would give him something to think about.

She had a feeling, after all, that they really had a lot in common.

"I think you've got it the wrong way around," she replied. "I think you're the one making assumptions." Rox ran the flat of her hand across his chest, unafraid.

Niall was utterly still as he watched her. He didn't even seem to breathe and his words were very soft. There was that blue light around him, a light that was both unreal and made his eyes seem more vivid. "Maybe I know all I need to know about risk." There was a shimmer of sparks beneath Rox's hand, a warm glow that made her knees weaken.

And she couldn't look away from his gaze. Niall had the bluest eyes Rox had ever seen. She stared right back at him and seriously wanted to jump his bones. A muscle ticked in his throat and she knew she was getting to him.

She could do better.

She could give him something to think about.

"Maybe this will challenge your conclusions," she whispered, then reached up and touched her lips to Niall's.

A spark leapt between them, searing Rox's lips and making her blood sizzle.

But Niall inhaled sharply, then stepped back. "Let's go," he said to Thorolf, impatience in his tone. He pivoted to stride away.

"No!" Thorolf waved his hands to intervene. "You can't do this! It's the firestorm!"

But Niall had already marched into the street. Every line of his body was taut; every step was filled with a denial of what Rox offered.

He was going to think about the kiss he'd had and the one he'd just evaded, though. She would have bet her last buck that he was thinking about it already.

Some forces were impossible to deny and the attraction between the two of them was one of them.

Maybe he needed to be reminded of that.

Maybe she wasn't going to settle for having her kiss declined.

Niall was on the move, putting temptation and the firestorm behind him as quickly as possible. He was compiling lists, deciding what had to be done first, and ignoring Thorolf.

He certainly wasn't going to think about Rox. His lips tingled from that fleeting touch of her lips, and his thoughts turned predictably to the promise of satisfying the firestorm. He'd wanted that kiss with a ferocity that could only mean trouble. Rox wouldn't be shy, and that enticed him.

It wasn't as if he didn't have enough to do. He strode even faster toward the café, pushing through the crowds, not caring whether Thorolf kept up or not.

Then someone seized him by the elbow and pulled him to a halt.

Someone with small fingers and a silver ring on her pinkie.

Niall looked down at a punker chick with flashing eyes and enough eyeliner for a dozen women. Yellow light flared from the point of contact, feeding that languid pulse of desire in his veins. Rox propped her hands on her hips to glare at him, her gaze knowing.

She, apparently, wasn't content to fade into the background of his life.

"Just answer me one question," she said before Niall could speak.

It wasn't an unreasonable thing to ask, seeing that she was his destined mate, given what they'd just experienced together. He folded his arms across his chest and waited, letting the crowds stream around them.

"How did you do that? How many of you are there? Why don't you do it all the time?"

"That's three questions," Niall retorted, turned on his heel, and kept walking. He wasn't surprised to hear

Rox's boots as she hurried behind him. For a small woman, she could cover territory.

And she was persistent, too. He admired that.

"Okay, then, why don't you do it all the time?"

Niall didn't slow down, but she kept pace with him, undaunted. "Don't you think people would notice?"

"Maybe that would be a good thing. Shake up their preconceptions." Rox gestured with her hands as she strode beside him. They moved through the crowds with the same ease, and Niall dared to consider that this woman might be a good partner for him. Thorolf loped along behind them. "I mean, there has to be a point to your ability, right? Thorolf couldn't see it, but you seem to have your shit together a bit more than he does."

"Thank you," Niall said, feeling himself start to smile. "I think."

Rox didn't smile. "No, really. You can do this amazing thing. What do you plan to do about it? Or do *with* it?"

It was a good question, but not one Niall often heard. It was tempting to tell her about the *Pyr*'s mission to guard the treasures of the earth, about his own quest to eliminate the shadow dragons, but he wasn't one inclined to confide in others. He glanced her way, intrigued by her curiosity and a bit worried about it, and asked a question of his own. "Why should I tell you?"

Rox slanted him a glittering look of such intensity that Niall caught his breath. "Because declaring your intentions is the first step to getting anything done. Once you decide your goal, it's easy to plan how to achieve it."

Niall stared at her, struck by how determined she was. Had her kiss been a declaration of her intentions? His body responded predictably to the notion of Rox's having her way with him.

He was trying to think of a good reply when Rox suddenly glanced past him. "Stop!" she said, putting her hand on his arm. That spark lit and sent a glow of desire

surging through Niall, one that stopped any clear thinking in its tracks.

Her command also halted him in his tracks.

Rox stepped in front of him, hunkering down in front
of a kid sitting against the wall. Niall had noticed the
teenager, but he hadn't thought much of his presence—
there were street kids everywhere in the city. The boy
looked to be twelve or thirteen years old. Dressed in
grubby clothes, he was dirty, his hair disheveled and his
gaze wary.

"You got any place to stay?" Rox asked, as direct as
Niall was coming to realize she was. He knew he should
move on, leave her behind, but he was curious as to what
she would do.

"What's it to you?" the kid retorted. He pulled his
knees up to his chest and wrapped his arms around
them, his expression turning hostile.

"A lot," Rox said flatly. She reached into her pocket
and pulled out a business card, then handed it to the kid.
Niall would have liked to have seen her card himself.
"You change your mind about how great this corner is,
you come and see me. We need someone to sweep up in
the shop. You can sleep there, if you take a shower first."
Rox pushed to her feet as the kid read the card.

"It's a tattoo shop," he said, his surprise showing as he
looked up at her.

A tattoo shop?

"That's right. And I'm one of the owners. Roxanne
Kincaid." She pointed to the card. "Deal only stands if
you don't break the law and don't take any drugs. Other
than that, you can hang as long as you want to."

The kid's brow furrowed, and Niall knew it had been
a long time since anyone had made him such an offer.
He looked up at her, wariness mixed with hope. "Why
are you doing this?"

"Because I've been on this corner, or one a whole lot
like it, and I know it sucks."

Niall blinked in astonishment at this confession.

But Rox turned away, her defenses back in place. She continued to march in the direction she and Niall had been walking, then turned to point at the kid. "Think about it."

"Yeah. I will," the kid said, tucking the card into his pocket.

Rox carried on, content with what she had done, and her indifference to her own safety enraged Niall. He strode after her, and this time he was the one to seize her elbow. "What the hell are you doing?" he demanded.

Rox was untroubled by his tone. "What do you think I'm doing? I'm trying to make a difference."

"But you don't know anything about him!"

Rox pivoted to confront Niall, staring him down even though he was so much taller than she. If nothing else, this woman was unafraid to challenge him. "I know he's a kid. I know he's got nowhere to live. I know he's hungry and I know he's scared." She spread her hands. "What else do I need to know?" And she kept walking.

Her lack of concern for herself lit a fuse within Niall. This was his mate! And she was utterly careless about her own safety!

Niall could see, though, that she wasn't inclined to listen to dissenting perspectives. "But he could trash your shop. He could have a history of violence, or of mental illness, or any one of a number of things."

Rox laughed beneath her breath. "Let's remember that I let a dragon stay in my spare room for three years." She met Niall's gaze. "Having this kid work in the shop is a much lower risk."

"But you can't jeopardize your safety like this!" Niall argued. "It's too risky!"

"Risky?" Rox halted again, and one more time confronted Niall with her hands on her hips. Just how many of his expectations could this woman challenge in one day? "Okay, let's talk about risk. There are two options here. One is what I just did. I try to make a difference. I offer this kid an option, a way out of his situation. Maybe he takes advantage of that and maybe he doesn't. I can't make his choices for him. Maybe it works out; maybe it doesn't. I can't predict the future, either."

"Picking people up off the streets is risky," Niall said.

"Sure, but we have to choose our risks. What if I take option number two? What if I walk on by, as if I haven't even seen him? What if I don't do anything at all, except look out for number one?" She leaned closer, her expression fierce. "What if I read in the news tomorrow that this kid got beaten up, or killed, or raped? What if I realize that I had the chance to help him but didn't do anything?" Rox held Niall's gaze unswervingly. "There is risk in reaching out, but I think there's more risk in trying to live with yourself if you don't try to change the world."

Niall was astonished by this argument, by this determined little woman who was his mate. "But you could be hurt."

"And I'm not saying I haven't been"—Rox shrugged—"but I have to choose the greater good. I have to try."

"But what does your family say about this?"

Rox rolled her eyes. "There are families of choice and families of blood. I've picked which kind I like best, and that family was formed exactly like this. We give each other chances and stick together."

"But . . ."

"If I'm not afraid, then why are you?" she interrupted him to issue her challenge. "You're a *dragon*!" She leaned closer while Niall tried to think of an answer that would satisfy her. Her eyes were bright as she put her hands on his chest. Sparks fell like fireworks where her hands landed on him, and Niall's heart nearly lurched to a stop. "Which brings us back to my question. What do you do with this power of yours? What's your plan?"

"I can't tell you that."

Rox smiled. " 'Cause you don't have one," she guessed. She heaved a sigh, feigning disappointment, but her eyes were sparkling when she looked up at him again. "Too bad. I thought you were the one with promise."

While Niall sought a good answer to that, Rox reached up and touched her lips to his. When he didn't move, she deepened her kiss, sending a jolt through Niall that drove all rational thought from his mind. He reached to catch her around the waist, to pull her closer, to have more of her intoxicating touch, but Rox stepped away.

She was flushed and smiling. "On the street?" She winked and tut-tutted. "That's not very conservative, Mr. Talbot."

Once again, Niall was at a loss for words. He felt his neck heat.

Rox pushed her card into his hand. "You've got a choice. Give me a call or I'll find you. I'm not going to let an opportunity like this slip away."

Then she spun and marched in the other direction, her hips swinging beneath that plaid skirt. She cut through the crowd as if she owned the street, and Niall could only look after her in amazement.

As he tried to still the thunder of his heart.

"Some mate you got there," Thorolf said.

Niall blinked. Thorolf could say that again.

Neither Niall nor Thorolf saw the jade and gold salamander slip out of the crevasse before Niall's apartment and climb to the lip of the pavement. The cloud of dust from the falling building obscured their view of the ground, and they were both too intent on ensuring Rox's safety to look around.

Once in the alleyway, they couldn't have seen the salamander even with their sharp *Pyr* vision. They couldn't have smelled the salamander, even though it was a *Slayer* in alternate form, because this particular *Slayer* had drunk of the Dragon's Blood Elixir and could thus disguise his scent. They didn't see his astonishment, either.

Nor did they see the elderly Chinese man who darted through the crowd with surprising agility, ignoring the commands of the emergency crews, and snatched up the salamander.

That man shoved the jade and gold creature into a plaid plastic shopping bag and zipped it closed before disappearing into the crowd once more.

Chapter 4

Niall couldn't forget the sizzle of Rox's kiss.

He also couldn't forget her challenge.

He would have liked it to be easy to ignore his firestorm, to take a pass on the opportunity of a lifetime. He would have liked Rox to maybe have been afraid of what he was, to not challenge his assumptions, to not be so damn interesting.

He liked how clever she was. He liked that she wasn't afraid to speak her mind or even to provoke him. He was startled that she took so much in stride, especially when it came to the realities of his nature. He admired her conviction and her fearlessness.

He really wished she looked different than she did, even though he had to concede she was right—it was shallow to judge someone on appearances. The punk look didn't work for Niall, because of its implications.

Funny how he found Rox attractive despite that.

And he loved the husky sound of her voice. Her words haunted him, echoing in his thoughts, ensuring he couldn't put her out of his mind.

Good plan. Throw back the one person who's actually trying to teach you something. Niall had been shocked to have Rox back him up in his anger with Thorolf, especially with such a scathing comment. But then, she had been there and done that, and she knew the frustration of trying to get Thorolf to pay attention.

We sound like parents. There was a reminder of the firestorm's import that Niall hadn't needed.

I would have thought that a Pyr *with his keen senses would have seen beyond the surface.* That stung. Niall wasn't like Thorolf, but he respected her criticism. He'd judged her by appearance, but he had been intrigued as soon as she started talking.

His mother's terror of his father's *Pyr* ability would never be echoed in a relationship with Rox. She hadn't been shocked by his change or terrified of him. In fact, she seemed to like pushing him. She was confident he would never injure her, and her assurance was alluring.

What was behind Rox's surface? Why did she dress the way she did? What did the firestorm know that he didn't?

The funny thing is you don't look dead to me. Oh no, Niall wasn't dead. He was simmering and aroused, his blood hot and his breath coming quickly. His mind was filled with thoughts of sex, thoughts that hadn't needed the encouragement of Rox's kisses to distract him from the very real threats he faced. Surviving the assault on his home and office had only heightened his body's need to prove that he was alive.

And Rox was ready to volunteer. Niall, who loved being in control, was spooked by how readily she got to him.

Was it the firestorm?

Or was it Rox?

Maybe you're afraid to take a chance. Well, she'd nailed that in one. Niall knew the stakes, he knew what was at risk, and he wasn't going to bring a son into this world with so many challenges stacked against one boy.

Maybe he *was* afraid to risk more.

And maybe that was the smartest choice of all.

That didn't mean it was easy to do.

Niall eyed the sky, which was still dark and tumultuous with roiling clouds. The wind was cold, too cold for the month of June, and he had a feeling that whatever had started wasn't done.

He was still in danger.

Niall moved quickly away from the damaged area and focused on real-life details. He thought about Rox while he called his landlord and left a message for the insurance company. He replayed Rox's kisses even while he confirmed that JFK was undamaged and traffic continuing as scheduled. Niall was an expert at balancing a thousand details simultaneously, but Rox—her defiant attitude, her challenges, and her touch—tormented him throughout this round of problem solving.

He was aware of Thorolf dogging his footsteps but didn't start a conversation. He marched into the café, ordered carrot juice, and claimed a table. Thorolf, predictably, took longer because he ordered more.

Niall wasn't sure if the other *Pyr* was hungry or avoiding another confrontation. He tapped his toe until Thorolf came with his loaded tray, then shook his head. Two ham and cheese bagels, a large cinnamon roll, two bags of potato chips, and a Gatorade were not an ideal snack in Niall's world.

"Tell me what happened with Rox," he said, knowing his thoughts had betrayed him. He'd meant to ask Thorolf about his plan for the future.

But he wanted to know more about his destined mate. Niall was hungry for details, even knowing how dangerous temptation could be.

Thorolf shrugged. "She saw me shift, and there was trouble. Rox stood by me, and she insisted the others were too drunk, that there was no way I'd become a dragon right before their eyes." He took a big bite of bagel. "She's pretty persuasive when she wants to be."

Niall believed it. He could almost taste her kiss; it had been short but very persuasive. "I hope you at least won the fight."

Thorolf rolled his eyes. "Please. I kicked his ass all the way to Kentucky. That's why his buddies were so determined to discredit me. Like I *cheated* by shifting shape. If he could have done it, he would have." He eyed Niall. "I didn't know anything about beguiling. All I knew was that this tough-talking little punker chick knew the truth but lied for me."

"She wasn't drunk?"

"Rox doesn't drink. She's straight edge."

Niall glanced up. "What's that?"

"She doesn't drink, ever. No stimulants or mood-altering substances; she's all natural and organic." Thorolf shook his head at what he obviously saw as misguided behavior and finished the first bagel. "Like you."

Niall found himself fascinated by this detail. Did he and Rox have a similar code in terms of respecting their bodies?

No, Thorolf was just trying to sell him on the firestorm.

"Right," Niall said, knowing he sounded more skeptical than he was. "Then what was she doing in this club? If it was like the one where I found you, it was operating illegally and after hours."

"Well, yeah, but Rox goes out to look for business."

That didn't sound promising. Niall felt his lips tighten.

Thorolf gave him a glare. "She's a *tattoo* artist. People get ink when they're loaded, but Rox, she never takes advantage of them. She's the voice of reason in the middle of the night. And if someone does get a tattoo, Rox does it in the shop, all nice and clean, no nasty surprises or infections later."

"A tattoo *artist*?" Niall couldn't imagine that the two words belonged together. "But tattoos look dirty. . . ."

"Right! Who do you think did mine?" Thorolf stretched out his left hand, displaying the blue dragon that embellished his skin there. Niall had always been impressed by that tattoo.

He had a good look at it in the café. The dragon was in flight on the back of Thorolf's hand, majestic and powerful, his tail coiled around Thorolf's wrist and forearm. The scales were carefully delineated, and the dragon looked fierce. Thorolf had other tattoos, as well, but that one was outstanding.

Art.

Challenging his expectations and assumptions.

Just like Rox.

"She did that?"

Thorolf nodded and smiled at it, then reached for the second bagel. "You know, she's like you. She said I've got to use my powers for good. Gotta make something of myself. Gotta make a difference. Blah blah blah."

"It's not a bad idea."

Thorolf took another big bite. "She took me in, tried to clean me up. I kept partying and coming home wrecked." He nodded at his left hand. "She did this when I was still passed out one morning—she said it was a gift from her, one to remind me of what I am and what I could do. Hurt like the bejabbers, but she said the best lessons do."

That sounded familiar to Niall—and this time, he wasn't surprised to find himself and Rox making the same argument. He started to wonder whether he really should have walked away from her when he should have been thinking about his tours coming home.

Thorolf cleared his throat and looked worried. "I could have really messed her up by not beguiling her, couldn't I?"

Niall nodded grimly. His heart clenched at the risk Thorolf had unwittingly taken. He thought of his mother and recognized that some women were more resilient to the *Pyr*'s truth.

But no *Pyr* should count on that.

"Okay, time to get serious," Thorolf said, squaring his shoulders. Niall looked up in surprise. "It's more than trying harder. I gotta help you take care of Rox."

To Niall's astonishment, Thorolf put down the bagel, took a deep breath, and stared unblinkingly at Niall. He conjured a flame in the depths of his eyes, one that flickered as if it burned in the middle of the pupil.

"Good start," Niall said, wanting to encourage him.

Thorolf managed to make the beguiling flame brighter and larger, as Niall counseled him in old-speak. Niall reminded him to compose his thoughts and to focus, and to Niall's astonishment, Thorolf made rapid progress.

"That's great," Niall said, impressed.

"That's nothing. Check this out." Thorolf stood and went to the counter. Niall heard him start to chat up the serving girl and assumed he was getting more food. Niall pulled out his laptop to start through his e-mail.

When he put it on the table, he realized the big *Pyr* had left his wallet there.

Niall glanced up in time to see Thorolf return with another cinnamon roll, a triumphant smile on his face. "I told her she forgot to give it to me," he said, as delighted as a kid with a new toy. "She believed me." He took a big bite of the cinnamon roll, his eyes shining.

Uh-oh.

"Wait a minute, wait a minute," Niall chided. "Beguiling isn't supposed to be used for theft. You have to pay for that."

"Come on, I done good," Thorolf complained, giving Niall a cocky grin. "I'm learning, aren't I?"

"You're trying and that's a good start." Niall smiled

at Thorolf, then shrugged. "Maybe the hundredth second chance was the one you needed, after all."

Maybe Rox had been right.

Thorolf grinned happily and inhaled the cinnamon roll. He went back to the counter and put a couple of bucks in the tip jar, then checked out a woman at the other end of the café.

Niall shook his head.

Some things would never change.

Would he ever get Rox out of his thoughts? Niall tried to stop reliving Rox's kiss, the sparkle of intellect in her blue eyes, that impish smile that made her look clever and mischievous and completely alluring. He wasn't sure he wanted to forget Rox, and that was a big part of the problem.

He opened the e-mail message from Ginger, Delaney's mate. Niall's heart sank at the length of the revised list she'd sent him. With Erik's help, Ginger had been tracking the genealogies of the *Pyr*, trying to identify missing *Pyr* who could be recruited to fight against the *Slayers*.

The result of that spreadsheet was a list of dead *Pyr*, with asterisks beside those who might not have been exposed to all four elements within twelve hours of death. Any or all of them could have been roused by Magnus with his Dragon's Blood Elixir and made into shadow dragons.

Niall hated how long the list had become.

In a year and a half, he'd killed twenty shadow dragons; then he and Thorolf had destroyed another the night before. It was exhausting work, given that the shadow dragons fought on even once they were injured. They had to be dismembered and incinerated—Niall was starting to believe he'd never get that smell out of his nostrils.

Niall hadn't yet managed to locate the refuge of the

shadow dragons, even though he knew there had to be one. It made sense, given their staggered attacks. The wind had led him underground countless times, but he always came to dead ends. He quit the software application and shut down, discontent, only to find Thorolf watching him closely.

"What about you?" Thorolf challenged. He glanced around the nearly empty café, then leaned over the table, dropping his voice. "What about the firestorm?"

"I have other responsibilities," Niall murmured, knowing Thorolf could hear him.

"*Bullshit!*" Thorolf bellowed in old-speak, the echo of his anger in Niall's own thoughts making Niall blink.

"I have a lot of obligations," Niall said, hearing his father's inflexibility in his tone again.

That list of potential shadow dragons was long, too long. What would happen to a son he conceived, if Niall couldn't be around when that boy was growing up? He was in no way convinced that he'd survive this quest. Niall had only to look at what had happened to his own twin in their father's absence, how his brother Phelan had been persuaded to join the ranks of the *Slayers*, for an example.

He couldn't risk adding to the *Slayers*' ranks.

Thorolf jabbed his finger through the air at Niall. "Bullshit. Your primary duty is to the *Pyr*, and your main responsibility to the *Pyr* is to consummate your firestorm, no matter what you think of the options available."

"Suddenly you sound like Erik."

"What can I say? He's made an impression on me. Rafferty, too. Maybe I have learned something, but it's not something that's convenient to you." Thorolf laughed at his own stroke of brilliance, then polished off the last bite of bagel.

Niall ignored him.

Thorolf leaned closer, his eyes gleaming. "Come on. You can't judge a person on appearances. Sure, no one would imagine you and Rox together, but I saw the sparks, man. I saw the firestorm and I felt it. You can't just pretend that didn't happen."

Niall felt his lips tighten and heard his father again in his summary of reasons why he couldn't surrender to the firestorm. "We're too different. I can't just consummate the firestorm and leave."

"So get married. Whatever."

It was impressive how the big *Pyr* could work his way through a cinnamon roll so quickly. "It's not that simple."

"Come on, it's *sex*. Rox is cute. How bad can it be?"

Niall eyed his companion as he had a troubling thought. "You haven't."

Thorolf straightened and held up his hands in surrender. "Absolutely platonic, right from the get-go. Rox and me, *never*, man."

"Why not?"

Thorolf shrugged and took another bite of cinnamon roll. He gestured with the remainder. "She's not my type." But he fidgeted as he tried to lie.

"She's female," Niall felt compelled to observe. "She's your type."

"Okay, okay." Thorolf cast a glance down the café, then leaned across the table. "Rox has this whole thing about making the world a better place and using your abilities to the max. She was pretty disappointed that I just passed out in her apartment after that fight and didn't know any more dragon stuff. I might have gone for it—you know, with a little encouragement—but she shut me down the first morning."

Niall was pleased that Rox showed some discretion. "Why?"

"Well, you know, they have this joke at the shop.

They call her Sister Rox, because she never takes anyone home. She's, like, chaste." Thorolf grimaced at this
unfortunate choice.

"Maybe she's waiting for the right guy," Niall said,
respecting the choice. It was a lot like his own code.

Maybe she wasn't as cavalier about her own safety as
he'd assumed. He thought again of her assertion that she
had been there and done that, and he wondered about
her own history.

Was there a reason she dressed to keep everyone at
a distance?

That wasn't too dissimilar a policy to his own inclination to keep the world at arm's length.

"I guess. She's not someone I'd expect to be a romantic, but there you go." Thorolf dismissed the issue as he
ate.

Was there more to Rox than met the eye? That certainly hadn't been the kiss of a woman committed to
celibacy.

Had she been waiting for *him*?

"Why didn't you answer her?" Thorolf asked. "You
know, about the point of being *Pyr*."

"I can't just tell anyone who asks about us," Niall retorted. "We have to have some discretion. We have to
protect our truth."

Thorolf raised his brows. "If you can't tell your destined mate, dude, who are you going to tell?" And he
licked icing from his fingertips as Niall thought about
that.

The scary thing was that Thorolf was making sense.

Niall relived Rox's kiss at the worst possible moment,
and he knew sex with Rox wouldn't be bad at all. But the
timing was terrible, and the risks were high. He could be
distracted at the worst possible moment and put them
both in danger.

After the mistakes his father had made with his

brother, Niall was determined to do better. He wanted
to provide the best environment possible for his son.

If he ever had one.

If he didn't consummate the firestorm with Rox, he
never would have a son. He told himself it might be better that way, but he didn't believe it.

"I'm not going to be irresponsible," he argued, his
heart not really in the protest.

Thorolf was characteristically dismissive of any reservation. "Tell you what—you go to Rox. You try to work
it out. You consummate the firestorm. And if it all goes
to hell, if you two can't stand each other or you get fried,
I'll be sure your son knows everything he needs to know
to be *Pyr*."

Niall eyed the big *Pyr*, surprised by the offer. "Except
that you don't know much about being *Pyr*."

"I'm determined to learn now," Thorolf insisted. "So,
you can teach me more and I can be motivated to learn
more, and we'll both know that Rox is okay. Hey, it could
work for everybody." He wiped cinnamon and sugar
from his fingers and offered his hand over the table.

"So now you're a matchmaker."

"I'm playing for the team." Thorolf stretched his hand
out a bit farther and gave Niall a challenging look.

Niall had never seen Thorolf commit himself to anything beyond fighting and pleasure, and he was touched,
in a way, that the *Pyr*'s newest recruit was so determined
to see Niall's firestorm negotiated with success.

Still, his gut warned caution, and he was going to trust
his instincts.

"What?" Thorolf demanded, evidently seeing Niall's
doubts.

"It worries me when yours is the voice of reason,"
Niall admitted, and Thorolf laughed.

"Limited time offer, you know," Thorolf said, then
sighed with mock dismay as he opened the Gatorade.

"I just think you shouldn't mess up your firestorm. I got an exclusive going on being the only fuckup in the *Pyr*, you know."

Niall laughed despite himself. "Don't want to cut into that."

"Better," Thorolf said, and gave him a playful punch in the shoulder. "You're a whole hell of a lot better looking when you lighten up." He raised his hands. "Not that you're my type or anything."

"Great Wyvern forbid," Niall growled, and the pair of them chuckled together.

Then Niall's laughter was cut short. He caught a whiff of a chill as cold as the grave, the smell of rot and mold. As previously, it was wet, and he wondered again where the shadow dragons hid.

"What?" Thorolf demanded, proving that he was paying attention.

Niall was already on his feet, his bag slung over his shoulder, without uttering a word. Thorolf got up in a hurry, sending the cheap chair flying backward. When Niall looked back, the big *Pyr*'s eyes were round.

"*Another one!*" Thorolf declared.

That was progress—Thorolf had smelled the shadow dragon without even being told to try.

Things were looking up.

Once on the street, Niall saw the indistinct silhouette high overhead, like a deeper shadow against the evening sky. His heart clenched, then raced. If the shadow dragons kept coming to him, he might never have to find their lair. It would be nice if the battle didn't drag on forever, though. He could use some sleep—and needed to be done by December. He hated that the shadow dragons, mindless zombies that they were, were setting the schedule.

But he'd worry about that later. Niall raced into an alley and shifted shape, tearing into the sky, primed to fight.

"Bring 'em on," Thorolf muttered as he flew right behind Niall. "I'm ready for a good fight."

Now that Thorolf was committed to making a difference, Niall was pleased to have the latest recruit by his side. They reached the roof line only to discover that another shadow dragon was lying in wait for them. Niall and Thorolf roared as one, breathed dragonfire, and the fight was on.

One way or the other, Niall was going to cross these two off Ginger's list before the night was done.

It would have been nice for Rox to not be obsessed with a certain blond hunk, a tanned Adonis with muscles to spare, a guy with snapping blue eyes and the ability to turn into a dragon at will.

Never mind a dragon determined to protect her.

But she was. It wasn't supposed to work this way. She was supposed to be patient, cool, and composed while she gave him an increment of time to come to his senses.

This way, she'd be jumping his bones the next time she saw him.

As an amorous approach, that lacked some finesse, and she guessed that Niall liked finesse.

But that heat seemed to linger in Rox's body, coaxing her mind in earthy directions, filling her imagination with fantasies of doing it with Niall.

It was more than distracting.

She might have to hunt him down sooner than anticipated. Maybe tonight. The prospect made Rox catch her breath and fantasize a little more.

She had been angry with Niall for judging her by her appearance, for making assumptions about her character based on the way she looked, but as Rox thought things through, she knew she couldn't hold that against him.

That was the point, after all.

Her way of dressing was a deliberate choice to present a certain side of herself to the world. Rox had chosen the look because of its implications, because people would assume that she didn't care about convention or anything else, that she was a rebel and maybe even a troublemaker. They'd stay away from her and leave her alone. They'd know she didn't want all the conventional trappings of love, romance, marriage, and babies.

Her appearance kept others from asking questions, from being curious about her, from making demands.

It was her armor.

And it was working like a charm on Niall. For the first time in years, Rox was impatient with the results of her own choices. The look had been her protective shell for so long that it was second nature. Niall's reaction made her aware of its power. ·

Rox didn't want to keep Niall at bay, but his reaction—and the obstacle it placed between them—was her own fault.

That was the real root of her restlessness.

She checked the news and discovered that the earthquake's damage had been very localized. Her impression had been right, and she could think of a couple of good reasons why Niall could have been targeted by someone or something. It was Rox's tendency to defend those she cared about, and even though Niall wasn't (yet) in that company, she worried.

She was honest enough to admit—to herself at least—that it wasn't just because Thorolf was with him. The world could do with more dragon shape shifters, in Rox's view, not fewer of them. She liked the idea of their being in the world.

She liked the idea of what they could accomplish.

Rox had a sense that Niall was a good teacher, and maybe just stubborn enough to get through the concrete that Thorolf seemed to have for a skull. She respected that he had lost it without being verbally abusive in his frustration. She knew Thorolf could try the patience of a saint, but Niall had kept his criticisms to specific examples. It seemed to be working. It was possible that one of Rox's projects would get the direction he needed, if not from her.

Maybe that was why she was restless. The possibility niggled at her that her own life might be the one that needed some tweaking.

No one at the tattoo shop seemed to notice she was a bit out of sorts, but then, it was a place where people came in all moods. Chynna, the lead of the three partners, had taken the night off, and she was the most perceptive of them all.

Rox persuaded Neo's apprentice to take on the delivery job at the organic grocery, reasoning that it would keep him from partying too much at night. Rox's other partner, Neo, was pretty much a lost cause in that department, but he was old enough to take care of himself. Rox figured they'd argued for the last time about his leading his apprentice astray. Jimmy was responsible and he'd keep his hours with Gary.

She gave herself points for a deed well-done.

Then she thought some more about Niall's kiss.

The shop was comparatively quiet for a Saturday evening. Three of the other artists were in, Neo and Tom having scheduled appointments, and the music was blaring. If nothing else, it was a noisy and familiar routine.

Rox settled at her table to work on the sketches for more of Chynna's roses, but she wasn't entirely satisfied with them. Chynna was Rox's oldest friend, as well as the tattoo artist who had started Imagination Ink. She'd found Rox on the streets all those years ago and had taken Rox in. Chynna had taught Rox everything she knew once she'd seen Rox's drawings, and in recent years had made Rox and Neo her partners. She was outrageous and outspoken, fiercely talented and an unabashed romantic.

Chynna didn't have to open her mouth to explain any of that—her tattoos said it all.

That was the point.

Chynna had also given Rox her most important tattoo, the one she loved the best and hid from the world. It was her private emblem and a glorious piece of work, even though it was yet unfinished.

Rox knew she owed pretty much everything to Chynna, and that her life could have turned out very differently without Chynna's help. Chynna wasn't one for grateful gestures—she, in fact, had been the one to teach Rox to "pay it forward" by passing good deeds along.

But Rox had finally managed to persuade her surrogate big sister to let her even the score—Rox was giving Chynna the pair of tattooed sleeves she'd long dreamed of having. Ultimately, Chynna wanted all of her skin embellished in one integrated array of images, a choice that tattoo aficionados called a "full suit." Tattoos that wound from shoulder to wrist were called "sleeves" because they covered the skin of the arm like a garment sleeve.

The problem with this kind of work came in the person's existing tattoos. Few people chose initially to have a full suit—it was a decision they reached in time, after already having a number of tattoos. So those existing tattoos, which might be quite different from one another, had to be integrated into a cohesive whole.

At least, they did if the tattoo artist was as obsessive as Rox was about making beauty. It was the kind of design challenge that Rox usually welcomed. She was especially determined to do a great job on Chynna's sleeves, both because the tattoos were a gift and because Chynna had some fantastic work on her skin. Despite all of that, on this particular Saturday night, Rox had a hard time concentrating.

She drew dragons on her sketch pad.

Blond wrestlers, all pumped up, tight jeans on every one of them.

They possessed a remarkable similarity to one another.

Rox crumpled the sheet and chucked it, telling herself to focus.

Rox had done Chynna's left sleeve first because it had been the easier one. That sleeve wound from the back of Chynna's neck to her wrist, a dozen large full-color roses tumbling down her skin.

The roses were detailed and realistic, to the point of having dewdrops on their petals and even a few small insects lurking on the stems and leaves. Rox had had more than one customer come in for "a rose like Chynna's."

Roses were the perfect image for Chynna—pretty, lush, romantic, but thick with unexpected thorns. The dozens of insects and butterflies secreted between the flowers made Rox think of all the lives Chynna had helped along.

Chynna's right sleeve was the work in progress, and it was more challenging because of her existing tattoos. Rox had photographed and traced them all to prepare her sketch. There was no escaping these older tattoos' not being in ideal positions, but Rox hadn't yet thought of a way to blend them in.

Even the roses Rox drew on this night looked a bit too stiff, less exuberant than she'd managed on the other sleeve.

Maybe she just wasn't in the mood for romantic imagery.

She drew a dragon breathing fire over the existing tattoos traced on her sketch, incinerating them so she wouldn't have to deal with them.

She colored the dragon amethyst and platinum, recognized that her romantic impulses were leading in different directions, then crumpled the sheet and tossed it in the trash.

By then it was almost eleven, and Rox thought seriously about going home early. At Neo's request—because he was in the midst of shading a large and splendid koi fish—Rox balanced the till before leaving. They took a lot of cash payment, and the partners liked to ensure that the money stayed where it belonged. Balancing the till was a rational and reassuring task, more rational and reassuring than worrying about a man who could become a dragon and might be targeted by earthquakes.

Rational and reassuring didn't do a damn thing to stop the sizzle in Rox's veins, though. Rox licked her lips and got an unexpected taste of Niall, one that filled her body with an urgent need. She remembered the hard, muscled strength of him under her hands, and the tender power of his kiss. She could smell his subtle cologne on her own skin, and it teased at her nostrils, driving her thoughts in predictable directions. He'd smelled good, fresh from the shower, and she hadn't smelled his cologne until her face had been pressed against him.

That was the best kind, in Rox's opinion. The scent was private, then, intimate, something shared only with lovers.

She broke the pencil lead and swore softly. She should have overwhelmed Niall with kisses and been done with it. She should have dragged him home and talked about the details later.

That decided it—she'd leave early and go after him.

She worked more quickly with her decision made. When the balance was finally done, Rox carried the deposit back to the safe and set up a new cash drawer.

When she headed back to the front of the shop, she

paused to shout at Neo that she was going to leave, juggling the new drawer, then strode down the last bit of corridor. She was startled to find a man leaning on the front counter.

Waiting for her.

He was blond.

He was built.

He was wearing sunglasses, and he would have looked just in from the beach if not for his black leather jacket and scarf. He looked as buff and dangerous as a dragon shape shifter should look—Rox was awed that he had worn the jacket, just for her. He'd listened to her criticism. He even seemed to have a bit more swagger and less of that stern manner than he had earlier.

"Hey, gorgeous," he said, exuding smooth charm. "I wanted to come by and apologize."

And he smiled a killer smile.

Rox's heart went thump and her knees went weak. It had worked out just as she'd hoped. Niall had changed his mind. He had listened to her and taken her words to heart.

If that wasn't sexy, Rox didn't know what was.

The *Slayer* Chen ducked into the apothecary shop with his precious burden, liking that the ancient proprietor pretended to not even see him.

The old man was learning.

Chen strode to the back of the shop, past the dried roots and leaves and jars of preserves, then ducked through a beaded curtain. He quickly folded back a plush rug, revealing a trapdoor in the floor. He glanced over his shoulder to ensure that he was alone and was reassured that the beads were stilling again. He let his right nail shift to a dragon talon, unlocked the trapdoor with his nail, then opened the door.

The scent of damp earth, rock, and rot assailed him

from the darkness below. Chen didn't hesitate, simply lowering his plastic shopping bag with its precious cargo into the hold, then following it. He used a string to tug the rug back into place when the trapdoor was half closed over his head, then secured it from the underside.

He descended into the darkness, shifting shape at the bottom of the ladder. The roar he emitted was intended to keep the curious aboveground, and so far, the strategy was working well.

But shifting shape put Chen more in tune with the elements of the earth as well as sharpened his vision. He heard the shadow dragons struggle against their restraints far below him and smiled. He heard Magnus stir in his plastic prison and smiled a little more.

The elements of the ancient spell were coming together beautifully.

Chapter 5

Niall had to admit that he and Thorolf fought well together. Thorolf was particularly fierce on this night—Niall hoped he'd never have to fight against the big *Pyr*. He attributed the change to Thorolf's new dedication to the *Pyr*.

It was about time.

The two shadow dragons didn't have a chance. The pair targeted the two *Pyr* separately and tried to divide them, but gradually Niall and Thorolf gained the upper talon.

When the first shadow dragon lost a wing, they set on him together, slicing him apart with terrifying efficiency and incinerating the pieces before they fell to the earth. They didn't even need old-speak to anticipate each other's moves.

When only torso and head were left, Niall snatched at the shadow dragon, holding him aloft. The shadow dragon breathed a feeble stream of dragonfire.

Thorolf, meanwhile, attacked the other shadow dragon.

"*Your name!*" Niall demanded in old-speak, and tightened his grip.

"Finish what you've started," the shadow dragon snarled. *"Unless you're afraid to do so."* He lunged at Niall and snapped, his powerful jaws closing on open air.

Niall noticed a dark mark shaped like a tiger on the side of the shadow dragon's neck, like a brand. He'd never seen anything like it.

"Your name will gain you mercy," Niall insisted.

"Mercy?" the shadow dragon echoed.

"You know your state is unnatural. You know you cannot heal without the Elixir. Look at what you've become!" Niall leaned closer. *"I could drop you, leave you to suffer in this state with no chance of redemption or peace. I could torment you for hours. Or I could destroy your body now, so you can rest. The price of mercy is your name."*

The truth was that Niall had no taste for tormenting even shadow dragons, but his opponent didn't need to know that. And if he surrendered his name, it would be easier to match his identity with those lost *Pyr* on Ginger's list.

The shadow dragon's eyes flashed and he would have held back any confession on principle alone. But Niall demanded again in old-speak, forcing his question into the shadow dragon's thoughts. He pushed hard, harder than he ever had before, and saw surprise in the shadow dragon's expression.

The shadow dragon shuddered violently. *"Anson,"* he admitted with obvious reluctance. *"Son of Guthrie."*

That was all Niall waited to hear. He breathed fire as he decapitated Anson, then roasted the falling pieces to cinders. Thorolf left his fight and joined the effort, breathing fire of glorious orange and yellow. In moments, all that was left of Anson was ash, floating on the wind.

The second shadow dragon was badly battered after his fight with Thorolf. He was barely able to remain aloft and appeared exhausted. His wings were torn and there was a large gash in his side. His back leg hung from a mere tendon while his front claws appeared to be useless. When he saw what had happened to his companion, he tried to flee.

"Mine," Thorolf said. He raced in pursuit and seized the shadow dragon from behind. Thorolf made short work of him, lopping off both of his wings with savage power. Niall joined him to finish the attack, that shadow dragon struggling against his body's destruction.

"Barth!" he cried, and Niall loosed his dragonfire.

Barth pivoted in the dancing flames and Niall had a glimpse of a similar tiger mark on his neck. The fire devoured the shadow dragon, though, frying that mark to nothing in a heartbeat. Barth whimpered, then sighed as his body was destroyed. Niall and Thorolf were left, watching the swirling ash ride the wind to oblivion. Both of them were panting in satisfaction as they hovered high above the city.

"I don't smell any more of them." Thorolf said.

"Me, neither," Niall admitted, not missing the other *Pyr*'s pleasure in his perception. "I wonder where they're coming from," he mused. "I'm sick of being surprised every time."

"Do you think they can manifest in different places at will, like Magnus could?" Thorolf asked.

Niall wasn't persuaded, even though he couldn't think of another answer. "It seems to be a hard talent to master. I can't believe that Magnus managed to teach all of the shadow dragons to do it."

"Much less that he'd want to," Thorolf said with a frown. "But Rafferty destroyed the academy. They can't be going back there."

"I keep thinking they must have found another refuge."

Thorolf's skepticism was clear. "But where? It would have to be close. And why?"

"Did you see the mark on their necks?"

Thorolf nodded. "Barth had a black mark, like a brand on his scales. It looked like the outline of a tiger."

"Anson had it, too."

"Weird. Do you know what it means?"

Niall shook his head. He closed his eyes and asked the wind for tidings. As had so often been the case of late, there was no immediate response. Niall had an affinity with the element of air, but the wind was agitated and distracted, and less likely to heed his call in these days.

If nothing else, he doubted they'd be attacked again—three shadow dragons in less than a day was a new record.

Was the tiger mark a coincidence? He wished he'd looked more closely at the other shadow dragons he'd destroyed.

The wind was disinclined to confide in him on this night.

But one facet of Niall's abilities was working just fine. He didn't need Rox's business card to locate her presence, especially after a battle in which he'd been triumphant. He couldn't resist the temptation.

Knowing where Rox was and savoring the firestorm—the only one he'd ever have—wasn't the same as conceiving a son, after all. He inhaled deeply, savoring the flickering heat of the firestorm. It was like a beacon in the wilderness, directing him to the precise location of his mate.

He inhaled deeply, letting the golden shimmer slide through his body. It was like being filled with firelight, or like breathing sparks, a totally different sensation from anything he'd experienced before. It was seductive and marvelous, making him recall Rox's magical kiss, prompting him to wonder how much more potent it would be if they did consummate the firestorm. It kindled his questions and curiosity about her, tempting him.

"Are you feeling the firestorm, even from here?" Thorolf asked with amazement.

Niall didn't answer because the next time he took a deep breath, he sensed something else.

Something darker.

Something far less good than a firestorm.

It was a smell he knew well, one he'd expected to encounter again but one he wanted as far from his mate as possible.

What Niall sensed was the presence of his twin brother, Phelan.

And the shadow of their shared past.

"Another shadow dragon," Thorolf spat, flexing his muscles. "Where is he?"

"Not just any shadow dragon. It's Phelan."

"Your twin," Thorolf muttered. "Big trouble."

Phelan's presence came from the same direction as the heat of the firestorm. It wasn't a coincidence.

"Worse than that," Niall muttered. "He's with Rox."

"No!" Thorolf cried, but Niall was already on his way. He flew straight uptown, the heat of the firestorm drawing him like a trout on a line, hoping that he would get to his mate in time.

Rox's knees went wobbly and she had a hard time catching her breath. Niall was every bit as sexy as before, but she felt oddly hesitant about following her gut instincts.

He looked different somehow.

He sounded different somehow.

Her intuition was less convinced of his merit.

It wasn't like her to lose her nerve.

She dropped the till into the drawer of the cash register with an impatient gesture and shut the drawer. That gave her a moment to collect her thoughts. It also gave her the chance to hold on to the counter. "I didn't think I'd see you again," she said, keeping her tone light. "Not unless I came after you."

He leaned closer and she caught her breath at how handsome he was. It ought to be illegal for a man to look so good and be a dragon besides.

"You thought wrong." His voice was low enough to give her shivers of the very best kind.

Rox knew he was watching her, because she could feel the weight of his gaze on her, but she couldn't see his eyes because of the sunglasses. "What changed your mind?"

"As I said, I owe you an apology." He leaned across the counter and caught her hand in his. "And besides, how could I let the most gorgeous woman I've met in years just walk away?"

His words should have charmed her, but his fingers were so cold that Rox jumped.

There was something odd about him. Niall looked shadowy and a bit indistinct around the edges, like a tattoo with a smudged outline. Or one with a faded perimeter. Really old tattoos often got that look, especially if they'd been done in a hurry or with primitive tools.

But Niall hadn't looked indistinct earlier. Rox would have noticed. In addition, his skin was icy and his voice made her shudder.

At least there were no sparks. She wondered whether she'd imagined that.

"I'm really sorry about earlier," he said, his voice dropping into a lower zone of sexy. At least it should have been. Something about him made Rox want to run. "I was just surprised, both by you and the earthquake."

Rox could understand that. She'd been surprised, too, and pleased that he'd been so determined to protect her. He *had* had a lot to worry about. A few of her reservations dissolved. "Are all of your people okay?"

"Yes." He nodded, sliding his thumb across the back of her hand in a slow caress. If his skin hadn't been so cold, it would have been an enticing gesture—as it was, she had to fight her urge to pull her hand away. "And that's a huge relief. I was pretty worried about that trip coming back tonight. Imagine coming home to disaster."

"But none of them are?"

He shook his head. "No. It seems like most of the damage was in Chinatown, and there were no clients from that part of town."

Rox smiled a little, knowing that the kind of person who worried about his clients would have been relieved by that. She appreciated that he'd come to apologize to her, too, and admitted that having your home demolished by an earthquake might affect anyone's mood. She tried to make conversation, even though she couldn't ignore the iciness of his touch.

He'd been warm when she'd kissed him.

Very warm.

Did dragon shape shifters have big swings in their body temperature? She hadn't touched Thorolf enough to know. Despite her uncertainties, she recognized that Niall had come to apologize and felt the need to meet him halfway. "It was nice of you to offer to check on friends and family for them."

His smile flashed again. "Just the kind of guy I am. Responsible. Thoughtful. Reliable." He leaned closer and Rox tried to keep from bolting. What was wrong with her? "When do you finish work? We could go somewhere and really talk."

Talking was one thing. Leaving with him was another.

Rox pulled her hand away and stepped back, cautious. This afternoon, she hadn't been able to get close enough to Niall Talbot, and now that he'd come to apologize to her, she didn't want to be near him. She didn't want to tell him that she'd been about to leave the shop for the night.

What had changed? Niall hadn't had sunglasses on earlier, in the daytime when there had been at least some prospect of sunshine. Why wear them at night?

And although she appreciated that he'd put on a leather jacket in response to her suggestion, it was pretty warm outside.

But then, his skin was frigid. He tugged off the scarf and started to play with it, sliding it through his hands. There was something both hypnotic and menacing about the movement, an impression that was amplified when she realized he was watching her intently.

Smiling just a little.

As if she'd make a good midnight snack.

He was giving her the creeps, something Rox wouldn't have believed possible just hours before. Niall's behavior and attitude was about as different as possible from this afternoon.

"Where's Thorolf?" she asked, hearing suspicion in her tone.

He straightened and his smile broadened. Was his smile calculating? Condescending? She wished again that he'd take off those sunglasses so she could see his eyes. "I thought three would be a crowd, but if you want me to find him, I will." His smile broadened, giving him a predatory air. Rox's heart skipped. "Whatever works for you, babe."

Babe? No one had ever called Rox "babe," and she would have bet her last buck that Niall wouldn't have been the first.

What had changed? Did he have some kind of split personality problem? Either way, Rox was going to listen to her gut.

She wasn't going anywhere with him.

"Too bad I've got to work late," she lied, forcing a smile. "Thanks for the apology. Give my best to Thorolf. I hope the mentoring goes well." She turned to go into the back of the shop again, wanting only to put distance between them. Neo's apprentice could watch the till.

"Oh no," Niall said softly from behind her, the threat

in his tone making her shiver again. "You're coming with me."

Rox pivoted to glare at him. "No, I'm not."

He laughed, and it wasn't a friendly laugh. Then his body shimmered blue around the edges in a disconcerting way. Rox didn't wait to see what happened—she turned and ran toward the back of the shop while she could.

She managed only two steps before his arm locked around her waist. His grip was tight and his arm as hard as a rock. He jammed that scarf in her mouth so her scream was muffled, moving so quickly that she knew he'd planned it that way. The threat she'd sensed had been real. He was strong, stronger than she'd imagined, and even though Rox fought hard, her efforts made no difference.

She wasn't nearly as certain that he wouldn't hurt her. That terrified her.

Rox could hear Neo, so close at hand, but Neo didn't miss a word in singing along with the loud music. Besides, she'd told him she was leaving. With the speakers blaring and the other artists chatting or working in the back, no one had a clue what was happening to Rox. Rox panicked as she realized she was on her own.

She fought harder, guessing she was fighting for her life.

It made no difference. Niall lifted her off her feet effortlessly and tossed her over his shoulder. He turned and ran, Rox struggling with all her might. He shifted shape as soon as he was over the threshold of the shop. He was airborne in two steps, soaring toward the sky, Rox captive in his grasp.

To her astonishment, the few people outside the shop didn't seem to even notice him.

Maybe they were hammered, like the people who had seen Thorolf shift shape in that bar, three years before.

Maybe it didn't matter. They weren't going to help her, anyway.

Niall's scales were different from earlier in the afternoon, too. Instead of shining with inner light, looking like faceted gems, they were clouded and dim. The platinum edges didn't gleam and sparkle—they looked more like tarnished silver. He looked more like a dead fish than a piece of jewelry.

And there was a smell about him, a rotten, dead smell, one that made Rox gag. She spit out the scarf and it fell toward the pavement. As she stared at it, shocked that he had flown so high so fast, she saw his sunglasses tumbling toward the pavement, as well.

She looked into his face and her heart stopped cold. His blue eyes had become black, soulless pits. She couldn't even see the difference between the pupil and the iris—they were all black. He saw her surprise and laughed, revealing an impressive array of sharp and yellowed teeth. There was a mark of a tiger on the side of his throat, one that hadn't been there earlier.

He wasn't Niall, after all.

At that realization, Rox screamed.

Niall bolted toward the heat of the firestorm, drawn to the heart of the blaze and following his instincts. He landed on St. Mark's Place and shifted shape, seeking Rox and knowing she was close. There were crowds of people filling the sidewalks, but Niall shoved his way through them, ignoring their protests of his rudeness.

He had to get to Rox before Phelan did.

He should have gone to her sooner.

In fact, he should never have left her.

He'd forgotten the obligation of the firestorm. He owed it to Rox to protect her, to defend her against *Slayers* and shadow dragons. He'd been so caught up in his own responsibilities that he'd overlooked the possibility of Rox's becoming prey.

It was his past, occurring all over again.

Niall hoped that this time he had the chance to fix his mistake.

He heard Thorolf shouting behind him, but he left that *Pyr* to work out his own details. He heard a scream and saw a shadowy dragon fly high over the buildings, a woman in his grasp.

Phelan.

Niall leapt into the air, shifting shape on the spot. A group of people gasped and parted, staring at him in shock. Niall didn't look back. If Thorolf wanted some practice with his beguiling skills, he could get it right there and then.

Niall had other things to do. He headed straight for Phelan, slicing through the air like a well-honed knife. Niall had only been so enraged once before in his life, and anger gave him power. He was on Phelan in a heart-beat, snatching at his twin brother's back with his talons extended. His claw dug deep, but there was no blood from the wound.

Rox looked terrified; then her eyes widened as she looked between the two brothers.

"About time you turned up," Phelan said smoothly, pivoting to evade Niall's assault. His tone made Niall wary. "I only just managed to save your mate from Jorge and the *Slayers*." He flew a short distance, eying the cut on his hip with disgust. "That's some thanks for watching your back."

Niall hesitated for a critical moment. Was Phelan truly on his side? There had been times when they had defended each other's backs, so to speak, times when Phelan had lied for him when they were children.

But that had been before Phelan had chosen the darkness.

"Liar!" Rox shouted, and aimed a kick at Phelan's gut. "He grabbed me when I wouldn't go with him. He pretended he was you."

"What was I supposed to do?" Phelan cried. "The city is full of shadow dragons, and you get a firestorm in the middle of it all. Why can't you believe that I'd defend your mate? Even if I had to deceive her to take her into my custody, we're working together, Niall." Phelan smiled. "Like old times."

"What a crock," Rox said. "You weren't going to protect me."

"Quiet!" Phelan bared his teeth at Rox.

To her credit, she didn't flinch.

In fact, she spat at him, her defiance filling Niall with pride. Phelan sputtered in shock and Niall seized the moment. He snarled at Rox, showing no protective tendencies at all, and Niall didn't hesitate to defend his mate. He struck Phelan across the face with his tail. Phelan had never fought fair, and Niall wasn't going to fall for his ploys again.

Not when the stakes were so high.

Phelan cried out and fell backward, pretending to be more injured than he had to be. Then he pivoted and raged at Niall, talons extended. He had no fire to breathe, another reminder of his decayed state. Niall breathed fire, even knowing it wouldn't stop his opponent. It was instinctive, as was his directing the dragonfire away from Rox.

The dragonfire startled Phelan, though, and singed his scales on one side. That seemed to enrage him. "There's the thanks I get," Phelan snarled. "I thought we could share. I thought you might show some graciousness to your only brother, to your twin."

"You turned *Slayer*," Niall retorted. "You chose the darkness."

"I had no real choice." Phelan looked regretful and Niall hesitated. "At least that was what I thought." He stretched out a talon. "Only you can help me, Niall." His voice fell low and Niall was torn. "Help me. Help me come back to the light."

"Liar!" Rox said, and kicked Phelan in the gut.

"Ungrateful bitch." Phelan's eyes flashed and he flung Rox high into the air. Rox screamed and flailed as she fell. Niall made to dive after her. Phelan snatched at Niall's claws, catching him close in the traditional fighting pose.

Niall watched Rox fall and struggled against his brother's grasp on his claws. Niall's heart leapt with fear as he realized how strong Phelan was.

"Once, we were the best of friends," Phelan murmured, and Niall knew it was true. "Once, we looked out for each other. Once, we shared everything." His eyes lit. "Share your mate with me."

"No!"

"Why should you be the only one to have a mate? Why shouldn't we share?" Phelan murmured. Niall saw that his brother had that same strange tiger mark on his neck. What did it mean? "Don't be so selfish. I shared the horse Mother gave to me."

It was true. There had been good times and shared amusements. Could Phelan be healed? Did he really want to be?

Aware that Rox was falling fast, Niall surprised Phelan as he pulled his brother into a tighter embrace, then tore at his twin's tail with his back claws. The threat to his mate awakened something fierce and primal within him. Phelan didn't let go. Niall ripped his twin's cold flesh, intent upon escape.

He had to save Rox.

Phelan bit into Niall's shoulder with savage force. The seconds ticked past with terrifying speed as the two battled, rolling end over end. Phelan didn't bleed, even though his tail was shredded. He didn't even seem to notice the injury, his own teeth digging deeply into Niall's shoulder.

Niall thrashed hard against Phelan's grip, thumping Phelan with his tail and breathing fire. He could feel

Rox's anxiety, courtesy of the firestorm. He could feel her racing pulse and his own breath came in terrified gasps, echoing her own. The awareness of her fear fed his own urgency, giving him the power to hit harder.

He tore one of Phelan's claws loose and spit it aside. Phelan fell back in dismay, losing the rhythm of flight for a precious moment. "Why are you hurting me?" he wailed. "Aren't we two halves of a whole?"

And they were. Identical twins. They had been partners and friends, comrades and confidants.

Niall saw the long scar across his brother's belly and recalled a horrible night, one that still fueled his nightmares. The wound had healed white, but puckered unevenly, probably mended by the Dragon's Blood Elixir that had roused Phelan from the grave. By then, he'd been dead more than a century, and the cut flesh, the wound that had been his death knell, would have been rotten and uneven.

There was a lightning flash of opportunity, a chance to rip Phelan wide-open and finish what his father had started, but Niall couldn't do it.

Was there truth in Phelan's words? Had his brother made a mistake in choosing the darkness? Could he be healed, as Delaney had been? Niall was keenly aware of their father's failures in raising his twin sons. He heard Rox's assertion that some people needed a hundred second chances.

His father had allowed for no such reconsideration.

Niall had to make the right choice.

Niall swore, flung his twin aside, and dove after Rox.

He caught her when she was a dozen feet from the roof of a building. He felt her shudder of relief, just as the firestorm flared between them; then he soared upward with her safely in his grasp.

"About time," she muttered.

"You're welcome," Niall replied tightly.

"The sparks *are* real," Rox breathed as she eyed the firestorm's sizzling flames.

Niall had no time to explain it. The heat of the firestorm seared his skin and surged through his body, giving him new determination to win. Phelan was headed straight for them, every beat of his wings filled with purpose.

"There *are* two of you," Rox whispered.

"My twin brother, Phelan," he said, calculating Phelan's course. "I'll explain it once we get out of this," he said, passing her to his back talon as Phelan raged closer. "Just hang on." At least his brother couldn't breathe dragonfire. It would be harder for him to injure Rox that way.

Especially as he seemed determined that neither of them enjoy a firestorm alone.

"Deal," Rox said grimly, and gripped his claw tightly. "I'd appreciate not being dropped again."

"I'll do my best."

Niall tried to make a choice without enough information. He thought of his *Pyr* friend Delaney, forced to consume the Elixir but healed of its effects. Could Phelan be healed? Was there any chance of recovering the brother he had known?

Niall had to be sure. He'd have to ask Sloane, the Apothecary of the *Pyr*. He had to give Phelan the chance their father had never given him.

Just in case.

But first, Niall had to save Rox.

Without killing Phelan.

This would be a challenge.

The fight didn't proceed as Rox would have expected.

Niall flew away from his twin, deliberately slowing his speed to let his attacker draw near. He flew with leisurely ease, spreading his wings wide. Rox couldn't figure it out. It was as if they were out for a Sunday ride.

And his brother was closing fast. She peered around Niall to watch. Phelan looked pissed off.

Niall continued to fly slowly. He had a cut on his shoulder from Phelan's previous assault and she feared the wound was worse than it looked.

"Are you okay?"

"More or less."

"Then why don't you just kick his ass?" Rox was perfectly good with there being one fewer dragon shape shifter in the world, so long as the delegate of choice was Phelan.

"Shhh," Niall urged softly.

Okay, he had a plan. Rox took another look around and realized he was flying toward a brick chimney. And by spreading his wings so wide, he was probably blocking Phelan's view of that obstacle.

When the chimney was just ahead, Niall sped up. Rox held tightly, sure they were going to run straight into it.

She heard a rumble like a freight train, although it was impossible to hear one here. The vibration seemed to emanate from Niall's chest.

Something happened, though, because both brothers sped up. She peeked over Niall's shoulder again and saw Phelan looming large, his teeth mere yards from Niall's tail. He opened his mouth wide to bite and she bit her own knuckles to keep from screaming a warning.

She felt Niall's muscles go taut. She remembered those keen *Pyr* senses and knew he was aware of his brother's precise position. She felt his grip tighten on her, took one last glance between chimney and twin, then gasped in shock.

Niall abruptly changed course, mere yards from the chimney, and skyrocketed upward.

Phelan surged after Niall in the same instant, his jaw snatching at air just before he slammed headfirst into the brick. Niall was high above him by then, and Rox cheered.

The force of Phelan's impact was enough to crack the mortar, and the chimney began to sway dangerously. Phelan roared with fury, shook himself, then raced after them. Niall headed for the stars, spearing through the sky. It was a thrilling ride, but Rox would have preferred not to be pursued.

Especially not by someone so bent on destruction. She looked between the two brothers, her heart pounding.

Rox clutched Niall's shoulder. "You can sense his position, right?"

"Right," Niall said grimly.

Rox shut up, rather than distract him. All the same, Phelan was fast. He spiraled directly toward them, his dark eyes shining with what had to be malice. He stretched his talons toward them and opened his mouth—Rox had a terrifying glimpse straight down his rotten gullet.

Her fingers dug deeply into Niall. Once again, Phelan came closer and closer, close enough that she could smell him and almost feel his anger.

Then Niall folded his wings shut.

He dropped like a stone. Phelan shot past them, swore, then changed course again.

There was no question of Rox's hanging on. They plummeted toward the earth and she fought the urge to scream.

"You're avoiding him," she accused. "Nothing will get solved like this. You've got to take him out."

Niall was adamant. "It's not that simple."

"Can't you just kill him?"

"Shadow dragons have to be decapitated and each piece has to be incinerated, until their ashes are dispersed by the wind," Niall said tersely.

"So, do it."

"No. I have to be sure." He sounded a bit annoyed that she was questioning his tactics, but that didn't frighten Rox.

"Looks as if that's what he's trying to do to you," she said, touching the wound on Niall's shoulder with tentative fingers. Niall flinched, then spread his wings, halting their fall. "Better him than us."

"It's not that simple," Niall said through gritted teeth. "If nothing else, I'll tire him out."

"What's complicated about it? He's trying to kill you." Rox was skeptical. "And he doesn't look tired to me."

She saw Niall's eyes narrow and followed his glance. A familiar moonstone and silver dragon emerged from between the buildings below them, and Rox felt relief that there were two good dragons on the scene.

"Time for Plan B," Niall said.

Rox didn't ask for details. It seemed to be important to Niall that she trust him, and she did.

Mostly.

Even if it made zero sense that he didn't want to kill his brother.

She gasped aloud when Niall launched himself directly at Phelan, and the pair locked talons. Rox had a close-up view of a scar on Phelan's belly, one that had healed in a ragged white line. The pair tumbled head over tail, biting and snapping and thrashing.

At least Phelan never touched her—Niall made sure of it.

There was that train rumbling again, which made no damn sense.

Then Phelan reared back and swung his tail in Rox's direction with deadly purpose. Niall moved quickly, evading the blow just before it connected. Phelan missed, the force of his momentum sending him for a tumble through the air. Niall attacked his brother, seizing his damaged tail and spinning his weight. Phelan roared, twisting to snap at Rox. She squeaked and flinched as his powerful teeth moved closer.

But his jaw snapped shut on empty air.

Because Niall suddenly flung Rox into the air behind him.

She saw him pounce on Phelan, ripping his chest and then tossing him in the opposite direction from her. Phelan soared through the air, desperately trying to stop his own fall.

Rox screamed.

Instead of coming after her, Niall went after Phelan.

He seized his brother by the wings and bit into the tendon of Phelan's left shoulder before his brother could twist away. Phelan thrashed in Niall's grip, intent on gaining his freedom if not evading the pain.

Rox was shocked that Niall had abandoned her. What had changed? He had protected her before. Why would he toss her to her death? She looked down at the ground that was approaching far too fast and feared she'd never have the chance to find out.

Then Thorolf snatched her out of the air.

Rox thought she might have a heart attack in her relief.

"Assignment completed," Thorolf said, and hovered with Rox safely in his grasp.

Rox tried to catch her breath as her heart hammered. "What assignment?"

"Niall told me to catch you." Thorolf chuckled. "Gotta listen to my mentor, just like you said."

So, Niall was still ensuring her safety, even as he tried to trick his brother. It couldn't have been easy fighting with her in his grasp, especially now that she saw how hard the two were battling.

But Rox hadn't heard Niall give any command to Thorolf. There had been only that rumbling sound. . . .

Rox knew then that there was more going on than she'd realized and that she had lots of questions for Niall. Just then she saw another dragon appear over the tops of the buildings, one that appeared to have scales made of opal and edged in gold. He was larger and moved with a slow elegance, but Rox had no doubt he was powerful. Which team was he on?

Phelan shook free of Niall's grasp. He took one look at the new arrival, glanced back to Niall and Thorolf, then fled.

Okay, the new arrival was a good dragon.

Niall didn't give chase. He just let Phelan go.

Why? Rox was sure there was a reason, and she intended to find out what it was.

Chapter 6

Phelan returned to the lair of the shadow dragons.

He hated his compulsion to return. He knew Chen would be displeased with the outcome of the battle with Niall, and he doubted the old *Slayer* would be kind in expressing his dissatisfaction. He certainly had no desire to be fettered with his fellow shadow dragons in darkness again.

The darkness in his mind was much worse than that of Chen's physical prison.

But Chen had the powder that let Phelan escape the mental state of being a shadow dragon. It might not be addictive, but the return of his intellect and initiative was a powerful incentive to doing Chen's will.

Never mind the promise Chen had made him, the one he would fulfill when Phelan succeeded.

Phelan had failed this time, but he wouldn't the next. His thoughts were already clouding, the shadow of limbo descending over his mind. He hated that state of being; he despised being no more than an automaton under the command of another.

Unfortunately, only Chen offered the opportunity for change.

He had a limited amount of time to plead his own case, so he had to make it count. Phelan slipped into the hidden entrance, easing into the cold shadows of the darkness beneath the city even as his mind grew more dull. He hurried through the trapdoor at the back of the apothecary shop, hoping he would find the old *Slayer* there.

Chen was waiting for him in the little room beneath the apothecary shop, the one he used as an office. He was clearly annoyed. "You failed," was the sum of his greeting.

"I tried! I will try again. I will do whatever . . ."

"And a most unfortunate moment for a failure," Chen said, and Phelan braced himself for the worst. The *Slayer* was in the form of a young man, dressed in jeans and leather, a look most evocative of his nature.

Or maybe not.

"I'll try again." Phelan felt coherence slipping away, along with his power to think for himself. His words fell in panicked haste. "You promised. . . ."

"*Promised?*" Chen repeated, his tone arch. He spun to face Phelan and folded his arms across his chest. "I promised nothing. I never promise anything." His voice dropped. "I said I would try."

"And I will try. Please!"

Chen turned to the window, appearing to listen to the rain. "There are other *Pyr* coming. The window of opportunity is closing." There was unusual urgency in his tone. "Do you understand what I am saying?"

"Another chance!"

Chen moved quickly, crossing the room in a blink of an eye and seizing Phelan by the throat. "Time is running out," he muttered, then repeated a rhyme.

> *When the Dragon's Tail turns in the sky,*
> *When the year of tiger rises high,*
> *The Phoenix and the Dragon mate,*

Desire does their child create.
But at this junction the old charm,
Can be performed to make great harm.
Elements four in union do conjure,
The chance to invoke the fifth's measure.
Master the four, command the thoughts
of all Gaia's populace.

The verse startled Phelan, who had never heard it before. He had a hard time making sense of it, given the dulling of his faculties, but he understood it was important. Chen changed to his female form with astonishing speed, those red-painted fingernails digging sharply into Phelan's throat.

"I will try again," Phelan managed to whisper.

"I have waited centuries for this junction," Chen insisted. "I will not live to see it again, and I will not watch you waste it." He tightened his grip and leaned closer. "I am the last of the *Lung wang*, the last of the Dragon Kings, and this is my opportunity to secure my stewardship of the earth." His grip tightened. "I chose you for a reason. Do you intend to disappoint me?"

"No! No!" Phelan heard his tone turn pleading. "I'll succeed next time. I was only surprised."

"No. You were outwitted." Chen cast Phelan aside with surprising strength and paced the room again. The cloud of oblivion began to settle more resolutely over Phelan's mind and he tried once more to bargain.

His words, though, came out as gibberish. He fell to his knees, gabbing like a fool, and reached out one hand in entreaty.

More powder.

Another chance.

Chen turned to watch him, a smile playing over those red lips. "I shall think about giving you another chance," he murmured; then Phelan felt the iron fetter close around his ankle.

He moaned as the darkness claimed him fully, felt the chill air of the shadow dragon's dungeon, then knew nothing beyond the resonance of the command Magnus had planted in his thoughts so long ago.

"Kill. Kill. Kill."

It was the stuff of nightmares, but once the shadow claimed him, Phelan knew nothing else.

"I don't understand it," Ginger murmured as she heard Delaney come into the kitchen from the barn. She sat in front of the computer, in the office off the kitchen of the Ohio farmhouse she shared with Delaney, and glared at the screen. It was late.

Ginger held their seven-month-old son, Liam, in the crook of her left arm as he slept. The amber and silver ring on her left hand was a reminder of the vows Ginger and Delaney had exchanged before Liam's birth. The amber shone as if lit with a fire of its own.

"What don't you understand?" Delaney asked. He leaned over her, stroked the baby's cheek, then bent to kiss Ginger just below her ear.

She shivered with pleasure. The firestorm might be sated, but the man still had the ability to make her heart pound. "Erik is ducking my question. It's irritating."

"That's not like Erik," Delaney said, pulling up a chair beside her. He leaned closer and Ginger smelled earth and wind and the scent of his skin. Ginger began to think about things other than spreadsheets. "He's got to be the most direct *Pyr* I know."

"But no matter how much we work on this genealogy of the *Pyr*, he refuses to tell me about Gaspar's children. I really could shake him"—Ginger shrugged—"except that he's in Chicago."

Delaney smiled, then sobered. "Wait a minute. Gaspar? Wasn't that one of the original high council members?"

"Right. We worked back as far as Erik could remember, and now are working forward. He gave me the biographical details for the members of the high council that his father established; then we've worked down the centuries from there."

"What are those names in the column on the right?"

"The list of dead *Pyr*." Ginger frowned. "Well, not all of them. The ones Erik knows were exposed to all four elements within twelve hours of death—"

"Half a solar day," Delaney supplied.

"Aren't included in the list. They just have death dates where they appear in the genealogies."

"So this is a list of the potential shadow dragons," Delaney said.

"Magnus would have had to find their corpses, force the Dragon's Blood Elixir into them, and raise them from the dead," Ginger agreed. "But he sure got around." She scrolled the display so Delaney could see the list of confirmed shadow dragons and he whistled through his teeth.

"At least Niall is getting through them."

"Twenty-one confirmed dead since he took on the quest," Ginger agreed. "I'm trying to correlate the eliminated ones with my list, but we don't always know who they were."

Delaney pointed to the screen. "Quinn had four brothers and you have only three listed as shadow dragons."

"Right. Because the eldest, Jean, was with Quinn's father when they both died. Erik was there and exposed them both to all four elements. We know they're dead for good." She showed him the difference in notations and he nodded.

"But the other three made the potential shadow dragon list."

"Quinn said the three of them were shadow dragons and had attacked him at the end of Donovan's firestorm. Both Quinn and Donovan confirmed that two of them were destroyed then."

"One left," Delaney said, his gaze dancing over the display. "Both Sloane's father and Rafferty's grandfather were turned into shadow dragons, but they were destroyed when Magnus's secret academy was trashed."

Ginger was impressed that Delaney could so casually mention the academy, where he had been imprisoned by Magnus and forced to consume the Dragon's Blood Elixir.

"But not Niall's twin brother, Phelan. He was just injured," Delaney continued. "You sent that list to Niall?"

"I sent him the updated file earlier. He's working through it."

"Mr. Detail, that's what he always called himself. The list looks pretty complete," Delaney said with admiration. "You've even included the Dragon's Teeth Warriors."

"Only what we know about them. I'm hoping Rafferty can corner their commander, who is pretty uncommunicative from what I understand, and learn more."

"At least we know none of them have had a firestorm in the last couple of thousand years," Delaney teased, referring to the fact that those warriors had been snared by a spell for millenia. "That saves on your paperwork."

"The irritating thing is Gaspar's line," she complained. "Erik won't tell me anything beyond Gaspar's name."

"Maybe he doesn't remember."

"I find it hard to believe that Erik forgets much of anything."

Delaney chuckled. "Maybe he has a secret past that he doesn't want Eileen to know."

Ginger laughed despite herself. "Eileen would have gotten it out of him by now, if that was the case." She frowned at the screen. "Did you know Gaspar?"

Delaney shook his head. "No. And I never heard anything about him. That first council was way before my time."

Ginger pursed her lips. "I think Erik's ignoring me,

I'm sure of it even though I don't know why." She highlighted the cell in the spreadsheet and turned it red, putting her question in larger and bolder type.

Then she saved it and sent the file to Erik.

Again.

"Well, he can't miss that," Delaney teased, and she looked up to find him smiling at her. He braced his hands on the chair and leaned over her, his expression so intent that Ginger tingled.

"I've been thinking," Delaney said in a low voice.

"A sure sign of trouble," Ginger teased.

"Maybe Liam needs a brother."

"It's good for siblings to be close in age," Ginger agreed solemnly. "But I don't think anything is going to happen while I'm breast-feeding, hotshot."

"Practice. It can't hurt to practice," Delaney murmured. "Besides, it's too late to keep working." Then he leaned down to capture her lips with his.

Ginger had no complaints about that.

Sara, the Seer of the *Pyr*, awakened with a start. She was at home, the home she shared with Quinn, the Smith of the *Pyr*, and she was reassured that he slept beside her still. He had been restless lately, although he didn't want to talk about it.

Sara knew she simply had to wait. He would tell her what troubled him when he felt the time was right.

She wondered whether he suspected she was pregnant again and was protective of her as a result. She, too, was choosing her time to share the news.

But in this moment, Sara's dream was still vivid in her thoughts and she knew she had to record it. She reached for the flashlight, pen, and paper she kept beside the bed and scribbled quickly.

> *The Phoenix sheds her former skin,*
> *Clothes herself to begin again.*

Injuries and debts unearned,
Consigned with her hide to fire's burn.
The Dragon loses but one scale,
To keep nigh intact his coat of mail.
But not all things should survive,
And not all burdens help him to thrive.
Can he learn Phoenix's song,
And leave his past where it belongs?
Learn the DreamWalker's dance
And usher in the world's new chance?

Sara frowned at what she had written, recognizing the format of the prophecies of the *Pyr*. As usual, she couldn't make much sense of the verse.

She wondered at its source. She was the Seer of the *Pyr*, but these verses always came from outside of her. They could have been missives from another world, the world of the *Pyr*, which Sara didn't completely understand.

In the past, the Wyvern Sophie had sent Sara the prophecies that linked with the firestorms of the individual *Pyr*. But there had been no Wyvern since Sophie's death eighteen months before.

The *Pyr* had speculated that Erik's daughter was the new Wyvern. Zoë had been conceived in Erik and Eileen's firestorm, and as a female *Pyr*, she should be the Wyvern. She was just a little girl, though—Sara was skeptical as to whether Zoë would have any powers yet even if she was the new Wyvern. Male *Pyr*, after all, came into their abilities at puberty.

But there were hints of Zoë's identity. Erik had been convinced of Zoë's role from the outset. And Rafferty believed that she had given him a dream. Then there had been the strange exchange between Zoë and Garrett during Delaney's firestorm.

And now Sara had received this dream. Sara couldn't imagine where else this verse could have originated.

But why now? The next full eclipse would occur in December. She and Alex and Eileen kept track of such events now, so they wouldn't be surprised with the need to travel. Life was more complicated with toddlers.

Was Zoë still refining her abilities? Had she sent the message too soon? Or was Sara herself learning more about attracting prophecy? Either way, there'd be no firestorm for months. She tucked the verse into the journal she kept at her bedside.

At least she'd know where to find it come December. Sara turned out the flashlight, curled up beside Quinn, and went back to sleep.

Magnus was rudely awakened when the plaid plastic bag was tipped upside down and he was dumped out of it. He landed on a bare wood table, the zipper teeth abrading his skin as he slid past it. Green onions and long beans scattered all around him, and he was outraged by the indignity of his situation.

He was not *groceries*.

He immediately looked around for the old Chinese man who had snatched him up in his iron grip.

Magnus was in a small room, a room containing little other than that wooden table. It was dank and cold, like an old cellar. An embossed and foil-stamped calendar on the wall proclaimed 2010 to be the year of the tiger. Beyond that, the room was austere.

But a massive red dragon filled the space, his tail curled across the floor and a wisp of steam rising from his nostril. The dragon's lacquer red scales with their gold edgings told Magnus his identity.

"Chen!" Magnus murmured. Chen had been one of the last to sip of the Elixir, a young man Magnus had encountered in Beijing. He'd assumed the young angry *Slayer* to be a gang member, volatile and restless. Such an individual, kept in one's debt, could be useful.

Chen inclined his head in acknowledgment, his

small golden horns catching the light. He seemed larger than Magnus remembered, more muscled and powerful. Chen's scales were a richer shade of red, closer to blood than the ruby Magnus recalled, and the gold of his talons glittered dangerously.

They looked to have been sharpened.

Chen's gaze was as steady and as dark as Magnus remembered, the *Slayer*'s thoughts just as difficult to read. Magnus scanned his prison, acknowledged there was more to his captor than he'd initially realized, and felt a frisson of fear.

He sensed a familiar darkness and glanced toward the only doorway. Steps wound down into darkness, but Magnus knew that sound, that smell. "The shadow dragons!" he said with relief. "You've retrieved them from the destroyed academy." His own fortunes had taken a turn for the better. "And now I can lead them. . . ."

"I've gathered them for my own purposes," Chen corrected softly.

"But I command the shadow dragons!"

"You did. Once."

That was when Magnus heard the rattle of fetters. He stared at Chen.

"They are my tools now," Chen murmured. "Since you cast their stewardship so carelessly aside."

"I was attacked! I was trapped. . . ."

"And how did you become free?"

"My song. I sang the song of the earth, and Gaia released me." Magnus's conviction faded along with his voice as Chen shook his head deliberately. He had wondered why his song had suddenly begun to work, and now he guessed.

"I gained your release, which leaves you in my debt."

"So, we can be partners. . . ."

Magnus could have sworn that Chen smiled, right before he shifted shape.

To Magnus's astonishment, Chen took the shape of a

beautiful woman. She wore a tightly fitted red and gold blouse, a cropped cheongsam of embroidered silk. It hugged her curves, as did her black leather pants.

She smiled at Magnus's astonishment, her red lips curving into an expression that wasn't at all friendly. That smile didn't touch her dark eyes, either. They tipped up at the corners and were outlined in black, the makeup adding to her exotic appearance. Her long, carefully tended fingernails were the same deep red as her lipstick, and her straight dark hair was tugged into a sleek ponytail.

Magnus stared. Chen could take *two* different human forms? Magnus could take three forms—dragon, man, and salamander, the last being a particular point of pride as the salamander form was traditionally reserved by the Wyvern. But all *Pyr* and *Slayers* Magnus had known took the same human form each time.

Had the old man been Chen, as well?

What else could Chen do?

The woman who was Chen turned and took down a jar that Magnus hadn't noticed before. It was a large clear glass sealer. Chen dropped Magnus into the jar, then closed the lid and locked it down. There was a rubber ring around the lip, one that sealed the contents completely.

"I won't have any air!" Magnus cried.

Chen smiled. "I have no need of a partner, not now when everything is coming together so well."

"But I can share my knowledge!"

Chen laughed. It was a chilling sound. "You have nothing to teach me, old man."

"Then why ensure my release?"

Chen leaned down, his face magnified and distorted by the glass. "Because I don't trust you, and I like to keep track of those I don't trust."

Magnus scurried around his new prison, more agitated than he had ever been. But he was still tired, still weak from his ordeal, still without the power to change his circumstance. Magnus tried to manifest himself on the outside of the jar without success.

And he would only grow weaker with every passing moment.

The woman who was Chen leaned against the wall to watch him with a bemused expression.

"I could break it," Magnus murmured.

Chen smiled. "It is fortified with my will."

"I will bargain with you!" Magnus cried. "Let's come to terms."

"Such a charming offer," Chen mused, "but unfortunately you have nothing left that I want or need."

Magnus couldn't believe it. He wasn't obsolete. He couldn't be dismissed, but Chen clearly did not care about his powers or his agenda.

He stared at the other *Slayer*, realizing only now how he had been deceived.

Too late to do anything about it.

Then Magnus heard the steady drum of rain against a metal roof. He heard it slap against glass somewhere above him, as if the drops were large and heavy. Then he heard gurgling begin far far below, followed by the rush of flowing water.

Was there a sewer down there? Or an underground river?

"Dragon rain," Chen said softly. That enigmatic smile curved those red lips once more as he looked upward. Then he surveyed Magnus once again, his smile fading to nothing. "The best kind."

Chapter 7

Niall was uncertain that he'd made the right choice in letting Phelan retreat. He didn't doubt that his brother would be back, or that Phelan would play by his own rules. Niall would have to be on his guard 24-7.

And he'd have to guard Rox with his life.

He'd taken a risk, and that wasn't his favorite choice of options. All the same, if he killed Phelan, there was no undoing his decision.

Niall wanted to be sure. He owed his brother that much. His father hadn't given Phelan another chance, but Niall was determined not to make judgments in anger. It was possible that this was the lesson of his firestorm.

Or it was a big mistake. Niall wished he'd had enough sleep recently to let him think more clearly, but he was out of luck on that.

It didn't look as if he'd be getting much sleep anytime soon.

He could do without the paranoia of feeling targeted, too.

Niall heard Rafferty's greeting in old-speak and returned it, then looked toward Thorolf. Rox was as undaunted as ever, her eyes bright and her gaze fixed upon him. She was resilient and he admired that. It was good not to have to worry about her mental health.

On the other hand, one look told Niall that Rox had questions, probably some that he wasn't going to like answering.

Maybe Thorolf was right, though, about confiding in his mate.

The rain began to fall in fat drops that splashed on Niall's scales and beat on his wings. He flew toward Thorolf and extended a claw toward Rox. "*Good job*," he said in old-speak to Thorolf, who looked ridiculously proud of himself.

"There it is again!" Rox said. "What is that rumbling? Are you two talking to each other so I can't understand it?"

It wasn't that surprising that Rox would figure out old-speak before he could explain it. Niall heard Rafferty's deep chuckle.

"My favorite part of the firestorm," Rafferty said quietly. "When the mate learns about old-speak."

"What about beguiling? I thought that was your favorite part," Thorolf teased.

It was clear that Rox had a whole lot of questions, but when Niall took her in his grasp again, her lips softened. She seemed to lose her train of thought, and he could understand that.

Golden heat rolled through his body at the contact, making his heart pound and his breath catch. He felt a profound relief that she was all right, but that relief was tinged with excitement. Little sparks danced from every point of contact between them and the rain sizzled on Niall's scales.

Was it burning hotter?

It certainly was more distracting.

Rox sighed with contentment, then slid her hands

across his chest. She looked up at him and smiled, a promise in her eyes. "Thanks for coming after me. I'm thinking this is worth celebrating," she murmured, her voice so husky and low that Niall couldn't help but think of the last time she'd shown gratitude.

Rafferty gave a low whistle of appreciation and appeared to bask in the heat. "I do love a firestorm," he murmured.

"What's a firestorm? Is that what causes the sparks?" Rox asked, glancing up at Niall, her curiosity clear. "What's wrong with your brother's eyes? And what's with the tiger mark on his neck?"

"The what?" Rafferty asked, his voice sharp.

"The two shadow dragons we took out tonight had it, as well," Niall said. "It looks like a brand and is shaped like a tiger."

Rox looked between them. "If they're all shadow dragons and they have this mark, it could be a gang mark." She nodded at Niall. "Happens with tattoos all the time. People mark their bodies to show their allegiance, especially criminals." She winced. "Getting the mark isn't always their choice, but once they have it, they have to live by its code."

That wasn't news that Niall wanted to hear, although it made a lot of sense. Could someone else have assumed leadership of the shadow dragons? That would explain their having a different strategy. "Let's get out of the rain to talk." He looked around, targeted a likely site, and headed for it.

"*Excellent choice*," Rafferty murmured in old-speak. "*I like the awning.*"

Rox caught her breath, but Niall would explain in a moment. She was showing a remarkable ability to accept his *Pyr* nature, and he found her more attractive with every exchange. Plus she was smart, and she brought new ideas. Niall was starting to think the firestorm might have led him in precisely the right direction.

And he was definitely thinking about Rox's suggestion of a celebration.

The trio of dragons descended in an elegant spiral, landing on the terrace of a penthouse apartment. They shifted shape in unison, ducking under the shelter of an awning affixed to the building. The lights were out in the apartment, and the rain fell steadily on the flagstones of the terrace all around them.

Rox had been amazed by how gracefully and quickly the three *Pyr* had shifted shape, dragons one minute and men the next. Niall had been holding her against his scaled chest, flying with her through the air. It could have been her wildest dream come true.

A heartbeat later he had been carrying her in very muscled arms, with her cheek against his chest and his T-shirt soft against her skin. He was the buffest guy she'd ever known, so being in his arms could have been another wild dream.

It was a bit startling to experience them back to back.

But good. Definitely good.

Thorolf had been the slowest of the three of them in making the shift and Rox thought she caught a glimpse of him unfolding his clothes. It was as if they had been stashed beneath his scales when he was in dragon form. The back of his neck turned red when he caught her staring and Niall exhaled with what could only have been exasperation.

So, humans weren't supposed to see that. Rox made a mental note to watch Niall more closely when he shifted.

In Niall's embrace, Rox felt that shimmering heat again, that sizzle of desire that distracted her in a most basic way. She'd been feeling it since she came into Niall's proximity, since he'd come zooming out of the night to help her, and it made her dizzy.

The lust it awakened was impossible to ignore. Niall's touch was as different from his brother's cold one as could be imagined. Rox was keenly aware of Niall's strength, and that he seemed to be warm everywhere he touched her. There was that light, too, as if they stood at the middle of a bonfire.

She couldn't explain how much she wanted to jump his bones, either. Her reaction seemed way out of proportion, almost a compulsion, and much stronger than any lust she'd ever felt before. It was hard to think about anything else, which wasn't like her at all.

She wanted to run her hands all over him. In either form. She wanted to know where his tan ended in human form, whether all of his hair was that golden blond, whether there was any bit of him that wasn't hard-muscled strength. She wouldn't have minded checking out his dragon bits, either, exploring the smoothness of his scales and feeling the power of his body beneath them. She wanted to nibble on him and kiss him and, well, embark upon a major exploration from there.

She wished the others would disappear so she could get this urge out of her system.

Niall looked down at her, his eyes gleaming, and Rox's mouth went dry. The other two *Pyr* were behind her, but she forgot about them for the moment, losing herself in his bright gaze. She felt his hand slide up her back, a proprietary gesture that was hot, hot enough to almost sear her skin.

Had lightning struck?

She blinked, then inhaled at the tidal wave of desire that rolled through her as Niall pulled her closer. It made her blood heat and her knees go weak. The sensation was stronger than before, more demanding and impossible to ignore.

Was it her imagination that Niall's eyes had darkened to indigo? That his heart seemed to be pounding faster beneath her fingertips? She couldn't be imagining the radiant light emanating from every point they touched.

"First things first. This is the firestorm," he murmured, his voice low and seductive. "It's the mark of a *Pyr* finding his destined mate." Rox parted her lips to ask for more detail, but Niall bent his head and kissed her instead.

She realized she had initiated their other kisses, because this one was different. It was potent and hot, demanding and driven. It was precisely the kind of kiss a dragon would initiate—one that swept Rox away on a tide of sensation, one that was determined to cultivate her passion and fearless as to where that desire might lead. Niall's kiss left her shaking and unsteady on her feet, glowing with desire and hanging on to his shoulders tightly. He was the only fixture in her universe, and really, the only one she needed.

When he lifted his head, his eyes glittered. He smiled crookedly at her, well aware of the tumult he had raised within her. Rox exhaled unevenly and he ran a fingertip down her cheek.

"Mate?" she echoed, hearing unsteadiness in her words.

"Surrendering to the firestorm's call means conceiving an heir."

That was plenty of news for Rox. Although it wasn't easy, she stepped away from Niall. The heat diminished with distance, giving her some ability to think clearly. She hung on to the pillar that supported the awning and tried to catch her breath. "Like a child?" she said.

"A son," Niall said, as if there could be no doubt of his child's gender. Rox blinked and looked around.

An heir. A son.

As if.

Rox forced herself to check out their surroundings instead of Niall. It was time to think of something other than sex. They had a sparkling view of the city spread before their feet, the rain glistening off glass and pavement. Rox thought it would be magical to live in such a place.

Then she glanced guiltily at the darkened windows of the penthouse. "It's lucky they aren't home while we use their terrace," she said.

"Not lucky," Niall corrected. "We could hear that this apartment was empty. Rafferty thought the awning made it a good choice."

Rox looked from one to the next, but couldn't read their expressions. "I didn't hear him say anything," she said carefully. "Are you psychics or telepaths?"

"We just have sharper senses," Niall said.

"The ones Thorolf mentioned," Rox said, remembering, and Niall nodded.

"We can hear at higher and lower frequencies than humans, and also hear sounds from greater distances. Old-speak is low—it sounds like thunder to humans."

She'd been right! "Except that we can't hear the words," Rox said, feeling obligated to note. "It's like a secret."

Niall winced as Rafferty chuckled. "Not exactly a secret. It's not meant to be, anyway."

Rox nodded, realizing that Niall for one wouldn't use his ability to deceive. That might not be true of all his fellows, though. "So that's how you told Thorolf to catch me?"

Niall folded his arms across his chest and leaned against the opposite pillar supporting the awning. His hair was wet and his T-shirt clung to his muscles. He looked imposing and delicious.

Rox licked her lips in memory of that kiss.

An heir. Just the prospect of a baby was enough to quench her desire a little bit.

That Niall calmly answered her questions just made him more appealing. "I needed the element of surprise. If I'd called to him aloud, then you and Phelan would both have heard. Your shock distracted Phelan just long enough that I could keep him from attacking you."

"But you were still counting on Thorolf."

Niall smiled. "Someone suggested I give him another chance."

Their gazes locked and held for an electric moment; then Rox frowned. "Wait a minute. That means you can talk to one another without humans knowing what's going on. Without *my* knowing what's going on."

"Well, yes," Niall admitted.

"I don't like that. You should speak out loud."

"Funny how mates always make the same request," Rafferty mused, then continued at Rox's glance. "I'm Rafferty Powell." He offered his hand and Rox immediately responded in kind.

"Roxanne Kincaid."

Rafferty smiled as he shook Rox's hand. "Always delighted to meet a mate and feel the heat of a firestorm."

He was an older man, one who moved with tranquility and deliberation. Like Thorolf and Niall, he was trim and fit. He had his dark hair tied back in a ponytail and his eyes were darker than dark. He wore a strange ring on his left hand, one that seemed to be made of black and white glass spun together.

There had been no sparks when he'd shaken her hand.

All the same, it was incredible to be in the company of not one, but three, dragon shape shifters.

"Okay, let's get to it." Niall spared a glance at the sky and Rox thought she could see him organizing his list of what needed to be done. Then he met her gaze, and Rox was pleased to find herself a priority. "We can hear, for example, whether anyone is home," he said. "If they were here, we'd hear their breathing or the rustle of their movements, even at a distance." He flicked a glance at the large glass windows. "They do have a cat, but she won't likely give us away."

Rox perched on a wrought-iron settee. She was determined to learn as much as possible in the time available. "How do you know it's a cat? It could be a dog or another small pet."

Niall touched the tip of his own nose. "Cat. Spayed female."

"You don't know her name?" Rox teased.

Niall smiled and Rox's heart thumped. "She's not telling."

"You might be making that up. . . ." Rox fell silent when she glanced at the window. A sleek cat the color of soot had come to sit on the sill, her eyes wide and yellow. Her paws were white, as if she'd stepped in paint or wore socks. Her tail flicked as she stared at the intruders.

"Okay," Rox said, impressed. "Okay. Tell me more about the firestorm." Niall caught his breath, but he didn't kiss her.

He caught her hand in his, though. There was a shower of sparks; then a radiant glow settled around their clasped hands. Rox swallowed as lust rolled through her, seeming to emanate from the point of contact. She was keenly aware of the strength of Niall's hand and of his holding his power in check to protect her from injury. She looked up, met his gaze, and acknowledged that she liked how he talked to her, too.

"An heir?" she asked, and he grimaced and nodded.

"The firestorm is a dream come true," Rafferty said with undisguised satisfaction.

"How many of you are there?"

"Not enough," the three men said in unison; then Thorolf grinned.

"That's what Erik always says," Rafferty said, a sparkle in his eye as he clearly anticipated Rox's next question. "Erik is the leader of the *Pyr*."

The count was up to four. They'd mentioned Erik before.

"*Pyr.*" Rox tried out the word on her tongue.

"Dragon shape shifters," Niall supplied. "The ability passes through the male line."

"From father to son," Rox said, understanding. "So you have relatives. And there must be female *Pyr*."

The three shook their heads as one. "Only one at a time," Niall said. "She's called the Wyvern and has prophetic powers."

"Well, fathers don't get sons without a female being involved," Rox said. Niall frowned, and she wondered why he was at a loss for words. "It's just basic biology. Unless there's something really odd about you guys."

Niall shook his head and Rox was relieved.

"That's where the firestorm comes in," Rafferty said, his tone encouraging. They fell silent, Rafferty and Thorolf studying Niall. It was apparently up to him to explain.

"Each *Pyr* has a destined mate," Niall said, his gaze fixed on the flagstones. "Once in a lifetime, a *Pyr* will find the woman who can conceive his son—or sons, if he's lucky—and that mating is marked by the firestorm. The firestorm is a sign of that opportunity," Niall said quietly, then smiled slightly. "One that you're not supposed to miss."

"I guess not." Rox had to be sure it was clear. "So I'm your destined mate?"

Niall averted his gaze. "You're the woman who can conceive my son, if we choose to consummate the firestorm."

Rox couldn't ignore her impression that Niall was less than thrilled to have a firestorm, or maybe a mate.

She certainly didn't have babies in her ideal future. Maybe this was something else they had in common.

"What happens if we don't?"

Niall looked toward Rafferty.

"The firestorm keeps burning, hotter and hotter," Rafferty said with a shake of his head. "Firestorms are disinclined to be ignored." He smiled at Rox. "They are magical and marvelous opportunities."

"Have you had one?"

Rafferty shook his head slowly, his regret clear. "I've been waiting twelve hundred years for the right woman to cross my path"—he shrugged—"and I will wait twelve hundred more, if the Great Wyvern decrees it should be so. There are things worth every increment of patience they demand."

Rox was stuck on one thing he said. "Twelve hundred years? As in, twelve centuries?"

Rafferty nodded, amusement curving his lips as he watched her accept his claim.

"How can you possibly be that old?"

"We age slowly before our firestorms. It's common for people to think us immortal as a result, but that's not technically true." He smiled broadly. "I like to think I don't look a day over four hundred years."

Niall chuckled and Rox turned her attention on him again. "How old are you?"

"Barely two hundred years," he admitted.

She looked at Thorolf.

"Not sure," he admitted with a shrug. "At least eight hundred."

"Kids," Rafferty scoffed as Rox tried to accept what she was being told.

"So, you have a firestorm at some point, have sex with your destined mate, make a son, then start to age more quickly," she said in review, keeping her tone neutral. Niall watched Rox, and her sharp awareness of him became even stronger. This heat made it too easy to imagine being intimate with Niall, to think of his strong fingers sliding over her skin, to imagine the hard press of him against her. "But what if they don't conceive a son?"

"Then the *Pyr* misses the opportunity of a lifetime," Rafferty said quietly. He held up a single finger. "It's a onetime offer." He smiled easily. "But then, who needs more than one chance to get it right?"

"But the firestorm lasts until the woman conceives the *Pyr*'s son?" Rox insisted.

"Apparently it takes only the once," Niall said.

"That can't be true," Rox argued.

Niall sat beside Rox then, his presence and the firestorm's heat setting her nerves on edge. His shoulder bumped hers and sent an imperative through Rox's body. "That's what Ginger said. And Eileen and Sara and Alex."

"Who are they?"

"*Pyr* mates identified by firestorms," he said, then smiled at her. "All have had children since their firestorms—children conceived during their firestorms."

The *Pyr* and his mate got to do it only once before she conceived? Rox crossed her legs, not liking the sound of that. A sexy beast of a dragon man was one thing. Potentially having a relationship with someone who defended her was another. But conceiving his child immediately did not fit into Rox's life plan.

"But what happens after that?" she asked, trying to hide her reservations.

Rafferty sat on Rox's other side. "There are two schools of thought among our kind."

"Get in and get out, make more while you can, and never look back," Thorolf said with enthusiasm.

Both Niall and Rafferty regarded him unhappily.

"That is one perspective," Rafferty continued, "while others believe that mate and *Pyr* complement each other's strengths, that the firestorm is the mark of an opportunity for each to become more than they could be alone."

"The firestorm shouldn't be satisfied outside of marriage," Niall concluded. "It should be a permanent commitment."

Marriage now, too?

Rox had heard enough. "I don't think so," she said, her words hurried as she pushed herself to her feet. She had to put distance between herself and Niall before the firestorm coaxed her into making a big mistake. "I don't do permanent; I don't do long-term. I don't do marriage and I won't do babies. The planet is crowded enough without making more."

"Even more *Pyr*?" Rafferty asked softly, his eyes shining.

"Even then," Rox said with resolve.

"But it's the firestorm," Thorolf protested.

"We should talk about it." Niall rose to his feet and stretched out a hand toward her. That he had the most reasonable perspective only made it harder to keep her distance. Rox knew that if he touched her, she'd lose her resolve.

The firestorm was on his side, after all.

"Thorolf, will you give me a ride home?" Rox asked, spinning away from Niall's bright gaze. "Like, *now*?"

Niall watched Thorolf carry Rox away, a jumble of reactions churning inside him. He wasn't convinced that a crowded planet was the real reason she didn't want to have children. Her comments about the long term only made him fear that satisfying the firestorm would lead him to repeat his father's mistake.

Once again, he wondered about Rox's history.

Could Rox's perspective be changed? Maybe she was dealing less well with his reality than he thought—she had experienced a lot in a few hours and been in danger several times.

Niall ran his fingers over the cut on his shoulder, reassuring himself that the damage wasn't too extensive. He felt a bit overwhelmed by all the responsibilities he needed to manage. He fought against that pervasive sense of dread.

Instead he thought about his tours coming home, about the people he'd promised to check on, about no longer having a home or an office, about his working without a partner and logging too many hours, about needing to train Thorolf, about the shadow dragons who were still out there, about his twin brother's determination to interfere with his firestorm, about the challenges Rox herself offered, and he had to sit down again.

"*You have to change her mind*," Rafferty said softly in old-speak, and Niall bowed his head.

"I don't have time!" He flung out his hands in frustration. "There isn't time to court a mate, much less seduce her, much less raise a son."

Rafferty smiled. "I would wager that Roxanne is much closer to seduction than you believe."

Niall frowned and shoved his hand through his hair. Rafferty might be right, but Niall didn't believe he could juggle another responsibility at this time. "I really wanted my firestorm to be different. I really wanted to do it differently from my father—to make better choices and take more time."

"The Great Wyvern does not bless us with any burden we cannot carry," Rafferty said, his tone soothing. "There is a way, but you must find it."

"You heard Rox—she doesn't want kids. That's fair. She gets to make those kinds of choices for her own life."

Rafferty pursed his lips and studied the sky. The rain fell steadily as he thought. "She would not be your destined mate if there was no chance of conception."

Niall pushed himself to his feet, lacking Rafferty's confidence in a great plan. "Maybe after the shadow dragons are eliminated, I can attend to the firestorm," he said, already guessing what Rafferty would say. "Maybe then Rox and I can build a relationship. We need to take some time to know each other. . . ."

Rafferty interrupted Niall sharply. "We can both guess that the elimination of the shadow dragons will be linked to the consummation of your firestorm."

He was right. Niall sighed, displeased with this idea as much as he'd anticipated it. "But it's so dangerous for Rox."

"The danger exists already. You must face it to be rid of it. In fact, consummating your firestorm could make her safer."

Niall met the confident dark gaze of the older *Pyr*. "Because there won't be the heat of the firestorm to attract danger."

Rafferty raised a brow. "You cannot evade the danger, just as you cannot evade the destruction of your brother. Your task would have been simpler if you had destroyed him tonight."

So Rafferty had noticed his reluctance to destroy Phelan, as well. "I can't help but think of when we were children together, before he turned *Slayer*."

"That is the treacherous power of the shadow dragons. They prey upon our emotional response and memories, although they have few themselves."

"No, it's more than that," Niall argued. "I thought of Delaney. He was forced to consume the Elixir and he was healed of its effects. He was returned to the *Pyr*." Niall appealed to Rafferty. "What if Phelan can be healed, as well?"

Rafferty winced. "He chose in his life to turn *Slayer*. That is no portent of success in this endeavor."

"But I don't think it was his choice." Niall sighed and shoved a hand through his hair. "I think he didn't have all the information, and he made a mistake. He asked for my help."

Rafferty folded his arms across his chest. "Was he not inclined to deception, even before he turned *Slayer*?"

It was a truth that Niall couldn't evade. "But what if seeing the darkness made him realize what he lost? What if all he needs is another chance?" Rafferty looked unpersuaded. "Rox, you know, is always giving people more chances to redeem themselves. I wondered whether this is the lesson of my firestorm, that I learn how to be less judgmental."

"From Roxanne," Rafferty murmured, then nodded thoughtfully. "It is a possibility. But the fact remains that your choice to let Phelan survive leaves your mate in greater danger."

Niall met Rafferty's solemn gaze. "How can I create a son without knowing for certain that I'll be around to teach him what's right?"

Rafferty considered the question for a long moment, as the rain beat on the awning overhead and the flagstones all around. "You cannot," he said finally. "None of us can truly be certain." He heaved a sigh and put a hand on Niall's shoulder. "But you must trust in the wisdom of the Great Wyvern. You must try. You must discover whether the answer to your concern lies in the nature of your mate."

Niall grimaced. "I knew you would say something like that."

Rafferty chuckled and squeezed his shoulder. Just the presence of the older *Pyr* made Niall acknowledge that obstacles might be overcome.

That a resolution to all of this might be possible.

He just needed some sleep to restore his perspective.

And that gave him an idea.

"You know," Niall said as he watched the rain fall, "I need a place to stay for a few nights. I need to ensure Rox's safety in the short term by keeping guard over her."

"Dragonsmoke is no longer the effective defense that once it was," Rafferty agreed. "Vigilance is best."

"Plus Thorolf just moved out of Rox's spare room. Maybe it's still available."

Rafferty smiled encouragement. "You see? The Great Wyvern is moving mountains for you."

Niall smiled despite himself. "All I have to do is persuade Rox to let me in."

Rafferty met his gaze steadily. "A firestorm is never without its obstacles."

There was nothing Niall could say to the truth of that. He sent an old-speak message to Sloane, requesting his presence and his advice regarding Phelan as soon as possible.

As he took flight from the terrace roof, his heart leapt with the prospect of seeing Rox again. There was far more to his mate than met the eye—Niall just hoped they could survive and find a middle ground.

In the pouring rain, with his awareness of the shadow dragons hunting him, it seemed a lot to ask.

Rox was unsettled.

She didn't feel safe in her apartment, for the first time ever. It was true that she hadn't lived alone since she'd dragged Thorolf home in an attempt to save him from himself, but Thorolf had always gone out in the evenings. Rox had given up on waiting for him pretty quickly, as he was better equipped than most to fend for himself.

And he had a cell phone, in case he needed to call her for help.

Like the two times he'd needed her to post bail after he'd gotten busted in bar fights that spilled into the street. Thorolf meant well, and he had a great big heart, but he was too quick to use his fists.

Rox had told him that umpteen gazillion times, to no discernible effect.

She couldn't help thinking that Niall's restraint was more admirable. She respected that he used his power with discretion and had tried to find alternative answers. He'd taken her comment to heart about giving Thorolf another chance, and it seemed to be working.

It was also true that she'd told Thorolf not to stay with her on this night, mostly because she sensed his desire to return to Niall. If nothing else, Thorolf had taken to this mentorship like a fish to water.

Or a dragon to the fire.

That was good and she was glad for Thorolf.

A child. Rox's heart clenched at the word that kept echoing in her thoughts. Niall's son. She could never bring a child into the world, could never go the whole marriage-and-babies route. It wasn't her style.

It smacked of her past, of pain and heartache and emotional journeys she was determined to avoid.

Were there more dragon shape shifters? It was tempting to consider that a different one might be the right one for her, but her fascination for Niall and admiration of him undermined that.

She wanted Niall.

Without the firestorm's suite of obligations.

Rox was out of luck.

So she paced around her apartment, restless.

The rain kept falling hard and fast, so hard and fast that Rox thought it might never stop. She stood at the window and watched the raindrops pelt against the pane. The water turned the streets dark and slick, the puddles reflecting the streetlights. She usually liked the rain, but on this night, it gave her the creeps.

She decided to make herself a cup of herbal tea, pacing while the kettle came to a boil. Each time she looked at the dark, wet windows, she thought of the dead eyes of Niall's twin and shuddered. She lowered the blinds in every room and played some soothing music, but still.

She couldn't settle down.

The tea didn't help.

She really needed to get some sleep.

She had a quick shower and washed both the mousse and the temporary color out of her hair. Then she tugged on a favorite pair of red silk pajamas. She was heading to the kitchen to make another cup of tea, when there was a knock at the door.

A decisive knock.

She froze and stared at the door, then at the clock.

It was past two in the morning. Who would be at her door?

Rox was actually quite sure who it was.

And she was honest enough to admit that she was glad.

Rox crossed the living room on silent feet, the warmth that grew stronger with every step supporting her theory. She splayed her hands on the door, letting the heat of the firestorm spread over them. It embraced and enfolded her, filling her with a seductive and welcome heat. Rox savored the sensation for a minute, then looked through the peephole. Her body simmered even before she saw him.

Niall stood in the corridor, looking straight at her. His hair was wet and curling at the ends from the rain, his shoulders were soaked, and his T-shirt clung in all the right places. He had that black laptop bag slung over his shoulder and his left hand rested on top of it. He looked impatient and grim and absolutely scrumptious. Rox's heart skipped a beat, then skipped again when he waved two fingers in a curt salute.

Rox opened the door as far as it would go with the chain still on. It was stupid, because even in human form, Niall could have broken down the door, but in a way, it made her feel more in control of the situation.

"Hi," she said.

"Hi." Niall cleared his throat and looked uncertain of himself for a moment. "I was wondering whether you're as worried about my brother as I am."

"What do you think he's going to do?"

Niall grimaced. "Something sneaky."

Rox had exactly the same feeling, and she doubted that anything good would happen to her after that. "What do the bad *Pyr* do to mates?"

"*Slayers*," Niall corrected. "And they kill mates." He didn't flinch and he didn't put a gloss on the truth. Rox appreciated that, even though she didn't like his answer.

"If you think about it, that's the easiest way to eliminate the chance of making more *Pyr*."

"Did you come to defend me or to watch?" Rox asked. It was supposed to be a joke, but it sounded a little more defensive than she'd intended.

Niall frowned, then glanced up and down the hall. He took a step closer, leaning his free hand on the door frame, and that heat rolled through Rox with renewed strength. His eyes were dark with intent, almost indigo, and his voice dropped low. "I know we didn't start off on the right foot," he said, "but maybe we could try again. Maybe you could let me protect you tonight."

Rox's heart pounded so loudly in her ears that she felt dizzy. Even though she'd refused to have his child, he had still come to her. His presence made her much happier. "Maybe you just want a place to stay tonight."

Niall grinned, looking daring and sexy. Rox's heart went thump. "Well, there's that, too. But if you say no, I'll just keep watch from the roof."

Rox was surprised by the offer, but she believed it.

"That's where Thorolf and Rafferty have been while I picked up my stuff."

"Why?"

"Because I asked them to." His gaze bored into hers and she could feel his determination. "Whether we work anything out or not, Rox, your defense is my responsibility as long as the firestorm lasts."

"How long is that?"

He looked away and she guessed he didn't like this answer. "I don't know anyone who's managed to resist it long enough to find out."

Rox could understand that. Even with the door between them, her desire was raging, making her skin tingle and filling her thoughts with the persistent notion of sex, sex, and more sex.

"Maybe you just think you can seduce me in the night," she teased.

Niall shook his head, his smile fading. He held her gaze, his own expression solemn. "No, I respect your choice. The world doesn't necessarily need more babies, and children are a long-term commitment." He arched a brow. "Even if I don't believe that's your real reason."

Rox changed the subject, although she figured Niall would guess why. He was too perceptive. "Why does it sound like I'm not the only one with an issue with consummating the firestorm?"

"I don't have a problem with the consummation," Niall admitted, the wary twinkle in his eye making Rox smile. "It's the bit after that. It's the baby. Especially now."

Rox knew she shouldn't have been surprised that they had something else in common. "Why?"

"It's complicated." Niall cleared his throat. "Look, I came to tell you what the point was, the point of my being able to do what I can do. I thought it was too long a story before, but you've seen a lot more now."

"Okay," Rox said, leaning against the door frame. She was curious. "Tell me the point."

To her amazement, Niall did.

Chapter 8

Niall glanced up and down the corridor before he leaned close to Rox. His voice dropped to a whisper that made her shiver with delight. "In the beginning, there was the fire, and the fire burned hot because it was cradled by the earth. The fire burned bright because it was nurtured by the air. The fire burned lower only when it was quenched by the water. And these were the four elements of divine design, of which all would be built and with which all would be destroyed. And the elements were placed at the cornerstones of the material world, and it was good."

Rox watched him, fascinated.

"But the elements were alone and undefended, incapable of communicating with one another, snared within the matter that was theirs to control." Niall held her gaze steadily. "And so, out of the endless void was created a race of guardians whose appointed task was to protect and defend the integrity of the four sacred elements. They were given powers, the better to fulfill their responsibilities; they were given strength and cunning and longevity to safeguard the treasures surrendered to their stewardship. To them alone would the elements respond. These guardians were—and are—the *Pyr*."

"I knew you had to have a higher purpose than kicking butt and looking good doing it," Rox whispered.

Niall's smile was quick. "We don't just defend the elements. We protect all of the treasures of the earth—that includes the elements and humans, too."

It was a philosophy that perfectly meshed with Rox's own.

"And that's the kicker," he continued, "because I've taken on a quest, to eliminate the shadow dragons, and I want to be sure I'm going to survive before I bring a child into the world."

"Why wouldn't you survive? I mean, isn't there always going to be a threat?"

Niall sobered and his eyes narrowed. Rox liked that he was giving her questions serious consideration. "There's something different this time. I can't explain it, but I feel targeted, as if something or someone is out to get me. As if maybe there's no escape. I know it sounds crazy, but it's throwing my game."

Rox knew that feeling all too well. "But what's that got to do with creating a son?"

Niall looked pointedly at the chain. "Long story."

Rox understood. If she let him in, he'd tell her. She was tempted, seriously tempted. If nothing else, the firestorm proved that Niall wasn't his twin. There was no case of mistaken identity, so long as the firestorm was raging.

"Give me your hand," she said, and Niall blinked. "Just to check. Before I let you in."

He lifted his hand to the gap between the door and the frame. Rox touched his palm with her fingertips, watching as a brilliant orange spark burst from the point of contact. She felt its heat roll through her and caught her breath at its power. Niall swore softly. She watched him swallow, noting the sizzling blue of his eyes, and was aware of the warmth of his skin beneath her hand.

There was no doubt that he was Niall.

Her destined mate.

In another time or place, with another history behind her, Rox might have found the whole notion romantic and appealing. As it was, the prospect of a permanent bond terrified her.

But Niall's concern, both for the child that would result from the firestorm and for defending the treasures of the earth, was his passport back into her life.

Or, at least, into her apartment.

Rox shut the door, removed the lock, and opened the door to Niall, refusing to consider whether this was the dumbest thing she'd ever done. She had a feeling that nothing would be the same if she let her life become entangled with Niall's.

On the other hand, it already was.

On the third hand, it was healthy to shake things up once in a while and take on new challenges.

This was going to be a big one. Her heart said to trust Niall, so Rox tried. She had a policy of not letting fear govern her choices, and this firestorm was testing her determination.

Rox stepped out of the way and held her breath, trying to see her home with Niall's eyes. She wasn't worried about the furniture from the thrift shop, or the spartan decor.

Niall stepped into her living room and froze. Rox felt his astonishment, but she was mostly aware of his presence in her home. He seemed larger and more buff, filling the space in a way she hadn't anticipated. She felt self-conscious then, because her dreams were truly displayed in her home.

They covered the walls. Niall stood and stared at the myriad images of dragons. He was silent, as if struck dumb with wonder, his gaze roving over the drawings again and again and again. The quiet made Rox fear his reaction, and she had to say something.

"So, no getting a son on me while I'm asleep," she joked, feeling as if her heart and soul were laid bare.

Niall turned and glanced over his shoulder at her, his eyes glittering in a way that reminded her all too well what he was. His smile was slow and seductive, the sight of it enough to make her heart thunder.

"Invitation only," he murmured, his gaze sliding over her with obvious appreciation. "But feel free to invite me anytime."

Uh-oh.

Rox could have been a different woman.

Niall had thought when she opened the door that he might have the wrong apartment. Even the sliver of her figure that he could see was utterly different from expectation. Her hair was damp and her features were devoid of makeup. Her eyes seemed more vividly blue, and she looked more delicate.

Feminine.

Pretty.

He appreciated that he was seeing her without her shields up, and he was awed that she'd opened the door to him at all. When she'd let him in, there'd been the surprise of her lustrous red pajamas, the silk covering her completely but sliding over her curves.

Just the way Niall would have liked to slide his hands over her.

And if that wasn't enough to shake Niall's assumptions, there was Rox's apartment itself. It was in a big six-story building, a Beaux Arts building more typical of the Upper West Side than so far downtown. He wasn't surprised by the high ceilings or the grandeur of the rooms or the elaborate plaster on the ceilings, even though the entire building seemed out of place.

He was shocked by the artwork. The walls were filled

with framed posters of dragons, and one wall was actually painted in a fresco of a dragon in flight.

No, they weren't posters—they were original paintings. He'd never seen so many images of dragons, let alone so many that were so beautiful. Each dragon was unique, each image rendered with a loving hand and an eye for detail.

The living room, otherwise, had only a pair of vintage couches. They were slightly different, but covered in the same natural cotton. Their backs were low enough that they didn't obstruct the view of the art. The floor was hardwood, polished to a sheen and devoid of any rugs. White rice-paper blinds covered the windows, which must have been large, judging by the expanse of closed blinds. The only color was from the art, which seemed to glow on the walls.

No doubt about it, the dragons held court.

Niall couldn't stop looking at the paintings. He moved around the room, examining each in turn, well aware of Rox's nervous silence as she watched him.

There was one dragon perched on a mountain aerie; another flew low over a lake as clear as a mirror, his scaled belly reflected perfectly in the water. There were two fighting each other, their tails locked together and their teeth bared. There was a dragon sleeping beside his hoard, one eye open a slit as an intrepid woman ventured closer. The fresco was of a moonstone and silver dragon, raging on the attack. Each dragon was so realistic that Niall wouldn't have been surprised to hear the rumble of old-speak in his thoughts.

He gradually realized they had been created by the same hand. There were commonalities in the way the scales were articulated, the way the eyes had been drawn, the assumption of the musculature beneath the scaled skin. He saw an *R* in the bottom corner of one, an *R* executed with flourishes, and he knew why Rox was self-conscious. He remembered Thorolf's tattoo.

He turned to look at her.

She was watching him, her arms folded across her chest, her eyes filled with doubt as she nibbled one thumbnail. He'd never seen her uncertain, and his heart clenched with the reason why she felt vulnerable.

"Did you create all of these?" He heard the wonder in his own voice and didn't try to hide his awe.

Rox nodded once; then she swallowed.

"They're wonderful." Niall couldn't help but look again. The level of detail was fascinating, and he could have studied each work for hours on end. "Do you sell your work?"

"No." There was no question in her tone. "These dragons are for me." She marched past him, keeping her gaze averted as she headed toward the kitchen. Again, she seemed vulnerable to him, and Niall followed her with caution. He didn't want to make a mistake and it seemed increasingly clear to him that the firestorm had made his match in one. "Do you want some tea?"

"If you're making it, sure."

Rox was moving quickly, uncertain as Niall had never seen her. "Herbal okay? I don't do caffeine."

"Me, neither, so that's perfect, thanks."

She flicked a quick glance his way, as if skeptical, and Niall smiled, hoping to reassure her. "I try to avoid stuff like that."

She blushed and turned her back on him, as if he had spooked her. *Blushed*. Rox blushed. Niall couldn't have imagined her blushing just twenty minutes earlier. Fascinated, he put his laptop bag down by the kitchen table, then leaned in the doorway, giving her lots of space.

No wonder she'd been able to accept so much dragon lore. She knew about Thorolf and she was obviously interested in his kind.

Rox filled the kettle and put it on to boil, then rinsed out the teapot, moving with that same energy. When she had put in the tea bags and laid out the mugs and run out of tasks to do, she almost vibrated in place.

"Why dragons?" Niall asked quietly.

She exhaled and stared at the counter, still avoiding his gaze. The back of her neck was a smooth curve of pale skin, one that he was tempted to caress.

"I've always been fascinated by dragons, always thought they had to be the most beautiful and magical creatures."

"Always thought they were real?"

"Dragons are real!" she said, pivoting to face him abruptly.

"You don't have to persuade me," Niall agreed, and her cheeks were touched with pink again. "Most humans would argue otherwise."

"True." Rox kept her distance. She folded her arms across her chest again, looking both defiant and fragile. She looked a bit, actually, like the woman brave enough to invade the dragon's hoard in that one illustration.

Intrepid but cautious.

Determined.

"It started when I was a kid, when my dad died," she admitted softly. "I wanted to become an animal or another creature, to fly away maybe."

There it was again, that hint that her childhood hadn't been idyllic.

"No fairies or butterflies?" Niall asked lightly.

Rox laughed. "Too vulnerable. They can be squished." She lowered her lashes, once again ensuring that she didn't meet his gaze. "I wanted to be fearless. Dragons are still beautiful; they still can fly, but they don't have to be afraid of anything."

He heard the resonance of truth in her words. Her defiance and resilience made Niall angry, making him want to take a price out of the hide of whoever had hurt her. "What happened, Rox?"

She shook her head, then turned her back on him. "I

always knew dragons were real, no matter what anyone else had to say. I *believed*."

Niall respected her privacy enough to leave the subject alone. He couldn't help looking back at the fresco, the painting that was obviously of Thorolf. "And then you saw one."

"Thorolf. He called himself T." Rox grimaced, then shook her head, her mood lightening. "I thought he was my destiny. I thought my every dream had come true. And when he needed an alibi, someone sane and sober to insist there hadn't been a dragon there, I was quick to volunteer." She smiled, rueful, and Niall felt bad that Thorolf had unwittingly disappointed her.

On the other hand, he was glad of it.

"You brought him home."

Rox made a gesture of futility and turned to the kettle, hiding her expression from Niall. It wasn't a coincidence and he knew it—the kettle wasn't quite boiling yet. "Call it a weakness," she said lightly. "I'm always trying to save people from themselves, or give them a chance to start fresh. Sometimes a second chance even works."

"But not with Thorolf."

She made a sound of frustration. "He had—*has*—this incredible power, and all he wanted to do was get drunk, brawl, and seduce women."

Niall fought a smile, knowing he'd accused Thorolf of the same thing.

"What's so funny?"

"He accused me of not respecting him last year and we had an argument. I told him I couldn't respect someone who hadn't bothered to learn to use his powers, and only wanted to drink, fight, and, um, get lucky."

Her unexpected smile was mischievous and made her eyes dance. "I'll bet you used a different word."

Niall grinned at her. "You'd win that bet." He'd accused Thorolf of wanting only to party, fight, and screw.

Rox laughed, the most delightful sound Niall had ever heard, then flung out one hand. "I couldn't understand it. All those powers, yet he just wanted to slide through life and achieve nothing. I've had to work for everything I've got, and it just drove me crazy that he wouldn't even try."

That sentiment sounded pretty familiar to Niall. "I hear you."

Rox swallowed and looked down.

"You were right, though," Niall said quietly, and she looked his way, startled. "About giving him a second chance. He did well tonight."

She smiled. "You got through to him."

"Be serious," Niall scoffed. "He's scared crapless of you. I think you softened him up for me."

Rox laughed, then blushed again. It seemed warmer in the kitchen, more intimate and welcoming. "What about you?"

Niall recognized that the question wasn't an idle one. "Well, as I mentioned, there are these shadow dragons. I've taken it as my quest to eliminate them all." Anticipating her question, he explained. "Shadow dragons have been fed the Elixir, the Dragon's Blood Elixir that confers immortality. The thing is that they didn't ingest it by choice—they were raised from the dead and forced to consume it. It makes them into zombies that a *Slayer* can control."

"Is that what's wrong with your brother's eyes?" she asked, and Niall nodded. "Then why didn't you kill him?"

He exhaled and stared at the floor. "Well, that's just it. I'm not sure he really knew what he was doing when he chose to turn *Slayer*. I wonder whether he was tricked."

"Because he wasn't really bad?"

"Just misguided." Niall shrugged. "Looking for the easy way and living on charm."

"Like Thorolf."

"Exactly. And what happened today made me wonder whether Phelan just needed another chance."

Rox stared at him, her eyes wide.

"He even asked me to help him."

"Oh. Is that possible?"

"I'm not sure. You see, my friend Delaney, who is also *Pyr* and used to be my business partner, was forced to drink the Elixir. It really messed him up, but he didn't exactly become a shadow dragon. And it was possible to save him, to drive the Elixir out of his body and make him whole again."

"You think you can save your brother," Rox whispered.

"I don't know. I do know that I need to be sure, so I sent a message to Sloane. He's the Apothecary of the *Pyr*, and I asked him to come and help me work it out." Niall grimaced. "It leaves both of us in more danger in the short term. . . ."

"But you're giving him a chance."

Niall met her gaze steadily. "Yes. I want him to have the second chance my father never gave him." He smiled. "Just like you suggested."

Her lips parted in wonder.

"Rafferty thinks firestorms are intended to teach us something about ourselves, and I'm wondering whether that's it. I've got to be sure." Niall fell silent then and stared into the endless blue of Rox's eyes.

The kettle boiled, startling them both with its shrill whistle.

Niall took the opportunity to step farther into the tiny kitchen. He heard Rox catch her breath as he reached past her for the kettle.

"Let me," he murmured, then filled the pot with steaming water. She was so close, so alluring, so delicate. He put his hand on the counter beside her and, to his relief, she didn't move away. His hand looked large beside her, making her seem more tiny and feminine.

More precious.

He looked down and was startled to find her watching him closely. Her eyes weren't just blue, it turned out, but mingled with gray and gold, wide and thickly lashed. Her skin was so fair, her mouth so full and soft. She was lovely, far prettier than he'd imagined, and he wondered again why she took such effort to hide her beauty.

There was a tattoo at the outside corner of one eye, one that he hadn't noticed before. It was a tiny heart, no more than a quarter of an inch in diameter, outlined in blue. There was a jagged line right across its middle.

He was surprised by the choice of tattoo, of the hint of fragility that belied her attitude. But he'd glimpsed it several times, this vulnerability of Rox's, and it was no less fascinating to discover a tattoo that echoed his own observations.

What was Rox hiding from the world? And why? Niall wanted to know.

"A broken heart?" he murmured, unable to keep himself from raising a finger to touch the minuscule tattoo.

They gasped in unison as the firestorm's spark leapt between his finger and her cheekbone, and Niall caught his breath at the sight of Rox bathed in golden light. The heat slid under his skin, through his hand, up his arm, and pierced his heart.

"A reminder each and every day of the price of trust," she said, and he was surprised by her words and her bitterness.

"Every day?"

"When I look in the mirror, it's there. Every time." She shrugged and smiled, trying to soften the edge of her words. Niall knew her tone was indicative of an old wound, only tentatively healed. But she smiled for him. He ached that her smile was wary, and he found it utterly seductive. "No chance of forgetting ever again."

Niall found himself wanting to defend Rox from anyone who gave her trouble, anyone who challenged her

obvious desire to fend for herself. He studied her, seeing again the shadow that lurked beneath her bold manner, and let his finger ease down her cheek. It caught
at his heart that anyone could have been cruel to her;
it angered him that anyone dared to deliberately hurt
her. "I'm sorry," he murmured, and she swallowed, her
lashes dropping to hide her thoughts.

"Yeah, sure," she said, her tone dismissive of his
sympathy.

Niall saw the tear, though—he saw it slip onto her
cheek before she rubbed it away. He understood that
she didn't want anyone to understand or show compassion. He respected her attempt to defend herself, but he
knew she didn't have to defend herself from him.

He'd never break her heart.

He instinctively wanted to console her, and there was
only one way to do it. Niall lifted her chin with that one
fingertip, tipping her face toward his. When she didn't
fight him, simply met his gaze steadily, he bent and
touched his lips to hers.

The heat was incendiary, flaring instantly between
them and making both of them inhale in unison. But
Niall didn't retreat from the flame. He closed his mouth
over Rox's soft lips, claiming her with a kiss, even as he
cupped her jaw in his hand.

And when she opened her mouth to him, he thought
he would explode. He wrapped his other arm around
her waist and lifted her against him, loving the way she
twined her arms around his neck. She kissed him back,
meeting him more than halfway, just as she had the last
time, and her response melted his reservations even
more quickly.

He deepened his kiss and she made a little growl of
pleasure, one that made him wonder how she would
look, how she would sound, when she came.

Never mind all the things he could do to prompt that
reaction. He could feel her heartbeat accelerating, and

he felt a bit dizzy as his own heart matched its pace. He heard his breathing synchronize with hers and the sensation made him tingle. He caught her closer and the firestorm's heat surged through him, obliterating awareness of anything other than Rox's soft lips.

Niall slid his hands over Rox's curves, the smooth silk still too much of a barrier to his touch. He kissed her beneath her ear, feeling her sigh in his hair, then unfastened the silk top and eased his hand inside. Rox was tiny and perfect, her breasts pert and her nipples responding to his caress. He cupped one breast in his hand, slid his thumb across the nipple, smiled when she gasped and swallowed.

But she didn't move away. Her eyes were dark and her cheeks were flushed, her lips parted and swollen from his kiss. He could see the edge of another tattoo on her shoulder, but Niall didn't care about such details.

He wanted Rox.

Niall bent, closed his eyes, and took her nipple in his mouth, teasing and caressing, loving how she arched against him. She locked her fingers in his hair and moaned, drawing him closer and closer. The firestorm crackled and snapped, illuminating her kitchen with its fiery glow, touching her artwork with golden light. It drove every conscious thought from Niall's mind, incinerated every reservation, eliminated everything from his universe except the splendor of his mate.

There was no pretense with Rox. No posturing, and no lies. She was what she was, and she was unafraid to show it.

Even a dragon could learn from her courage.

He didn't want to create a son. He didn't want to inflict the *Pyr* agenda on Rox, but he wanted to give her pleasure. More pleasure maybe than she'd ever known. He wanted to show her that trust was sometimes of merit.

He wanted her to trust him.

Niall bracketed her waist with his hands and pushed

her pajama bottoms to the floor. "Not that," she protested, her words breathless.

"Not that," Niall agreed, looking her in the eye. He smiled. "Something else. Trust me."

It took her only a heartbeat to smile.

That was all the encouragement Niall needed. He scooped Rox up, holding her in his arms while he kissed her again. When he was dizzy with desire, he put her on the counter, parted her knees, then bent to touch her with his tongue.

Rox cried out and dug her nails into his shoulders. She locked her thighs around his head and Niall caught her butt in his hands. He lifted her to feast upon her, flicking his tongue so that the flames of the firestorm danced between them.

Rox writhed. She was wet and he was hard.

"Trust you," she muttered, her fingers locking into his hair. Her hips began to buck of their own accord. "Just don't stop."

Niall didn't have any intention of stopping. As much as he wanted to prolong Rox's pleasure, he had a feeling she wouldn't last long. She moaned and twisted. He caressed her with sure strokes, alternating an aggressive tease with a touch as soft as a butterfly's wings. He let her pull away when she tried to evade him, loving that she kept sliding closer to him for more.

He teased her and he touched her, and the firestorm crackled against the night. His heart thundered and he felt it match Rox's own pulse. They breathed in unison, moving as one, their passion kindling ever higher and hotter.

When Rox came with a cry of delight, Niall barely restrained himself from joining her orgasmic cry.

He should have known he couldn't have hidden his response from Rox. She reached down, her face flushed and her hair mussed, and unfastened his jeans. She caught his erection between her hands and caressed him boldly.

Irresistible.

He couldn't last. He didn't last. He was overwhelmed too quickly, already on fire from giving her pleasure. Niall came with a roar, his seed spilling over her hands. He gripped the counter to catch his breath, as Rox regarded him with an impish smile.

"Fireworks," she said, touching her finger to his shoulder. The spark flared between them and her smile broadened at the sight.

"And that's not half of it," he managed to say. Their gazes locked, the air between them heating with the unspoken promise of the firestorm. Rox ran her tongue over her lips and Niall watched the gesture hungrily. He would have reached for her again, but a key turned audibly in the front door.

They froze as one.

Rox was in very deep trouble.

Niall protected her. He was both a dragon and a hunk. He listened to her and changed his direction on the basis of her opinion if he agreed with her. But more than that, Niall wanted to give his brother a second chance, maybe another second chance, despite whatever he had done and what he had become.

Because what she had said to him made sense.

Rox already suspected that she could count on Niall, and that he would keep any promise he made. He'd given her pleasure without sex, and he would have denied himself if she hadn't intervened.

This was the kind of man she'd always wanted to find.

Never mind that he kissed well enough to make her forget everything she knew, every promise she'd made herself, and every vow she'd ever sworn. Never mind that he brought her to orgasm as if he had written the book on seduction.

Rox could lose her heart to this *Pyr* warrior.

With another guy, she might have thought he was just saying what he needed to say to win her agreement to have his child. But Rox already knew Niall wasn't that way.

She was tempted, even knowing what she knew, to drag him into her room right that minute and spend the night making love to him. She was ready to know more about making love to a dragon dude, about what would certainly be the best sex ever. She was tempted to challenge this *Pyr* conviction of "first time every time" and just savor the pleasure once.

Someone unlocked the door just in time to save Rox from her unreliable impulses. Niall spun at the sound, and Rox could see him shimmering blue around his perimeter. He was ready to defend her from anything or anyone.

There was nothing to dislike about that.

"Thorolf and Rafferty," he murmured.

Rox washed her hands pronto. Niall was doing up his jeans with similar haste. She heard him take a steadying breath, then another, slower one for good measure. That shimmer faded to a faint gleam. She got her pajama bottoms on and her top buttoned just in time, the way he winked at her making her heart go thump.

"Saved by the key," he murmured, and Rox bit back a smile.

Thorolf appeared in the kitchen doorway then, his hair and shirt completely soaked. "Dude! It's, like, pissing out here. Can't we crash on the floor?"

Rafferty was a dark shadow behind him.

Rox didn't know what Niall intended to say, but she knew opportunity when she saw it. The presence of two other *Pyr* would ensure that she didn't lose her senses.

Yet.

"It's okay," Rox said, hearing her voice waver. "There's room."

"It's up to Rox who she lets into her apartment,"

Niall said, his tone stern once again. "You should have knocked instead of using your key."

"Relax!" Thorolf said. "It's not like you were doing it or anything."

Rox felt her mouth fall open. Would the *Pyr* have been able to hear from the hall if she and Niall had been doing it? Niall gave her a glance, as if he'd guessed her thoughts. He nodded once and Rox resolved to be more careful around this bunch.

Of course, the neighbors had probably heard her climax.

Rox fought the urge to blush. Niall stood in front of her like a barricade, clearly unpersuaded that they needed company.

Rafferty hesitated in the hall, waiting for an invite. "If this is a bad time . . ."

Maybe his hearing was keen enough to sense nuance.

"Would you prefer they went elsewhere?" Niall asked, his gaze flicking to her work. "It's up to you."

Rox liked that he was protective of her privacy. "I don't think any of the *Pyr* are going to laugh at my paintings," she said, and beckoned to the two arrivals.

"I knew I should have taken your keys," she said to Thorolf, "or changed the locks."

The big *Pyr* grinned, unabashed, and jingled the keys. "Points for initiative, Niall?"

Niall put out his hand in silent expectation.

Thorolf looked between the two of them, sobered, then gave Niall the keys. Niall immediately surrendered them to Rox, and she appreciated his gallantry.

Among other things.

But she had to keep her reservations in mind so she wouldn't make an irrevocable mistake.

Rox stepped past Niall, the sizzle of the firestorm diminishing as she put distance between them. "Couch or floor, that's your choice," she said to Thorolf.

"What about the spare room?" Thorolf protested. "I like some privacy."

"Privacy?" Niall echoed, his tone incredulous.

The back of Thorolf's neck turned red.

He *had* heard.

"You moved out," Rox reminded him. "Niall can use the spare room." And that way there'd be a wall and a couple of doors between them. Every increment had to help.

She smiled at Rafferty, who was listening avidly. "Please, come in. I should have thought to invite you sooner, but I wasn't thinking about the rain."

Thorolf snorted and Niall gave him a killing look.

"I don't want to impose," Rafferty said.

"Two *Pyr* or three," Rox said with a smile. "It's a full house either way. And I kind of like the idea of having lots of good dragons around me when the shadow dragons are on the hunt."

Rafferty stepped into the apartment and his eyes rounded with surprise at her art. Rox watched him look from drawing to drawing, his gaze flicking over the fresco of Thorolf, then back to the drawings again.

"So I see," he murmured. Rafferty stepped toward one drawing with caution, as if he feared it might disappear before he could more closely examine it, and stood in silent awe for a long moment. "Marvelous," he said finally.

Rox knew she'd made the right choice to let them in.

Niall followed her from the kitchen. "I have to stay closer to you than the spare room. Maybe Rafferty could guard that flank." Rox didn't answer.

Rafferty touched the *R* of Rox's signature, the glass over the drawing keeping his finger from touching the actual image. He turned to smile at Rox. "You are wondrously talented," he said, and there was no doubting his sincerity.

"I thought I would hear old-speak from them," Niall agreed, and Rox felt her face heat.

"It's just what I do," she said, flustered by their praise.

"You could illustrate our history," Rafferty said, then eyed Niall. "If, of course, your firestorm became a permanent relationship."

"I don't do permanence," Rox repeated. She then yawned elaborately, making an excuse to disappear. "Time for bed, guys." She felt Niall's gaze on her and doubted he was fooled by her performance. "You work out the sleeping arrangements yourselves. I've got to get some sleep."

With that, she left them all in her living room, retreating to her own bedroom.

Once inside, she turned the lock on the door. It didn't truly pose an obstacle to Niall, in either human or dragon form, but Rox knew he'd hear the lock turn. She wanted her message to be clear.

She was going to sleep alone.

Even if it felt like a stupid choice.

Niall's decision was made.

He'd seen Rox's mask slip, and he had glimpsed the vulnerability it protected. He'd heard her perspective and appreciated her intellect. He found her incredibly sexy, and he respected her advice.

He thought about that broken heart tattooed on Rox's cheek and about the sweet fire of her kiss, and knew that resisting Rox's charms would be impossible.

The firestorm was right.

As it always was. Niall sensed that Rox could help him avoid his father's errors and lead him to a new understanding of his nature. He knew Rox had wounds of her own in need of healing and he knew he could help.

Niall knew they would be stronger together than apart.

This firestorm was his destiny, and Rox was precisely the right mate for him.

He still had two problems. The first was Rox herself. It was clear that she was disinclined to trust him. Yet. The second was his pervasive sense of being targeted, that awareness of Phelan lurking in the vicinity, that fear that he might not survive this quest.

Niall suspected that trusting he had a future was a big part of ensuring it would be so. If he focused upon eliminating Rox's reservations while he continued his hunt for the shadow dragons, then he might win everything.

He was also unlikely to get much sleep.

He should be getting used to that.

Niall watched Rox retreat to her room, knowing that she needed some distance but regretting her departure all the same. Niall's body demanded that he celebrate the power of life. He'd killed two shadow dragons on this night and fought another. He'd survived an assault on his home that had destroyed the building. He had a gash on his shoulder and a taste of his firestorm, and he instinctively wanted to spend the night making love to Rox over and over again.

But Rox needed time.

Niall would give it to her, at least as much of it as he could. He guessed that he could pursue her tonight, overwhelm her with the insistence of the firestorm, win the battle but lose the war. Niall didn't want a one-night stand or a son left without a father.

He wanted more.

So he had to bide his time. Niall settled in her living room, checked his e-mail and voice mail one more time, and thought about his mate all the while. He considered her reputation as Sister Rox, and her refusal to bring anyone home—with the exception of *Pyr*, like Thorolf and himself. No, with the exception of men she imagined might be the right match for her. She was a romantic, albeit one with barbed wire fences in self-defense.

He thought about her love of dragons being founded in their ability to defend themselves against anyone, their lack of fear, and suspected he had found the shadow in her past that he needed to help banish. He thought about her passionate response to his touch, and he dared to hope she already believed in the firestorm.

He dared to hope for success.

When he'd finished reassuring everyone on his travel team, Rafferty was already breathing dragonsmoke slowly and steadily, weaving a protective shield around the apartment. Thorolf sat on the couch and tried to do the same, although his line of smoke kept breaking.

Niall put his laptop away and shifted shape, stretching his dragon form across the hardwood floor. It was easier to steady himself and close his mind to other influences in this form. He felt more primal in his dragon form, more in tune with his body and the elements, more instinctive.

More powerful. That counted when he intended to defend his mate.

Niall entered the meditative state required for breathing dragonsmoke with somewhat more difficulty than usual, knowing that the persistent hum of the firestorm was responsible for that. Then Niall exhaled slowly, creating long tendrils of dragonsmoke that would surround his temporary lair, create a boundary mark, and keep Rox safe from some potential attackers. It wasn't a perfect defense, but it was better than none.

And it gave him something to do besides think about Rox.

Chapter 9

Rox didn't think she'd sleep, not with Niall so close by, but she did. She fell asleep immediately, then slept deeply and dreamlessly. When she awakened, her alarm clock revealed that it was after noon.

She supposed she shouldn't have been surprised, given the activity of the day and night before. And it was Sunday, so there was no rush to be anywhere. The light was silvery gray, the rain slanting against the windows with steady persistence. That it was still pouring rain was yet another reason to sleep in.

She could hear Niall in the living room, the rhythm of his breathing telling her he was still asleep. His presence and his protectiveness worked for Rox in a big way.

Could there be a more potent guardian and defender than a dragon? Niall could have shredded her without any trouble at all, but instead he had defended her. Repeatedly. And he listened to her—the proof was in his determination to give his brother a second chance. He could have been one of her fanciful drawings come to life.

But so much better.

Rox stared at the ceiling, acknowledging that she had

lied to him about the whole baby issue. It wasn't about long-term commitments. It wasn't about there being too many babies on the planet already.

Rox's reservation was about fear. It was about that broken heart tattoo on her cheek, about loving someone so much that when that person goes away, the whole world ends.

Or loses its meaning.

Would Niall leave her? Rox suspected he would. They looked so different, they lived differently, and he'd already shown that he had a number of assumptions about her and what she must think. Plus dragons, Rox was sure, needed to be free. The *Pyr* had their mission, after all, and Niall had his quest. She was sure that mates were left behind once the deed was done.

Rox had a feeling that after they had sex, after the firestorm was satisfied, Niall would be gone.

She really hoped she was wrong. But she was already falling in love, and she knew that physical intimacy— never mind bearing Niall's son—would only make it worse.

She needed to know for sure that he wanted to be a permanent fixture in her life.

She needed to know that he was planning to stay.

She couldn't survive another broken heart, not if it could be avoided with a little foresight and temperance.

Events could intervene in anyone's life, Rox knew that, but she needed to be more sure of Niall before she risked her heart again. It wasn't deceptive. It was self-defense. She had a feeling that if she explained it to him, he'd understand.

Niall had some pretty high protective walls of his own.

And really, if he could be scared off by appearances, if his desire for her was only skin-deep, she'd prefer he left sooner rather than later.

She knew exactly what she was going to wear on this day. Armor. Studded leather armor and lots of black makeup. Her attitude would be defensive, too, and if she saw the chance to point out a difference between them, she'd do it. She wanted Niall, but she wanted him with his eyes wide-open or not at all.

It sounded like such a good plan, and her resolve was complete.

So long as she was alone in her room.

Rox slipped out of bed. She approached the bedroom door, feeling that the room became warmer with every step. She heard the sound of Niall's slow, steady breathing get louder and realized he must be sleeping right across the threshold to her room.

Guarding her. The very idea made her tingle, and the firestorm kicked that tingle up to a hum. She pressed her palms flat to the door and savored the sparks of the firestorm.

Niall was there.

His decision caught at Rox's heart. She opened the door silently, only to find the living room filled with soft silvery light. Rafferty slept on one of her couches and Thorolf on the other, both of them in human form.

But there was a majestic amethyst and platinum dragon coiled across the threshold to her bedroom. The bottom fell out of Rox's world at the sight.

Niall was larger than she'd realized, or maybe he looked bigger and more dangerous in her apartment than he had in the night sky. He was so utterly motionless that she could barely discern his breathing. His scales could have been made of gems, but they didn't disguise the musculature that gave him his power.

She started when she realized she could see the glitter of blue beneath his lids. He was awake. He was watchful. He was dangerous.

Fearless.

Right then, Rox knew for sure that one night was never going to cure her of her desire for Niall and his fiery touch. She was going to want him for the duration.

All the more reason for both of them to be absolutely sure.

Filled with purpose, Rox made to step around him. She knew the instant Niall's eyes opened wide, the second his gaze fell on her. She swallowed and faced him, raising her chin. "Did you sleep?"

"No." He seemed impatient, though whether it was with primal urges or his brother's interference, Rox couldn't tell. "Close your eyes," he said then, his voice making her shiver, but not with cold. "I'll shift."

"No." Rox held her ground and let defiance fill her tone. "I'd like to see you better."

His eyes glittered and he surveyed her with care, as if he'd noticed the change in her tone immediately. Rox wondered how transparent she really was to him, and she feared she knew the truth.

Dragons were supposed to have really sharp eyesight. Could Niall see her thoughts? Her secrets? Her every motivation?

His tail slid across the floor as he considered her, its weight lazily sweeping back and forth. Rox wasn't fooled. He could move quickly if he so chose. His eyes shone like gems. His wings were folded across his back, his scales gleaming in the pearlescent light. That wound in his shoulder had a red scab, one that looked like a line of rubies. "Are you sure?"

"Who wouldn't want to check out a real dragon?" Rox had another good long look. The light was perfect for highlighting his physique and the details of his body. She watched how the light touched each scale, how the scales were each distinct from one another. She noted how his muscles were evident beneath his armor, how potent and powerful he was.

Her mouth went dry. He was more beautiful than she'd ever imagined dragons could be.

And that was saying something.

"There is a story among our kind that humans can be driven insane by the sight of our shift," Niall said. "You need to look away."

"We're not that fragile," Rox scoffed.

"Some are. My mother took to her rooms after seeing my father shift for the first time. She refused to be in his company for almost thirteen years."

Rox was intrigued by the notion of Niall having a family, of *Pyr* families having complications and dynamics like a human family. She'd met his brother, but she hadn't thought about his parents. If the tendency passed through the male line, then his mother must have been human.

A mate.

And Niall must have been conceived in a firestorm.

"But was she crazy?"

Niall averted his gaze, his thoughtfulness clear even in his dragon form. "She was troubled by his truth. He hadn't been honest with her."

Rox immediately saw the connection. "Is that why you've tried to answer everything I ask you?"

"Yes." Niall looked back at her, and Rox suspected he would have changed back to human form by now if he hadn't been afraid of her witnessing the change.

She kept her eyes wide-open, determined to not miss a thing. "It didn't make me crazy to see you change before. Maybe some of us chicks are made of tougher stuff."

"It's possible," Niall ceded, but he still didn't shift.

Rox decided to find out. She reached toward him, watching his eyes brighten. She was in the mood to be daring, to push him, maybe to provoke him.

It was her nature to challenge the status quo. If Niall didn't like that inclination, he knew where to find the door.

With closer proximity, the heat of the firestorm turned her thoughts in a predictable direction. It filled the room with that brilliance that grew brighter with every inch she bent, heating her skin until she was sure she'd flush crimson. She heard his breathing accelerate and knew he wasn't turned off by her curiosity.

Otherwise, Niall remained motionless.

Rox told herself that she was doing research for her art and knew it was a lie. She put her hand on his tail, anyway. A flash of orange lit the apartment, making Rox close her eyes against its brilliance and catch her breath at its heat. It seared her palm.

And made her yearn. She thought of Niall's kisses and she remembered his touch. The firestorm's welcoming heat made her spread her hand across his flesh and slide her palm up the length of him. She felt his muscles and his strength, and she spread her hand wider. Niall caught his breath and shivered. Rox liked that she could have such an effect upon him.

"That's enough," he said tersely.

Rox smiled and put her other hand on him, sliding them both higher. Niall's eyes opened wide. They shone brilliant sapphire, daring her to challenge him further.

He was irresistible.

She eased one hand over his hip, guessing what she'd find and wanting to know for sure. Niall started and pulled back. His tail swirled across the floor, sweeping past Rox with vigor.

"Close your eyes," he commanded.

"Never!"

Niall swore. Then he twisted away from her. He shifted shape as he turned his back on her, making the transition so quickly that it seemed like a blur to Rox. Then he closed the distance between them and caught her chin in his hand. He backed her into her bedroom door and bent, his lips just the breadth of a finger from hers. The firestorm's sparks snapped and crackled between them, and Rox couldn't break her gaze away from his intensity.

"You've made it clear you don't want a child," he whispered in a low voice. "But if you do that again, I won't stop." He inhaled sharply, his hot glance sweeping over her. "I won't be able to," he added quietly, then brushed his lips across hers.

His touch burned Rox's lips and weakened her knees.

It felt so good.

But Rox believed Niall. She put her hands on his chest and pushed until he stepped back, knowing that if he kissed her when she was this riled up, she would be the one who couldn't stop. It didn't help her resolve that Niall was responding to her challenge with such gusto, as if he liked to be provoked.

As if they maybe were meant to be together.

Better not to think about that.

Yet.

She felt him watching her as she practically fled into the bathroom, but he didn't make a move to stop her. That was the only reason she made it, and she knew it.

The door locked behind her, Rox stopped to survey her reflection. Her eyes were shining. She looked awake and alive, more invigorated than she ever had. Her lips were swollen and soft and reddened; her cheeks were flushed and her nipples were pert.

No doubt about it—the firestorm wasn't taking no for an answer.

Rox had to do something, if she wasn't going to surrender to raw urge. She had to keep herself from potentially making a mistake. She turned on the shower, then peeled off her pajamas as she considered her options. If Niall was determined to seduce her, Rox knew she'd lose. Her body was already on his side.

Her roughest, meanest, most shocking punk armor it would be.

*　　*　　*

Niall wasn't at his best. He was tired, he was hungry, he had denied his desire too many times in a row to be a cheerful houseguest. He hadn't slept—again—out of his determination to protect Rox. That persistent sense of being stalked niggled at him, as did his conviction that Phelan intended to surprise him. He didn't trust his brother, even though he had to consider Phelan's request for help, and he didn't like how the shadow dragons seemed to have developed a plan.

And now something had changed with Rox. She was challenging him, deliberately trying to get a response out of him.

Trying to get rid of him.

That realization improved Niall's mood enormously. Rox could only be trying to ditch him because he was wearing down her defenses. He recalled her comment about dragons not needing to be afraid, and he wondered again what Rox feared.

Niall was going to find out. Rox wasn't stupid and she wasn't irrational—whatever had happened had scarred her deeply, and she was trying to learn from her mistake.

He could relate to that.

It was another tendency they had in common.

Niall peeled off his grubby T-shirt and wished he had another. He could have used a razor, as well. He didn't much like that, ready to seduce his mate and needing to erode her resistance, he was destined to do it at less than his best. He liked to look crisp and well-groomed.

There was little chance of that, with Thorolf being his best shot for a change of clothes.

Niall headed for the kitchen and put on the kettle, remembering where Rox kept the tea. He made a pot of green tea and drank two cups in thoughtful silence.

"What's for breakfast?" Thorolf demanded of the

world in general. He had pulled a T-shirt over his head, one that didn't look any cleaner than the other Niall had discarded, and the hem hung unevenly over his khaki shorts. He looked even more rumpled than usual. "I could eat a horse."

"That's one thing I don't have in the fridge," Rox said as she joined them in the kitchen.

She looked like a different person than she had earlier, but Niall was determined not to stare. The lime color in her hair, the way it was teased into spikes, and the stark contrast of her makeup was probably intended to keep him at a distance. Niall didn't doubt that she was wearing the torn Ramones T-shirt, the black leather pants that fit like a second skin, and the stiletto boots with studs to tick him off.

He disliked how well her ploy worked. He knew better than to judge by appearances—even if Rox had deliberately chosen every item to be as unfeminine and unappealing to him as possible.

She even wore leather bracelets studded like pit bull collars. He wanted to toss her over his shoulder, carry her back to the bathroom, strip her bare, and wash her black makeup off.

Then move on from there.

At least she couldn't stop looking at his bare chest. Niall decided it was a good thing he hadn't yet asked for a T-shirt from Thorolf.

Maybe he'd wait a bit longer.

Maybe he'd be in Rox's way a bit, so the firestorm's sparks could argue his case. Rox, he guessed, might be prickly and argumentative, particularly if she was determined to keep him at a distance. She wasn't immune to the firestorm's call, after all.

He would do his best to undermine her reservations. If she wanted to find ways in which they were different, he'd make note of what they had in common.

It could work.

"All I've got is organic and vegan," Rox pronounced, seemingly daring the two of them to argue with her.

Thorolf wrinkled his nose. "Man does not live by organic vegetables alone."

"Are you so sure of that?" Niall asked, and saw Rox's surprise. "I seem to be doing all right with it."

Rox's eyes narrowed as she confronted him. "Be serious."

"I am."

"No. Men like you eat steak and potatoes every day of your lives. Dragon dudes need their meat, or so I've been told." She gestured to Thorolf, who grinned. "I know. I've lived with one."

"Not this one," Niall argued, leaning in the doorway right beside her. He watched her swallow, then glance sidelong at him. He saw her inhale sharply, watched her eyes narrow, and smiled at her.

She spun away from him. "I have organic yogurt, granola, and fresh fruit," she said, that challenge in her tone.

"Perfect." Niall smiled. "It's what I eat every day."

Rox blinked, glared at him, then opened the fridge. Niall could still sense her accelerated pulse and the quickness of her breathing. He could smell her perfume, its scent becoming stronger because she was warm.

His plan was working beautifully.

"Bacon," Thorolf insisted. "Bacon and eggs, toast and coffee. That's a real breakfast. Maybe steak and eggs, if you're feeling flush."

"It's past lunch," Rox said, sounding cross.

"Whatever," Thorolf insisted. "Give me meat, and lots of it."

Rox wrinkled her nose and stared in the fridge.

Niall decided to accent their similar choices. "Have you tried that yogurt from the organic dairy in New Jersey?" he asked. "It's really good, no additives or other garbage, and probably as local as we can get."

Rox lifted a container of yogurt, her expression wary. "This one?"

"Great minds think alike," he said cheerfully, reaching into the cupboard for bowls. Niall could feel her gaze on him, then heard her put the yogurt on the counter.

Hard. He stifled a smile.

"Don't mess with my preconceptions," she said, shaking a finger at him. "You're a dragon dude, too. You're on the red-and-dead plan, just like him."

"I avoid red meat," Niall said. "Organically raised chicken or farmed fish are easier on the planet when I need that kind of protein. Matching amino acids and eating vegan is better."

Rox's eyes narrowed. "Be serious."

"I am. No leather. Minimal plastic. Nothing from sweatshops or countries where people are taken advantage of. Vintage over new. Reduce, reuse, and recycle. We dragon dudes *are* in the business of taking care of the planet." Niall looked into her astonished gaze, saw her approval, then filled the two bowls. He fought the urge to whistle.

Everything was coming together perfectly.

"It's true," Thorolf complained, and Niall could have hugged the big dope. "Niall eats exactly like you. It's like you two are meant for each other. No matter which one of you I live with, I have to eat like a rabbit."

"Rabbits don't eat organic yogurt," Niall observed, pleased that Rox fought a smile.

"There's an advertisement for getting your own place, maybe a reliable job," Rox countered.

"It's depressing," Thorolf continued, ignoring her. "Give me a big old four-egg omelet, with ham and cheese, instead. Or get three orders of steak and eggs, and I'll eat yours."

"Always helpful," Niall said under his breath.

"Always a bottomless pit," Rox agreed with a wary smile.

"Always a lean, mean, fighting machine," Thorolf corrected.

Rox made more tea while Niall popped a couple of slices of multigrain bread into the toaster. He remarked on her unpasteurized buckwheat honey and asked where she'd gotten it. They had started to compare farmers' markets and organic grocery stores, and she was just warming up again when Thorolf yawned like a lion.

"All right, all right, it's like fucking kismet," he said. "Now, what's *really* to eat?"

Niall heard Sloane's arrival, heard Rafferty greeting the Apothecary, heard Sloane admiring Rox's work.

Rox took a step back, her wariness restored, just as Rafferty and Sloane appeared in the doorway. He made introductions smoothly, and Sloane expressed gratitude for the cup of tea Rox poured for him.

"I'll go out to get coffee and bacon, if necessary," Rafferty said, amusement in his tone. As usual, the older *Pyr* smoothed over the moment.

"And white bread, please," Thorolf said. "This multigrain stuff is like a loaf of bird seed. One day I've been gone and I see it's reverted to nature central around here."

"Nothing changed," Rox said. "It's not as if you ever bought any groceries. You just complained about the ones I bought."

"Sure I bought groceries!"

To Niall's amusement, Rox turned on Thorolf, determined to set him straight. "Bringing home a two-pound steak from the store, grilling it, and devouring it in five minutes or less does not constitute buying groceries or cooking."

Niall laughed, but Thorolf looked insulted. "Why not? I go to the store, buy food, cook it, and eat it."

"Why don't I go for groceries?" Rafferty suggested.

"Bonus!" Thorolf said, nodding approval. "Bring

something wicked bad for us. Donuts, maybe. Iced ones."

"That stuff will kill you," Rox began hotly, but Thorolf straightened up and tapped his chest with pride.

"Eight hundred years and counting, getting better every day," he said.

"That is a matter of perspective," Rox countered.

Thorolf laughed. Sloane shook his head. Rafferty and Niall exchanged a smile; then the older *Pyr* left.

"I think he might not have been the best candidate to make deliveries for the organic store," Niall noted.

Rox grimaced. "I thought they might teach him something."

"You didn't. That proves he's immune to good lessons." Niall ate a spoonful of granola and yogurt.

"Except from you," Rox ceded.

"So maybe there's hope, after all." Niall smiled at her and saw her eyes widen. "I still say you softened him up."

She smiled back and Niall dared to be encouraged. He winked and she flushed crimson. The firestorm was right, contrary to his initial perceptions.

This could work out beautifully.

It would have been easier to hold tough if Niall hadn't been bitably sexy, half naked in her kitchen, and interesting, too.

Who would have guessed they ate the same way, and tried to live the same way? Who would have guessed he worried about his ecological footprint, too?

Still, Rox tried to ignore both him and his effect on her equilibrium. Sex was all good, but this was about bigger stakes. She had to play it right.

Even if her punker look didn't seem to bother Niall.

In contrast, having Niall standing barefoot in her kitchen, wearing only his jeans—which fit very well, thank you—and advocating a locally sourced vegan diet had completely messed with her own convictions.

Never mind that he spoke to her as if she had a brain and he respected her opinion. Never mind that he listened. Never mind that he looked good enough to eat.

Rox had to get a grip.

The new *Pyr* arrival, Sloane, was dark haired, tall, and slim, clearly a thoughtful type. He wore jeans and Blundstone boots, a red T-shirt, and a faded chambray shirt over top.

Sloane's handshake had been firm, and Rox had already decided he must be the strong silent type. He looked a bit tired, actually.

He smiled at Rox and saluted her with the tea she'd poured for him. "Long flight. This is perfect."

Niall ate his granola and yogurt in silence, then moved to put the bowl in the sink.

His chest was tanned a rich gold and Rox could tell he spent a lot of time working out. He was exactly as muscled as she'd expect a dragon dude to be, and Rox caught herself ogling.

She thought Sloane caught her, as well, because she saw his quick smile.

The firestorm, with its constant flickering heat, didn't help, either. Rox wished her life had been different, that she could have been the kind of person to not think so much about these kinds of decisions. She wished she could just go with the flow. Rox could do that with the little stuff, but not with something like this.

The big one.

She needed to stop thinking about sex—sex with Niall, Niall's fabulous kisses, and the heat of the firestorm.

"So, did you guys sleep well last night?" she asked, needing the distraction of conversation.

"We hardly got any zzz's after we breathed enough smoke to make His Highness happy," Thorolf complained, jerking a thumb toward Niall.

"Excuse me?" Rox said. "I don't see any smoke."

"You can't see dragonsmoke," Thorolf said. "Humans can't."

"Some feel a chill when they pass through it," Sloane said.

"Dragonsmoke is a boundary mark," Niall explained.

Rafferty returned then, entering the kitchen with a bag of groceries. Rox started because she hadn't heard the older *Pyr* come into the apartment. The *Pyr* weren't surprised, though, courtesy of their sharper senses.

"I assumed you wouldn't have a coffeepot," he said, setting down two large cups of take-out coffee. "And Sloane always prefers tea." The new arrival nodded in agreement and topped off his mug. Thorolf took the lid off one coffee cup and poured nearly half a cup of sugar into it before taking an appreciative swig. Rafferty shook his head, then began to unpack his purchases as Thorolf watched with interest.

Niall continued. "We exhale dragonsmoke and weave it around a specific area to mark its perimeter. Another *Pyr* or *Slayer* cannot cross the dragonsmoke without the permission of the one who breathed it." He grimaced. "At least that's how it used to work."

"Before the Elixir," Sloane said.

Thorolf hooted with joy when he saw the box of donuts Rafferty had bought. The *Pyr* smiled and Rox rolled her eyes.

"But what's the difference between *Pyr* and *Slayer*?"

Niall turned, as attentive as always to her questions. Rox liked that he didn't ignore her, or dismiss the notion that she could help. "We're all born *Pyr*. Only the *Pyr* have firestorms, so only the *Pyr* have the chance to conceive a son."

There was that word again. Rox refused to get seduced by interesting dragon lore. She finished her yogurt as quickly as she could.

Niall turned to Sloane. "That's what I wanted to ask you. I need to know if Phelan can be healed, rather than destroyed."

Sloane grimaced. "That he turned *Slayer* in his lifetime makes it a serious long shot."

Niall was resolute. "Even given what happened to Delaney?"

"Delaney hadn't turned *Slayer*," Sloane noted.

"But he was cured," Niall insisted.

"How?" Rox asked, unable to help herself.

"It was because of the firestorm he was having with Ginger." Niall eyed Sloane. "Can my firestorm heal Phelan?"

Rafferty clicked his teeth. "So risky."

"He's changed, too, regressed back to how he was when he was alive. He's not a mindless shadow dragon anymore."

Sloane frowned. "That's weird. I wonder what happened to him."

"Maybe he just needed another chance." Niall turned and smiled at Rox so quickly that she couldn't evade his gaze. "Some people need a hundred second chances, right?"

That Niall was giving his twin another chance was a noble choice. It was possibly foolish, but his choice made Rox's heart squeeze so tightly that she could hardly breathe. It put Niall at risk of a surprise attack, but he was determined to do the right thing despite the potential cost.

That was a perspective that Rox could understand.

And it was one she respected.

He stood in her kitchen, looking grim and golden and determined, and Rox couldn't decide if he was more appealing in dragon or human form. As much as she'd loved the amethyst and silver splendor of him coiled across her bedroom floor, there was a lot to be said for his human form. He looked like a surfer dude, just in from the beach, his hair tousled and his eyes vividly blue.

But he looked a lot more resolute than surfers usually did.

Oh, she was in serious trouble.

"I don't think so," Sloane said. "I think you're going to have to do the deed."

"I need to be sure," Niall insisted. "Especially since he asked for my help. Especially now that he seems more like his old self."

"Sneaky," Sloane murmured.

"Animated," Niall corrected.

"Maybe it's the firestorm," Rafferty suggested.

Niall turned an intent look on Rox and she knew she had to do something before she surrendered to temptation.

It was time for some fire walls.

She straightened up from the counter. "Hey, look at the time. I promised Neo I'd open today and I have sketches to do." Thorolf left the kitchen while Rafferty and Sloane quietly conferred.

"I'll be coming with you," Niall said, stepping away from the counter.

"You'll only be in the way," Rox argued, knowing she'd lose.

Neo would probably salivate a puddle onto the floor of the shop.

"You're not going alone, not with Phelan out there and all the shadow dragons attracted to the firestorm," Niall said, and his uncompromising tone made it clear that there was no room for argument. "I'll be inconspicuous."

"I don't think so," Rox argued.

"I do," Niall countered.

Thorolf returned with a lime green T-shirt. "This will make it easier," he said.

"Hardly." Niall rolled his eyes at the skull logo on the front.

"Well, you can't go without a shirt," Thorolf said with a wink at Rox. "Some tattoo artist will get ideas about the blank canvas."

And how. Rox didn't even want to start thinking about applying a stencil to Niall's skin, about leaning close to him for hour after hour. . . .

"Besides, it's kind of cute," Thorolf said with a grin. "The shirt matches Rox's hair, like you're a couple."

Niall gave Rox a mischievous glance, then ducked into the bathroom before she could protest. He was back so quickly that Rox had no time to evade him. He'd tugged the shirt on, then grabbed his laptop bag. He leveled a very blue glance in Rox's direction. "Whenever you're ready."

Inconspicuous.

Rox had never heard anything so ridiculous in her life. Niall might be many things, but "inconspicuous" would never make the list. It had nothing to do with the way he dressed—even though he obviously tended to be conservative in his taste—but it was the way he moved.

Niall was decisive. Confident. Controlled. Powerful. He wasn't as tall as some men, but he was muscular—not only was his body a balanced machine, but he knew its abilities with a precision beyond that of most people.

Inconspicuous. Hah. Walking beside Niall under her huge black umbrella proved to her that it wasn't as big as she'd previously thought. Her shoulder brushed his arm, lighting a continuous sizzle of tiny sparks, sparks that sent a frisson of excitement through her body.

Rox was aware not only of her own response to Niall but that of other people. There weren't that many out on the streets, given the driving rain, but more than one woman came to a window to watch them pass.

Rox saw her own admiration echoed in more than one expression.

She realized that Niall could never blend in, no matter how conservatively he dressed, that human gazes would always be drawn to his confident stride. People, she thought, instinctively understood that there was something special about him.

If Rox had seen him on the street, she would have assumed he was a commando. In a way, he was. She understood that he worked out because his strength, and his responsiveness, could make the difference between life and death in a fight with a shadow dragon or *Slayer*. She respected that he took his body and his abilities seriously, and that he tried to be the best he could be.

But inconspicuous? The very idea made her laugh.

When Rox and Niall got to the shop, there was a lump in front of the door. Only when she stepped closer did Rox realize it was a person.

Not just any person. It was the kid she'd given her card to the night before. He was soaked to the skin and shivering when Rox nudged him awake. He kept his face turned away, as if ashamed that he had to ask for help.

Rox was really glad to see him, but she understood that showing as much would probably spook him into disappearing again.

"Hey!" Rox said. "Crappy place to sleep." She reached over him and unlocked the door.

"Hey," the kid said, getting to his feet. There was uncertainty in every line of his body, a lack of confidence that became only more pronounced when he glanced sidelong at Niall. "Guess I got here past closing time." He shuffled his feet.

"And?" Rox prompted.

The kid pulled her card from his pocket, waved it at her, and stuffed it away again. All without looking straight at her. "Your offer still stand?"

"You bet. But you have to work, stay out of trouble, and stay clean."

"No worries," the kid assured her. He ducked his head so his hair hung in his eyes, his wariness noticeable. Rox had time to wonder what had changed his mind when Niall moved quickly to touch the kid's chin.

He had a shiner rising on the eye he'd tried to hide from her.

He blushed and Niall lifted his hand away.

The kid exhaled then, and looked straight at Rox. "Sometimes something happens to change your mind."

Rox was sorry he'd been hurt, but a black eye wasn't the worst thing that could have happened to him on the street. "I hear you. Come on in and get warm."

His smile was fleeting but honest. "Thanks. I won't let you down, you know."

"I know," Rox said with breezy confidence. "You got a name?"

"Barry."

She turned in the open doorway and shook his hand. "Hi, Barry. Welcome to Imagination Ink. There's a shower in the employee restroom at the back, and I'll see if I can find you some clean clothes while you're in there."

"Thanks!"

A hundred second chances. Niall thought of Rox's philosophy as she directed Barry to the shower and found him some jeans and a T-shirt. He had a feeling Barry would willingly lay down his life for Rox.

There was very little risk in helping him. Niall saw that now. Barry was just a scared kid. And part of why he trusted Rox was that Rox understood what Barry was facing.

Maybe she even guessed why.

He wondered again at her own history.

Niall had never been in a tattoo shop, and he hadn't

known what to expect. If pressed, he would have said it would be a dirty little hovel, the walls covered with Gothic text and satanic symbols, the logos of motorcycle manufacturers and Americana. Convicts had tattoos, as did sailors and hobos. Tattoos were not ladylike and they were not beautiful.

Except for the one Rox had done for Thorolf. That dragon was something else.

Imagination Ink surprised him even more than Thorolf's tattoo.

"It looks like a hair salon," he said, staring as Rox returned to the reception area.

"Maybe a Goth one," Rox agreed with a smile.

Niall was having a good look around. The decor was intended to look best at night, but it wasn't grubby at all. In fact, it had a kind of elegance to it, given the plaster work on the ceiling and the candelabra mounted on the gold walls. Niall liked the black and white checkerboard floor—it was just like the stone-tiled foyer of his father's London town house.

That building was probably long gone—or converted to condos. Niall had sold it when his father died, without ever going back for another look. He hadn't thought about it since and realized the transaction had been more than a hundred years ago.

There was a reception area with several chairs and a pile of tattoo magazines, presumably to give customers ideas. There was a cash desk with a wall of images behind it. Niall was surprised by the diversity and quality of much of the artwork. The stock images he'd expected were there, the anchors and hearts and astrological signs, but there was other work of much better caliber.

"Those are called flash," Rox said. "They're stock designs. Customers can pick a design and have it colored in however they like."

"I don't see anything like the tattoo you gave Thorolf."

Rox laughed. "That was a custom piece. A one-off. I just drew it on his skin with a marker and made it up as I went along."

"It's a beautiful piece of work," Niall said, and he wasn't joking. He was impressed to think she had just drawn it freehand. He smiled and felt the room become warmer as Rox stared at him. "A good reminder for him, too."

Rox pivoted quickly and he knew she was shutting him out. "Yeah, well, we all do what we can." She marched away, leaving Niall to do what he wanted.

He followed her, still looking.

Behind the reception area was a corridor complete with a copier and what Rox said was a stencil-making machine, then a line of a half-dozen rooms. In each room, one or two tattoo artists could work. There was a black padded couch in each room like a massage bed as well as several smaller padded stands and a couple of chairs, lots of lights, and drawers of tools.

As in many hair salons, each artist had customized his or her space. The walls in Rox's workroom were painted burgundy, and on her side of the shared space, those walls were covered with thumbtacked sketches. Rox offered no explanations. She pulled out a sketchbook and sat down at the drawing board, ignoring him.

Niall wondered about Rox's own tattoos. He'd glimpsed some script on her shoulder the night before, but hadn't taken the time to read it. And he'd seen the broken heart on her cheekbone. That one was hidden today, lost beneath a black curlicue of eyeliner. He'd seen another tattoo through those fishnet stockings the day before. Did she have more tattoos? How many did she have?

Where were they?

What images had she chosen? Did they all have meaning, like the heart? Were they specially chosen as reminders, like the tattoo she had given Thorolf? Niall wondered.

She didn't look inclined to confide in him.

Niall wasn't interested in being shut out and he knew the firestorm was on his side. He moved closer, savoring the golden heat that grew more radiant with every step.

"You'd better stay on the other side of the room," she said without looking up. "Everyone will notice the sparks." She shrugged. "Then they'll want some."

Niall smiled at the creative way she had found to ensure that he kept his distance. He wasn't fooled, though. He knew that Rox was aware of him and that the firestorm was winning.

Chapter 10

Niall smiled and backed up a bit. "But what are you doing?"

Rox sat back, gesturing to the drawing. "This is the sketch for a sleeve."

"What's a sleeve?"

"Tattoos covering the skin from shoulder to wrist." Rox grabbed her portfolio and opened it, showing him a photograph. "This is the other sleeve I did for Chynna."

Roses tumbled down the arm of a young woman in a tank top, looking so lush that they could have been a photograph. There were close-up images of the dewdrops on the petals and several small insects hidden in the leaves.

"You can almost smell them," Niall said with admiration.

"That's what Neo said."

"Who's Chynna?"

"My partner. Actually she started Imagination Ink, then let Neo and me buy in recently." Rox indicated her sketch. "Now she wants the other sleeve to be similar, but she already has a couple of tattoos on that arm." Niall saw that Rox had those designs on tracing paper, as if she had traced them from Chynna's arm. One of them was the logo of a heavy metal band, while the other was a cute fairy. He found himself moving closer, fascinated.

"You need to integrate them into the design," Niall guessed.

"And I don't like where they are." Rox grimaced. She put the tracing paper over the sketch, showing Niall how the images worked together. "I don't like *what* they are, either."

"Can't you cover them with another image? Or remove them?"

"Removal is painful. I think the fairy can be worked out. See? If I put a rose right beside her, a darker one, that would make her smaller. Her face could be peeking out from around the flower."

"Like the insects," Niall said with a smile. It was an ingenious solution. "It fits."

"Plus it's the tattoo Chynna really likes, and the face is her favorite part. Otherwise, I'd bury the fairy in the middle of a flower. She's faded enough that it could be done."

"Do all tattoos fade?"

"Only the crap ones." Rox raised her brows. "Like this one. I'll redo the part that's going to survive." She tapped her pencil. "But the band logo is solid black. It'll never be covered."

"Can you make it into something else?" The angular lines of it reminded Niall of his mother's garden at their country house, of the roses she had grown that could have modeled for Rox's rose tattoos.

"Sure. But what?"

"Well, some roses grow on a trellis," Niall suggested. He took her pencil, ignoring the spark, and sketched lightly on her tissue. "You could maybe turn it into a grid, like this. I'm no artist. . . ."

"But that's brilliant!" Rox's face lit up. She seized the

pencil and made magic of Niall's idea. She worked over the sketch rapidly, adding bits of a black trellis throughout the sleeve, so that the covered logo looked like just another glimpse of the structure. She glanced up at him, her eyes dancing. "Thank you! I've been sweating this for more than a week."

Niall saw her pride in her work, and her pleasure in what she could do. She was enticing when she sparkled like this and he bent his head, intending to capture a small reward for his contribution.

Rox looked as if she would welcome his kiss, then suddenly her eyes flashed and she pushed him hard in the chest. Niall took a step backward, then heard the footfall in the corridor that he should have heard sooner.

His heart sank with another reminder that the firestorm—and his fascination with Rox—left him vulnerable, which was the last thing he needed. He had to find the shadow dragons, before one of them found him.

Niall had only just retreated to his corner and leaned against the wall, arms folded across his chest, when company appeared.

"Got one for you, Rox," the arrival said, sticking his head around the door frame. He was a slim guy in his thirties with dyed black hair and lavish eyeliner to rival that of Rox. His earlobes held large earplugs that could have been made of ebony.

"My partner, Neo," Rox said. "This is Niall, Neo."

Neo gave Niall an appreciative once-over. "Sister Rox sticks in her thumb and pulls out a plum," he said, then grinned. Before Niall could reply, he continued speaking to Rox. "This lady wants a memorial tattoo. Name's Laurie and she's asking for you specifically."

Rox nodded. "Okay."

Neo considered Niall again. "I gotta say, Rox, that this one looks like he has it together more than your usual projects."

"Maybe I'm not a project," Niall said quietly.

"Oh, like a date?" Neo grinned. "Then you're the one with the odds stacked against you. Sister Rox is the last bastion of chastity on the old East Side. . . ."

"Don't you have something to do, Neo?" Rox demanded. Her face was red. "Like maybe in LA? Or Hawaii?"

Neo laughed, as untroubled by her manner as Niall was. "Just sayin'." Neo winked at Niall. "Rox is the most *disciplined* person I know."

"Nothing wrong with discipline," Niall said. He was enjoying this conversation and what it told him about Rox.

"Nothing at all," Neo agreed, ignoring Rox. "As long as everyone understands the deal from the outset."

Rox was annoyed. "Neo! There's a kid named Barry in the restroom. He's going to work here, help out. Maybe you could show him around."

"He's the project," Niall said softly. "Probably needs a meal."

"Got it," Neo said, leaning in the doorway, his gaze bright with curiosity. "So, tell me where you two kids met."

"I thought customers came first," Rox said.

Neo swore as he remembered the waiting client and darted down the corridor.

"What's a memorial tattoo?" Niall asked.

"A tattoo to honor someone who's died," Rox said in an undertone. "Probably half the tattoos we do are memorials. It's bread and butter."

Then she stepped forward to greet the client who appeared in the doorway. "Hi, I'm Rox. It's Laurie, right? Come on in and tell me what I can do for you."

Niall was intrigued by the change in Rox's manner. She was effusive and friendly, more approachable than she had been when he had met her.

He settled back in his corner, pleased to have the chance to watch her doing what she did well.

*   *   *

Something was wrong.

Erik Sorensson, leader of the *Pyr*, studied Ginger's spreadsheet on his laptop screen for what had to be the hundredth time. He needed every talon he could muster in the war against the *Slayers*, and Ginger had the expertise to track bloodlines well.

The *Slayers* would be tougher to document, as they deliberately tried to hide themselves from the perception of Erik and other true *Pyr*. Erik also tried to keep his mind from following the dark paths the *Slayers* regularly trod. On the upside, the *Slayers* could no longer breed.

They could, however, recruit. It was entirely possible that some of the missing *Pyr* had turned to the darkness, which was news that Erik refused to anticipate until it was confirmed on a case-by-case basis. It would be bad enough to confront the loss then. He didn't like the length of the list of potential shadow dragons, even though Niall was eliminating the ones he found. Donovan was working through the list, too, visiting sites to confirm those *Pyr* who remained dead.

Why did the shadow dragons reveal themselves at intervals? Erik shared Niall's frustration with that fact, and couldn't explain it, either.

It didn't help his mood that Erik could feel the distant blaze of a firestorm. He'd felt it since shortly after the eclipse had ended the previous day.

Erik didn't like coincidences—that the *Pyr* who had volunteered to eliminate the shadow dragons was having a firestorm before those shadow dragons were all found and dispatched smelled like trouble to him.

That was nothing compared to the irritation of his laptop.

This latest version of Ginger's spreadsheet, like all the others, had been returned by Ginger with questions. She wanted death dates and birth dates, names and birth-places of sons, last-known locations for each, et cetera, et cetera. The level of detail was impressive, and Erik was glad he remembered as much as he did.

But there was a note in red on this one. Obviously, this was a detail Ginger had requested before, and Erik hadn't yet supplied it. The odd thing was that he couldn't read her note. He could see the red type from the periphery of his vision, so he knew it was there, but when he looked straight at the screen, the cell appeared to be empty. Erik knew it had to be right in the middle of the screen with Ginger's question in red type, but he couldn't read it because he couldn't see it.

He tried, over and over again.

Was there something wrong with his laptop's display?

Erik was nearly ready to chuck the expensive piece of junk at the wall, when Eileen unlocked the door to their apartment. She looked weary when she nudged open the door with her boot and Erik went to take their daughter, Zoë, from his partner's arms. The toddler was sleeping, as boneless as a rag doll in Eileen's embrace.

But considerably heavier.

"The sitter said she was chattering all day, but she's slept the whole way home," Eileen said, dropping her satchel onto the floor and stretching her shoulders. "How did I end up with so much stuff tonight?" she asked no one in particular. "I'm going to rent myself a forklift instead of taking public transit."

Zoë, twenty months old and more adorable to her father with every passing day, sighed and dozed on his shoulder. Her hand curled, her grip tightening and her fingers entangling themselves in his T-shirt. He felt her relax even more, just as she always did when he carried her.

Her hair had darkened even from birth, becoming

the same inky black that his own had once been. Yet it was clearly going to be curly like Eileen's. Zoë's eyes were also resolutely blue, like her mother's.

Eileen smiled and kissed his cheek. "Did you get a lot of work done today on that pyrotechnics project?"

Erik glanced toward his desk with some guilt. The whole reason Zoë had gone to a sitter and Eileen had done research in the library on a Sunday was to give him a chance to work, but he hadn't accomplished anything, thanks to his various irritations.

"No, actually, I was quite ineffective today." He heard the annoyance in his own voice, and shrugged at Eileen's glance.

"That's not like you." She grimaced. "But then, I was running in circles all day today, too. Maybe the stars are aligned against us. Or maybe they just don't approve of people working weekends."

"There was a partial eclipse yesterday."

"Is that why you've been out of sorts this weekend?"

"Part of the reason. It presaged a firestorm, too."

"Whose?"

"Niall's."

"Delaney's firestorm started on a partial eclipse." Eileen went into the kitchen and took a bottle of mineral water from the fridge. She took a glass out of the cupboard and, at Erik's nod, added a second. She sliced a lime, then poured the sparkling water over it in the glasses. She took a sip and sighed with appreciation.

Erik leaned in the doorway with their dozing child. "But Delaney had been a shadow dragon. He'd drunk the Elixir. I don't understand why Niall's firestorm would be linked to a partial eclipse." Erik frowned at the murmur of distant old-speak, knowing that Eileen was watching him. "Fortunately, Rafferty and Sloane are already there. Thorolf, as well." He still felt restless and impatient, lacking a piece of the puzzle.

Never mind his stupid computer.

"But there's more than that, isn't there?" Eileen flashed him a smile, and Erik was glad his mate understood him as well as she did. "Are we going to the firestorm?"

Erik glared across the room at the laptop.

"You have that contract," Eileen noted.

"Fourth of July. It's just over a week away, a huge display, and I'm not as organized as I'd like to be."

"Which means you're probably as organized as normal people manage on their good days," Eileen said wryly. "You are the high master of controlling all the variables, my love."

"It only makes sense," Erik said. "Pyrotechnics aren't toys. . . ."

"And you've never had a single injury on your team. I know." Eileen raised a hand and smiled. "It's all good." She opened the fridge, pulling out dishes of leftovers and setting them on the counter. The toddler awakened, predictably, and began to bounce in anticipation. "Well, Zoë's got to eat, no matter what you decide."

"Could you do me a favor?" Erik asked as he bounced their daughter. "Would you look at the file displayed on my laptop and tell me what the red type says, please?"

Eileen glanced across the room. "I can almost read it from here."

"I can't read it at all."

"You're joking." She smiled at him. "Are you going color-blind after all these centuries of perfect vision?"

"Very funny." Erik wasn't in the mood to be teased.

Eileen abandoned Zoë's dinner and crossed the room to peer at the display. "This is that file you're working on with Ginger, right?" She didn't wait for an answer. "Mmm, Ginger wants to know about any sons Gaspar might have had, what surname he assumed, if any, and when he died." She glanced back at him and smiled. "She sounds a bit impatient, as if she's asked you this before and you've ducked her."

"Gaspar," Erik repeated as he frowned. Gaspar had been one of his father's compatriots, and a member of the original high circle of *Pyr*. He had a glimpse in his mind's eye of that *Pyr*, then couldn't recall what he had looked like.

Or even that he existed.

"What was the name again?"

Eileen gave him an odd look. "Gaspar."

The memory flicked briefly, then disappeared. Erik's annoyance grew as he forgot the name once more.

Eileen was watching him, probably seeing more than he suspected. "You really couldn't read it?"

"I can only see the red type from the corner of my eye. When I look straight at it, it disappears."

"That's weird."

"It is, indeed." Her comment made Erik wonder whether there was anything magical at work. He returned to the desk and tried to see the red type, but no luck.

"It bugs you, doesn't it?"

"It has nearly driven me mad."

"I can imagine, but I don't think you're quite there yet." Eileen heated up Zoë's dinner in the microwave and Erik pulled out the high chair. Zoë clapped and chattered as he set her in her chair, so adorable that the sight of her nearly broke Erik's heart.

If anything ever happened to this child . . . He couldn't even think about the possibility. She gave him one of those intent looks, as if she could sense his concerns, then smiled sunnily.

Was she trying to reassure him?

Erik fastened on her bib as she fidgeted, clearly hungry. She clapped her hands when Eileen presented her dinner and took her spoon in her hand with such resolve that Erik's mood was lightened. "She's determined to eat like an adult," he marveled. Zoë concentrated, putting her spoon into the vegetables slowly.

"As stubborn as her father," Eileen teased.

"Not her mother?"

She grinned. "So, what about Gaspar?"

Erik was puzzled by the reference. "Who?"

"Gaspar!"

Gaspar. "That's the thing," Erik admitted. "We've just exchanged one frustration for another."

"You don't remember? But you remember everything, Mr. Mind-Like-a-Steel-Trap." Eileen laughed. "You could give me some of that, you know, one day when you decide you have overstock."

"You don't do so badly yourself, Dr. Grosvenor."

Zoë, two spoonfuls successfully delivered to her mouth, cast the spoon at the floor and reached into the vegetables with her bare hands. Her dinner was smeared across her face in a heartbeat, her eyes dancing with delight, and Erik could only hope that some made it into her mouth.

Eileen rolled her eyes. "Just don't throw any of it," she admonished, getting another spoon and feeding the little girl with experienced ease. Zoë shoved the occasional fistful into her mouth, even so.

Eileen continued her conversation with Erik. "Then why did I spend all day chasing my own tail around the library, following lead after lead after lead and getting nowhere? The strange thing is that it was all about Venice. Venice! Everything led to Venice, as if that made any kind of sense when I was trying to research the various urban legends of sewer dwellers."

Venice. Something shook free in Erik's memory, then disappeared as surely as if it had never been there. It could have been coming to the surface of a dark lake, then sinking without leaving so much as a ripple.

"Sewer dwellers?" he echoed.

"Don't get me started. They don't even have sewers in Venice; they have the canals. It was the stupidest loss of a day ever."

Zoë was, as usual, an enthusiastic eater—that had to be why she was growing so fast. Erik wanted her to grow faster, to become capable of advising him, given his belief that she was the current Wyvern who could aid the *Pyr*.

"So tell me about Gaspar," Eileen invited. "I'm up for an entertaining story that makes sense. We're not going anywhere until Zoë eats, anyway."

Erik frowned and leaned against the counter. "That's just it—I don't know."

"You mean you forgot."

"No."

"You never knew?"

"No. I knew. I know that I knew. And I feel like I remember. Or I should remember. I just can't pull it into my thoughts. I can't even keep a grasp of his name. What was it again?"

"Gaspar!"

"Gaspar." Erik flung out a hand in frustration. "It's like that red type I've spent all day trying to see. There's something keeping me from it."

Eileen glanced up at him, the loaded spoon in midair. "Sounds like you've been beguiled," she said quietly.

"Don't be ridiculous." Erik was dismissive. "*Pyr* can't be beguiled. We beguile humans, but we cannot beguile one another."

"Oh, okay, then you are going crazy. I'll pick up some adult diapers for you at the grocery next time, just in case you lose your grip on the world completely." Eileen spoke lightly, but Erik knew she was giving him a hard time.

He was insulted. "You will not."

She laughed. "I have to tell you—I like the idea of your being beguiled a whole lot better than the prospect of your losing your jelly beans."

"We *Pyr* do not experience neurological disorders. . . ."

"Then you give me your explanation." There was a dare in her tone, one Erik couldn't ignore. She turned to look at him, her eyes bright. "Why can't you remember Gaspar?"

Erik tried to recall Gaspar, but that *Pyr* disappeared from his thoughts as surely as a shadow runs from the sun. Even his name was slippery.

"I can see him in my mind's eye, but not clearly and not for long," Erik said, pulling out a chair.

"What did he look like?"

Eileen's question seemed to tease the memory into making a reappearance. "He had dark hair and dark eyes. Handsome and flamboyant."

"Errol Flynn as a *Pyr*," Eileen said with approval. "That works."

"It worked for lots of women," Erik admitted. "I remember my father's complaining that Gaspar was more interested in seducing women than in defending humans as a whole. He could usually be found with at least one woman and was easily distracted by another. He claimed he needed to be immortal to appreciate all the feminine beauty in the world."

Eileen smiled. "I gotta tell you, fidelity is a whole lot more sexy." She winked at Erik and he smiled slightly.

"He was persuaded of the merit of that after his own firestorm." Erik paused, finding that barricade in his thoughts again.

"Well?" Eileen prompted.

"I don't know," Erik admitted with irritation. "I remembered some of it, but then no more."

"You mean you know you know, but you can't think of it."

"Exactly!"

"I thought beguiling was a kind of hypnosis that persuaded humans that things were true even though they knew they were not."

"Well, it is. . . ."

"Like your thinking that you don't remember about Gaspar, but knowing in your heart that you do."

"That *Pyr* was one of my father's best friends. I *know* they kept in touch until the end, and I *know* I knew about him."

"Gaspar," Eileen repeated, then gestured to the pen and paper.

Erik wrote down the name. "There's no way that I could not have known! His firestorm happened long before my father died."

"Then he must have had a son."

It was true.

If anything, the barrier in Erik's mind grew more impenetrable, which told him a great deal. "He had a firestorm, so he must have had a son," Erik agreed, then rubbed his forehead with the inevitable realization. "And he or his son must have beguiled me."

That feat alone was impressive, never mind the question of why any *Pyr* would have seen fit to beguile Erik. What could Gaspar and his son have been hiding? What had become of them?

Erik didn't know, and he supposed that had been the point.

Still, Erik Sorensson had been beguiled. It made sense, given the data at hand, except that he'd never believed it possible. He fought to wrap his mind around the inescapable yet astonishing fact.

"You look insulted," Eileen said, laughter in her tone.

"I am insulted! It's outrageous that some *Pyr* would have the audacity to attempt to beguile me. . . ."

"To *succeed* in beguiling you," Eileen corrected. "He must have been pretty good at it."

Erik pushed to his feet to pace. "It's a breach of propriety! *Pyr* should not beguile each other, and no one should even consider beguiling the leader of the *Pyr*."

"So now you know how humans feel about beguiling."

"That's different."

"Is it?"

Erik exhaled, not troubling to hide his irritation. One thing he admired about Eileen was her ability to face the truth, however discomfiting it was, and adjust her course accordingly.

He could use some of that in this moment.

She threw him a mischievous smile, knowing exactly how to dissolve his foul mood, and it worked like a charm. "It's good for you to have your assumptions challenged once in a while, Erik. Good for everybody."

Erik smiled despite himself. "I still would have preferred for you to be wrong."

"Sure, but it's kind of interesting. Opens up a number of new possibilities."

"None of which I like."

"Well, there has to be a way around it," Eileen said, showing her usual practicality. "Now that we know the barrier is there, we can define its perimeter and maybe find a way around it. Hypnosis has its weaknesses, too. You already remembered some things about Gaspar because I asked different questions, so let's work with that strategy. We'll poke and prod and see if we can find a pathway into your memories that this son overlooked."

It was as good a plan as anything, and Erik was—yet again—glad of Eileen's clear thinking. They made a good team, and he was encouraged that they could resolve this together.

Then he realized that Zoë, her eyes gleaming, was watching him intently, as though following their discussion. He leaned forward closer. "Can you help me, Zoë?" he asked softly. "Does the Wyvern have the power to undo a beguiling?"

Zoë smiled, turning her attention on her mother as if she hadn't understood him at all. She reached for the spoon and carefully managed to feed herself another bite.

Erik wasn't persuaded. There had been something evasive about her gesture, something that put him in mind of the last Wyvern, Sophie.

Did Zoë already know more than he did?

And how could he persuade his daughter to share? If she truly was like Sophie, he wouldn't be able to force her to tell him anything more than she intended to tell him.

That was when he knew what he had to do. This was a distraction and a potentially dangerous one—he couldn't let himself be diverted from his duty to the *Pyr*. That was his priority.

"We have to go to New York," Erik said, narrowing his eyes and casting his thoughts into the future. "I'll hope that we're back in time for the big display."

"*Pyr* come first?" Eileen teased.

"You know they do, especially now. There are some things I can't delegate."

"Just tell your team that you have a family emergency," Eileen suggested. "It's pretty much the truth."

Erik grabbed his cell phone and punched in the number of the most talented and thorough man on his pyrotechnics team. He knew he'd be making Steve's dream come true.

He was right.

When he'd made the arrangements and promised to stay in touch with Steve, he felt even more confident in his choice. "I'll have to revise my notes and e-mail them to him tonight, then cross-check the list of supplies and send that, as well."

"And you have to try to remember about Gaspar."

Erik nodded in agreement, wondering how he would manage all of this while flying his family east in his dragon form.

Eileen was two steps ahead of him.

"So, we have to drive," she said firmly. "You can work and Zoë can sleep."

"But," Erik began in protest, knowing where this was going and not liking it one bit.

Eileen grinned. "Yes, I finally get to drive your shiny new car. No alternate possibilities, Mr. Sorensson, so you're just going to have to get over it."

Erik frowned, already having gotten over the car seat in the back. He'd never imagined any vehicle in his possession would be so equipped, and was surprised only by how little he minded.

And his beloved Lamborghini, carefully stored for the time being, had been spared that indignity.

"You can't do everything." Eileen patted his shoulder on her way to the sink with the dirty dishes, showing a perkiness that Erik didn't trust. "Don't worry," she said with a grin. "I'll try to stay under one hundred."

The client at Imagination Ink wasn't a woman Niall would have expected to get a tattoo. Laurie looked as if she were on a day trip from the suburbs, her chestnut hair deftly styled and her makeup light. She was dressed in expensive casual wear and carried a designer purse. She seemed hesitant, her gaze flicking to Niall.

"He's my apprentice," Rox said quickly, then cast Niall a mischievous smile. "He'll just watch and hopefully learn something."

Niall found himself smiling in turn, trying to put the client at ease and help Rox. "There's always hope, when a person gets enough second chances."

Rox flushed.

"I didn't know there'd be an audience," Laurie said, gripping her purse more tightly.

"There often is an apprentice," Rox said kindly. "Don't worry—he'll just blend into the wallpaper. Inconspicuous, that's Niall."

Niall knew she was teasing him, and he swallowed his smile.

Laurie smiled quickly. "I doubt that." She hesitated

on the threshold, clearly nervous at what she'd decided to do.

"Come on in," Rox said, her tone encouraging. "How did you find Imagination Ink?"

"I heard this was a good place to come and that you were the person to see." Laurie looked between the two of them. "My neighbor's teenage daughter has a butterfly on her shoulder that you did." She touched her left shoulder with a fingertip.

"Oh, the blue and purple one?" Rox asked. She grabbed the fat binder of her portfolio and opened it, fanning to the page. "That was Stephanie. She knew exactly what she wanted. It came out nicely."

"Yes, that's it!" Laurie's face lit up at Rox's remembering, and she tapped the photograph with a fingertip.

"I'm glad she was pleased." Rox smiled. Niall respected that she took such pride in her work.

The tension eased out of Laurie's shoulders. "I thought it was so pretty, for a tattoo. Feminine."

Niall nodded, knowing exactly what she meant. "Rox does good work," he said, and meant it.

"So, who's the memorial for?" Rox was relaxed and friendly, her question putting Laurie even more at ease.

Niall sensed that she wanted to talk.

"My sister, Anna," she said. "She died last month. She always said she would get a tattoo, but she never did." Laurie swallowed and smiled slightly, her tears rising. "She was always the rebel, you know, while I always did what I was told. When she first said she'd get a tattoo, our mom went wild."

"Which only made her more determined to do it," Rox guessed. She was pulling out small mechanisms and lining them up on her worktable, much as a dentist would line up his tools.

Laurie nodded and loosened her grip on her purse slightly. "But then she got sick, and—" Her throat worked and she blinked rapidly.

Rox moved to change the subject with an ease that told Niall she'd done this a thousand times before. "What kind of image were you thinking of? Do you have something special in mind?"

"A Celtic cross." Laurie indicated her left bicep. "And I want it here."

Rox stood up and headed for the door. Niall was ready to follow her. "There are a lot of crosses in the flash."

"I wanted something unique," Laurie said firmly, and Rox halted. "Something no one else has. That's why I came here."

"A custom piece is more expensive," Rox warned, "because it takes more time."

"I don't care." Laurie squared her shoulders. "It's the only tattoo I'll ever have, because Anna was the only sister I ever had. The price isn't the point. That it reflects Anna is."

Rox smiled and Niall understood that she preferred to do custom work. She moved quickly then, pulling down binders from her own shelf. The two women began to discuss the piece, Laurie pointing out what she liked and didn't like while Rox sketched on a piece of tracing paper.

Niall tried his best to be invisible, even though he was itching to look through those binders. He was aware that the firestorm's sparks could spook Rox's client, so he stayed put.

Within fifteen minutes, the two women had a design they both liked. Niall was impressed again by Rox's skill—and also by her ability to draw information from the client that would make the work particularly meaningful.

The Celtic cross indicated the family's Irish heritage and sustaining faith—the knots on it were intricate, even though Rox had just drawn the design freehand. The two lush peonies below the cross were intended to evoke the two sisters, and Rox was going to color the tattoo so it looked as if light were coming from behind the cross. *In Memory of Anna* would be drawn in script that arched over the cross like a rainbow, colliding with the peonies at either end.

The design was quite pretty, to Niall's eyes. The women discussed and agreed upon the price, then Rox set to work.

He could see that the routine was reassuring to Rox. She made a stencil in the corridor, giving him a look when he followed her. At least she didn't argue as he stood vigil.

"Apprentices have to learn," he whispered, and saw the quick light of her smile.

Back in the room, she pulled on her surgical gloves. She cleaned the skin and applied the stencil in position on Laurie's arm. Laurie checked it out in the mirror while Rox chose sterilized needles and inks.

"We can break the session in half if it's too much for you," she said. "I can do the color at a later date, so just let me know how you're feeling."

"How long will it take to do it all?"

Rox eyed the stencil. "Two hours, give or take. The outline will take about forty minutes, but the color always hurts more."

"I want it all done now," Laurie said, then laughed. "Otherwise I might lose my nerve. And I might not get such a good parking spot the next time."

The women laughed together, and Rox turned on the tattoo gun. "Just a little line first to get you used to the feel of it," Rox said, her tone soothing. Laurie's eyes widened at the first prick of the tattoo gun, then she relaxed.

"It's not actually that bad," she told Niall, and he smiled to reassure her. He wasn't at all convinced. He'd seen the cluster of needles that fit into the tattoo gun and he knew he was hearing the sound of them impacting the skin over and over again.

Rox was focused on her work, her face close to the lines she was drawing. The stencil had left a purple outline on Laurie's skin and Rox carefully retraced every line with the black ink. Niall could see the skin swelling and reddening from the impact of the needles, and Laurie fell silent.

To his surprise, Rox began a conversation. "Tell me about your sister," she said. "What was Anna like, besides being the rebel?"

Laurie heaved a sigh and closed her eyes.

Then she talked.

Laurie talked about the two girls growing up together, about her sister's need to push the limits, about their differences and commonalities. She talked frankly about her sister's illness and the challenges it had offered to the whole family. She talked about her feelings of loss and love, her mother's devastation, and the sustenance they'd all had from their faith.

Niall thought about siblings, about the bonds between sisters and brothers. He realized he hadn't wept when Phelan had died.

He had wept when Phelan turned *Slayer*.

Interesting.

Laurie talked and talked, responding to Rox's occasional prompts, emptying her heart as the image grew on her skin. Niall could almost feel the pain she shed, could almost see it being discarded on the floor. She wept when she described Anna's last moments, surrounded by everyone she loved, and Rox's eyes glistened in sympathy.

That was when Niall understood the transaction being made.

Laurie ran out of memories and pain at roughly the same time Rox put the last touch of pink in the heart of the second peony. When Laurie stood to study the tattoo in the mirror, she stood straighter, as if she'd surrendered a burden. Laurie touched the swollen skin carefully, marveling at the tattoo's intricacy, and then she cried.

Rox had a big box of tissues at the ready. She gave Laurie a tissue and a hug, then turned Laurie to the mirror to fix her makeup while Rox cleaned up her tools to give her some privacy. Rox blinked back tears, trying to keep Niall from seeing them, but he knew she'd done this before.

Many, many times.

Niall was amazed by the gift of healing Rox gave so readily. It would have been cheap at twice the price.

Laurie composed herself and Rox put a bandage over the fresh tattoo. Niall didn't think Laurie heard the care instructions Rox gave her, but he noticed that Rox also gave her a sheet with those instructions along with her change.

Laurie smiled at Niall from the doorway. "I think you have a good teacher," she said, a new sparkle in her eyes.

"I know you're right," he agreed.

Laurie gave Rox another tight hug, thanked her profusely, then strode out of the shop.

Rox started to clean up her station. Niall could see her lifting her defenses back into place and knew he didn't have long to reach her.

And there was something they needed to talk about.

Or more accurately, something he needed to say, something that might make a difference to her perspective.

This was his chance.

Chapter 11

"Laurie looks taller," Niall said as Rox cleaned up her work area. "Happier."

He leaned in the doorway, his eyes bright as he watched her. Rox had the definite sense that he was barricading her into the room, that he wanted to say something and was going to be sure she listened.

She was tired, as she always was after doing a memorial tattoo, and was pretty sure Niall had noticed. She turned her back on him, trying to compose herself before he saw too much.

She dropped the used needles into a hygienic trash container, fighting her awareness of Niall. "It's a kind of therapy," she said lightly. "Chynna always says the physical pain helps heal the emotional pain."

"You don't sound as if you believe that."

Rox frowned but still didn't glance up. "There's an exchange, but I don't think that's quite it."

"The transaction is the passing of grief," Niall said, no equivocation in his tone. "In talking about her pain, she left its energy here. The tattoo is a souvenir of that surrender, but not the exchange itself."

Rox glanced up at him in surprise. She'd suspected

as much for a long time but would never have expected anyone to come up with the same conclusion.

Much less someone practical like Niall.

"I'll bet you feel tired after you do a memorial tattoo," Niall said with conviction. "I'll bet it wears you out."

Rox nodded, then sat down heavily. "I told Chynna and Neo years ago that one a shift is my max."

"Because you took on the burden of her grief. She passed that negative energy to you." Niall shrugged. "It's not that different from bartenders listening, or priests hearing confessions. Putting the pain into words cuts it loose."

"Hairdressers," Rox said with a nod. "They listen, too."

"But a tattoo takes longer than any of those things. Maybe that's why it works so well."

Niall smiled, the connection between them as hot and strong as ever. Rox felt dizzy just looking into his eyes, and he was on the other side of the room.

The firestorm tingled and teased, reminding her just how fabulous Niall's kisses were. She found herself watching his lips as he spoke.

Wanting.

"Just because you can't see the transaction doesn't mean it isn't happening," Niall insisted. "We pass energy to one another all the time, good and bad, and how we feel is shaped by that. Talk to a friend who's sad, and you'll feel blue. Talk to a friend who's busy and happy, and you'll feel energized."

He was right.

His ability to see so clearly behind her barricades was a bit spooky.

"Hey, Rox," Neo said, leaning around the door. A familiar figure lurked behind him, looking much cleaner than before. "I'm taking Barry to Mickey D's. Kid's going to faint wiping the floor if he doesn't get something to eat."

"Okay, great."

"It's dead quiet today," Neo continued, casting a mischievous smile at Niall. "Why don't you lock up when you're done and go play with your friends for a while?"

Rox threw a towel at him. Neo laughed and ran, Barry fast behind him. When they were gone, Rox got to her feet and turned to put her inks away. Her thoughts were stuck on Niall's comment, and he seemed to be waiting for her reply. "That sounds pretty flaky for a practical problem-solving guy like you."

"Not that flaky. I have an affinity with the element of air," Niall said.

Rox turned to look at him, surprised one more time. "What does that mean?"

His gaze was steady and vibrantly blue. Rox was aware that the shop was empty except for the two of them. "Because we guard the elements, some of us have affinities for a specific one. Actually, it's usually two elements."

"Isn't fire a gimme?"

He smiled. "Pretty much, although there are exceptions."

Rox was fascinated, one more time. "So what does an affinity with air get you?"

"The ability to speak to the wind, to ask it for news, or send messages on it. The power to summon the wind . . ."

"Like calling up a storm?"

"Something like that. There are variations. Erik's affinity with air manifests as foresight, because the element is associated with ideas and intellectual activity and energy."

Rox understood then why he had understood the transaction so well. It was right up his elemental alley.

Niall stepped closer and she felt the firestorm heat the room a notch. She put her paints away more quickly.

"Rafferty says that a successful firestorm brings two

halves together to make a whole that is more than the sum of the parts." Niall was close, his voice dropping to an intimate tone that turned Rox's knees to butter. "We each have an affinity to one element, but it's really for two because we're pretty much all empowered by fire. It's common for a mate to have an affinity for the other two elements, so that the union indicated by the firestorm is complete with all four."

Rox saw her own fingers tremble just a little as she put the last jar of ink away. "Which would make me water and earth."

Niall smiled, well aware that she was listening. "Empathy and pragmatism. I think the firestorm has it exactly right."

Okay. It was time to set him straight.

Or maybe herself.

Rox turned to face Niall, defiance in her eyes. He was closer than she'd expected, which made her talk tougher. "I told you that I don't do long term," she said. "I don't do forever. I don't do permanence or lasting bonds or marriage or kids, and neither you nor the firestorm will change that."

Niall folded his arms across his chest, unpersuaded. "Who are you trying to convince?"

"You!"

He arched a brow. "For how long was Thorolf your project again?"

"Three years. Accident, not design."

"Who ended it again?"

Rox tightened her lips. "He did. Accident, not design."

"How is giving someone a hundred second chances not long term?"

"That's different. You're talking about something a lot bigger, a much longer commitment . . . ," Rox began, but Niall shook his head and strolled closer.

"I don't think so. How long have you lived in that apartment? You look pretty well settled there."

"It has rent control," she said through her teeth. "And a great location. I'd be insane to move. I'd get a closet for twice the price."

"That's not the issue, Rox." Niall looked all too confident of his conclusions. "The lady protests too much."

Rox wished he weren't so right. "The *Pyr* is seeing things from his own perspective."

"Really?" Niall smiled. "What about tattoos? Aren't they permanent?"

Rox smiled and turned her back on him again. Anything to ignore how close he was. "You're right. Only ink is forever."

He halted right behind her. Rox was sure she could feel his breath on the back of her neck. She could feel the firestorm's persistent tingle and smell the clean scent of his skin.

She was sure she knew what he was going to do.

But Niall surprised her. "I'm sorry that I misjudged you at first," he said softly, and Rox blinked in astonishment. "I'm sorry that I assumed I knew the kind of person you were because of the way you dress."

Rox glanced over her shoulder, wary. "No harm done."

Niall held her gaze. He was close, too close, impossible to ignore. "That's the point, isn't it? You dress punk and talk tough to keep people at a distance."

"You don't know anything about me," Rox began to argue, but Niall didn't stop.

"It's your barbed wire fence and you need it, because once you come in here, you take on the grief of your clients and all the boundary lines dissolve." He was confident even though Rox was shaken that he had seen through her so well. "Like dragonsmoke before *Slayers*. It doesn't work against serious opposition, when the stakes are high."

"You sound even more flaky," Rox said, hoping to make him stop.

"But I'm only just getting to the heart of it," Niall said, his eyes brightening. "You have to have defenses to protect yourself, because you're a giving person, more giving than most. You give right here in this room. You give to any stranger who walks into this shop with a wound in need of healing. It's your nature to heal."

Rox straightened. "So what if it is?"

"What about the imbalance?"

"What imbalance?"

"What about you, Rox?" Niall's tone softened. "Who gives healing energy to you?"

Rox spun away from him then. "I don't need to be healed."

"Then tell me what taught you to build those protective walls in the first place."

Rox caught her breath and eyed him, her heart in her throat. "I don't have to tell you anything about that."

"No, you don't," Niall said quietly. "But think, Rox. What if the firestorm is your second chance?"

Rox knew she should run. She knew she should hide. She knew she should do everything she could to escape this man who was so determined to turn her world upside down and make her forget everything she knew.

He leaned closer. "It's not about babies, is it? It's not about permanence and it's not about commitment. Is it about trust, Rox?"

Niall was just too perceptive. In a day, he was seeing her truth, working his way into her heart, burning her barricades, ensuring that she'd never forget him.

And Rox was snared by his gaze. His eyes were so bright, his manner so intent, his concern almost tangible. He took the only step between them and caught her shoulders in his hands. Rox should have run, but she closed her eyes against the sweet heat of the firestorm, surrendering to its power.

When Niall bent to capture her lips beneath his own, she just waited for his touch.

* * *

Kissing Rox got better every time. Niall couldn't have believed it; he wouldn't have believed it if he hadn't experienced the truth. This kiss scorched him, touched him, stirred him; it made him burn for her. She was sweet and vulnerable and utterly exposed.

And he wanted to defend her forever.

Her kiss even took Niall to the cusp of change. She was always so responsive, and her passion made him feel each time as if they came closer to a perfect union. He felt his heartbeat match hers, felt his breathing resonate with hers. He swore he could feel her desire build, his own keeping perfect time. The tumult to shift grew within him, overwhelming him, and he had to step away to regain control.

Niall broke the kiss with an effort and leaned on the absent tattoo artist's station with both hands, trying to control his response. He was well aware of Rox's gaze upon him. Even with distance, he was keenly aware of her, yet he could make some effort to think clearly.

Rox leaned against her own station, visibly catching her breath. "Those are some kisses," she murmured, his own wonder echoed in her tone. She fanned herself and made a joke. "Dragons are dangerous for more reasons than I might have imagined."

Niall could only nod. He risked a glance her way and his heart clenched. Her eyes were filled with starlight and her cheeks were flushed, her lips rosy and inviting. He *wanted* as he had never wanted before, even though he knew he shouldn't. And each time he touched Rox and each conversation they had only heightened his response. He wasn't fooled by her light response. She felt exactly the same way as he did.

The firestorm had it right.

But Rox had to surrender to the firestorm willingly. Niall was never going to force her, and he was never going to compromise her right to decide her own future.

Even if his body demanded otherwise. He looked down at the floor, fighting the tide of desire, striving for control.

"You're shimmering blue," she whispered. "I can't tell where you end and the shimmer begins."

"It's the cusp of change," Niall admitted, clenching his hands. "Just give me a minute to get it under control."

Rox tilted her head to watch him. "Why now?"

"It must be because of the firestorm."

"I thought it was a defensive posture."

Niall nodded, breathing deeply as he fought the urge to change. The tide was growing within him, gaining ascendancy, driving his body to act against his will. He could smell Rox's skin, remember the feel of her under his fingertips, hear the accelerated pace of her heart. His keen *Pyr* senses betrayed him, providing him an array of detail that made it harder to do what he knew to be right. "It *is* a defensive posture. We fight in dragon form, or protect others."

"Then why would the firestorm make you start to shift?"

Niall looked up, his thinking clarified by her question. It wasn't Rox's kiss making him begin to shift; it was danger he had sensed.

"Because I must sense a threat to you," he said, scanning the room.

Rox started to ask, but Niall raised a hand. He sought the threat, the clue that had put him on the cusp of change. It had to be present, but it must be subtle. He narrowed his eyes and inhaled deeply, taking the scent of the wind and the air of Rox's shop. The firestorm hummed in his veins, tempting him to indulge in pleasure, but his body hovered on the threshold of change.

Niall concentrated. He smelled ink and the antiseptic Rox had used to clean Laurie's skin before applying the stencil. He smelled latex gloves and Rox's floral shower gel. He smelled the rain on the pavement outside the shop and the storm riding on the wind. He heard the discordant note of the earth's song, and had a heartbeat to be surprised that he could hear it so clearly.

Then the floor rippled and bucked.

Another earthquake.

Targeting him one more time.

No, it targeted the firestorm.

He had to save Rox!

Niall shifted shape in the same moment that he reached for Rox. It was his worst nightmare all over again. The building broke in half, ceiling plaster falling all around him as the rain began to slant through the cracked roof. Linoleum tiles flew in every direction as the foundation of the building cracked wide-open. Rox toppled on the edge of the crevasse in her stilettos, but Niall caught her close.

Rox swore and hung on tightly. "Barry and Neo?"

"Long gone," Niall said, checking for their scents. "They're fine." He felt her relief, noted his own surprise that she understood what she could expect of him, and was amazed.

In the same instant, he made to leap into the air, but the earth rumbled with sudden vigor. The crack in the floor gaped wide, then abruptly snapped shut.

His tail was caught in the floor.

Niall tugged but couldn't pull free.

The earth rumbled some more and the building fell around them. He pulled his tail again, thrashing, but it made no difference. The floor began to vibrate and he suspected the building would fall. They had to get away.

But he couldn't move. In fact, it felt as if the foundation of the building pulled him deeper.

"Rip free!"

"I can't!" Niall spoke through gritted teeth. "It's holding me too tightly."

Rox reached to tug at his tail, as futile as that effort was. Niall struggled, but he was trapped.

The earth was sucking him down into its maw.

He thought that fanciful, until he felt the rough edges of the floor scrape over his hide. He *was* being pulled deeper! He roared and fought, using all of his strength. He held Rox high above his head, knowing that she was the target of this attack.

Just as she had been at his apartment.

A *Slayer* was targeting his firestorm, choosing moments to attack his mate when he and Rox embraced and the flames burned brightest.

The earth devoured another increment of his tail.

Someone was commanding the earth to terminate his firestorm. The earth would stop only when it had destroyed Rox. What *Slayers* had an affinity for earth? Niall couldn't think of any, except Magnus.

The earth chewed down on his tail, crushing him in its grip. Niall felt his bones grinding and his scales being crushed. The pain was tremendous.

But it would be nothing compared to the loss of Rox. How could he ensure her safety, when he was trapped? If he sent her running through the building, he had no doubt that another crack would open.

Niall fought and bit; he roared and breathed dragon-fire. Frustration filled him, followed quickly by fury. The earth sucked back another increment of him. Niall had time to panic before Rafferty soared through the gap in the roof.

"*Take Rox!*" he roared in old-speak. He cast his mate toward the ancient *Pyr*, knowing that having Rox out of harm's way would help him gain his freedom.

He felt cold without Rox in his grasp, chilled without the steady burn of the firestorm against his skin. He bellowed again and struggled, believing the earth would release him.

It didn't.

It drew down another increment of his tail.

In fact, there was a definite tug from beneath the building's foundations. Niall felt himself sliding inexorably into the earth's grip. He thought of being crushed by Gaia. He wondered what he had done to deserve such a fate. Was this the vengeance of Magnus, for Niall taking on the quest to eliminate the shadow dragons? The broken concrete ripped at his scales, but Niall couldn't stop the course. He was being pulled into the earth.

At least he knew that he'd been right all along—he *was* being targeted.

He just didn't know why.

And it looked as if he wouldn't have the chance to figure it out. He raged against the hungry earth, to absolutely no avail.

Then Rafferty began to sing.

Rox watched in horror. The floor might have been quicksand, the way it was pulling Niall down. His struggles to release himself only seemed to make him disappear more quickly.

"Help him!" she cried to Rafferty, who had already started to hum.

Thorolf appeared against the silvery sky, as ethereal as a moonbeam. Another dragon was right behind him and Rox guessed that it was Sloane. His scales were like tourmalines edged in gold, shading from green to purple and back again. He was large and sleek, and he moved with the thoughtful intent that she already associated with Sloane.

Sloane and Thorolf dove to the shattered floor, each of them seizing one of Niall's arms. They bared their teeth and pulled with all their might, trying to take flight with the other *Pyr* held fast, but Niall was still being pulled down.

Rox saw his fear.

She certainly shared it. She watched his blood flow

across the floor from his torn scales and wished there
was something she could do to help.

"The earth's songs are too slow!" Sloane complained
as Rafferty's hum began to increase in vigor.

His song became a chant, as insistent as marching
music.

Niall was sucked down to his waist. "No!" he roared,
pounding on the floor and battling mightily. A wind
swirled in the broken building, perhaps a manifestation
of his distress, and Rox felt as if she were caught in a
tempest.

"It's not enough!" Thorolf complained. He set to ripping the floor and foundation himself, trying to break
Niall free. Each piece he tore loose seemed to fall back
around Niall's trapped body, though. He was pulled
steadily deeper and the building began to crumble
around them.

Rafferty's song grew louder and more insistent.

"There's another song," Sloane said. "I hear Rafferty
competing against it."

Rafferty nodded once, not risking a break in his tune.
He sang louder and deeper; he sang so vigorously that
Rox's bones resonated with the tune. She hung on to
him as he hovered over the scene, watching in horror as
Niall's wings disappeared into the earth. He was buried
to his underarms.

Sloane looked between the two of them, then raised
his voice to join Rafferty's. It was clear to Rox that the
Apothecary didn't know the chant as well as Rafferty,
but he added his voice where he could. Thorolf continued to rip at the building, anxiety making him move
faster and more powerfully.

It wasn't enough.

The earth devoured Niall to the shoulders. He shouted
in rage and managed to punch one claw free. He
breathed dragonfire. He clearly kicked and struggled; he
bellowed in terror as his neck slipped into the crack.

"No!" Rox whispered.

Just when it seemed that Niall would disappear forever, the foundation began to resonate. Rox saw that it moved in the same rhythm as Rafferty's song, the same cadence that vibrated in her own body.

"Louder!" she cried. "You're winning!"

Rafferty's song became bombastic, an anthem demanding that every force surrender to its beat. He tipped back his head and roared, the volume of his song making the walls shake. The foundation began to shudder, caught between two competing forces. Niall gave a cry of pain as he was pulled into the crevasse.

Only his one talon remained above the floor.

Rox squirmed from Rafferty's grasp and jumped down to the floor. She ran to Niall and caught his claw in her hand. "Fight it!" she demanded, the spark of the firestorm lighting the room. She held fast and pulled.

Rafferty sang.

Sloane sang.

Thorolf forced open the crack and grabbed Niall by the shoulder. Rox pulled. The floor shook as if they were in an earthquake. It rocked so violently that Rox feared she'd fall, but she held on tightly. The wind swirled around them, whipping Rox's hair against her face and driving debris against her skin.

And with an abrupt shudder, the crack opened wide.

Niall erupted from the space, bounding toward the sky as he caught Rox against his side. Thorolf was on his other side, urging him to greater speed. Rox cheered, even as she saw how his scales had been damaged.

Rafferty and Sloane followed Niall, even as Rafferty concluded his song to the earth.

Rox hung on to Niall, ferociously glad he had escaped.

He raged into the gray sky as the rain pelted on his scales, carrying them both away from harm. It was around six, but the sky seemed to be turning a darker shade of pewter. The water beaded on Niall's hide and fell away, his protective embrace keeping her warm against his chest. He was like a mailed warrior.

And he was safe.

Wounded, but alive.

Flying away from potential disaster was thrilling. Rox felt the wind in her hair and her torn T-shirt snapped in the breeze. It was exhilarating to be so free and yet not be in danger. She leaned against Niall's chest and heard the steady pounding of his heart, its accelerated pace telling her that he wasn't as calm as he appeared.

It was more than the firestorm heating her body, and Rox knew it.

Rafferty's eyes flashed with annoyance. His opalescent scales seemed to be edged in gold, while Thorolf's scales more closely resembled moonstones edged in silver. Rafferty's wings were golden, like gilded leather, while Thorolf's were silvery. They both seemed ethereal in the rain, ghostly, and not quite real. Rox felt the muscled strength of Niall even as he held her with care, and she knew these dragons were real.

Just as she'd always imagined. The firestorm made a rosy glow between Rox and Niall, illuminating every point they touched and filling her body with that delicious heat of desire.

Her cell phone rang, startling her with its sound. It seemed strange to answer it as she soared through the sky in Niall's embrace, but Rox went with it. The caller was Neo, wanting to check on her. He'd seen something of the building's destruction, but Rox assured him she'd left. She pretended to know nothing of the disaster, and Neo said he'd solve everything.

She ended the call, aware that Niall had heard the whole conversation. She was blushing at Neo's last suggestion of what she should do with her day—and with Niall—and thought she detected a satisfied smile.

So she changed the subject. "I thought you *Pyr* defended the earth."

"We do," Niall said, his tone grim.

"Then why did it try to eat you? It's just like yesterday, when your building was the only one destroyed." If anything, Niall looked more grim. "Face it—the earth is after you."

"It's not the earth," Rafferty said with conviction. "Gaia was seduced by a song, a strong song sung by an old singer."

"But it can't be Magnus," Thorolf said. "Is it someone he taught?"

Rafferty shook his head. "No. I didn't recognize his voice, except that I heard it yesterday, as well." The older *Pyr* shook his head. "He sings differently from Magnus, as if his chant is in another language than the one I know. The only reason I prevailed is that he tried to make Gaia act against her principles. He's strong. I could have lost."

"You might lose next time," Rox said, feeling obliged to note this possibility. Niall caught his breath.

Rafferty nodded. "That's why we need to figure out what's going on first."

Rox's heart clenched. She realized Niall might leave her, but not due to his own choice. He might be *taken* from her.

This was a puzzle she needed to help the *Pyr* solve.

They convened in Rox's kitchen one more time, but this time, Rafferty opened a bottle of wine. Sloane accepted a glass of it. Thorolf treated himself to a beer instead. Rox made a pot of ginseng tea for herself and Niall.

"Okay," she said when they'd all calmed down a bit. "Walk me through this, and let's see if we can solve it. We have *Pyr* and *Slayers*, good dragons and bad ones, and the bad ones target firestorms. Although they usu-

ally target mates, this time they're going right for the
Pyr."

"No," Niall said. "This has to do with the shadow
dragons. Magnus created the shadow dragons and he
also had an affinity with the earth."

"How did he create them?"

"With the Dragon's Blood Elixir," Niall said, his
words tight. "The shadow dragons were another way
for Magnus to increase his power. He discovered that
those *Pyr* or *Slayers* who had died but had not been exposed to all four elements within half a solar day of their
demise—"

"Twelve hours," Rox said, and Niall nodded.

"Could be raised from the dead with the Elixir."

"Ick. That's why Phelan's scales look so dull compared to yours." Rox shuddered. "He looks decomposed
because he is."

"Ick is it," Sloane said, then took an appreciative swig
of wine.

"Who's Magnus?" Rox asked.

"An old *Slayer*," Thorolf said, then took a gulp of his
beer. "A dead *Slayer*, which is the best kind."

Rafferty continued. "Magnus created the Dragon's
Blood Elixir. It was a rumor for a long time, but he made
it a reality. The Elixir conferred immortality among those
who drank it, and it allowed them to heal more quickly
from injuries. It also gave some of them the power to cut
dragonsmoke and move through it, without the permission of whoever had breathed it."

"But the Elixir doesn't exist anymore," Sloane said.
"Delaney destroyed its source last year."

Niall gave her a look. "And you don't want to know
its source."

"I can guess from the name." Rox made a face.

"But this voice inciting the earth to violence is unknown to me," Rafferty insisted. "I am certain he was
not tutored by Magnus. His song is too alien."

"It has to have something to do with the shadow dragons," Niall insisted. "Someone doesn't like my taking them out."

"So how do you hunt shadow dragons?" Rox asked.

He grimaced. "I wait until they attack."

"But where are they hiding?" Rox asked.

"That's the thing," Niall acknowledged. "The Elixir was destroyed about sixteen months ago, along with Magnus and the academy where he had created the shadow dragons. The shadow dragons had used that academy as a refuge and a rallying point, but then were dispersed. We've been eliminating them ever since."

"Ginger has been helping to make a list," Rafferty said.

"And that's all good," Niall said, his expression intent. "But the thing is, I didn't think we'd need a list. I thought they would just all attack, pretty much immediately, and keep on attacking until they were all eliminated. They had already been commanded to attack, and there was no one left to change their command or to call them off. I thought the job would be wrapped up pretty quickly."

"You're right," Rafferty said thoughtfully. "That would have been characteristic of them."

"Couldn't they make a plan?" Rox asked.

"Shadow dragons as a rule are not really home." Niall tapped his temple to illustrate his point. "They just inflict damage and will do anything to win. They keep fighting until they can't."

"What's happened instead?" Rox asked. She was thinking about Phelan, and trying to reconcile his manner with the idea of his being a shadow dragon.

"They appear, one or two at a time, usually weeks apart. It's as if they're being released at a controlled rate." Niall frowned. "Although there have been three this week already. It's weird."

"Maybe it's the eclipse," Thorolf suggested.

"Not the eclipse," Rafferty corrected. "The firestorm.

It draws us, regardless of our allegiance, like a song in the blood. We all feel one, no matter the distance, and they probably do, too."

Rox thought about the two earthquakes that had targetted Niall. Did that mean the shadow dragons were hiding in the earth?

"So, the firestorm is drawing them from their refuge, wherever it is," Thorolf said, "because there's still some *Pyr* in them?"

"No," Niall argued. "It makes no sense that they would be able to hunt out and find a new refuge, never mind plan these spaced-out attacks. They aren't strategic planners. They'll attack and fight until they either win or are outnumbered, in which case they'll retreat and attack again."

"Could they have a new leader?" Rox suggested. "Or be under the control of someone else?"

Niall nodded agreement so ruefully that she knew he'd thought of that. "I've been wondering. But who could control them, other than Magnus?"

"Magnus's *Slayers*, Jorge, Balthasar, and Mallory, have disappeared," Sloane said. "No one has seen or smelled them since the Elixir was destroyed."

"And they were injured, without any Elixir left to heal their wounds," Thorolf said.

"But Jorge at least can disguise his scent," Niall reminded the others.

"It could still be them," Sloane said.

"I don't think so," Rafferty said. "They lack the skill. And this voice is new to me, that of a different *Slayer*."

"Could Magnus somehow be alive?" Niall asked the oldest *Pyr*.

"I have wondered," Rafferty admitted with a sigh. "I trapped him in the earth and persuaded Gaia to crush him to oblivion." He grimaced. "I did not see his body, though, and Gaia's song has become dissonant of late."

"Can't you ask the earth for the scoop?" Thorolf demanded.

"Rafferty has an affinity with the element of earth," Niall told Rox. "And he knows many songs that move Gaia to act."

"Or not to act, as the case may be." Rafferty shrugged. "Magnus also had an affinity for the earth, which is why we were once friends, before he chose the darkness. I thought it might be his song, here in New York, which was why I came. I needed to listen more closely."

"But?" Sloane prompted.

Rafferty shook his head. "This is the work of another, stronger singer, one whose voice I don't recognize. There aren't that many of us who sing to the earth."

"Great," Sloane said, and finished his wine. "Just what we need—new strong enemies."

"In this era, when so much is at stake, we must anticipate that old forces will reveal themselves," Rafferty said softly. "There is opportunity in adversity."

Silence reigned in the kitchen for a minute and the rain drummed on the windows.

"Tell me more about having an affinity for an element," Rox said.

"Some of us have strong connections to one element," Rafferty said, seeming to welcome the chance to explain something. "Niall has an affinity with the element of air, just as I have one with earth. It means we have mastered the songs to which that element responds."

Rox nodded, having heard some of this from Niall.

Rafferty continued. "Quinn, the Smith of our kind, has an affinity for fire. He can take the assault of dragonfire and convert it to build his own strength or that of his forge for the repair of our armor."

Rox spared a glance for the rain still slashing against the windows and tried to lighten the mood. "Well, whoever has an affinity for water should talk to the rain

about stopping. We'll all float away otherwise." She'd
meant it as a joke, but the *Pyr* exchanged glances and
Niall caught his breath. "What did I say?"

"An affinity for water is a rare relationship in our
kind," Sloane said. "Only Delaney and Donovan and I
have it."

"Three isn't a lot?" Rox asked.

Sloane smiled. "Not over thousands of years. Our affinities take the form of empathy with others, not control over rain."

"Mates often bring the element of water into the balance," Rafferty said.

"Why? Because water douses fire?" Rox guessed.

Rafferty shrugged. "I would assume so. Associations
with the other three elements are far more customary,
although only the affinity is inborn. To master an element and persuade it to do one's will takes work and
practice over many years."

"No one can control rain? Seriously?" Rox asked.
When the *Pyr* shook their heads, she stood up with purpose. "You must not have any Chinese dragons in your
company, then," she said. "In their folklore, dragons do
control the rain."

Niall was both impressed and surprised by Rox one
more time. He'd never thought about dragon lore from
human cultures, having assumed it would always offer
only part of the story. On the other hand, Erik's mate,
Eileen, always insisted the most persistent myths and
stories had their toes in the truth.

The trick would be deciding where to draw the line
between fact and fiction.

Rox returned, carrying a big coffee-table book on
dragons.

"Bet the illustrations aren't as good as yours," Niall
said, and she blushed.

"There are a lot of historical images in here," she said,

fanning the book. "From illuminated manuscripts and old carvings. I don't like all of them, especially the ones that associate dragons with the Devil."

"I have never been fond of those, either," Rafferty said.

"But it provides a lot of inspiration and information." She put the book down on the counter. Sloane and Rafferty immediately turned to it, leafing through its pages. Rox talked about the mythology illustrated or explained on each page, giving them an executive summary of human lore about dragons.

Niall listened avidly to Rox's explanations. He was amused at her disgust over the assertion that dragons were only interested in virgins, princesses, and damsels in distress.

"A woman in need of defense does have a certain appeal," Rafferty said softly. Niall watched Rox turn on him before she evidently saw the twinkle in his dark eyes.

"You're teasing me," Rox accused, and Rafferty laughed.

"I think you're on to something here," Niall said to Rox. "We might learn more by tracking specific affinities." He booted up his laptop, found a WiFi connection—he loved living in the city—and e-mailed Ginger. He asked whether she could add another attribute to each *Pyr*'s individual record, so they could gather information on affinities.

In the meantime, he could keep notes. If Donovan and Delaney both had an affinity for water, did that mean affinities ran in families? Those two were brothers, the only *Pyr* brothers Niall knew about other than himself and Phelan. Did Phelan have an affinity for air? Had he ever done anything to hone it? Niall wasn't sure, but he doubted it.

"It might even help locate some of the missing *Pyr* and *Slayers*," Rafferty said. "Maybe we die near our associated element."

"I gotta get me an affinity," Thorolf muttered.

Niall refrained from comment upon that.

"So, are affinities for defensive purposes?" Rox asked.

Sloane shook his head. "An affinity can manifest in different ways. Both Niall and Erik have an affinity with air, for example, but they use that gift differently. Erik's affinity gives him foresight, whereas Niall's lets him communicate with the wind."

"I can summon a storm, but once the wind gets rolling, the storm often takes on a power and direction of its own." Niall frowned, then uttered the strange thought he'd had with increasing regularity of late. "I suspect there's a consciousness in the element that can be awakened, and once it is stirred, it makes its own choices for the future."

To his relief, no one laughed.

"I have often thought as much of the earth," Rafferty said. "Although it sounds far-fetched, there is a determination and unpredictability about Gaia that cannot be explained by simple cause and effect."

"Isn't any unpredictability a result of the earth's being under duress?" Rox asked. "What with pollution and there being so many of us on the planet now, stretching resources thin?"

"That is a variable, to be sure," Rafferty said, "but sometimes I also have an awareness of sentience, another consciousness at work"—he shrugged—"and anger."

"Did Phelan have an affinity with air?" Rox asked.

"If he did, he never did anything about it." Niall was amazed he had never thought of such a thing before this day.

"It takes many years of diligent practice to cement such an affinity," Rafferty said. "I do not believe it was Phelan's inclination to spend such time on his studies."

"I can understand that," Rox said, "and believe it,

too." She smiled at Niall. "Maybe you two weren't so identical, after all."

"Maybe not," Niall agreed, returning her smile. The air heated an increment in the kitchen, until Rafferty cleared his throat.

"You look exhausted, Niall," the older *Pyr* said softly. "And sleep will help you recover from your ordeal."

"Shift and let me have a look at that tail," Sloane advised.

"But . . . ," Niall began to argue. He saw welcome in Rox's eyes and was ready to capitalize on advantage. She retreated, though, hiding her thoughts once more.

"We'll defend Rox," Thorolf said.

Rafferty tilted his head. "Erik is en route. He will have more ideas of what should be done, if not a glimpse of the future to guide us."

"I think sleep is a great idea," Rox said, and yawned so luxuriously that Niall knew she was pretending to be so tired. "Maybe it'll all make sense in the morning. Breathe smoke, dudes, so we can all sleep soundly." With a perky wave, she retreated once more to her bedroom.

Without Niall.

Chapter 12

Phelan was surrounded by fog.

It was the darkness of impenetrable shadows, the fog that had initially been pierced only by Magnus's commands. He had been able to accept Magnus's dictates and act upon them, but no more than that. Initiative had been sacrificed long ago, along with the fire of life.

Until recently.

Phelan heard the old man murmuring to himself. He spoke a language Phelan didn't know and didn't understand—he assumed it was an Asian language, given the old man's appearance. It was rhythmic, though, like a chant, and its familiarity sliced through the fog that enveloped Phelan.

Eliminating it.

Dispersing it.

Creating anticipation. The brush of those cool fingertips against his throat, then the imprint of the strange coin upon the mark that Chen had placed upon him, had Phelan following the old man.

Blindly and wherever he led.

They halted somewhere—Phelan didn't care where—

and Phelan felt the old man force his mouth open. He tasted that strange metallic flavor on his tongue.

And his mind sparked.

Like an engine being restarted, his thoughts began to dart like quicksilver. He recalled more than this spell, more than Magnus, more than the fog that enveloped him as a shadow dragon. Phelan remembered everything, in fact, that he had ever known. He remembered everything he had lost, everything his twin had stolen from him, every injustice and imbalance.

And with the memories came the lust for vengeance, the power of intiative, the conviction that he could achieve whatever he desired.

Phelan wanted what Niall possessed. It had always been thus between them, and even choosing the darkness to gain more than his twin had only intensified Phelan's jealousy.

Now Niall had a firestorm and Phelan did not.

Now Phelan had been given the magical powder and remembered.

Chen alone held the power to give Phelan what he most desired.

The old man murmured as he had before, his cool fingertips touching Phelan's eyelids each in turn. Phelan's eyes flew open at what must have been a command.

He found himself standing in that basement room, the one that was effectively the office of Chen the *Slayer*, and caught the merest glimpse of the old man's departure. His heart leapt. No sooner had the door closed behind the old man than it swung open again and Chen strode into the space in the form of a young man.

Phelan fought his urge to cringe—without success.

This *Slayer* was unpredictable, ancient, inclined to violence. Chen was as unlike Magnus as Phelan could have imagined—but he made better offers.

He saw with one glance that Chen was displeased with him.

And Phelan feared the *Slayer* would withdraw his offer.

"A waste," Chen whispered, and began to pace the width of the room. That he smoothly shifted shape during each turn, becoming by turns a young woman and a young man, did little to reassure Phelan. Phelan clenched his hands, burned with desire, and waited.

It had to be a good sign that he had been revived again.

Or maybe Chen simply wanted Phelan to be aware of his own destruction. Phelan swallowed in his uncertainty. It was worse in a way to have lost his sense of self and to have it restored—he knew what he had lost and knew what he would lose when he really died. It made him more determined to achieve his desire.

A calendar on the wall declared that 2010 was the year of the tiger. It seemed oddly ornate for the spartan basement room. An old wooden table that looked as if it had seen better days—and a few floods—stood in the middle of the room. There was one shelf on the wall, a wooden plank mounted on a pair of L-brackets.

There was a large sealer jar on the table and Phelan was sure there was something in it. Something alive—something gold and green that moved very little. The glass was fogged, though, presumably from the creature's breath, and he didn't dare tempt Chen's anger by taking a close look.

Chen pivoted to glare at him and Phelan tried not to quaver. Even his ability to feel sensation was returned with this strange powder, though it was a mixed blessing when Chen turned abusive.

"Against all expectation, you may still prove useful." Chen's eyes narrowed. "I ordered a larger increment of pulverized dragon bone for you this time. This time, you will be more cunning, more like your old self."

Phelan nodded in understanding. It was true. He felt sharper than he had the last time.

He wondered where Chen had obtained dragon bones, but he didn't think it wise to ask. Would he be a future source, if he failed in this task?

Chen gave a curt nod. "You are more alive than dead, for the moment."

"For the moment?"

"This increment of time is finite. The effect of the dragon bone does not last; it cannot last. You have only hours to bring me the mate. As I instructed you before, your brother will follow if you succeed in seizing her."

"And Niall will die?" Phelan loved the notion of cheating his twin of the satisfaction of his firestorm. He wanted to seize the woman immediately, to ensure that his brother did not have the pleasure he himself desired.

"He will wish for death first." Chen ticked off the elements on his fingers. "Gaia surrendered my enemy to my grasp in an earthquake, at my dictate, proof that I command the element of earth. A deluge continues to fall, at my instruction, as proof of my command of water. When the *Pyr* who commands the wind is a shadow dragon in my thrall, I shall control the element of air."

"And fire?"

"The firestorm, of course. I command its heat, as well. Didn't you know?" Chen smiled. "Look." He pulled some dark powder from his pocket and exhaled upon it.

As Phelan watched with astonishment, flames erupted from Chen's mouth and lit the powder. It glowed brilliant orange and shot sparks. Chen murmured a charm beneath his breath, then blew the burning powder across the room. The particles flared as they danced through the air, several exploding, others shooting sparks.

"We can guess what they will be doing when you arrive," Chen said, then smiled again.

"And then?"

"And the fifth element, that of spirit, will be within

reach and its conquest will be mine." Chen folded his hands together. "Finally!"

"And then I will have my firestorm?"

Chen's smile broadened. "I will try." He arched a brow. "But the quicker you are in succeeding, the more effort I will expend upon your wish. I will surrender no more of my precious ground dragon bone upon you."

Now or never. Phelan rattled his fetter, anxious to be off.

Chen bent, let his index finger change to a dragon talon, and loosed his captive. As Phelan lunged into the night, he thought he heard the old *Slayer* laugh far beneath him.

But he didn't care. He knew what he wanted, he knew he would succeed, and he believed Chen would grant his fitting reward.

Late at night, in a car seat strapped into the back of a black Maserati sedan that raced eastward, a toddler stirred. She saw the moonlight glimmer in the loose red hair of the woman driving. She saw the laptop's light gleam on the sharp features of the man in the passenger seat. There were a few approaching headlights on the interstate and the instruments on the dashboard gleamed. Jazz music played softly and the car engine hummed.

The toddler felt the tug of the moon, the shadow of the recent eclipse, the glow of a distant firestorm. She felt the spark of the Great Wyvern burning brightly and remembered what she had been born to do.

She routinely forgot the impetus to her existence in the hurly-burly of the day, in the hustle and bustle of learning to command her body and communicate with those around her, in the frustration of growing up.

But in the middle of the night, she remembered everything.

She was young, but her soul was ancient. Her body was weak, but her purpose was potent. She had a small vocabulary to express herself, but she was filled with the knowledge of what had been and what might be. She knew her legacy and her responsibility; she knew how imperative it was—she knew all of this in the depths of her heart.

She was the new Wyvern and the future was hers to shape.

She was Zoë Sorensson, the latest in a long line of female Wyverns sent to aid the *Pyr*. The last Wyvern, Sophie, had abandoned tradition: rather than remaining remote, she had mingled with the *Pyr* and dipped her fingers into the conflict of life. She had not been indifferent—she had dared to fall in love and be intimate with another *Pyr*, breaking an old injunction. Sophie had paid the price with her choice, sacrificing all for love, but even so, Zoë was determined to continue on the path Sophie had forged.

The world was caught in a period of adjustment called the Dragon's Tail, the astrological phase governed by the moon's descending node. Karmic balances would be corrected in this phase, past debts would come due, and lessons learned would manifest in change. A modification of roles was a critical element in the *Pyr*'s successful navigation of this nine-year phase, but it wasn't the only part of the puzzle to be resolved.

The first three total eclipses had occurred within the Dragon's Tail and the critical firestorms marked by those eclipses had been successfully resolved. But that was just the beginning of three tests—three by three, the eclipses and the critical firestorms came in trios, each one marking another milestone to be conquered.

The second set of three total eclipses would begin in December, a mere six months away, and Zoë knew the firestorms they lit would be similarly critical to the *Pyr*'s triumph. They would bring new challenges, and new opportunities. She also knew there were forces arrayed against the *Pyr*, forces that had to be removed for that success.

In this moment, Zoë could help.

She looked out the window at the glow of the moon, which was just a hair past full. She raised her clenched hand so that the moonlight touched her skin, closed her eyes, and—unbeknownst to her busy parents—cast a fistful of dreams into the starry night.

Rox stared at the ceiling and itched with desire. She wanted Niall even more badly than before, her mind replaying the sight of him as he climaxed.

He'd been all power and masculinity, and she'd been shocked by how much she'd wanted him inside her.

Even then.

Another day and the heat was even worse. Was it possible that the firestorm did burn brighter and hotter until it was sated?

She knew he was just beyond her door.

She knew he was agreeable.

She knew it would be amazing.

She did not know, however, that she could trust Niall to stay, not with someone inciting the earth to gobble him up whole.

Rox tossed in her bed, thinking more about sex than shadow dragons, listening to the *Pyr* breathe smoke. It was hours before she slept, but then she dreamed in glorious color.

She could have been in a Jane Austen movie. She walked through a glittering ballroom, resplendent with crystal chandeliers and bright with candlelight. Richly dressed people on all sides laughed at one another's bons mots and drank sparkling wine. She heard music and followed its summons. The women's dresses swung as they danced, taffeta and silk gleaming in the light. Gems flashed and hot glances were exchanged, chaperones scowled, and starlight shone through an entire wall of large glass doors.

A man leaned against the opposite wall, drinking as he watched. He could have been Niall, blond and muscular, but his expression was too stern. He was older, too, a bit thicker through the middle although still trim. As she came closer to him, she saw a few lines of silver at his temples, the silver almost disappearing in the gold gleam of his hair.

His eyes were the same resolute blue as Niall's, his gaze as direct. Rox had a sense that he was uncompromising, though. She couldn't imagine that he would kiss like Niall did, all soulful heat.

He watched the dancers as he drank, fixed on them with an intensity that made Rox curious. She followed his gaze and realized that his attention was snared by a woman. She could have been made of porcelain, she was so beautiful, and the man watched her with heat in his gaze.

"You should dance with her, Nigel," came a man's low voice. A dark-haired man with dark eyes and amusement in his tone had joined the blond man.

Rox started. It was Rafferty.

He was dressed in clothing similar to Nigel's, with tall boots and a white shirt, a tailored jacket, and his dark hair queued in back. Rox noticed that he didn't have the black and white ring.

He clearly wasn't threatened by Nigel or worried about annoying him, despite his manner. Rox assumed they were friends.

Niall had said he was two hundred years old. Was Nigel his father? Was the woman Niall's mother?

Nigel's mate?

"I do not dance," came the quick retort, as cutting as a knife.

"You should," Rafferty replied easily.

"Have you no matters of interest of your own?" Nigel demanded.

"Dance," Rafferty urged, his voice as soft as a whisper.

Nigel straightened. "It should hardly be a concern of yours whether I dance or not."

"You will paw a hole in the floor if she dances with another man," Rafferty said with a smile. "I think only of the finish of our hostess's floors."

Nigel's eyes narrowed as he turned on Rafferty, and Rox almost saw a puff of smoke rise from his nostrils. "You are impertinent and—"

"And you are squandering the rare gift of a firestorm," Rafferty replied. His voice was still soft, but there was an undercurrent of steel to his tone. "Your lady wife knows your secret, and the chasm between you is of your own making. Repair it."

Nigel glanced around with agitation before glaring at Rafferty again. His next words came low and hot. "Our son has turned to the darkness. How can I go to her, knowing that?"

Rafferty didn't move. "How can you stay away from her, knowing that?"

Nigel hissed through his teeth and threw back the rest of his drink. Rox guessed that it wasn't tea. "You don't understand a whit of it."

"Nor, sadly, do you. There is nothing to be gained in silence. Did you not learn that the last time?"

But Nigel had turned away. He dropped his glass on a servant's tray before he strode out of the hall and left his lady behind.

Without a word.

She wasn't as oblivious to his presence as she had appeared. Rox saw her stumble in the dance, her smile fading as she watched her husband leave the ballroom. He moved so decisively that there could be no mistaking his identity.

Or her adoration of him. The lady's mask of pleasure slipped for a moment, leaving her heart revealed. Rox knew that Rafferty was right about the couple's needing to work together to find a solution. Each was obviously the only person in the room unaware of the truth of his or her spouse's feelings.

Nigel, though, was gone.

The lady summoned a smile for her partner and continued to dance. If Rox hadn't seen her dismay, she might have guessed the lady was having a wonderful time.

Where was Niall?

Rox scanned the room again, marveling at how ornate it was. The music changed and Rox couldn't see any sign of Rafferty. She surveyed the dance floor, but couldn't find the beautiful woman anymore. She felt a moment's fear and moved closer.

Then she spied the lady who must be Niall's mother approaching the large glass doors on the far side of the ballroom. She was chatting to the man who accompanied her, her hand on his elbow. She seemed utterly at ease, even though this man hadn't been in her presence earlier. How had he appeared so quickly? He was a younger man with golden hair, who charted a direct course for the French doors. He was slimmer than Nigel and moved like a young man.

Twenty or thirty years old. Rox's heart skipped a beat.

Was it Niall? He moved the same way and was the same height, maybe a little slimmer. He held the woman's arm with a gallantry Rox associated with Niall, listening to her and nodding. The woman laughed up at him, rapping her fan on his arm.

Rox followed, hoping to catch a glimpse of the man's face.

On the threshold of the garden, the man glanced over his shoulder. Rox saw the familiar darkness of his eyes.

It wasn't as complete as it was now, but there was menace there.

Phelan.

His smile was unkind. He had a dark plan, Rox was sure of it, and his mother was going to pay the price.

Where was Niall?

The lady was oblivious, still chatting to her son, apparently unaware that anything was amiss.

Someone had to do something!

Rox tried to cry out. She tried to shout a warning. She tried to push through the dancers, but they dispersed to mist in her hands. The scene faded as she thrashed in her sleep, disappearing as if it had never been.

Rox awakened gasping, the sheets clutched in her fists as her heart pounded. She was in her room, all alone, her heart pounding.

What had Phelan done to Niall's mother? Rox doubted it was anything good.

Her own memories supplied an array of horrible possibilities and Rox thought she might be sick. She lay in the darkness and stared at the ceiling, fighting against the shadow of her own past, even as she feared for a woman who must be a century dead.

That was when Rox realized she had company.

Sara awakened with a start, her breath caught in her throat. Another verse had spilled into her thoughts, one that came with a charge of insistence. She turned on her flashlight and wrote it down, puzzling over it when she had written it all.

What did it mean?

> *When the Dragon's Tail turns in the sky,*
> *When the year of tiger rises high,*
> *The Phoenix and the Dragon mate,*
> *Desire does their child create.*
> *But at this junction the old charm,*

Can be performed to make great harm.
Elements four in union do conjure,
The chance to invoke the fifth's measure.
Master the four, command the thoughts
of all Gaia's populace.

This time, Sara realized that Quinn was awake and watching her.

"A dream?" he asked.

"A prophecy," Sara corrected. "It's the second one. I had one last night, and now this." She pulled out her journal and showed him the first verse, knowing that he would be more likely to catch any references to *Pyr* lore.

"I had a dream, as well," Quinn said softly after he scanned her words. "I dreamed of my brother Michel, the one who is still a shadow dragon." His gaze slid to the window, his concern clear. "I dreamed that he came here, that he awaited me in my shop."

"Wouldn't he have come after you already, if it was his plan?"

Quinn nodded slowly. "I think it was a warning. Niall must face his shadow dragon brother, just as I must confront mine. We should go to New York, to assist him."

Sara was confused. "Niall? But why now?"

Quinn cast her a shimmering look. "I felt the eclipse yesterday and then felt his firestorm. I wasn't going to go. . . ."

Sara heard the uncertainty in his voice. A *Pyr* in the midst of his firestorm often needed the services of the Smith to repair his armor, and Quinn was loyal to his fellows. She glanced down at this recent prophecy, her heart in her throat because she knew what Quinn would choose if he read it.

But he wasn't the only one loyal to the *Pyr*. Sara silently handed Quinn the second verse and watched his lips tighten.

"Let's go," he said, moving quickly. She knew he would collect their son, and hastened to pack a few things, the truth about her pregnancy catching in her throat. She didn't want to tell Quinn now, didn't want to interfere with the fulfillment of his duty.

But she was afraid.

Quinn halted on the threshold, then strode back to catch her close. "I know," he whispered, smiling when she glanced up at him in surprise. "Your skin is different, softer somehow, when you are pregnant. You sleep more deeply." He ran a strong fingertip down her cheek. "And you seem more precious to me than ever."

Sara heaved a sigh. "If I'm the Seer, how is it that you know all my secrets?" she complained good-naturedly.

"Because you are my mate, my wife, and my life," Quinn whispered, a glint of determination in his eyes as he looked down at her. "Never imagine that I will let anyone or anything steal you from me." And he kissed her with the surety that dissolved her fears, each and every time.

They would go to New York and ensure that Niall's firestorm came out right.

Alex Madison decided that life was good.

She was rubbing more suntan lotion on her legs, relaxing on a chaise lounge on the whitest sand beach she'd ever seen. The ocean was a glorious azure and the sky was completely clear. The palm trees were lush and green; the cocktails were cold and came with little paper umbrellas in them. The cabana boys looked good enough to eat, and the all-inclusive resort had excellent day care.

She'd been working full-out for the past two years, getting her Green Machine into production and into a test market. It had been grueling work, filled with technical challenges and exciting chances to learn. San Francisco was filling with prototypes of the vehicle, more investors were coming on board with every bit of good news, and Alex was finally able to take a vacation.

Sort of. She and Donovan had taken on a job to contribute more to the quest of the *Pyr*. The challenge facing the *Pyr* was to determine how many shadow dragons still existed. Donovan had had the idea that there might be a difference in the soil beneath a fallen *Pyr* warrior depending on whether his remains had been undisturbed or raised by the Elixir. Alex had managed to identify three trace elements that existed only at the sites where *Pyr* had been raised by the Elixir.

Not surprisingly, mercury was among the contenders. The other two trace elements were unusual enough, especially in combination, that their presence made it clear not only that the right site had been identified, but that the shadow dragon had been raised.

Ginger had supplied a list of approximate death sites of *Pyr*. Some were hundreds of years old. Some were more recent. Donovan had used his *Pyr* senses and his affinity with the elements to locate the sites specifically, then taken soil samples for Alex.

The scheme had worked brilliantly. Ginger supplied locations, and Alex and/or Donovan visited the sites to collect the samples; then Alex tested them and sent the results back to Ginger.

This site, off an island in the South Pacific, had been the location of a much mythologized battle between *Pyr* and *Slayers* several hundred years before. Alex liked that it had proven to be roughly located where old maps were marked *Heere be Dragones*.

She also liked that Donovan had found an all-inclusive resort close enough for him to dive the site, and that they had taken their first comparatively normal family vacation. Ever since she and Donovan had become a couple, her brother had been pestering her that both families should vacation together. On this day, Nick was in the hotel day care with his two older cousins, while Alex's brother and his wife had gone on a sightseeing day trip.

Alex was content with the view on the beach. She dug her toes into the hot sand, adjusted her sunglasses, and watched her partner stride out of the surf in his black wet suit.

Just like Sean Connery in *Thunderball*.

But better. Oh, so much better. Donovan, the Warrior of the *Pyr*, was tall and lean, muscled in all the right places. A week and a half in the sun had tanned his skin to a rich golden hue, which seemed to make his hair look more russet and unruly. It certainly made his eyes look even more like green glass.

He glanced around the beach, saw her, and headed straight for her. His teeth flashed white as he smiled, and Alex straightened a little on her chaise lounge.

Maybe it was time to make Nick a brother.

Maybe today was the day.

Donovan unzipped his wet suit as he strode out of the water, tugging it open as he pulled off his mask. He shook out his hair and grinned at Alex like a pirate, then placed his net bag of samples on the side of the chaise lounge.

"Got the last five, gorgeous," he said with satisfaction.

"Good job. Want some margarita?"

To Alex's surprise, Donovan shook his head. "No, thanks." He scanned the sky and she sensed his concern.

"What's going on?"

"A firestorm." He frowned and shrugged, then did take a swig of her drink. She could tell he didn't even taste it. "I thought it wasn't important, since it was only a partial eclipse, but there's shit going down."

Alex felt suddenly chilled. "Whose is it?"

"Niall's. New York."

"But he's been fighting the shadow dragons."

Donovan nodded, his gaze sweeping over the beach. "Will your brother freak out if we leave?"

"How much shit is going down?" Alex asked, sitting up so abruptly that she knocked over the bottle of suntan lotion.

"Enough that I'm needed." He met her gaze steadily. "There's turmoil in the earth, a vibration I can feel even from here."

"What do you think it is?"

"I'm wondering whether Magnus has been replaced."

That was a sufficiently frightening prospect to get Alex moving. "We'll just tell Peter that you got called back to work. He bails on vacations all the time for that reason." Donovan helped her gather her towel and accessories. "I can run these tests in the room."

"I'll get Nick and pack," Donovan said, moving with that resolve Alex knew so well.

She trusted Donovan's instincts and she knew they were telling him to hurry. The *Pyr* must have need of the Warrior, and she wasn't ever going to be the reason he arrived too late.

Ginger looked up when Delaney bolted into the house from the barn. He was moving too quickly for there to be nothing wrong.

"It's time," he said. "We have to go to New York."

"Niall's firestorm?" Ginger asked.

Delaney shuddered involuntarily, then gave her a hot look. "Something's going wrong. Something with the shadow dragons. I feel them stirring. I feel their shadow stretching long."

"And you've got to help." Ginger knew better than to ask too many questions. "Five minutes to pack Liam and I'll be ready."

Delaney eyed the sky. "Faster would be better. It'll take hours to get there."

And he feared he'd be too late. He didn't have to say that out loud for Ginger to understand.

She took the stairs to Liam's room three at a time.

Eileen yawned as she and Erik walked across the parking lot of the rest stop and stretched. Erik was carrying Zoë.

"Halfway there," Eileen said, eying the sky. She touched the lock on the car keys, and the horn of the only Maserati in the lot gave a soft beep.

"You could have let me drive," Erik said. They were both tired, but he was ready to take a turn.

Eileen smiled and tossed the keys from one hand to the other, keeping them out of his reach. "I haven't wrecked your car yet."

"I can't help thinking you mean to get even with me for that ride in England," Erik teased, knowing she'd never take a risk with Zoë in the car.

"You did terrify me. I should get even," Eileen said. "Tell me more about Gaspar and I'll think about it."

Erik bent to put the toddler into her car seat. He cast his mind back into the past, trying to envision Gaspar. He couldn't quite grasp the image, which was irritating.

He felt someone watching him and assumed it was Eileen, but when he glanced up, it was Zoë's solemn gaze that was locked upon him. He was startled when she reached up and touched the middle of his forehead.

Then he caught his breath as the images spilled into his thoughts. He saw a flurry of falling shadows, like a dark curtain torn to shreds and discarded. Zoë's touch ripped down the barricade in his memory and Erik fell back against the car in surprise.

They were doing it again.

Erik and Zoë had had a powerful connection right from the beginning, and Eileen could only watch it grow stronger with every passing day. She saw the baby's left hand land on Erik's forehead, right where his father's rune stone had been used to patch the wound of his missing scale. When in human form, Erik appeared to have a mole right between his brows, the rune stone of his father visible in its full detail only when he was in dragon form.

Erik stumbled in shock and Eileen moved to his side.

"Easy!" Eileen said. She supported Zoë's hand and watched Erik carefully. He looked dazed, almost over-whelmed, and she guessed that the baby had somehow compromised the beguiling.

"Tell me," she said. "In case you forget again."

"Gaspar's son," Erik murmured. "His name was Sal-vatore di Fiori."

"Gaspar used that surname?"

"Never. It was the mother's name. She was a Vene-tian noblewoman."

Venice again. Eileen eyed her daughter, wondering whether it had been Zoë who had infected her research with all those false trails.

Zoë stared fixedly at Erik, her intensity of focus fit to rival Erik's own.

Erik frowned. "She defied her family to be with Gas-par. The son was illegitimate, but the human grandfa-ther had adopted him as his grandson. I think she was quite formidable and no one dared to whisper about her indiscretion."

"Did she marry?"

"I don't think so."

"It sounds as if Gaspar might have been a lover who was hard to forget."

Erik smiled, his gaze fixed on the distance. "Salva-tore was raised with every advantage." Erik blinked, frowned, then looked at Eileen in shock. "My father sent me to teach him how to be *Pyr*, because Gaspar refused to return to Venice and his mate refused to part with their son."

"Maybe she hoped to tempt Gaspar back."

Erik shook his head, uncertain. "Maybe. Maybe he was afraid to go, afraid he might willingly surrender his freedom to be with her. Theirs was rumored to have been a passionate union."

"And Salvatore?"

"I liked him. He had that easy charm that comes from being raised with wealth, and an ability that I envied to enjoy the moment. I remember the richness of their home. I was dazzled by that place and by him. Salvatore took me everywhere, introduced me to his friends, taught me to speak their dialect of Italian, included me in his jokes. We ate and gambled and danced. It was a remarkable winter, one I never wanted to end."

"And he got to know you, so he knew best how to beguile you."

"Yes and no," Erik said, his gaze colliding with Eileen's. "Beguiling was Salvatore's particular passion and he had a remarkable skill. It amused him to make people believe what wasn't true, and he learned everything I could teach him, then did it better. But he didn't beguile me."

Eileen frowned, not understanding.

"It was his son who beguiled me." Erik nodded with resolve. "Lorenzo di Fiori, son of Salvatore and the most beautiful courtesan in all of Venice."

Zoë gurgled then and her hand fell from Erik's brow, her small body showing its limitations. She fought sleep valiantly and tried to reach for him again, but Eileen's maternal instinct won. She tucked her daughter into her car seat and kissed her forehead.

"That's enough for one night," Eileen said softly, and Zoë's eyes fluttered shut. "One overachiever is plenty in this household, especially one who pushes himself too far to do his duty."

"Only one overachiever?" Erik teased.

"Have you smuggled someone into the family while I was at work?" Eileen asked with false innocence. Erik laughed and the pair smiled at each other with affection.

She offered him the keys. "You drive. I'll make notes of what you told me and dream up some new questions. This beguiling thing has to be important if Zoë's leaping in to help you."

Erik frowned. "I wonder what ever happened to that son."

"Lorenzo," Eileen said. It seemed he couldn't remember the names of any of them.

Erik snapped his fingers. "Lorenzo."

"I'll bet you already know, and I'll bet it's important." She shook her head. "He's good, that's for sure."

Erik opened the passenger door for her. "Let's get to New York."

"Try not to get a speeding ticket," Eileen suggested.

"I'll just beguile the officer in question," Erik said, starting the car and squealing the tires as he pulled out of the lot. He eased into traffic with that rapid assurance that made Eileen catch her breath.

"My past is repeating itself," she complained, not looking at the dashboard.

Erik smiled slightly, so completely focused on his driving that she knew they were safe.

Erik's beguiling, though, was troublesome. Eileen was going to get to the bottom of that, and quickly. Zoë's concern revealed its importance and Eileen didn't need to be nudged twice.

She turned on Erik's laptop and Googled Lorenzo di Fiori. It took a bit of digging, but what she learned by the time they reached Pennsylvania was interesting indeed.

Phelan was outside Rox's bedroom window.

He was in human form, standing on the sill, leaning

against the brickwork as casually as if he were at a party. He wore the black leather jacket again, and she didn't miss that his one arm appeared to be limp.

His eyes were as dark as obsidian and his smile was cold. The rain fell in sheets behind him.

"You think we're different," he said when she started at the sight of him. "You think you can tell us apart."

Rox sat up and eased away from him, finding her back against the headboard. She knew exactly whom he was talking about, and she didn't imagine that Phelan had come on a goodwill mission. "Maybe I do."

Phelan shook his head. "Appearances can be deceiving. Deep down inside, twins are the same. We're two halves of a whole, perfect echoes of each other."

"No. You're a shadow dragon and Niall isn't."

"Any *Pyr* can be made into a shadow dragon," Phelan countered. "He just needs to be unlucky enough to die and not be exposed to all four elements in half a solar day." His smile broadened. "It can happen to anybody."

His implication was clear. Rox didn't want to think about Niall's becoming a monster like his brother.

Phelan eased closer, spreading his hands across the glass. "So, the difference between my brother and me is just luck. Or the timing of our luck."

Rox knew he was trying to frighten her but wondered whether she could learn anything important from him.

"No. The Elixir's source was destroyed," Rox argued. "No one can make any more shadow dragons."

Phelan's conviction wasn't shaken. "Just because the Elixir is gone doesn't mean there isn't another way. A better way."

"I don't believe you," Rox said, easing backward.

"Maybe seeing is believing," Phelan murmured.

"Why does that sound like a threat?"

Phelan smiled. "What if Niall dies now? What if he doesn't get exposed to the elements in time? I know a

Slayer with the ability to make shadow dragons—Niall and I could be identical again, before the morning."

Rox's bile rose at the idea. "But Niall's not going to die."

"Are you so sure?" Phelan flattened himself against the glass. He seemed larger and more menacing when he blocked out the night, and Rox recoiled. "I could kill him. It would be easy. Then I'd have you all to myself."

"No!" Rox was on her feet.

"Why not? It would only be fair." Phelan chuckled. "Since Niall's the one who killed me."

"That's not true!" Rox backed away from the window. "I don't believe it."

"Oh, but you should. It's an expensive mistake to trust my brother," Phelan whispered.

Rox knew all about misplaced trust.

Had Phelan guessed as much?

Rox meant to run but made the mistake of glancing toward Phelan. She froze instead, snared by the sight of him. There were flames in the depths of his eyes, like bonfires burning in the night. They looked so welcoming, so tempting. She wanted to move closer to him and see them better, even though she knew that was stupid.

"Go ahead," he murmured, his words low and seductive. "Ask him about my death. I'm sure he'll tell you the truth."

I'm sure he'll tell you the truth. Rox found that easy to believe—so easy to believe that she almost repeated it. Niall would tell her the truth.

She tore her gaze away with an effort, shocked that she had even considered trusting Phelan. She remembered her dream and her dread. "What about your mother?" she demanded, knowing that nothing good had come of that encounter.

"Oh, he betrayed her, as well." Phelan clicked his teeth and shook his head. "Very untrustworthy, our

Niall, even though he looks so upright. You know, some people simply rely on charm."

Rox stared at him, intending to argue, but those flames undid her force of will. She just wanted to stare at them forever. She stood and looked, unable to move even as she wanted more than anything to do so.

"You should trust me," Phelan whispered, those flames leaping high in his eyes.

"I should trust you." Rox was stunned to find herself echoing his words.

"You should leave with me."

"I should leave with you."

"You should choose me over my brother."

Rox's mind screamed outrage. She fought the suggestion, knowing how wrong it was, but her mouth formed the words, anyway. "I should choose you over your brother."

Phelan chuckled. His nails scratched on the glass. "You should open the window," he murmured.

"I should open the window." Rox found herself reaching for the clasp, even as her mind raged in protest. Her breath came in agitated gasps. But her body moved against her own desire.

She unlocked the window. She pushed the window open and it creaked. She felt a waft of cold air sail around her ankles. The rain came over the sill and pooled on the floor.

Phelan smiled at her, never breaking eye contact as he offered his hand. "You choose me now," he murmured.

Rox stared into the flames, trapped, and nearly had heart failure. Her lips moved, but the words caught in her throat. She stared at his extended hand, felt the force of his will, and fought it with every fiber of her being.

She was terrified it wouldn't be enough.

Niall didn't sleep. He couldn't. Not with his body raging for a satisfaction it hadn't had, not with the taste of

Rox on his tongue, not with her scent on his hands. The firestorm burned hotter in the night, surging through him like an unchecked bonfire and demanding that he do something to sate it.

She was so close.

And the door, even with its lock, was no obstacle.

But Niall knew he could win the battle and lose the war. And he was becoming convinced that the firestorm had it exactly right—Rox was the woman for him, and if he gave her the time she needed, they could make the enduring match of which he'd always dreamed.

But still, he was hard and hot and ready.

He tried to be still. He tried to slow his body's rhythms. He tried to breathe slowly, and he halfway closed his eyes. He made his pulse slow.

He still didn't sleep, not really, but he dreamed. His eyes were mere slits, his breathing slow, as he lay coiled across the living room of Rox's apartment in dragon form.

He must have dozed, because the dream slid into his thoughts, as quietly as a mouse might slip into a kitchen in the night. His eyes were partially open, and he was aware of the haze from the streetlights that fell into Rox's apartment.

Suddenly it became dark as pitch. Niall thought the power had gone out. The world closed around him with suffocating intensity, and all light was extinguished. The air was still, like he was enclosed in small space, and he felt claustrophobic.

Sealed in a space with no exit.

Trapped.

Niall felt a panic, the kind of panic he didn't usually experience in darkness. He felt his pulse quicken and he peered into the shadow that seemed to have swallowed him whole.

Maybe he had been struck blind.

The prospect was terrifying, as terrifying as the notion of being imprisoned. He stretched out a claw and felt his surroundings, finding smooth walls beneath every talon. They might have been made of obsidian, or steel, but they were dark, so very dark, reflecting no light and swallowing every sound.

Except one.

Niall heard a child weeping. The sound was faint, as if at a distance, but it drew him closer. The child was a little girl; he knew it although he didn't know how or why. He saw her clearly in his mind's eye, lost in similar darkness, curled into a ball as she wept.

Inconsolable—except that he wanted to soothe her. Her hair was dark; her skin was fair. She wore a flannel nightgown and had tucked it fiercely around her knees. She turned a silver ring on the smallest finger of her left hand, turning it around and around as she wept.

Niall recognized the ring.

She wasn't that young, not as young as he had first thought. She might have been fifteen, but petite for her age. She lifted her head and he saw her dark lashes spiked with tears just before she glared at him.

Her eyes were blue, a blue mingled with gray and a bit of gold. Their expression was mutinous and terrified, her gaze filled with challenge and defiance.

Niall knew who this child must be.

Or, more accurately, who she had become.

Despite her attitude, he reached for her, because he knew her surface did not always reveal her truth.

He intended to comfort her, to tell her that nothing could be that bad, but he could not touch her. He found only that smooth obstacle on every side. He railed against it, battling his prison in darkness, but didn't make so much as a scratch on the smooth surface.

In fact, the air seemed closer. Warmer. Suffocating.

What could make Rox cry? Even as a child, she must have been resilient. Even as a child, she must have been strong.

Who had hurt her? And how?

And why couldn't he help her?

Niall shouted with fury and frustration, lashing his tail against the wall of his prison. It made no difference to his situation. Nothing cracked, nothing yielded, nothing opened.

The little girl stopped crying.

She disappeared.

Niall heard the terrified thunder of her heart. He heard her agitated breathing and her fear. He had time to fear that some terrible fate had befallen her, that her silence was a greater sign of distress than her tears. He had time to be afraid that she had run or hidden herself from him.

Then he caught a whiff of cold air, as fetid as a breeze from a crypt.

And he knew the peril was closer at hand.

"Rox!" Niall roared. He awakened and kicked at the door of her bedroom, ripping it out of the frame to get to her even as he hoped he was wrong.

But he wasn't.

Chapter 13

Niall saw Phelan at Rox's window, Rox frozen in place in front of him. She had opened the window and the rain was pooling on the floor. She didn't move away from Phelan; she didn't even glance toward Niall.

Niall saw the flames flickering in Phelan's eyes and knew exactly what was happening. Rox climbed onto the sill, moving like a woman in a dream, then stepped over the window frame.

"No!" Niall raged toward them, shifting shape en route. He snatched at Rox and missed, just as Phelan grabbed her and took flight.

Phelan soared into the night, Niall right behind him. The rain fell in silver drops from a solid layer of clouds the color of pewter. The city below looked dark and wet, slick and dangerous.

Phelan laughed as he raced upward. He was faster than he had been before and more animated. Niall wondered how this could be. Shadow dragons usually had no personality or initiative.

What had Phelan become?

And who—or what—had forced the change?

Niall leapt after his brother, who changed directions

abruptly. He caught a glimpse of Rox, hanging limply in Phelan's grasp, which worried him. It was more typical of her to fight.

Was the beguiling affecting her even more adversely than it did most humans? Niall feared the worst.

Then Phelan dove down into the city again, soaring between buildings with Niall in tight pursuit. He clearly had a destination, but Niall couldn't manage to catch a grip upon him. He dreaded his brother's intent, remembered a dark night in their shared past, and flew faster.

Phelan turned a corner suddenly and dove toward the earth. Niall realized that they were in his old neighborhood, that Phelan soared over the crack that had consumed Niall's building.

Phelan dropped the unconscious Rox into the rubble. She fell like a rag doll, sprawled in the broken debris, and didn't move again.

Niall leapt after his mate, but his brother pivoted, reared up, and locked talons with Niall.

"Now she's mine," Phelan taunted. "You wouldn't share, so if someone has to win, it'll be me."

"You can't steal a mate."

"I just have!"

"You're a *Slayer* and a shadow dragon. You don't need a mate."

"Oh, there's need and there's want." Phelan leaned closer to whisper. "And I *want* this one."

Niall wasn't going to let that happen. The pair struggled in the air above the demolished building. Phelan laughed all the while, exposing the yellowed teeth in his maw. His scent of death and rot was overwhelming; that old wound in his chest looked to be festering. Niall thrashed at his twin with his tail, struggling to free himself to save Rox.

"Don't worry," Phelan taunted. "Soon we'll be exactly the same, just as we were before."

Niall was horrified. "I'll never turn *Slayer*. . . ."

"You won't have to. You can just go straight to shadow dragon. You don't even need the Elixir." Phelan's eyes gleamed. He flicked a glance over Niall's shoulder and smiled a welcome. "Chen! I fulfill your command!"

Niall had time to twist, to glimpse the massive lacquer red dragon that had appeared silently behind him. In that same instant, he was struck down with a hard blow from the new arrival's tail.

His thoughts spun. Chen? Who was Chen?

Was this who had overtaken command of the shadow dragons?

What was his plan?

Niall fell into the rubble, not nearly close enough to Rox. Dust rose from the impact of his fall, then settled quickly beneath the assault of the rain. He was dazed but not out. He would have gotten up to fight, but there were two of them.

And he wanted to know Chen's scheme.

Niall pretended to be more seriously injured than he was. He dropped his head to the debris and sighed, letting his eyes close to watchful slits. His wings fluttered once, then fell limp on his back. He tried to suppress his breathing, even though his body was on full alert.

Chen chuckled. "The prize is finally mine."

How far away was Rox? Niall caught a whiff of her perfume and felt the spark of the firestorm on his right side. She was behind Phelan, perhaps a dozen feet away. He could barely feel her pulse.

He'd get them both out of here.

Somehow.

Chen's scent was disguised to the point of his not having one. So that meant he had drunk the Elixir. How old was he? What did he want? What powers did he have?

Niall felt Chen land beside him and smelled Phelan on his other side. Chen laid one heavy claw on his back. Niall didn't flinch, didn't move, even as the talons dug beneath his scales.

He needed the element of surprise to escape.

To save Rox.

"What about my firestorm?" Phelan complained. "When will you deliver? The mate is here—let me feel the sparks."

"Not yet," the *Slayer* murmured. "First I must make him mine. Bring the brand."

Niall's heart leapt. What brand? He thought of the tiger mark on the throats of the shadow dragons he'd killed, and the identical mark on Phelan's throat. He saw the flash of dragonfire through his lids and felt the heat of Chen's flames. Niall dared to look.

Chen heated a tool, just as Quinn the Smith did at his forge. He held the iron form between his talons, breathing dragonfire at it. The metal heated, turning red, then orange, then yellow, until its color was lost in the flames.

Niall thought he knew what it was. He recalled Rox's assertion that gang tattoos could be applied against someone's will, but that person then had to live by the code of the gang.

Was Chen's brand magical? Did it give him control over those he claimed? Was this how he was able to make shadow dragons without the Elixir? Was Chen the force behind the shadow dragons?

The brand neared the left side of Niall's throat, held in Chen's talons and hot enough to burn. It radiated white heat and a ripple slipped over Niall's flesh.

Niall felt his scales singe. He waited; he waited until the hot brand was treacherously close to his hide; then he thrashed his tail, breathed fire, and erupted from Chen's surprised grasp. He scorched the *Slayer* before rearing out of his reach.

"No!" cried the *Slayer*, but Niall struck him across the face with his tail. Dark blood ran from Chen's brow into the debris, and the iron brand fell from his claw.

It was shaped in the silhouette of a tiger.

Phelan seized Niall from behind, grasping a claw with each of his talons and winding his tail around Niall's. He exposed Niall's belly to the furious *Slayer*, who rose slowly and majestically before the *Pyr*.

Chen exhaled.

Chen glared.

Chen was larger than any *Slayer* Niall had ever known, and his disapproval was more than clear. "I am not fond of impertinence," Chen murmured. "Especially in those to whom I would grant opportunity."

"I don't want any opportunity you offer!" Niall struggled, to no avail. How had Phelan become so strong? He writhed and bit, and Chen's eyes gleamed as he watched Niall's struggles.

Then he picked up the brand from the rubble, blew the dust from it, and turned his dragonfire on the iron again.

When it was white-hot once more, he turned his glittering glance on Niall. "Shall we try again?" he asked, then moved closer.

Niall struggled. He fought. He bucked against his brother's powerful hold.

But he couldn't break free.

Just as the brand heated his scales, just as he turned his gaze from Chen's intent, just when he thought there was no escape, three *Pyr* came streaming out of the sky. Rafferty raged dragonfire and Thorolf bellowed. Sloane launched himself at the ancient *Slayer*, talons extended.

Chen was startled and looked up in surprise. He fell backward from Sloane's assault. Rafferty went straight to Rox, standing vigil over her.

When Thorolf attacked Phelan from behind, Niall broke one claw free and kicked at the hot brand. It burned his toe, but fell from Chen's grip. Chen and Sloane battled for possession of the brand. It danced from the grip of one to the other, seemingly possessed of a life of its own. Sloane snatched it from Chen, who reached to grab it back. The brand tumbled into the debris of the ruined building, finding a course down into the earth.

The *Slayer* swore and lunged after it, Sloane fast behind him.

Thorolf pulled Phelan skyward and thrashed his wings. Phelan cried out in pain and his grip loosened on Niall.

It was enough. Niall broke free and spun to attack his brother. He reopened that old wound with a slash of his claws and Phelan recoiled in pain.

Pain? Niall was shocked. Shadow dragons didn't feel pain. What had Phelan become?

Sloane attacked Chen, who defended himself only enough to retreat. To Niall's surprise, Chen shifted shape, becoming a red salamander. He then jumped into the wreckage of the building. There was a sound of scrabbling feet; then the *Slayer* disappeared into the debris.

At his disappearance, Phelan also retreated. He fled quickly down the street, Thorolf breathing fire as he flew in pursuit.

"Changed forms again," Rafferty muttered, staring where Chen had disappeared. "Only a salamander could get through that. I could try to go after him."

"I don't think we should split up," Sloane said, and Rafferty nodded in agreement. "What was that thing?"

"He was going to mark me," Niall said with a shudder, and the *Pyr* exchanged worried glances.

Thorolf returned, looking disgruntled. "I coulda thumped him," he said with some irritation, "but you've got this lame idea of saving him."

"Something's changed," Niall said. "We need to talk about it. But first, I have to get Rox back behind the dragonsmoke barrier." His heart clenched at the sight of her limp form amid the dust and broken plaster. The firestorm still burned, lighting his touch with a golden glow, so he knew she was alive.

He picked her up and she stirred, her eyes flying open in fear. She was pale, her pupils so tiny that he remembered her terror in his dream. "Are you okay?" he asked softly.

"I don't remember anything after seeing him at the window." Rox trembled violently, shaking from head to toe.

"He beguiled you."

"How did he make flames in his eyes?"

"It's something we can do. Humans are fascinated by flames and look at them, trying to figure them out."

Rox shuddered. "Then we get snared. Trapped." She slanted a wary glance at him. "He could have done whatever he wanted to me," she said, and he sensed her terror of that.

What had someone already done to her? Niall was ready to take heads in his mate's defense.

"You have to look away," Niall advised.

She nodded but still looked shaken, like someone who had awakened from a nightmare. And he supposed she had—she'd been attacked by a shadow dragon for the second time. Phelan had beguiled her, as well, no doubt in an attempt to have her move past the dragonsmoke barrier.

It was a relief to know that Phelan, at least, couldn't cross dragonsmoke. But then, one had to apply oneself to learn that feat, and Phelan had never wanted to work for anything.

Thank the Great Wyvern for that.

Niall heard the gentle rumble of old-speak from his fellows as they flew behind Niall. There was no scent of shadow dragon, which was a break, and Phelan had disappeared as surely as if he'd never been.

"Are they gone?" Rox asked.

Niall nodded even as he scanned the streets.

"Hiding again," Rox said, her tone showing that she shared his disgust for their game.

It wasn't the only thing they had in common.

The firestorm's light illuminated Rox with a golden radiance that comforted Niall as he flew back toward her apartment. Niall knew Rox was frightened and didn't want to frighten her more by introducing new threats. Rox's skin was chilled and she felt delicate to him. The firestorm's golden shimmer shone all around them, heating every point of contact and turning Niall's thoughts in a predictable direction. He held her tightly, aware of his growing conviction that she was a prize to defend forever.

"I couldn't run," she said against his chest, then shook her head. "I couldn't do what I wanted." She sounded frustrated, closer to her usual self, which reassured Niall. She looked up at him suddenly, the brightness of her gaze startling him. "He made me repeat things I don't believe," she said, incredulous. "It was awful."

"Beguiling is a kind of hypnosis."

"It's horrible," she said with disgust, then studied him intently. "Tell me you've never done that to anyone."

Niall would have loved to have pledged that to her, but it wasn't true. "I have worked crowds, persuading them that they haven't seen dragons when they have," he admitted. "It's pretty much the only use the true *Pyr* have for beguiling, because it protects us."

"And keeping your secret lets you better protect humans and the planet," Rox concluded with a nod of concession.

"We only beguile crowds when Erik insists it has to be done." Niall sighed. "I think it's kind of futile, myself, but he's the leader of the *Pyr*."

"Why do you think it's futile?"

"Because whenever there are a great many witnesses, it's hard to get to all of them before they talk. And I believe that humans aren't predisposed to believe in dragons." He smiled down at her. "Given time, they'll rationalize that they didn't really see us after all."

"That's what you said to Thorolf after the earthquake."

"It's what I believe."

He landed on the windowsill of Rox's bedroom then, and shifted shape. He stepped into the dragonsmoke barrier with care, hearing its resonant ping, then jumped down into the room and set Rox on her feet.

She stayed close. "Thanks," she said, and laid her cheek on his chest. She didn't seem to want to let him go.

Niall was good with a little physical reassurance. He caught her in a closer embrace and shut his eyes.

The firestorm seemed to Niall to burn brighter then, as if it responded to his being in human form. He felt the softness of Rox's curves pressed against him, smelled her perfume, and became aware that her fingers were running up and down his spine. He wondered whether she was aware of the caress, as she seemed to be thinking, but it definitely gave him ideas. He felt heat emanating from her fingertips, surging through his body, reminding him that he hadn't celebrated the triumphs of the day before. He felt his own arousal and wondered whether Rox was aware of it.

She'd have to have been dead, to use her own words, to not have felt him so hard against her stomach.

She glanced up at him again, a gleam in her eyes that he dared to find encouraging. Her voice dropped lower, to that jazz singer timbre that drove him crazy. "Have you ever used beguiling for anything else?"

Niall shook his head without hesitation. "Never."

Rox smiled. "I like that you're one of the good guys." Before Niall could ask her to explain herself, she slid her hands around his neck and pulled his head down. He felt her stretch to her toes and lifted her against him, bending down to capture her lips with his.

It was a kiss filled with relief and tenderness, a sweet kiss that turned hot enough to singe his skin. Rox opened her mouth to him and Niall deepened his kiss, claiming her mouth completely. She met him more than halfway, and when he grabbed her buttocks, she wound her legs around him as she had before.

Her passionate response drove him even wilder than before, given that it was unexpected. He liked that she could surrender to desire with such enthusiasm, and he understood that her emotional truths would be harder to decipher.

For the moment, it didn't matter. For the moment, the desire between them was sufficient.

Niall couldn't get Rox close enough, couldn't explore her thoroughly enough, couldn't fight the incendiary heat of the firestorm. They were on the bed without his realizing how they'd gotten there. Rox, sprawled beneath him, was pulling him closer. Niall braced his weight on one elbow, then cupped her face in his hand. He slid his thumb across her cheek, and she purred with delight at the resulting flurry of sparks.

He slid his hand lower, unfastening her silk pajamas and running his hand over her breast. The curve fit perfectly in his palm and she arched her back beneath his caress. Niall broke his kiss to watch her pleasure and smiled at the glitter of her half-closed eyes. Her lips were swollen, her cheeks flushed, and the firestorm's radiance touched her features with gold.

And he saw the second of her tattoos, the one he had glimpsed earlier. He pushed back the silk to examine the tattoo. It was in script, written across her collarbone in elaborate lettering. *carpe diem* it said, the Latin for "seize the day."

Niall thought the advice was more than apt.

As always, Rox's body was more forthcoming than she was. The truth was in her gestures, not in her words, and there was no lie in the way she welcomed his kiss. Her touch was utterly lacking in doubts or fears. She knew what he was, and she wanted him despite that.

Maybe because of it.

Niall realized that satisfying the firestorm would diminish its heat and make them both less of a target for *Slayers* and shadow dragons. Maybe he needed to trust in his luck, his skill, and his fellows, and assume his own survival.

Maybe they should satisfy the firestorm now.

He slid his thumb across her nipple and Rox moaned. He pinched the taut peak and rolled it between his finger and thumb, and she gasped. She writhed beneath him and playfully bit his shoulder, casting him a sparkling glance.

"Do you kiss all the damsels in distress like this?" she asked with an impish grin.

Niall grinned. "No. Do you kiss all the dragons like this?"

"No!" Rox's eyes flashed with pleasure; then Niall bent to take her nipple in his mouth. Whatever she had meant to reply became a low moan, one that excited Niall. She locked one hand into his hair and dug the nails of her other hand into his back in her need to pull him closer. Niall was more than happy to comply.

"Ahem," Rafferty said from the threshold behind them, and Niall was recalled to his senses. He braced himself over Rox, ensuring that her nudity was hidden from his fellows.

"We gotta talk," Thorolf said, and headed for the living room.

"All of us," Sloane agreed. In mere moments, Rox and Niall followed them, hand in hand.

Niall was ready to hear the other *Pyr*'s advice.

The *Pyr* gathered grimly in Rox's kitchen. She made a big pot of tea, pulled together some sandwiches with Sloane's help, and kept her ears open. Niall's protective embrace had made her feel safe again, even as the doubts Phelan had introduced gnawed at her thoughts.

She was even more afraid of losing her dragon warrior than she had been before.

She had to help ensure his safety. Rox couldn't fight dragons for him, but she could try to figure out what was going on.

She wished she at least remembered what had happened with Phelan, but her mind was completely blank. She'd seen him at the window; then Niall had scooped her from the ruins of his building. What had happened in between?

"What was going on there?" Sloane demanded. "What was that piece of iron?"

"He was going to nail you," Thorolf said, gesturing to Niall, and Rox's heart stopped cold.

"Who?" she demanded.

"That old *Slayer*. He's lacquer red and gold," Sloane said.

"Chen," Niall supplied. "Phelan called him Chen."

Rafferty looked concerned.

"He had a brand," Niall agreed, "and he was going to mark me."

Rox straightened in fear.

"Was it a tiger?" Thorolf asked. "Like the mark on the neck of those shadow dragons?"

Sloane nodded.

"Phelan has one, too," Niall said. "I don't know what it means, but as Rox said, I think it's a kind of gang mark."

Rox didn't like the sound of this in the least. Rafferty and Sloane also appeared to be alarmed. Thorolf was agitated, but Niall was utterly still. He frowned at the floor, trying to puzzle it out.

"It must have some kind of power," Rafferty said, "if he thought that putting it on you forcibly would make a difference."

A gang mark. Rox swallowed. "Some people think

that tattoos and brands have magical power, like talismans."

"This one must," Thorolf said.

"He was going to mark me with it," Niall said. He looked dismayed. "Phelan was holding me down. It was as if he had brought me to Chen as an offering, or something."

"Wait!" Rox said. "Phelan told me that you could both be the same by morning, that he knew a *Slayer* who didn't need the Elixir to make shadow dragons." Niall grimaced at the prospect. It was one that gave Rox the creeps.

"Do you think that's true?" Thorolf asked.

"But that's just the thing," Niall said. "Phelan isn't a shadow dragon anymore." Sloane glanced up in surprise. "I don't know what he is, but he has his old spark back. He's the way he was before he died." The hope that lit his eyes touched Rox's heart, even though she feared it was unwarranted. "Do you think he's healing? Or regressing?"

Rafferty frowned. "I'm skeptical. He chose the darkness of becoming *Slayer*, and that is an irrevocable choice."

"But what about this Chen?" Sloane asked. "Do we know anything about him at all?"

Niall shrugged. "It looks like he's gained control of the shadow dragons, and that the tiger brand is part of it."

Rox shivered.

"But how?" Thorolf asked, looking between the *Pyr*.

"The greater question," Rafferty said softly, "is why?"

"No," Rox said. "The question is why he wants Niall. Shadow dragons are made of dead *Pyr*, not live ones."

"It could be because of the firestorm," Rafferty said thoughtfully.

"I think it's something else," Rox said, struck by an

idea. "You were talking about affinities earlier," she said, working it out as she spoke. "Rafferty thought he sensed Magnus, who had or has an affinity for the earth. Chinese dragons have an affinity for rain. Someone has an affinity for earth and is causing the earthquakes that target Niall."

"Chen," Rafferty said with conviction. "I recognize his voice now. He is the old singer who persuaded the earth to move at his command."

"So that's two elements he controls, as well as the fire that you all have an affinity for." Rox leaned forward. "What if he's trying to capture Niall because of his affinity for air? What do you get when you complete the set?"

Rafferty's gaze brightened. "Never mind that you are in the midst of your firestorm. That could provide the fourth element."

"Or at least enhance it," Sloane agreed, his manner thoughtful.

"But why?" Thorolf asked. "What would be the point?"

Sloane frowned. "There is an old idea that when the four elements are brought into proper balance, they collectively allow a control over spirit, or mind."

"And Phelan's mind is intact again," Niall mused. "Maybe that has something to do with it." He shoved a hand through his hair and looked tired. "I can't think anymore. At least we know that Phelan can't cross the smoke barrier."

"You're right," Sloane said. "Let's get some sleep."

Rox remembered something Phelan had said, and she wondered whether it would shed some light on the puzzle. "But wait a minute. Phelan said you killed him," she said to Niall. "Is that true? Could that be part of it?"

Niall was clearly shocked. He turned away from her, leaving distance between them. "I don't want to talk about it."

Rox had a bad feeling about his evasiveness.

"I think it's a pretty good question," she insisted. "And I think I deserve an answer."

"I believe she is right," Rafferty said softly.

Niall braced his hands on the window frame and kept his gaze averted. He looked as if he might be sick.

Rox was frightened by his reaction. Was this the long story he'd avoided telling her so far?

Was it a bad one?

Did it show Niall in a bad light?

"I didn't strike the killing blow," Niall said tightly, "but it was my fault that Phelan died."

Rox was shocked by Niall's dismay. She expected him to simply call Phelan a liar. She hadn't thought she'd rattle him. He was always so impassive, so resolute. She hadn't thought for a second that she could hurt him.

Whatever had happened must have been really bad.

It seemed characteristic of him that he would blame himself for the results of his actions, even if he hadn't directly killed Phelan. Niall took the long view, which Rox respected. Actions had repercussions, although most people chose not to look that far.

Whatever had happened still upset Niall. On the other hand, he was prepared to give Phelan another chance to be healed. She admired Niall for that, and she knew there was more to the story.

She waited and hoped he would confide in her.

Courtesy of Rox's question, Niall was remembering a night that had been hell, remembering blood and fire. He swallowed, then heard his mother's anguished scream, his father's bellow of rage. . . .

He straightened up, then shoved his hands into the pockets of his jeans. He stared out into the rain and remembered the darkest night of his life.

Niall shook his head to dismiss his memories, but they wouldn't budge. He could feel Rox waiting. He knew she wouldn't forget her question, but he didn't want to talk about the past.

"Let's get some sleep," Sloane repeated. "With any luck, Erik will be here in the morning, and with his input, we can figure out a plan."

Rafferty nodded, and there was a murmur of consensus. Niall noted that one voice was conspicuously absent from the chorus.

Rox's.

He glanced over his shoulder and saw the uncertainty in her eyes. Whether he wanted to talk about this or not, he had to. He heaved a sigh and faced the fire.

For Rox.

"I promised you a long story last night," he said softly to her. "Here it is."

Rox raised her hands to her lips, her eyes shining. His heart leapt that she understood he was doing this for her and that it wasn't easy for him.

The *Pyr* settled back into their seats.

"There is a tendency in my family, apparently, for people to make irrevocable decisions too quickly. I think it comes from my father, because that was his inclination."

"Nigel was always decisive," Rafferty agreed.

Niall frowned. "My father didn't tell my mother about his nature before they were married. On their wedding night, they were attacked by *Slayers* and he shifted shape to defend her. She was so frightened of him that she refused to let him into her rooms the next day. He took her at her word, and left her alone at the country house while he returned to London. They would never have reconciled if she hadn't gone to him, thirteen years later."

"Why did she?" Rox asked.

Niall met her gaze steadily. "She had twin *Pyr* boys who were entering puberty, and she didn't know how to teach us what we needed to know. Our nature begins to assert itself at puberty, often through shifts that aren't entirely under our control."

"First time, every time," Thorolf said to Rox.

Niall met Rox's gaze steadily. "Evidently they were attacked *after* the firestorm had been sated." He folded his arms across his chest, remembering. "My father was hard on Phelan when he came back into our lives. He said my brother preferred to use his charm rather than work for anything, that he wanted everything for nothing, that he was lazy."

"Hey, sounds kinda like you and me," Thorolf observed.

Niall glanced up in surprise, knowing truth when he heard it. "I'm sorry," he said. "I always wanted to do things differently from my father, but it's not working out that way so far."

"Aw, don't be so tough on yourself," Thorolf said. "You've been encouraging since I decided to try. Maybe Phelan should have tried, and your dad would have been cool with that."

Niall was startled by the idea. "Maybe, maybe not. I think my father's absence when we were young and his inflexibility with Phelan contributed to Phelan's finding appeal in becoming a *Slayer*."

"But you didn't turn *Slayer* and you had the same experience," Rox noted.

"That might have been luck," Niall said. "And Father was tougher on Phelan."

"It might have been character," Rox replied, her tone firm.

Rafferty smiled.

Niall felt his lips set. He was not blameless in this, and he wouldn't let them exonerate him. "The thing is that I don't think Phelan knew what he was getting into, but once the choice was made, there was no coming back from the *Slayer* side."

"Don't you think your answer to whether he can be healed is right there?" Sloane murmured.

"I think he made a mistake, that maybe he didn't realize what he was getting into before he chose."

"Why?" Rafferty asked.

"Because he's my brother. He's my twin! We grew up together. We got into trouble together and we got out of trouble together. He was always impulsive, leaping before he looked." Niall shrugged, unable to explain it better.

"You can't believe he's bad to the bone," Rox said quietly, and he nodded in quick agreement.

"It's more than that, too. I have to live with myself when this is done," Niall said, his voice rising. "I already have to live with the fact that Phelan wanted to talk to me about turning *Slayer* before he did it and I refused to have any such conversation with him. I have to live with the fact that I turned him away, the person who had been closest to me in all my life. I let him down."

"The choice was his," Rafferty said softly.

"That's not all of it," Niall argued hotly. "I was the one who told our father what Phelan had done, so I was responsible for the fact that our father both shunned and disinherited Phelan. I was the one who insisted that Father not tell Mother, that he leave that task to me, because I knew how fond she was of Phelan. I was afraid my father's decision to disinherit Phelan would drive them apart just when they had reunited happily."

"Nigel never explained himself to anyone," Rafferty said with a shake of his head. "He was so certain that he was right, that his logic was infallible, that he would never trouble himself to justify his choices to anyone."

"Not even his wife?" Rox asked, her astonishment clear.

Rafferty shrugged and smiled. "It was a different time."

"King of his castle," Sloane murmured.

"He was inflexible," Niall said. "But I didn't go immediately to my mother. I put off what I feared would be an unhappy exchange, even though I had volunteered for the job."

"You tried to protect her from the truth," Sloane said.

"And Phelan took advantage of that. He went to her immediately and persuaded her to go with him."

"He escorted her out of that party," Rox said. "I saw it in my dream."

"What?" Niall asked.

"I had a dream tonight. I was in a ballroom. I saw your parents, I think." She pointed to Rafferty. "You were there. You told him he was wasting the opportunity of a firestorm."

They all smiled at that.

"That is a recurrent theme in my comments and advice," Rafferty acknowledged.

Rox frowned and introduced an idea Niall had never considered. "Maybe Phelan beguiled her. Maybe that's why she didn't realize there was anything wrong with him. She would have noticed his eyes, otherwise. I could see in my dream that they had started to go black."

Niall shook his head. "It doesn't matter. I still didn't do what I should have done."

Rox stood up and came to him. To his amazement, there was compassion in her expression. She put her fingertips on his arm and a golden heat touched Niall's heart. "What did Phelan do to her?"

Niall was grim. "Nothing, because he had no chance. He threatened to kill her, sending a taunt to my father in old-speak demanding a return to his former status."

"Bad choice," Sloane said, and rubbed his forehead.

"Truly bad," Rafferty agreed. "Nigel would never have negotiated over the survival of his mate. He would simply have gone for blood."

Niall nodded. "That's pretty much how it shook out."

"Nigel killed Phelan?" Rox asked.

"It was savage," Rafferty said with a nod.

"Yet I was dancing, avoiding the job I'd promised to do," Niall said bitterly. "I arrived far too late to intervene on my brother's behalf, thought my mother was chatting with friends, and danced while I awaited her return."

"A flock of shadow dragons couldn't have stopped your father," Rafferty said. He stood and came to Niall's side, putting a hand on Niall's shoulder in consolation.

Niall wasn't consoled. "I should have stopped it. I should have talked to him. I should have given Phelan a second chance when it would have made a difference," he said stubbornly, then looked at Sloane. "There is no way back for a *Slayer* who has no glimmer of the divine spark left in his heart, but I'm not convinced that my brother is in that company. Until I'm sure, I can't destroy him." He heaved a sigh. "His death shattered what was left of our family. I couldn't stay near my parents after my brother's death because I reminded them of the son they'd lost. I never saw them again. I left for good."

"You *were* identical twins," Rafferty said with understanding.

"And I couldn't look at my father without remembering the sight of him killing Phelan." He met Rox's gaze briefly, not wanting to see the disappointment in her eyes. "There's your story." Then he turned away, fully expecting her to condemn him for not helping his brother more.

"I think you have to finish him off," Sloane said.

"Even though he seems to have his old spark back?" Niall challenged.

"There's a slim chance, but it's slim," Sloane acknowledged. "But I'll double-check my references tonight."

"Be quick about it," Rafferty advised softly, and Sloane nodded.

"Phelan already attacked Rox," Thorolf said with

some agitation. "And we know that shadow dragons don't stop until they've finished what they've started."

Niall's lips set. "I'm not afraid to do what needs to be done—I just need to be sure."

"The trick is whether you can be in time," Sloane said quietly.

The *Pyr* fell into an uneasy silence at that.

Chapter 14

Rox understood that it wasn't just Phelan who was getting lots of chances. When Niall was intent upon her, when he wasn't judging her, that was when he was most dangerous.

At least to her own conviction that she needed to remain alone and self-reliant, shields up, and barriers intact.

It was Niall's determination, not just the possessiveness of his kiss, that weakened her knees—the way he kissed as if he had invented it. His kisses were like molten chocolate, luxurious and languid, and utterly fabulous. Addictive. They left Rox's toes curled and her body humming. They reminded her of the very best chocolate, too, in that one taste just left her wanting more.

She knew he was seducing her on purpose, that he was trying to wear down her resistance, and she also knew that his ploy was working like a charm. Niall had too many advantages on his side.

He was noble. He was smart and resilient. He cared about the earth and the future. He defended her and listened to her.

And he was a dragon.

Rox's defenses were burning fast, like wooden palisades burning around a medieval fortress.

His story caught at her heart. Rox knew what it was like to have a broken family. She knew how it could leave you rootless, how it could make you yearn for something you'd never had and knew you'd never find. She knew, too, what it was like to be mistaken for a sibling and to leave everything you knew, despite the risk that you might not find anything better.

Her chest tight, she slid her hand up Niall's arm.

The firestorm flickered and burned with a brilliance that sent a trickle of sweat down her back. She was instantly warm and filled with desire, wanting to drag Niall back to her bedroom and make him smile.

No, first she had to be sure he'd stay.

She couldn't think about Niall's coming too close to being marked by this *Slayer* Chen.

There were other things she didn't want to think about, too, such as how she should seize the day to make love to a dragon while she could, lest she regret it forever.

Rox didn't want to make that decision on impulse.

All the same, she stood and stared into his eyes, seduced by the heat of the firestorm and her understanding of what he was. She knew she should step away, that she was mostly sure but not quite, but couldn't bring herself to do it.

To her surprise, Niall provided the impetus she needed to get her shields back in place. "You've heard my story," he murmured. "Now how about yours?"

Rox was confused, but wary. "What do you mean?"

"What made you cry in the dark when you were younger?"

Rox took a step back in her alarm. "I don't know what you're talking about."

"Yes, you do," Niall insisted. "I dreamed it, earlier tonight, just as you dreamed of my mother."

"The new Wyvern stirs," Rafferty said quietly, but neither Niall nor Rox paid any attention to him.

"*Do you think Erik is right?*" Sloane asked quietly in old-speak, and Rafferty shrugged, even as Niall turned to Rox.

"Something or someone made you cry," Niall said to his mate with resolve. "I saw you. You were crying. You were wearing a flannel nightgown with pink roses on it, and you had folded it tightly around your feet."

Rox knew that nightgown; she remembered that night. She backed away in alarm.

Niall didn't give it up, but his voice softened. "What is it really that you're afraid of, Rox?"

She stared at him, knowing he wouldn't take less than the truth for an answer. The *Pyr* averted their gazes from the conversation, but Rox knew they could hear her.

Although the real issue was confiding this one story in Niall.

"I don't know what you mean," she lied, then pivoted before he could challenge her. "I need some sleep." She headed for the bedroom without waiting for a reply. She wasn't entirely disappointed when Niall followed right behind her. He caught the door to her bedroom with his fingertips, then followed her into the room before shutting it behind them.

The room was filled with potent silence.

And the persistent glow of the firestorm.

Shimmering, illuminating, intoxicating.

Rox stared at Niall and swallowed. He looked disheveled and grim, tired and determined. She didn't need the firestorm to want him with every fiber of her being.

If he touched her, her reservations would be toast.

"I can't leave you alone," he said, his voice rough. "There's too much risk."

Rox chose to take that at face value.

"I hear you," she agreed, glancing around the room. One look at the bed and she remembered his potent kiss

of less than an hour before. The memory made her yearn
for more. "And I don't really want to be alone so long
as Phelan's around." She swallowed. "You shouldn't be
alone, either, if Chen wants you in his gang."

Niall frowned and surveyed the room for a moment.
Rox took advantage of the opportunity to check him
out, then jumped when he suddenly looked back at her.
The firestorm's sparks snapped and danced between
them, gaining in brightness, as they stared into each
other's eyes.

"I won't talk about *that*," she said, establishing her
line in the sand.

It was shifting sand and Rox knew it, but she'd share
her story on her schedule.

If at all.

Niall's gaze swept over her, leaving Rox feeling hot
and flushed. How could the man have such an effect
upon her, just with his glance? He had to be six feet
away from her and she was melting.

Burning.

Falling hard.

And the scariest part was that it felt good.

She also knew that it was only a matter of time before Niall knew every single thing about her. Her heart
would be completely exposed. Would he abandon her
then, once all her secrets were unraveled? Was that what
interested him?

Or would he give up before that?

Would he be taken by Chen before that?

The possibility made Rox's heart clench.

"I think Rafferty has some ideas of how humans can
defend themselves against beguiling," he said quickly.
"We can ask him more in the morning."

"Right," Rox said, still not moving.

Niall exhaled. He walked to the window, keeping his
back to her. He pushed his hands through his hair and
stared into the rainy night.

Their gazes met in the reflection and Rox's mouth went dry. The silence hung between them for a long moment, seeming to be electrically charged.

Then Niall pivoted to face her. "We should get some sleep."

Rox got the message. And really, any decision she made to be with Niall was one she wanted to make with her thoughts clear.

And her body well rested.

"You're right." She nodded and slipped into bed, pulling up the blankets with a sigh of relief. She wondered what Niall would do, where he would choose to sleep, and she had goose pimples of anticipation. She closed her eyes, feeling Niall looking at her, then heard him stretch out on the floor beneath the window.

"You'll be cold," she whispered, both disappointed and relieved.

"Discomfort might clear my thoughts," he replied, a smile in his voice. Rox smiled into her pillow, liking that her dragon was sticking close in her defense.

"I'm skeptical," she teased.

Niall chuckled softly. When he spoke, though, his tone was sober. "No accidents, Rox," he murmured. "We'll choose our path together deliberately or not at all."

Rox looked in his direction to see the bright blue gleam of his eyes, his lids only partly closed. She heard his slow breathing and felt the warmth of his presence in her room.

Protective.

Vigilant.

Her destined mate.

She could get used to this.

Niall slept poorly and awakened early. He got his laptop and checked on his tours again, maintaining contact with his tour operators and managing the details.

It wasn't bad, managing his business on the run, but he needed an office.

And an employee.

But first things first.

Rox slept deeply, to his relief. He enjoyed the warmth of the firestorm, the sound of her breathing, the scent of her skin. It felt cozy to be in her bedroom, although he was there to defend her. It made him think of spending many nights and mornings together.

Without the threat of Chen and the shadow dragons to haunt them. Niall wanted that future; he wanted it enough to do whatever needed to be done to ensure it.

He knew the instant that Rox awakened. She rolled over to face Niall and he felt her gaze as surely as if she had touched him.

"Where did Chen go after he attacked you?" she asked.

Niall looked up in surprise. "He shifted into a salamander and disappeared into the rubble of my old building."

"That's it," Rox said, throwing back the covers and swinging her feet out of bed with purpose. "I know where the shadow dragons are."

Niall stared at her in astonishment. Once again, Rox surprised him. He supposed he should be getting used to that, but he hadn't managed it yet. "Where?"

"Let's talk about it with everyone," she said, and headed for the door. Niall shut down his laptop and followed. Thorolf was in the kitchen, judging from the sounds of food preparation. Sloane was watching the rain, keeping vigil. Rafferty emerged from the kitchen with a fresh pot of tea.

"Heard you waking up," he murmured to Rox, and she flushed.

"Rox thinks she knows where the shadow dragons are," Niall said, immediately capturing the attention of the *Pyr*.

"There's a network under the city of abandoned tunnels," she said, taking a gulp of hot tea. "Their refuge must be there."

"A network from subways?" Rafferty asked.

"And trains and other underground ventures," Rox said. "There are secret rooms, abandoned subway stations, service tunnels, and hidden basements."

"How do you know?" Niall asked.

"I go down there," she said to Niall's surprise. "Neo took me the first time, and it's kind of addictive."

"It can't be legal," Sloane said.

Rox shrugged, as uninterested in this perspective as Niall might have expected. "Some areas are privately owned, but a lot of it is just a forgotten part of the city. If you enter by an access point that's open or untended, I don't think it's wrong." She lifted her chin. "I think citizens have a right to know how their city works. It's an adventure."

Adventure. It was characteristic of Rox to head right into the fray, that much Niall knew, and he wasn't surprised that she was bold enough to explore uncharted terrain.

But was she right?

Even disheveled and straight out of bed, she looked tough and defiant, and Niall sensed he would have a battle on his hands shortly. Why? He guessed immediately. They would, of course, check out her idea. He would, of course, want her to remain safe, given that Phelan kept trying to capture her. Niall saw the glint in Rox's eyes and guessed what deal she'd want to make.

There was no way she was coming along. Rox met his gaze resolutely, he folded his arms across his chest, and the argument began before the terms were even stated.

"How do you get in?" Thorolf asked.

"I can't tell you how to get there, but I can show you," Rox said.

Niall shook his head.

Rox ignored him, but she lifted her chin a bit higher.

"Most cities have conduits underground," Rafferty said, "and subway stations that are no longer in use."

"It's huge here, though," Rox insisted. "There are lots of abandoned passages here. Layers and layers of them. There are rumored to be anywhere from eight to fifteen stories under Grand Central Station, for example."

"Well, how many are there?" Sloane asked.

Rox smiled. "Depends who you ask. I've seen only five."

"We need a map," Niall said with resolve.

"There is no map." Rox tapped her temple. "Just a lot of travelers who remember. I've visited only a small percentage of it, but I can get us in." She frowned. "It's harder now, since the security is better, but the passages are still there."

"That's an intriguing possibility," Rafferty said, as if he intended to take her idea under consideration.

Rox eyed Niall. "Even more interesting, the most tangled network is supposed to be under Chinatown."

Niall caught his breath. "If the refuge was there, that would explain how they could surprise me so easily and so often."

"It's where they're hiding," Rox said. "I'm sure of it."

"We need to gather more information," Sloane said. "We need to be sure. . . ."

"We need to go down there, right now," Rox said. "The only reliable data you can gather is what you collect yourself."

"The longer we wait, the better the chance of a shadow dragon attack," Rafferty ceded, and that decided it for Niall.

Sooner was better.

Niall nodded, decisive. "Rox is right. We need to check it out. We'll be able to follow our noses to the shadow dragons' lair, once we're into the network. We can check it out, then plan for an attack later."

"Good plan," Sloane said with a nod.

"Maybe we can surprise Chen," Thorolf said. "Kick his butt."

"You're not going without me," Rox insisted. "It's my idea."

"And sharing it is your contribution," Niall said flatly, watching her eyes flash. "I'll take Thorolf, while Rafferty and Sloane protect you. . . ."

"Forget it." Rox shook her head. "I won't show you the way in unless I go along."

"You'll be at risk," Thorolf argued.

"Life is full of risk." Rox glared at Niall, to emphasize her displeasure.

Niall glared back. "You're not going closer to Phelan, Chen, or shadow dragons. You can show me. . . ."

"No way. I've told you my terms."

"Forget it," he replied. "It's too dangerous."

"You'll never find the way in without me." Rox shrugged, her eyes bright. "Or maybe even the way out."

"Bull. We can do both."

"Prove it," Rox said, lifting a hand to gesture to the window. "Show me the way in."

Niall couldn't and he knew his irritation showed. He tried to appeal to her common sense. "Rox, you can't go with us. We're not positive how many shadow dragons are left, but there are more than four. They could easily outnumber us, and if they do, they could capture you."

"I know."

"And Phelan is out there, hunting you," Thorolf added.

"It's too risky," Niall said. "We'll find our own way in."

"No chance," Rox insisted. "At least not in a time

frame you'll like. Travelers don't just trust anybody, you know."

Niall turned away from her resolve and paced, trying to think of a way to persuade her to ensure her safety. The last thing he wanted to do was explore a potential refuge for an unspecified number of shadow dragons, guarded and managed by *Slayers* of unknown abilities, with his mate in tow and his firestorm burning hot.

Rox, however, refused to listen to him.

On one hand, he respected how she had negotiated; on the other, he wished she hadn't. He wanted her to be sensible.

"Let's go down there and rout them out, get shit done," Rox challenged the *Pyr*. "We can all go, and have strength in numbers."

"It does make sense to surprise them," Sloane said.

"Take the initiative," Thorolf agreed.

Niall felt the opinion of his fellows shift in Rox's favor. "We don't even know for sure where they are," he argued. "It makes more sense to scout out the situation, then make a plan."

Rox smiled. "If you aren't going to fight, then there's no reason *not* to take me along."

Sloane laughed. "Point to Rox."

Niall didn't appreciate the joke. He gestured toward Rox. "You're not going to the shadow dragons' lair. Period."

She shrugged. "Then neither are you, because I'm the only one here who knows the way in." She sipped her tea, looking audacious. "If I go with you, they'll be drawn to the firestorm."

"You're not going to be bait!" Niall cried.

"Brilliant idea!" Rafferty said at exactly the same time.

Niall turned on the older *Pyr*. "It's my duty to defend Rox. . . ."

"Time is of the essence," Rafferty said. He spoke with calm authority. "Your firestorm is a time of power, a resource that gives you strength. And Roxanne is correct in her thinking that an assertive strike may work wonders."

"Only one chance to make a first impression," Thorolf agreed.

Niall shoved his hand through his hair and paced the width of the roof. "Never mind the mumbo jumbo. . . ."

"Then heed the facts," Rafferty said, curt as he seldom was. Niall stopped to listen. "Rox knows some of the network. Rox has volunteered to guide you there. And the firestorm will draw them to you, thereby making your hunt all the more efficient. This is your opportunity to fulfill your quest and eliminate the shadow dragons."

Niall's lips set. "I don't like it. I don't want to endanger Rox."

"I'm a big girl," Rox said. "I'm going by my own choice."

"I'm going with you," Thorolf offered. "Watch your back."

"Maybe learn something," Rox said.

"Maybe kick some butt," Thorolf said, clicking his mug to hers.

"We'll all go with you," Sloane agreed. They were so jovial and cheerful, as if they were discussing a stroll in Central Park.

Niall flung out his hands. "Don't you understand? Rox will be at risk!"

"Everyone will be at risk," Rafferty insisted. "And the risk increases the longer we wait."

Niall exhaled, seeing that his friends were allied against him. "I don't like it."

Rafferty smiled. "We seldom like the conditions attached to the burdens we choose to bear," he said, then shrugged. "I think this is an admirable opportunity to assess the situation. When the *Pyr* are all gathered, we can attack in force, with more information."

Niall considered the three *Pyr* and recognized that he had lost. "All right. But Rox, you need to stay close. First sign of trouble and we are out of there, understand?"

"Deal," Rox said, and ran to the bedroom. She was back in a flash, wearing that plaid miniskirt, biker boots, and leather jacket. The lime spikes looked a bit worse for wear, but she had put on a dark purple lipstick and her eyeliner. "Let's go."

"You know, Rox could be wrong," Thorolf said cheerfully. "This could be a false alarm. Happens sometimes."

Niall, however, had a feeling that Rox was right. "Okay," he said. "Where do we start?"

"Basement of the building," Rox said, rummaging in a ginger jar on the kitchen counter. "There's a way in there. Here's the key."

Rox led the *Pyr* to the basement of her building and unlocked a door to the boiler room with a flourish. The massive boilers were cold at this time of year, and the floor was thick with dust. She could see where the coal chutes had been—they were sealed up now that the burners were converted to natural gas.

Rox crept past the boilers, ducking under the pipes and stirring the dust as she walked. She'd grabbed a flashlight and a screwdriver in her apartment, and she turned on her flashlight as they moved toward a back corner of the cellar. The exposed stone of the old foundation was visible here. There was a metal door in the wall, one almost obscured by dust and grime. It had no knob or handle, just a single keyhole.

And Rox had the key.

"How'd you get that?" Thorolf asked, his voice low. "Is this legal?"

"As if you would worry about that," Rox scoffed. "You just don't want to come along. Chicken." She made a clucking sound.

Thorolf looked back across the boiler room, his expression revealing that Rox had it right. "I'd rather not go underground, after what happened last time," he said.

Rox looked up with interest. "What happened last time?"

"We destroyed Magnus's hidden academy," Rafferty said.

"Earthquakes, flooding, and disaster," Thorolf supplied.

"Where did you get the key?" Niall asked, changing the subject.

Rox shrugged. "A couple of years ago, the super had a heart attack. They were taking him out on a stretcher when I was coming home from the shop. It must have been four in the morning. He gave me his keys and told me to look after things."

"Because he knew you were reliable and responsible?" Niall suggested softly, and Rox was surprised.

"I'd been here about five years by then, and he knew me," she admitted. "Anyway, there were about a halfdozen interesting keys, keys that didn't seem to be to apartments or mailboxes. It was kind of a puzzle to figure out what they were for." Rox unlocked the door and it opened silently—she had earlier oiled the old hinges. A waft of cold air assailed them, air that smelled of dust and dampness and old stone.

"What happened to him?" Niall asked. Rox could hear water dripping in the distance and a rumble that might have been a subway train. Metal stairs descended into the darkness.

"Oh, he's fine." Rox let her light play over the stone walls and metal railing. "I just, um, forgot to give him all of the keys back." She grinned, then stepped into the darkness. "He must not have needed this one, anyway, because he never missed it."

Niall was right behind her. He put his hand on the small of her back and the firestorm glowed golden between them, lighting the darkness like a beacon.

Rox had a moment's doubt about her own plan, but then she knew she was right.

"Shut the door," Rox said to Thorolf.

He hesitated. "You can get us back out, right?"

"Of course!"

Thorolf shut the door behind him with obvious reluctance. The five of them stood at the top of the stairs for a moment. Rox saw the *Pyr* narrow their eyes and take stock of the situation. It was fascinating to watch them. It was strangely cold in the corridor—cold enough to make her shiver. The heat of the firestorm at her back was reassuring.

"It's like a crypt," Sloane said.

"What do you sense?" Niall asked Thorolf, and she liked that he was still mentoring his student.

"Bad news," Thorolf said. Rox saw Niall's minute nod and Rafferty's lips tighten.

"They're down here all right," Sloane said.

"So is *he*," Rafferty said.

"Don't say his name." Niall gestured impatiently, then seized Rox's hand as they descended. At the bottom of the stairs, he turned to Thorolf. "Here's your chance," he said in an undertone. "Close your eyes; feel the darkness. Let it fill your pores and confess its truth to you. *Listen.*"

Thorolf squeezed his eyes tightly shut, concentrating, then opened them with surprise. "To the right!" he said, clearly startled by his own abilities.

"Why?" Niall asked. Rox looked between them with interest.

"It's darker there. Colder." Thorolf shuddered. "That's where they have to be."

"Right. Let's go." Niall led the way.

"I still don't like it," Thorolf muttered.

"Get over it," Rox said, talking tough but sticking close to Niall.

Niall almost glittered.

Rox could feel his intensity and the force of his concentration. She could see him so clearly in the light cast by the firestorm that she turned off her flashlight. Niall led them ever deeper into the network. He never hesitated, and he kept instructing Thorolf as to what he should be noticing. She knew he was considering the structural integrity of the tunnels they entered and gauging the distance to the shadow dragons. It was fascinating to watch him.

Once in, she knew he didn't really need her after all.

For the first time in the labyrinth, Rox was completely confident of her safety. She knew Niall would defend her and knew he would sense any threat long before she did. He led them into tunnels and passageways Rox had never explored.

That let her be a tourist. She had always been intrigued by the history revealed under the city, the various modes of construction, the purpose for each passageway, the scribbled signatures and tag marks from graffiti artists. She liked seeing the cables and telephone lines, the gas lines and sewers, the vital guts that made the city work. She liked the shadows, the mystery, and the timelessness. It was odd to have the sense of being so isolated—anything they said echoed down the tunnels, reinforcing that solitude.

Rafferty hung back at one point, the rumble of old-speak telling Rox that the *Pyr* had agreed on his choice. He stepped back from the path, so still that Rox couldn't discern him from the shadows when she looked back.

Only their footfalls made any sound as they progressed. Dust was stirred by their passage, subways

rumbled at close proximity, and Rox heard small creatures scuttling away from the light. It could have been
an interesting adventure, except that Niall was so taut
and watchful. Rox felt on edge just because he was.

And she wasn't in that much of a hurry to be bait. She
had no idea how far they had walked or how long they
had been beneath the city when Niall halted at a branch
in the tunnel.

To the left, the tunnel stretched into endless darkness.
Even the shine of the tracks faded to nothing after a
dozen feet. To the right was a subway station, but one
with a narrow platform and only one track. Rox heard
the vibration of a subway train passing overhead, then
garbled announcements being made to the passengers
there.

The platform to their right, in contrast, was silent, lit
only by the occasional light. The tunnel at the other end
of the platform was dark except for a red signal light.
Both Niall and Sloane were intent, clearly sampling
scent and peering into the darkness.

"How can his scent come from both tunnels?" Thorolf
asked.

"He's messing with us," Sloane replied. "Or maybe
he's so active that his scent is everywhere."

Rox knew they were talking about Chen.

"He's playing games," Niall insisted. "We must be
close if he wants to distract us."

"One of us should check each direction," Sloane
said.

"Time to part ways again," Niall agreed. "Rox stays
with me."

"One of us should stick with you and the other check
this out alone," Sloane said.

"I have a bad feeling about this," Thorolf said. "Go
ahead, tell me who gets to volunteer."

Sloane smiled and pulled a coin from his pocket. It
looked like gold to Rox, but she barely glimpsed it be-

fore he flipped it. Sloane caught the coin out of the air and slapped it onto the back of his hand, keeping it covered. "Call it."

"Heads," Thorolf said; then Sloane lifted his hand to show that it had come up heads.

"Must be your lucky day," Sloane said with a grin.

"You sure?" Niall asked.

"I won't go far. Twenty feet, then I'll wait for you here." He stepped into the shadows, his figure consumed by the darkness. Rox held Niall's hand tightly as the three of them stepped toward the abandoned station.

Niall stopped on the threshold.

Full garbage bags were piled in the middle of the platform and Rox recognized that this was a service tunnel. At some point, the garbage train would come, or workers might bring trash down from the platform above. She wondered what station they were beneath. There was a staircase at this end of the track, one finished with tiles, that led down into darkness. There was one light down there, but it didn't reveal much.

Niall's eyes narrowed as he looked between the platform and the staircase, clearly weighing his options. Rox leaned closer and realized that the light at the bottom of the stairs was a reflection. She took her hand out of Niall's, and both light and reflection disappeared. The water was dark down there, and she couldn't guess how deep it would be. She shivered, aware suddenly of the cold.

"Do we have, like, any clue where we actually are?" Thorolf asked, heaving a sigh of frustration. "Because, you know, I'm pretty much done with the tour. I could use some food." He turned and stared down the path they'd taken, which seemed darker than Rox recalled. "Let's get Sloane and find our way back."

Niall didn't answer. He had begun to shimmer blue all around the edges.

Rox knew that nothing good was on the menu.

*   *   *

Niall smelled *Slayer* with sudden intensity and the scent stopped him in his tracks.

Chen's scent disappeared abruptly, as surely as if it had never been. Niall knew he hadn't imagined it. It was as if the scent were being revealed and hidden again, as if the *Slayer* were messing with Niall's mind.

Teasing him.

Trying to trap him.

They were close.

Niall listened and he looked; he felt the stone and the concrete, seeking the clue that would tell him what he needed to know. He was keenly aware of Rox's presence beside him, of her vulnerability in this situation.

Chen wasn't a lightweight. Only those *Slayers* who had consumed the Dragon's Blood Elixir could disguise their scent, though he'd never encountered one who could toy with it like this.

It came again, flicking across the end of Niall's nose like a cat's tail. Then it vanished.

Chen knew they were here.

There was no dragonsmoke in the vicinity, perhaps because Chen also could cross that barrier without trouble. Perhaps he couldn't be bothered with a defense that might be ineffective.

An unbroken ring of dragonsmoke, after all, resonated with a kind of clarity, a ring that could be heard by all of their kind. Niall supposed that dragonsmoke might be as much of a beacon in the darkness as the firestorm could be.

That the scent came and went made it difficult for Niall to assess the distance to his foe. Being underground meant that he couldn't ask the wind for assistance.

He had a very bad feeling about both the staircase that descended even lower and the tunnel ahead. He feared he was stepping into a trap either way. At the same time, he had a conviction that if he turned away, an opportunity would be lost.

That Chen was trying to distract them told Niall that he had been surprised.

Chen's refuge must be close. Niall's pulse quickened. He could locate the lair, maybe compromise it, and have the element of surprise on his side for once. Chen would hide his lair deeper if Niall retreated, and Niall might never find it again.

Or he might not find it soon enough.

He was aware that Rox was watching him and that her eyes were wide. She seemed to be holding her breath and he glanced her way, noticing that he was shimmering slightly.

Danger, danger, he mouthed to her, and she nodded her understanding.

A defensive pose, she mouthed in reply, and swallowed as she scanned the platform.

The train rolled onto the tracks on the station overhead, squealing to a stop. The motion of the train overhead made the air shift and the pressure change; a current of air rolled down the quiet tunnel like a spring breeze.

It carried the scent of burned fuel, grease, and shadow dragons.

One shadow dragon.

Headed right for them. Niall smelled him before he saw him.

Niall had a glimpse of a pale but stocky man, before the shadow dragon coming down the platform shifted shape. Niall had already changed shape and lunged toward his assailant, claws extended. Thorolf was right behind him, also in dragon form.

Niall and the shadow dragon locked talons and tumbled down the platform, Niall breathing fire.

Thorolf slashed at the shadow dragon's tail with his claws, making a slash deep enough that it should have drawn blood.

But the shadow dragon had no blood. It was a telling reminder of what he had become. The Elixir had replaced everything within him, filling him with darkness and despair.

Niall ripped the shadow dragon's arm free and spat it onto the train tracks. It landed on the third rail and sparked, filling the station with the smell of burned flesh.

Thorolf turned dragonfire on the lost limb, incinerating it on the spot. There was a crack and a flash from the electrical conduit in the tracks; then an alarm began to sound.

The shadow dragon roared, then struck Niall hard. Niall rolled with the blow, falling backward, letting his opponent think he was more injured than he was. The station was rapidly filling with smoke and another alarm added its summons to the first. The shadow dragon looked between Niall and Thorolf, then came after Niall.

Niall kept his eyes narrowed; then, when the shadow dragon was almost upon him, he leapt upward. He slammed his tail into his attacker's genitals, to no discernible effect. He breathed fire with new ferocity and caught the shadow dragon by his other shoulder, digging his claws deep into his chest.

The shadow dragon screamed and writhed, making the wounds deeper with his struggles. He, too, had that tiger brand, although the sight only told Niall that this one was in Chen's thrall, as well. Niall burned the shadow dragon's right claw to cinders, singeing it to ash while it was still attached to his body.

He had a heartbeat to believe that the battle was nearly over; then Rox screamed behind him.

Too far behind him.

The shadow dragon saw Niall's dilemma and laughed. He latched onto Niall's talons so tightly that Niall was trapped. The shadow dragon's claws dug deeply, drawing Niall's blood, and his tail twined around Niall.

He leaned his face close and his dark eyes glittered with malice. "Something for everyone," he murmured, then looked down the platform.

Niall saw a red dragon drag a captive Rox down those stairs. Thorolf raced after the red dragon, which didn't reassure Niall nearly enough. He struggled with all his might, sinking his teeth into the shadow dragon's side.

A little too late, he realized that the shadow dragon had been a distraction. Niall not only had to destroy his attacker, but he had to do it quickly enough to save Rox. There were only twenty steps down into that murky water, so time was of the essence.

"*You'll be one of us soon*," the shadow dragon whispered in old-speak.

"*Never!*" Niall roared, ripping himself free of his attacker's grasp. He slashed and raged against him, and the shadow dragon recoiled from Niall's assault. Niall dismembered his opponent with savage speed, scattering his limbs across the platform, then incinerating them.

It took far too long, to Niall's perspective, and he hoped that Thorolf was having success. As soon as the last ash blew down the tracks, Niall raced after Rox.

He could only hope he was in time.

Sloane intended to go only a few feet down the side tunnel.

Once he was enfolded by its shadows and unable to see, his other senses sharpened. Sloane smelled *Slayer* even more clearly.

Chen.

The scent tempted him onward, drawing him ever farther into the darkness. He followed it, sorting out the way it dodged and feinted, moving farther and farther away from Niall and Thorolf without realizing what he'd done.

Rox watched Niall and Thorolf go after the shadow dragon. He was slighter than either of the *Pyr* and she was sure they'd make short work of him.

"The nine-sixteen is running late," a man mused from right behind Rox, and she nearly jumped out of her skin.

Rox spun in shock. She'd been so busy watching Niall that she didn't hear the man until he spoke. He looked to be in his twenties, Asian, and neatly dressed. He was consulting an expensive watch on his left wrist, as if there were nothing surprising about their situation at all.

A train rumbled overhead and a smile of satisfaction touched his lips. "There. Only fifty-two seconds' delay, after all." Then he looked up and met her gaze, the coldness in his eyes prompting her to take another step back. "Oh no," he murmured, and closed the distance between them again. "You're coming with me."

"I don't think so," Rox said.

The man shone blue suddenly, as if his aura had caught fire, and Rox didn't wait for more. She screamed and ran toward Niall and Thorolf as quickly as she could.

She felt a rush of wind behind her; then the train platform seemed to ripple beneath her feet. She stumbled and he leapt over top of her.

He was a massive dragon, one seemingly made of red lacquer edged in gold. He had small golden horns on his head and long golden whiskers trailing from his chin. He snatched Rox in talons that seemed to be gilded, then raced toward those descending stairs.

And that dark, still water.

Rox knew that nothing good was going to happen down there. She struggled and fought and bit, though it made no difference. She kicked him hard in the chest, aiming for a spot that looked a bit different from the rest. When her boot connected, he inhaled sharply.

As if in pain.

Rox could work with that. She kicked again, driving her boot into the spot, and he stumbled on the steps. He hissed at her, his eyes lighting with fury.

"Pesky human," he muttered, grabbed her by the throat, and shoved her head toward the still water.

He'd drown her! She squirmed and struggled, but his grip was merciless. He locked his other claw around her waist, holding her so she couldn't reach the spot she'd kicked. He forced her steadily closer to the water. Rox could smell its mire and see an oil slick on its surface. She closed her eyes and fought harder, even though it made no difference.

Rox couldn't think of a worse place to die, but she didn't have a lot of choice.

Her face was inches away from the water when Rox saw a silvery reflection. Before she could blink, brilliant orange dragonfire erupted around them. In the mirror of the water, the red dragon was silhouetted in flames. He arched his back and screamed.

There was a moonstone and silver dragon right behind him.

A big one.

And he was pissed. Thorolf exhaled smoke and more fire as he leapt down the stairs. Rox smelled burning dragon flesh.

The red dragon spun with a hiss just as Thorolf fell upon him in an assault of talons and teeth. The red dragon dropped Rox and she grabbed the handrail with one hand as she fell. She got her back and one shoulder wet, but kept her face out of the water.

Then she tried to get out of the way.

Thorolf slammed the red dragon's head into the lip of the higher platform. One of his golden horns broke and black blood flowed from the wound. He went limp, his tail sliding into the dark water, and Rox took advantage of the opportunity. She scurried past the red dragon, back to the comparative safety of the higher platform. He didn't even seem to notice.

But then, Thorolf was kicking his butt. He drove the red dragon's head into the platform again, and black blood ran from the other side of his head. His eye on that side looked to be swollen shut. Thorolf ripped his claws across the red dragon's chest and the red dragon grimaced in pain; then Thorolf decked him.

Rox wanted to cheer.

Thorolf winked at her, then moved to toss the *Slayer* into the water that flooded the lower platform. The red dragon was completely limp.

Until the moment Thorolf released him.

Then he suddenly came to life.

Chapter 15

"No!" Rox shouted in warning.
   Too late.

The red dragon reached back and locked both claws around the moonstone and silver dragon's neck. His eyes were bright with anger as he hauled Thorolf into the water. Thorolf shouted. He struggled. He raged against his attacker.

To no avail.

Rox screamed, hating that there was nothing else she could do to help.

The red dragon dragged Thorolf into the dark water. They struggled, making the water churn violently. Rox saw a tail and then a wing; then a cluster of bubbles burst on the surface.

After that, the water was still.

No. He couldn't take Thorolf.

But the *Slayer* had.

Rox was standing with her hands pressed to her mouth, terrified, when Niall came thundering down the stairs in human form. He was bleeding and bruised, but it didn't seem to slow him down.

Rox realized there were alarms ringing and smoke

wafting from the upper platform. "Where's the shadow dragon?"

Niall shook his head, his frustration clear. "Destroyed." He halted beside her and stared across the still water.

"The red *Slayer* took Thorolf," Rox whispered, and Niall nodded.

"Chen." Niall looked between her and the dark surface, clearly torn between his responsibilities. She understood and she admired him for it.

Then she made the choice for him.

"You've got to help him, before it's too late," Rox said. Niall opened his mouth to argue, but Rox didn't give him time. "And I don't wait for anybody, especially not in the dark with shadow dragons and *Slayers* around." She heard her own anxiety but kept talking as if unafraid. "You leave me here, Talbot, and we're done."

Niall looked at her and he almost smiled. Rox thought for a heartbeat that he would call her bluff, but Niall didn't argue.

"Deal," he said, then caught her around the waist. He dove into the water, slicing cleanly into its darkness. Rox wasn't nearly so graceful and she sputtered when they went under. She was glad Niall had a tight hold on her, because she might have sunk like a rock.

She didn't want to think about what might be lurking in the water's depths. As soon as they were submerged, Rox felt Niall shift shape. The powerful length of him was suddenly beneath her, his amethyst scales gleaming beneath her hands. He rolled her to his back even as he swam, and Rox hung on tightly. She was wet, but the glow of the firestorm warmed her.

Plus she knew that Niall would defend her against anything or anyone they encountered. She gripped his scales tightly, sliding her fingers beneath them for a better grasp.

To her astonishment, the one she held with her right

hand came away from his skin. She watched a small ripple pass over Niall's flesh, as if he had felt the loss.

Did the *Pyr* shed their scales periodically and grow new ones? Rox wasn't sure, and it wasn't a good time to ask Niall. That spot where she'd struck Chen could have been tender because of a missing scale.

She'd have to ask later. She managed to shove the loose scale into the pocket of her wet jacket, then grabbed another scale, her grip tentative at first. This one stayed put, so she tightened her grasp. Then she leaned her cheek against Niall's shoulder, keeping as low a profile as possible, as the end of the tunnel came ever closer.

The firestorm sparked along the length of her body, emanating a pale golden light where her body touched Niall's. It warmed her and excited her, making her aware of his muscled strength beneath her. The light flowed over the surface of the water, turning oil slicks into rainbows that disappeared in the shadows on either side.

There was another light reflecting on the surface of the water. It couldn't have been from a signal light, because the power was off in this tunnel.

It was white and it pulsed. They were headed straight for it.

Rox was really glad Niall hadn't left her alone.

Niall yet again felt that he and Rox worked well together. She'd instinctively understood and solved his dilemma about saving Thorolf. He wasn't entirely happy having Rox with him as he headed into danger, but it was better than leaving her undefended.

Yes, definitely better, although he did have a feeling that Rox wasn't that defenseless. The way she challenged him when she was so obviously afraid made his heart clench. She was a fighter, more resilient than anyone had guessed and more vulnerable than anyone knew.

Niall wanted to shield her from every threat, from this

day forward through forever. He wanted his firestorm to be the beginning of a long partnership. He knew he could love this woman, so fiercely determined to protect those she cared about, but he wasn't sure Rox would let him.

Niall intended to persuade her to do so.

He shouted for Sloane in old-speak, but had no response. That was worrisome, but Niall was compelled to prioritize.

First, they had to save Thorolf.

The white light at the end of the tunnel seemed cold, which Niall didn't like at all. He feared that nothing good was waiting for him.

But if he turned back, he also knew that Thorolf would be lost for all time.

Niall drew strength from the firestorm's slow burn, letting the passion it kindled within his body give him new resolve to defend his mate. He felt that an additional spark of the Great Wyvern accompanied him, lighting his path in the darkness, giving him hope. Maybe it would guide his blows and give him resilience. Maybe it would protect them both in the deepest darkness.

The white light ahead grew ever brighter. The tunnel must have sloped upward, because the water became more shallow. Niall felt his claws brush against the ground, against old metal tracks. Soon the water was only as deep as his knees, so he shifted shape. Rox slipped from his back to walk beside him, her hand locked in his. He could hear the racing beat of her heart and the anxiety in her breathing, and he gave her fingers a reassuring squeeze.

"I hate the dark," she whispered so softly that the words were almost inaudible.

"But you said you'd been down here before." Niall looked at her and saw that her pupils were huge and her skin was pale. She was trembling slightly.

But she summoned a brave smile and squared her shoulders. "You can't let your life be shaped by your fears," she said with a determination he associated with her. "You've got to face those fears, kick the stuffing out of them."

"Slay your own dragons," Niall suggested, wanting only for her to smile.

Rox did, briefly. "Something like that." She leaned her breast against his arm and swallowed. "Or maybe you just need to bring one of your own."

Niall wrapped his arm around her shoulders, guessing that she was having a harder time with this than he was. Was her dislike of darkness linked to what he had seen in his dream?

"The sooner we get him, the sooner we get out of here," he said, then strode onward.

Rox didn't argue with that. "Works for me," she said grimly.

They only went a bit farther before the tunnel branched hard, a dark opening yawning to their right. The tracks gleamed as they rose above the water, the tunnel ascending toward some unknown point.

The tunnel before them terminated with only a small opening, maybe three-by-three, set at the height of Niall's shoulders. It must have been covered by a metal plate before, the one that now lay discarded on the ground. The light emanated from that hole, beckoning him onward.

"This stinks," Rox whispered, hovering close to his side.

Niall nodded in agreement. He suspected they were moving into a trap, but there was nothing to be gained by shirking the inevitable fight. Chen already knew he was here and already knew he was coming. Niall saw no point in delaying the inevitable.

"Stay close," he said to Rox, and climbed through the hole.

"As if I wouldn't," she muttered from right behind him.

Beyond it was a mirror image of the tunnel they'd just followed, although this one was constructed of cinder blocks. They'd moved through a partition that divided the tunnel in two.

Partway down the second half of the tunnel, there was a hole in the roof, and Niall could hear the faint echo of the street far overhead. He looked but couldn't glimpse light.

"Vent," Rox said. "They're everywhere down here. Hurry."

At least if they were sealed into this tunnel, they might be able to climb out. Niall moved forward with purpose, half expecting the far end to be suddenly sealed against them.

It was too quiet for his taste. Too still. He couldn't smell anything other than concrete and wet metal, and he didn't like that one bit. The water rose again as they moved forward, coming up to his hips. Rox waded right behind him.

Niall reached the end of the passage and stepped abruptly into a large room filled with pulsing white light. The light glowed from the very center of the chamber, as if its source was on the surface of the water.

"A railroad turntable," Rox murmured in surprise, looking around. "Neo said he'd found one down here, but he could never locate it again. I thought he was putting me on."

It was exactly that, or had been at some point in the distant past. The chamber was round, perhaps the diameter of three train cars, and tunnels led off in every direction. There had to be a dozen openings. The water filled the tunnels half deep, only a dark crescent about four feet high showing the top of each departing tunnel. The converging tracks were submerged.

And in the middle of the space, the water rippled.

Niall took a step back. He would have pushed Rox behind him, but she was already there, her hands clutching his shoulders. He felt his body shimmer on the cusp of change as circles began to emanate from a central point.

He shifted when a dragon claw extended out of the obsidian water. It was red, with golden talons, and it held that iron brand. The brand was the source of the light. It shone coldly, the sight of it making Niall shiver.

Chen was ready to recruit.

Niall was startled when he saw movement in a flooded tunnel on the far side of the chamber. A dark talon appeared, a manacle shaking as it was extended in silent plea. Niall saw a silhouette appear behind it, then the gleam of dark eyes. A manacle rattled right beside them, and Niall jumped farther into the chamber. Talons reached from all the tunnel openings, clutching at the air.

Niall realized there were shadow dragons shackled in all of the tunnels. They moved in agitation, all stretching toward the radiant brand. Rox swore and couldn't have been closer to him unless she'd slid under his skin.

"Chen, Chen, Chen," they chanted in unison, the sound making Niall's flesh creep.

The water heaved below the upheld brand. A tail thrashed as Chen broke the surface; then a long, scaled back rose out of the water. It was red with scales edged in gold.

The crimson *Slayer* appeared, water beading on his neck and running from his long whiskers. One side of his face was badly battered and his horns were broken, dark blood running down his face. Niall wondered what had happened to Thorolf.

He had a bad feeling about that.

"Chen," he said, and the *Slayer* inclined his head slightly in acknowledgment.

Then Chen held the brand even higher. His eyes

glinted with malice as the shadow dragons chanted more loudly.

"Chen, Chen, Chen!" the shadow dragons cried, rattling their shackles. Their voices were hollow and monotonous, creepy for their lack of animation. The sound echoed through the chamber, bouncing off the water's surface and making the space feel claustrophobic. Niall thought the water was beginning to ripple in time with the chant and he felt Rox grip his shoulders more tightly.

"I offer you a choice," Chen said. The water heaved again as he hauled an unconscious Thorolf out of the water and gave him an impatient shake.

Rox caught her breath and Niall was shocked at the pale, still state of the big *Pyr*. There was a large wound on Thorolf's chest, and his scales seemed lighter in hue, as if he'd lost a lot of blood.

Was he dead?

Or just close to it?

Either way, Niall had to get Thorolf out of here.

"There have to be repercussions for one's choices, don't you think?" Chen asked no one in particular as the shadow dragons chanted. "We must pay for the injuries we inflict upon others, the damage we do to their appearance."

"Oh no," Rox whispered. "Not that."

Chen smiled. "Yes, *that*." His gaze brightened as he considered Niall. "Although I have need of only one recruit. You could take his place."

"No!" Rox said, clutching Niall. "Don't you dare get heroic on me."

Chen reared back and exhaled dragonfire at the brand. It glowed, becoming even whiter and brighter. Niall thought he could feel its radiant heat.

"Chen, Chen, Chen," chanted the shadow dragons, the volume of their voices growing louder and louder.

The water was resonating and the stones were vibrating. "Chen, Chen, Chen!"

Chen bent Thorolf's neck so that the left side was displayed. He exhaled to dry the scales. Then he moved the brand toward Thorolf's flesh.

"No!" Rox cried.

"No!" Niall bellowed, then dove toward the *Slayer*, talons extended.

Rox watched Niall leap toward Chen. Chen threw Thorolf aside and the big *Pyr* fell into the water with a splash. Thorolf stayed limp and any hope Rox had that he'd rally faded fast.

Niall meanwhile had locked claws with the *Slayer* and they wrestled through the water. Chen's tail locked around Niall's, twining about it and holding Niall back. The *Slayer* continued to hold the brand high overhead, which meant he had one claw fewer.

Niall slashed at his face, drawing dark blood, then breathed fire. Chen took a step back and Niall bit at his shoulder, ripping the flesh with force. Chen cried out in pain. His tail moved quickly to disentangle from Niall's, and he grabbed Thorolf by the back of the neck. He forced the big *Pyr*'s head underwater, and some bubbles rose to the surface.

"No!" Rox cried, but Niall had already seized the *Slayer* by the throat with both claws. He lifted Chen up quickly and slammed his head into the ceiling of the chamber so hard that Rox heard a crack.

Chen's grasp loosened on both Thorolf and the brand. Thorolf fell with a splash back into the water as Niall ripped the brand from Chen's claw. Niall coiled the tip of his tail around the brand's handle, then passed it quickly back to Rox.

"Don't lose it," he said tersely, and Rox understood. It was hot—hot enough to burn her hands even

when she held the handle. On impulse, she plunged
it into the murky water and heard it sizzle. The water
bubbled, boiling in its vicinity, and the iron slowly
turned black.

It couldn't be used to mark Niall now. Not unless
Chen had the strength to heat it again.

Talons free, Chen and Niall raged back and forth
across the chamber, biting and slashing at each other
with savage force. They breathed dragonfire, the flames
lighting the darkness, and Rox heard the rumble of old-
speak as they traded taunts.

Thorolf shifted shape where he had been cast, changing from dragon to man to dragon again, as if he couldn't
control his body. He moaned as his form changed, as his
form wavered, and she knew he was in bad shape.

Rox made a step toward him when something rep-
tilian locked around her ankle and tugged hard. She
slipped, the cold water sloshing past her waist. That
something tugged again, and she lost her footing. Rox
screamed in terror as she fell, and she got a mouthful of
cold murk as a reward.

Then she was hauled to some unknown destination
at lightning speed. There was only dark, cold water and
helplessness.

It was her worst nightmare, all over again.

No. She wasn't going there again. Rox tightened her
grip on the brand and struck at her assailant with all her
might.

Chen was messing with him. Niall knew it.

He'd gotten in a few good blows, but he knew the
Slayer wasn't giving the fight all he had. He sensed that
the *Slayer* was letting him think he was winning.

Or stalling for time.

Niall couldn't figure out why, not until Rox screamed.
He saw her fall into the water, as if she'd stepped into
a hole.

Or been tugged down from deep below. Then he realized he'd lost track of the *Slayer*'s tail.

Chen chuckled and withdrew rapidly, bolting toward one of the tunnels that left the chamber. "*You'll never find her again*," he taunted, but Niall wasn't going to tolerate that.

He leapt after the *Slayer* and ripped savagely at his tail. He dove into the water and sank his teeth into that tail, shredding it with all his might. Chen thrashed and struggled, but he didn't have nearly the motivation that Niall did.

There was a rumble and stone began to fall all around Niall. Slamming Chen into the ceiling must have compromised the structure. The water sloshed in the chamber and the shadow dragons chanted with renewed fury. Chen struggled but Niall held fast, gnawing with all his strength.

How long had Rox been underwater? Had she held her breath? Was she still alive?

The shimmer of the firestorm answered his question. Its golden presence gave Niall the last burst of power he needed. He felt the rhythm of something in the water, saw Chen suddenly flinch, and guessed what his determined mate was doing.

Niall ripped Chen's tail and immediately felt the *Slayer* race away from his severed tail. Niall worked down its length, found Rox, and carried her to the surface just as the side tunnels began to collapse.

The shadow dragons moaned and roared. Rox sputtered and clutched Niall, her breath coming in anxious spurts. "Thanks," she said, and shuddered right to her toes. She found her footing and stood up by herself, catching her breath.

He wasn't surprised she still had the brand. "I got a few good hits in," she said, swinging it like a weapon. Her show of spirit reassured him as little else could have done.

Niall grabbed Thorolf and shook him hard, dragging the big *Pyr* toward the tunnel that seemed to slant upward. Thorolf was in human form, but limp. Niall felt as if he were dragging a dead moose, even in his own dragon form. Rox moved quickly to grab Thorolf's other shoulder and tried to help move him.

Niall then heard a low chant, the sound of someone singing the song of the earth. He looked around, distrusting his senses.

Then he heard a competing voice, one that sang a different song of the earth. The two voices competed with each other, the first one fading as the second became more vehement.

Chen and Rafferty.

Niall guessed Chen was determined to trap them here forever.

Rafferty began to sing the song of steel, which made no sense to Niall. He didn't have time to think about it, though. The earth rippled again and the ceiling shook.

"Crappy place to be during an earthquake," Rox said, covering her fear with bravado. They pushed Thorolf through the narrow opening, Niall wincing when the big *Pyr* fell into the shallow water on the other side. He could have been a bag of rocks. Niall helped Rox through, then leapt through himself.

How were they ever going to make it out together?

Niall eyed the distance to the stairs, the ones that led to the active subway tunnel and a guaranteed exit.

They'd never make it.

He called again for Sloane and wasn't sure whether he heard a faint answer or not. Whatever had happened to Sloane, they were on their own for the moment.

"Come on, Thorolf. You've got to help if we're going to get out of here alive," Niall said. His words had no discernible effect, but Rox slapped Thorolf hard across the face.

That didn't help, either.

The ceiling groaned overhead. It cracked and crumbled, stone falling in chunks into the water. The shadow dragons screamed far behind them, a loud wail of pain that gave Niall goose bumps.

That sound made Thorolf's eyes open.

Fetters sprang open audibly. Niall met Rox's gaze, wondering what was happening. Manacles clattered, splashed, and fell. The earth roiled and the walls shuddered. The water sloshed from side to side.

Thorolf swore. The three of them managed to hobble toward the distant stairs, the ones that led to the service platform. The alarm was still ringing there, and Niall wouldn't have minded some helpful human company at this moment.

There came a sudden fluttering of wings, like a thousand bats on the move. Niall saw the silhouettes pour out of the side tunnels and saw the glitter of their eyes. His heart leapt with fear.

They weren't bats.

They were shadow dragons, they were unfettered, and there were dozens of them. They moved like a cloud of menace and Niall was afraid he'd have to fight them all alone.

But they had another agenda. They passed low over the three of them, a dark cloud of fluttering wings. Rox ducked and put her hands over her head as they raced by.

Niall smelled their rotten scent and felt the shadow of their passing. He saw them swoop up the stairway and into the lower subway station. He saw them scurry down various side tunnels and passageways, clearly seeking the surface.

They'd been commanded to leave. Niall shivered.

Thorolf took one look at the flock of darkness swooping over them and his eyes went round. He swore vehemently, then hauled himself toward the staircase, leaving

Rox and Niall behind. He was grim and pale, but he was moving under his own steam.

"Never fails. Bad shit happens underground," he muttered, hauling himself up the stairs as he winced in pain. He was pale but fighting against his own body's limitations.

"Talk later," Rox said, looking worried. "Move now."

"I'm with you on that," Thorolf said.

"I can help, but I can't carry you," Niall said, fearing the big *Pyr* would push himself too hard.

He caught a whisper of old-speak and was relieved. "*Sorry!*" Sloane said. "*Got distracted.*"

"*It probably wasn't an accident*," Niall replied, relieved to hear the other *Pyr*'s voice.

"Good job Sloane's close," Thorolf said as he tried to catch his breath at the top of the stairs. "That bastard Chen nearly ripped my guts out."

"Well, hold on to them for now," Rox suggested.

They had just climbed the stairs when rubble began to fall into the water behind them. All three of them moved faster, even though the earth had stilled. No one needed to say there could be another earthquake at any point.

Niall just wanted to feel the wind again.

The shadow dragons were gone, but the silence was ominous. Niall didn't trust it. He felt that the tunnel was breathing, that there were a thousand eyes watching them. There was no sign of Chen, which meant exactly nothing. Sloane was coming toward them, close enough that Niall could hear his quiet tread on the concrete. They moved out of the service station, entering the dark tunnel once more.

Niall had time to think they couldn't get out of this underground realm soon enough before they were attacked from behind.

It was Phelan.

And he went straight for Rox.

*   *   *

Rox heard Niall swear. A tingle of electricity passed over her skin, the hair standing up in the way it had whenever he'd shimmered blue. She spun to see the dark shadow of Phelan closing fast and Niall rearing high, amethyst and silver, to defend her.

Thorolf bellowed a warning, shoved Rox behind him, and shifted shape. He looked unsteady on his feet, if determined. If nothing else, he was a formidable obstacle. She heard Sloane begin to run down the tunnel toward them, but she feared he wouldn't reach them in time.

Then everything went wrong fast.

Niall leapt to lock claws with Phelan. Phelan dodged at the last moment and wove beneath Niall with lightning speed. He was as sinuous as a snake, his eyes shining like black mirrors. Niall pivoted but Phelan struck as quickly as a cobra.

He sank his talons into the back of Niall's right shoulder.

Rox was sure that was where the scale had come free, the one she still had in her pocket.

Niall bellowed in pain. He roared and breathed dragonfire, writhing in Phelan's grip. Phelan bit harder and shook Niall like a rag doll, then cast his brother aside. Niall fell to the subway platform and didn't move, his blood pooling red on the tiles.

Uh-oh.

Thorolf swore right before Phelan attacked him with savage glee. He thrashed and pummeled the big *Pyr*, biting him and pounding him. Thorolf tried to fight back, but he was already injured and in a heartbeat, he, too, was lying on the ground. He shifted back to human form, cycling between forms less rapidly than he had before, then became still.

Rox ran toward Sloane. She saw a shimmer of blue far ahead of her in the tunnel and raced toward him as quickly as she could. She felt the chill of Phelan's gain-

ing on her, heard his breath, and ran faster. She could see
Sloane raging toward her; she saw his talons extended
and the fire emanating from his nostrils.

She didn't see the vent overhead until it was too late.

Phelan snatched at Rox. His reach was long, his talon
longer.

Rox felt his claw cut a line down her back, from
shoulder to butt, and she screamed. It could have been a
scalpel of ice, so cold that its touch almost paralyzed her.
It left her dizzy. It made her stumble. It filled her with
cold and despair.

She fell as she felt the flutter of his passing over top
of her. The last thing she saw before her eyes closed was
Phelan shooting up the vent like a spiral of dark smoke.
Rox was aware of Sloane leaping over her, of his tourmaline and gold scales glinting in the tunnel's darkness.
He spoke to her, but Rox couldn't reply. A dark cloud
filled her mind and made it impossible for her to move.

She was numb.

She just wanted to sleep.

Forever.

Sloane immediately sent a summons to Rafferty in old-
speak. Then he surveyed the situation and set to work.
He'd curse himself for being distracted by the *Slayer*
when he had less to do. A little triage revealed that Niall
was the most likely to revive quickly, and the most likely
to be able to help.

Thorolf would heal with time and Sloane's familiar
array of unguents and songs. Rox might be lost—one
look at her injury left Sloane grim. Sloane concentrated
on what he could solve.

Sloane bent over the amethyst and platinum dragon,
wincing when he realized the shadow dragon had found
a spot where Niall was missing a scale. The skin was pale
there and so soft that Sloane knew it had only recently
been exposed.

He didn't know why Niall had lost that scale, but Sloane could guess.

The wound had bled copiously, which had helped to drive out whatever toxin might have been on Phelan's talons. Sloane counted his blessings where he could find them. The wound looked cold and blue, so Sloane knew there was still poison within it. He shifted to human form, bent over Niall, and sucked as much liquid out of the wound as he could. He spit it on the tracks, repeating the action until the wound looked red instead of blue.

Sloane didn't have his kit of potions and bandages, so he had to make do. He had his skill and his experience, and he had his song. While he worked, he repeated the song of healing in his thoughts, letting its rhythm guide him, letting its power fill his gestures. He felt Niall's wound become cleaner, and he tasted the blood running truer. He tasted its red cleanliness, the spark of the Great Wyvern, and the shimmer of the firestorm. He worked diligently and as quickly as he could.

He was relieved when Niall opened his eyes and shifted to human form. His fellow *Pyr*'s color wasn't great, but it was better than Sloane had expected. And Niall had shifted shape deliberately, which was a good sign. The blood was running clear red from the wound now, so Sloane knew he had done all he could for the moment. He tore the hem of his T-shirt and bandaged the wound. He continued to sing, but he sang aloud.

Niall winced and moved his shoulder tentatively, then scanned the platform with concern.

"He's gone," Sloane said. "Rafferty's coming. Thorolf's down hard, but he'll recover."

"And Rox?"

Sloane grimaced. He wasn't sure what to do to help her. Whenever humans encountered *Pyr* or *Slayer* substances, the results were unpredictable. All sorts of variables played a part, such as character, and Sloane knew he'd have to do some studying to help Rox.

He doubted this was the news Niall wanted to hear, so he kept his mouth shut.

"Did he take her again?" Niall was already on his feet, bracing himself against the wall as he sought a glimpse of Rox.

"No. It's worse, in a way." Sloane knew the moment Niall saw his fallen mate, because he paled again.

"She's hurt!"

"Touched by the shadow. Like you, but she's human."

"So?"

"So its effects are less easy to predict."

"What about treating them?"

Sloane frowned. "The wound is deep and she fell hard. I'm wondering whether the darkness found a resonance within her."

"Can you heal her?"

Sloane avoided the question and its answer. This wasn't the time or place for despair.

"We've got to get her out of here," he said softly, and Niall's lips tightened in understanding.

Sloane bent over Thorolf, surveying the big *Pyr*'s wounds again. The T-shirt was torn into bands then, and he wrapped the strips around Thorolf's chest to staunch the bleeding. It was a clean wound, even though it was nasty, and Sloane knew he could heal it. There was a deep gouge in the *Pyr*'s thigh, which he probed with his fingertips before he bound it, as well. He didn't find anything in the cut, but Sloane suspected there was something in it. It looked angry, but he needed tools and light to clean it properly.

With luck, he'd have both soon.

While he worked, Niall moved with determination toward Rox. Sloane glanced up as Niall bent down to touch her cheek with such tenderness that there was no doubt why Niall had lost that scale.

Would the firestorm heal her, as it had healed Delaney?

Sloane could only hope.

"She's so cold!" Niall said, fear in his expression as he looked back at Sloane. "We have to do something!"

"There's nothing we can do here," Sloane said. "Let's go."

Niall was afraid.

Rox was icy cold, her skin pale. The wound on her back looked ugly. He picked her up and cradled her against his chest, trusting no one else with the precious burden of her. The firestorm flickered between them, its feeble glow making him fear for her survival.

Rox couldn't be the one who paid the price for his choice. It wouldn't be fair.

But Niall was afraid he had made a fatal mistake.

He only hoped he had the chance to make it right.

He and Sloane worked together, trying to find their way back to the surface. Niall was disoriented and his shoulder was so painful that he couldn't think straight. It wasn't easy for him to help Sloane support Thorolf's weight, in addition to carrying Rox. Determination made up for his physical challenges. There wasn't room in most of the passages for Niall and Sloane to be in dragon form, so they made slow progress.

At least the tunnels stopped crumbling.

Rox's breathing was shallow. Niall feared with every step that he'd lose her before they reached the surface again.

They couldn't find an unlocked door from the service tunnel to the adjacent subway station, and the platform was crawling with emergency workers. Niall preferred not to draw their attention, so he and Sloane decided to find another way out.

Thorolf's stillness was spooky. Niall had always thought the big *Pyr* was pretty much invincible, as well as a good fighter, and it shook him to see Thorolf so weakened.

Especially as he'd fallen in defense of Rox.

Sloane was confident of the newest recruit's recovery, but Niall was worried. Had he been too hard on Thorolf? Had Thorolf committed to learning the skills of the *Pyr* too late? Had Niall unwittingly brought disaster on his friends by being his father's son?

Niall kept looking back, fearing pursuit.

Nothing.

Only silence carried to his ears.

In a way, that was worse.

Chapter 16

Quinn was descending into New York with Sara and Garrett in his grasp. He followed the heat of the firestorm, its pull guiding him unerringly toward one part of the city. He sensed shadow dragons and caught a faint whiff of *Slayer*—more important, he smelled the presence of his fellows. They had already gathered, and he changed his route to join them. Sara was dozing against his chest, but Garrett was wide-awake.

"*Feel the firestorm,*" he instructed his son, loving that they could already make this connection. Old-speak seemed the most apt way to Quinn to teach his son about the *Pyr*.

At Quinn's bidding, Garrett stretched out both hands, as if holding them to a distant bonfire.

"*Know the miracle of our kind,*" Quinn continued. "*The firestorm brings each* Pyr *the richest gem in his hoard, the chance to build a legacy, the opportunity to create the future.*"

Garrett locked one hand around Sara's arm and nodded. He listened intently to Quinn, as yet unable to respond in kind. Quinn knew his son would learn old-speak in time, although it might not be possible until he experienced the change.

"*Honor your firestorm, when you are so lucky as to have one,*" Quinn murmured. "*That is the lesson of my father, your grandfather.*"

Garrett mocked breathing fire.

Quinn targeted the roof of the building and made to land, aware of his son's sharp interest. He was five feet above the roof, on the verge of shifting shape, when the shadow dragon leapt out of the darkness and attacked.

It was the shadow dragon made of Quinn's brother, Michel.

Michel had died the day the church bell rang so many centuries before.

Michel had been turned into a shadow dragon by Magnus.

And now, Michel had come for Quinn.

This creature looked like his brother, but the resemblance was superficial. His eyes were dead, like mirrors reflecting a starless night.

The true Michel was long dead, his spark returned to the Great Wyvern. In fact, Michel had not aged in all these centuries—he was long and lanky even in his dragon form, like the boy of fifteen summers he had been when he died. Quinn was no longer the small child he had been, however, but an adult man—and a *Pyr* of fearsome power.

Just as Quinn had dreamed so many times this past month, the shadow dragon attacked when he was most vulnerable.

When he had his family in his grasp.

It was also when Quinn had the most to lose and the least patience with risk.

Sara awakened suddenly in Quinn's embrace, ducking instinctively when his plume of dragonfire blazed into the night. Garrett mimicked his father, baring his teeth and exhaling noisily, as if he, too, would breathe drag-onfire. Sara had a moment in which she wondered what kind of challenge it would be to have a teenage *Pyr* be-fore the shadow dragon attacked Quinn.

She snatched Garrett, giving Quinn one arm free. She held her son close and locked her arm around Quinn's neck. New York glittered wetly beneath them.

Quinn would defend them to his last breath. She knew it and she believed in his power; yet she always feared for him when he fought. Quinn fought fairly and was honorable.

Shadow dragons and *Slayers*, however, didn't ac-knowledge any rules. They cheated and deceived, and Sara always worried that her honorable *Pyr* partner wouldn't see through their lies in time.

Quinn's opponent was a shadow dragon, which didn't reassure her at all. He had scales of rusted steel. He re-minded her of abandoned factories, reminiscent of the past and almost forgotten. He was smaller and leaner than Quinn, as if younger, and looked insubstantial. He had a cut on his shoulder, one that didn't bleed. He looked down at her and ran his dark tongue over his teeth, the cold emptiness of his gaze filling her with dread.

Garrett, in contrast to his mother's wariness, breathed his imaginary fire at the shadow dragon, undaunted by his father's opponent or their precarious position.

"Hold tightly to me!" Sara told the boy, and he did as he was told. Sara heard thunder and knew the two opponents were trading taunts; then Quinn lashed at his adversary with his tail.

The shadow dragon hissed but had no dragonfire to breathe. Quinn's dragonfire lit the night with brilliant orange, blackening the scales of his opponent. Quinn slashed with his talons and cut off the end of the shadow dragon's tail.

The limb fell, and Quinn incinerated it with dragonfire before it could reach the ground. The ash fell on the roof of the building far below like a dusting of dark snow.

Garrett bounced in approval.

The shadow dragon leapt on Quinn's back, his claws digging deeply into Quinn's flesh. Sara gasped as she saw the wound and the red blood flowing from it.

But the shadow dragon was no match for the Smith on this night. Sara knew that the shadow dragons haunted those who had loved them in human form, and she wondered who this shadow dragon had been. He clearly had no emotional tug for Quinn.

Or maybe he did.

Quinn was more vicious than Sara had ever seen him. He spun and bit into his opponent's chest, ripping a large chunk out of the shadow dragon and spitting it earthward. Keeping one arm tightly around Sara and Garrett, Quinn shredded one shoulder of the shadow dragon. He pulled one arm free, then burned the falling parts to ash. He was savage and determined, immune to any familiarity the shadow dragon might have had with a lost *Pyr*.

Sara had seen Quinn fight with such resolve before, usually in defense of her, and guessed that the shadow dragon had lost any advantage by attacking Quinn while he carried his family.

The shadow dragon didn't appear to feel any pain as Quinn attacked him—nor did he bleed. He carried on, fighting viciously, even as Quinn steadily cut him apart and burned the pieces. It was a grisly exercise and Sara sensed Quinn's abhorrence of what had to be done. Their son watched with wide eyes.

Quinn roared, thrashed the shadow dragon with his tail, then severed his head from his body. Sara held Garrett's face to her chest, trying to shield his view. Quinn's dragonfire was savage and bright as the last pieces of his opponent fell, only ash emerging from the brilliant orange torrent of flames.

Sara sensed Quinn's regret as he hovered, watching the ash fall.

"You knew him," she said, no question in her tone.

He nodded once, then continued his flight, following the lure of the firestorm. That Quinn was so silent told Sara all she needed to know.

"Michel," she guessed.

Quinn nodded again. "The shadow dragons are loosed."

But the only one who could haunt Sara's dragon, the last one who could make him dread what had to be done, was no more than ash on the wind.

It was a start.

Sloane chanted softly as the small party made progress, bending his attention on first one patient, then the other. It seemed to Niall that Thorolf was responding to Sloane's healing song. Was his color better? There was no change in Rox that Niall could discern. If anything, she seemed colder.

Rafferty appeared so suddenly out of a side tunnel that he made them both jump in surprise. "Let me," he said, taking Thorolf's weight from Niall's shoulders. He also lifted the brand from Niall's grip, shoving its handle into his belt after he had grimaced at it.

They moved more quickly then, all bent on getting out of the nether world of the tunnels. With Rafferty's aid, Niall was better able to concentrate and use his affinity to help them.

Niall's sense of scent led them ever onward. He knew they were following a different path from the one they'd taken into the tunnels, but it smelled right to him. Eventually they reached a metal staircase that looked like it would lead to a basement. There was a steel fire door at the top of the steps, and Niall wondered what was behind it.

Was it better or worse than what they'd already faced?

Where were they?

Rafferty and Niall exchanged uncertain glances. Niall couldn't smell anything unusual, just basement, cheap carpeting, maybe a restaurant in close proximity.

Fifteen narrow metal stairs stood between them and the street.

"Almost there," Sloane said, addressing Thorolf with false cheer. He pinched the *Pyr*'s side and Thorolf flinched. "Come on, kiddo, help us out."

Thorolf groaned, grimaced, and opened his eyes.

"Otherwise, we have to drag you up these stairs," Sloane said, his tone teasing. "We're too tired to be gentle."

"Where are we?" Thorolf asked.

"The details are unimportant," Rafferty said, his tone soothing. "You need to help so we can get out of here."

"Then I'll fix you up," Sloane said. "Promise."

Thorolf eyed the steps, then looked at Rox. His gaze was solemn and his concern clear.

"She's here because you defended her," Niall said. "Thanks."

Thorolf nodded, took a breath, and gripped the railing. He hauled himself up three steps, his teeth bared.

"Easy," Sloane said. "Don't make the injury worse."

"We gotta get Rox out of here," Thorolf said, and Niall couldn't have agreed more. They were up the staircase more quickly than he'd anticipated, Thorolf helping to haul his own weight while Rafferty braced him from behind.

Niall reached for the doorknob in the steel door and turned it.

It was unlocked.

He opened the door and peeked around the edge. It led to a corridor, the kind of hallway that would be in an old office building. That hall was lined with doors to various offices, many of which had signs in both English and Cantonese, and bent to the right over its length.

Niall disliked that he couldn't see either end of the corridor. That probably wasn't the only reason the hairs were prickling on the back of his neck.

He gestured to the others and they quickly emerged into the corridor while it was empty. Niall shut the door behind them, noting that it had no sign on it.

It also locked from the corridor side. There was no going back.

They looked left and right, and Niall knew he wasn't the only one trying to get a sense of the place. He could smell herbs and roots, as well as some kind of hot food—steamed dumplings, maybe. There was a pervasive smell of mildewed carpet and a silence that buffeted at his ears. There was something familiar about the place, something he couldn't quite name.

He chose a direction, heading left and holding Rox close. Traffic sounded close at hand and he hoped there would be an exit. Sloane and Rafferty supported Thorolf, who was still unsteady on his feet.

An Asian woman in tight jeans and stiletto heels came out of one of the offices behind them. Niall didn't see which one; he only heard her quiet murmur when she wanted to pass them. He moved immediately to one side, knowing they were blocking the passage.

"I beg your pardon," Rafferty said quietly as he and Sloane moved to one side, as well.

She smiled as she drew alongside them, her gaze flicking over Thorolf with obvious appreciation. Her floral perfume was strong enough to make Niall's nose itch and her blouse was a vivid red. Her jeans could have been painted on, and Niall was surprised she could walk easily in heels so high. Thorolf stared after her as she made her way to the street.

The woman paused just before the door to the street and cast Thorolf a smile over her shoulder. There was a bruise on her cheek, albeit one she had tried to hide with makeup.

When Thorolf didn't respond to the invitation, she shrugged and stepped into the street. She strode to the left without hesitating, the door swinging shut after her.

Thorolf then took a few steps in pursuit.

"Not dead yet," Sloane muttered, and rolled his eyes.

Rafferty chuckled and shook his head when Thorolf's neck turned red.

Niall caught the door before it closed. He was surprised to find them on Doyers Street near his ruined building.

There was a Chinese apothecary shop to one side of the door he held and a dim sum restaurant on the other. That explained the smells. The signage overhead acclaimed the services of the acupuncture specialist and several other professionals located in the corridor.

"Holy crap," Thorolf said, looking around with amazement.

"I've walked past here a thousand times, with no idea," Niall agreed.

"No." Thorolf shook his head. "She's gone."

And it was true. Despite the number of people on either side of the street to the left of the doorway, there was no sign of the striking woman in the tight jeans.

"As surely as if she'd never been," Rafferty mused.

"Maybe she went into a shop," Niall suggested, but he had a feeling that wasn't the case.

Were there other entrances to the underground network in the vicinity?

Did the woman know about them?

Or was he just seeing threats where none existed?

It didn't matter. He had priorities right now. He indicated an alley and they hurried into its protective shadows. The *Pyr* shifted shape immediately, leaping into the sky as they carried their wounded back to Rox's apartment.

*　　*　　*

Rox dreams of the dark prison of the past.

She's back in that house, back in her bedroom, back alone in the darkness. She's fifteen again, fifteen, filled with attitude and frightened.

She's terrified of the night and what it brings.

Suzie has run away; Suzie who always protected her baby sister; Suzie who was the first.

The pretty one.

Rox curls herself up tightly in her bed, afraid to sleep. She knots her nightgown around her ankles. There is danger in the darkness. Evil things happen in the dark and she is without a defender. She doesn't dare sleep; she hasn't slept since Suzie left. Nothing has happened yet, but it will.

She hears a footfall in the corridor and knows it's his.

He's coming.

Her breath hitches and she pretends to be asleep. She wishes he would pass her door. She wishes he would go somewhere else. She wishes he would leave her alone. She wishes he would die.

But he opens her bedroom door. She can see his figure silhouetted in the doorway, this man who has moved into their house and changed everything.

Her mother called Suzie a liar.

She would call Rox a liar, too.

Rox swallows; she tries to sound as if she's asleep even though her body is frozen in fear. He comes silently into the room, closing the door behind him. He comes closer, ever closer, and Rox's heart pounds in terror.

He sits on the edge of the bed and the weight of his hand falls on Rox's hip. She fights the urge to scream, knowing it won't fix anything.

"Pretty," he whispers, his voice making her shudder violently. He pulls the hem of the nightgown loose from her ankles. Rox doesn't want to move and reveal that she's awake. "Now that Suzie's gone, it'll have to be you."

And his hand slides beneath her nightgown.

*There is nowhere to run, nowhere to hide, no way to
escape her stepfather. Rox is trapped in the darkness of
her past, unable to find an escape to her present.*

The *Pyr* were gathered in Rox's apartment. Niall was
relieved to see Erik and Eileen, Delaney and Ginger,
Sara and Quinn. Zoë was sleeping on her mother's lap.
Quinn's son, Garrett, was pretending to breathe fire,
to Delaney's encouragement. Delaney remained close
while Ginger nursed their son, Liam. Erik was pacing
in front of the large window and Eileen was flipping
through Rox's book on dragons, her thoughts clearly
elsewhere. Niall wasn't sure whether Quinn was hurt or
lost in thought—he seemed very still.

Erik and Delaney moved quickly to help Thorolf to
the one couch, a flurry of old-speak mingled with questions and answers. Niall knew they had to be curious
about Rox, but he carried her into her bedroom. Sloane
could tend her in some privacy.

Sloane followed Niall, instructing him to put Rox
on her stomach on the bed. He cut her T-shirt away,
lifting it from her skin to reveal the wound fully. Both
he and Niall caught their breath at the sight of Rox's
tattoos.

Niall had seen the *carpe diem* emblazoned on her collarbone and the small heart on her temple. Neither of
those had prepared him for the other truths inscribed
on her skin.

Because he was standing to one side, he saw the tattoo on Rox's left bicep first. It was a portrait tattoo done
in shades of gray. It showed the head and shoulders of
two women, who faced each other. The images were so
detailed that they could have been photographs. The
names Chynna and Suzie were inscribed beneath the
portraits. Around the portraits were written the words
Sisters of the Heart.

Niall appreciated that Chynna had an important

place in Rox's life, perhaps more of one than he'd realized, and wondered who Suzie was.

The importance of both of them to Rox was clear.

Sloane swore softly. Niall realized then the Apothecary was looking at a second magnificent tattoo.

Across Rox's back was a dragon in flight, or at least the detailed outline of one. The dragon was drawn in the Chinese style, coiled and powerful. His tail was at Rox's neck, his body winding from her nape down to the left and back up the right side. Wingless and sinuous, he was horned and had five talons on each claw. Flames were drawn all around his body, the brilliant orange accenting the fact that the dragon scales were only outlined in black. The dragon held a pearl in its front claw, and he snarled up and over Rox's right shoulder.

Niall's first thought was that this dragon was guarding Rox's back.

Not effectively, though, given the injury that marred her skin.

The wound missed the tattoo, slicing from Rox's right shoulder down to her waist. Her skin was puffed and bluish white, the cut silvery as if touched by frost. She was cold, but the wound was frigid, as though generating a chill of its own.

"Worse than I thought." Sloane swore under his breath as the two of them stared and Niall's heart sank. Sloane eased his finger along the cut, exploring its depth. He shook his head and frowned. "Nothing in it. Nothing I can pull out, anyway."

Niall leaned toward Rox and felt the firestorm glimmer between them. Its heat was feeble, which terrified him. The firestorm wasn't satisfied—was it fading because Rox was going to die?

Niall put his hand on Rox's shoulder and the glow became a bit brighter. Niall felt the others come into the room, but he was focused on Rox. The firestorm had no sparks, no flame—just a radiance.

Like that of glowing coals.

Dying coals.

Sloane caught his breath. "Touch the wound," he commanded with quiet force. "There's no time to look it up. Just try."

Niall laid one hand alongside Rox's cut. The firestorm's sparks sputtered weakly and disappeared, as if the flame had been doused.

Frightened, he put his other hand beside the first one, bracketing the cut between his index fingers. Three sparks danced between his hands and Rox's skin for a moment before there were no more. The glow remained, though, and he dared to hope it was brighter.

"Not much, but we'll work with it." Sloane put his hands on top of Niall's and began to chant. Niall heard the Apothecary's song and let it fill his thoughts. He let it drive his intent; he begged it to fulfill his wish.

And when he understood its rhythm, he added his voice to Sloane's. They sang together with force and yearning.

The firestorm responded, kindling a greater heat beneath Niall's hands. There were still no visible flames, but Niall felt as if someone had stirred those coals.

As if they might not die after all.

They needed fuel. Niall slid his hands up and down Rox's skin, trying to coax the toxin from her body, and he sang louder. He let the memory of her kisses fill his thoughts, recalled the vigor of the burning firestorm, and tried to summon her to the bonfire they could make together.

The firestorm sparked, its radiance growing.

Niall knew the moment that Delaney came to stand behind him. He felt the weight of Delaney's hand on his shoulder and when he glanced up, he saw that Delaney had put his other hand on Sloane's shoulder. Delaney added his voice to the chant.

The firestorm's flame erupted beneath Niall's hands.

He sang even louder and with more force, determined to bring Rox back from wherever she had gone. He knew there was a shadow in her past, and knew she had triumphed over it before. Phelan's touch must have reopened that old wound, revealing its hidden depths. Niall coaxed the flame with all his heart and soul. He sang Sloane's song of healing and marveled at the power of the crackling firestorm.

Rafferty added his baritone to their chorus, Erik's voice giving their song another voice of strength. Quinn lent his voice to the effort, as well. Niall dared to hope that they could heal his mate, that the firestorm could be rekindled to burn bright enough. Ginger, Eileen, and Sara added the weight of their hands and the force of their wills.

The flames danced beneath his hands, simmering and sizzling, taking on the sensual turn that he associated with the firestorm. The way the influence of his friends helped Rox brought tears to Niall's eyes.

He kept singing, his voice becoming even more urgent.

Sloane changed his song as the wound began to weep a dark fluid. He called to the toxin, summoning it forth, removing it as it revealed its dark shadow. It looked vile, like oil, but had a shimmer like mercury. Delaney's low voice reminded Niall of how Delaney had been able to follow the firestorm's song through the darkness. They worked together until the wound ceased to weep dark fluid.

Then the flames abruptly died.

A white line glowed coldly on Rox's back. She was utterly still, cold, and motionless.

Had she died? Niall felt for her pulse in fear. It was there, slow and feeble, but fluttering at her throat.

"It found an answering shadow within her," Sloane said with disgust. "It found a resonance in her mind."

"What the hell does that mean?" Niall demanded.

"That Rox has an old wound. The shadow found it and fed it."

"But the firestorm should be able to heal it," Niall protested. "It was working so well. . . ."

Sloane put a hand on his shoulder. "It began the process. It removed the taint so that it couldn't spread farther, but it had already taken root."

"But how do we finish what we started? How do we save her?"

"I don't know."

Niall stepped back, dissatisfied with this answer. "That's not good enough!"

"The firestorm brings opportunities we do not expect," Rafferty said. "Think of *Pyr* and mate becoming more together than the sum of the parts."

Niall was impatient. "Rafferty, I agree completely, but there is no firestorm unless Rox survives."

The older *Pyr* surveyed Niall. "And who do you think can best heal her wound?"

Niall scanned Rox's still figure and panicked. "But how can it be up to me? I don't know what to do, or how to help her. . . ."

Erik stepped into Niall's field of vision, crouching down beside him. "The firestorm can show us new facets of our abilities, or teach us to expand our talents. I lost my gift of foresight until I learned to rely upon Eileen as a partner."

Niall immediately thought of his own affinity for the element of air. "The wind hasn't been as cooperative lately, but I haven't lost my link with it. Rafferty has said the same about the earth—that it's a sign of distress."

"But there are other possibilities linked to the element of air," Erik said. Zoë came to her father's side, bracing herself on his knee, and smiled up at Niall. He smiled back at her briefly, knowing she didn't understand. "I have foresight as a mark of my affinity." Erik continued. "You can call the wind, but what if you can do more?"

"Like what?" Niall asked. "And how could that heal Rox? She's not even conscious. If something hurt her in the past, how could I even find out about it? How could I heal it?"

Sara came to his other side. "I have a clue for you. I dreamed of a prophecy several nights back. Until Quinn told me about the firestorm, I thought I had just gotten it early." She pulled out a sheet of paper and read what she had written.

Her words immediately caught Niall's attention, dismissing everything else from his thoughts.

> *The Phoenix sheds her former skin,*
> *Clothes herself to begin again.*
> *Injuries and debts unearned,*
> *Consigned with her hide to fire's burn.*
> *The Dragon loses but one scale,*
> *To keep nigh intact his coat of mail.*
> *But not all things should survive,*
> *And not all burdens help him to thrive.*
> *Can he learn Phoenix's song,*
> *And leave his past where it belongs?*
> *Learn the DreamWalker's dance*
> *And usher in the world's new chance?*

"Rox is the Phoenix," Niall said, his gaze darting over her still form. The metaphor helped him understand better why Rox had made the choices she had.

She had decided to leave her past behind and remake herself and her life in the way she chose. Whatever had hurt her had been expelled from her life, and she had chosen to define herself.

With a family of choice.

In contrast, Niall had been burdened by his own past, carrying the guilt of his role in Phelan's death and letting that guilt shape his choices. Because he hadn't struck Phelan down immediately, Rox had been injured.

And only a shadow dragon with no soul or a *Slayer* who had surrendered his soul could willfully injure a *Pyr*'s destined mate.

Phelan was the first and Chen the second.

There was a point of balance between their two perspectives. The past shaped a person, but the past needed to remain where it belonged. In denying her past, Rox had given it a hidden power. In giving it ascendance, Niall had allowed his to have too much power.

Niall had to help destroy the memory that haunted Rox and now held her captive. He had to help her to take the lesson of that old wound and move forward.

But he had no clue how to do it.

"Does the rest of the verse have meaning for you?" Erik asked, his gaze searching.

Niall nodded. "I know now what I have to do about Phelan," he said, "but I don't know what to do about Rox. How can I help her? How can I heal the wound she has because of my mistake? What's a DreamWalker?"

Before any of the *Pyr* could answer, Zoë moved quickly, proving that she did understand. Erik jumped and Niall was similarly startled when Zoë's small fingers clutched at his. She eyed him intently, her gaze as vivid and unblinking as that of a hawk, and the wisdom of the Wyvern flooded through Niall.

"Air governs dreams," he whispered. "Can I walk in Rox's dreams? Show me how to stop her nightmare, Zoë. Show me how it's done."

The little girl squeezed her eyes tightly shut. Niall saw Erik holding his daughter fast against his leg and he heard the *Pyr* collectively hold their breath.

Zoë took Niall's fingers and shoved them into Rox's wound, breaking the skin open again. Niall was momentarily horrified; then he closed his eyes and followed either his instincts or Zoë's instructions. Her ideas merged with his own so clearly that he couldn't tell where one ended and the other began.

In his mind's eye, Niall saw an obsidian ribbon unfurl from the wound and curl deeper. At Zoë's urging, he followed the ribbon of darkness to its root, uncertain what he would find or what he would do when he found its end.

He did precisely what the Wyvern suggested.

There was too much at stake to do otherwise.

Rox is lost in darkness and desolation. She is cold, colder than she's ever been in her life. In every direction, she can see only barren rock. There is no sign of another being, no light, no stars, no hope.

He has fondled her.

He will be back for more.

She has been called a liar by her own mother.

She has run into the night, desperate to find Suzie.

But Suzie is gone, vanished into the world without leaving a trace. In her determination not to be found, Suzie has left no trail for Rox to follow.

Rox is alone and she is cold. She is frightened; frightened to be awake or asleep. She wanders, knowing she'll never get anywhere and wanting only not to be so alone.

When she sees the yellow gleam of a distant fire, she doesn't believe it is real. She is so cold and hungry that she thinks her mind is playing tricks with her.

She heads for it all the same.

The fire becomes brighter and more real with every step she takes. The sight of it gives her strength; it feeds her confidence; it makes her believe she might survive after all. She sees the bonfire's flames lick the night sky with delight and power. She sees it cast sparks into the darkness with joyous abandon. She sees it shed light and heat in every direction, generous and limitless.

She sees it pierce the darkness. She feels it touch her own skin. She feels it banish fear and hopelessness, and she hurries toward it, moving her numb feet as quickly as she can.

*The flames burn higher and brighter, as if to urge her
on. It's a conflagration, an inferno, a tower of hungry
flames. It crackles and snaps before her; it sizzles and
flares as if in welcome.*

*Or acknowledgment. It becomes brighter and hotter,
turning from deepest orange to brightest yellow.*

*She raises her hands to its heat as she steps into the
circle of light it casts. It's so warm, so inviting, so perfectly comforting, she keeps walking, walking right into
its blaze.*

Fearless.

*Because nothing can be worse than where she has
been.*

*The flames leap around her as if recognizing an old
friend. Rox lets the heat sear her skin, incinerate her fears,
destroy her terror. She lets it turn her memories to ash
and dust, lets the fire cleanse and purify her. She feels the
fire revealing her forgotten strength, kindling new power
within her.*

*Her skin turns red and then gold, changing from flesh
to armor. She is gilded and new, remade and reborn. She
is strong and young, powerful and liberated. She has resources she never realized.*

*And she has a future she only needed the audacity to
claim. It has been hers all along.*

Rox just has to reach out and take it.

As fearlessly as she stepped into the fire.

*The flames fade, their heat and vigor diminishing once
their task is done. They drop on all sides, turning more
orange and red again, burning still but not as ferociously.
When they fall beneath her shoulders, Rox expects to see
Chynna, the "sister" who took her out of the cold.*

She is still afraid to hope for more than that.

*But when she sees the man waiting for her, she knows
she has every reason to be fearless.*

She has a dragon on her side.

Niall stands on the other side of the wall of flames, his

lips pulled into a crooked smile. There is admiration in his blue eyes, admiration and respect and desire. This is honest. This is true. This is the opportunity she's been waiting to find. The firelight touches his features with gold, gilding his face and making glints in his blond hair. He is so handsome and sexy, so thoughtful and intelligent, that Rox's heart stops with awe that he wants her.

There can be no doubt when he offers his hand to her. Rox's heart begins to thunder.

Fearless.

She reaches through the last of the flames and dares to put her hand in his. She dares to trust. She dares to take a chance.

And Niall's hand closes possessively over hers. He pulls her closer, drawing her through the flames, and urges her to his side. Rox goes, knowing she will surrender more than a kiss to him and have no regret.

Without a word, he bends and kisses her with that sweet heat that will always curl her toes. This is the future. This is the promise he brings.

Then he lifts his head. He winks and he turns away from the fire, his hand locked around hers. He guides her away from its blaze. Rox sees the wound on his shoulder and knows he's been hurt where that scale had come off in her hand.

Then Niall shimmers blue. He shifts shape, becoming a magnificent amethyst and platinum dragon. He draws Rox onto his back and smoothly takes flight. The wind lifts her hair and makes her heart sing. The horizon becomes clear as the sun touches its lip. And Niall carries them both away from the desolate shadows that have governed Rox's heart too long.

To their shared future.

To the promise she has dared to claim.

"Her breathing changed," Sloane said, and Niall felt the Apothecary's hand on his shoulder. "That's good."

Niall opened his eyes, the vision fading from his thoughts. He was exhausted and exhilarated, filled with a hope that he had made a difference. Could he be a DreamWalker? Could he do this again, without Zöe's help? He wanted to try.

The wound on Rox's back wasn't inflamed anymore. It had closed neatly and Sloane was easing an unguent over it. Her skin was rosier and her breathing was deeper.

Niall dared to be relieved.

"You're next," Sloane said, and Niall remembered the injury to his own shoulder. "I need to make sure it's clean, so don't give me any back talk."

"Here comes the tough love," Rafferty noted with a smile.

"Well, I've seen the opposite and this is way better," Thorolf said, and Niall guessed he wasn't the only one surprised. "You guys are the closest thing to family I've ever had, and I'm going to prove to you I'm worth the trouble."

At that moment Niall realized that, like Rox and Chynna, he also had a family of choice.

"You already have," Niall said, knowing it was the moment to give the newest recruit some encouragement. "You defended Rox twice, plus you've worked on your beguiling." He addressed the others. "Thorolf committed to giving his training all of his effort, and he's made huge progress in just a day."

The *Pyr* congratulated Thorolf, each in his own way. Erik gave a nod of approval, warmth in his gaze. Rafferty shook his hand and Sloane gave him a thumbs-up. Delaney gave Thorolf a shoulder bump with his fist and Quinn shook his hand.

Thorolf beamed with the attention; then his gaze fell to Rox. "She's going to be okay, isn't she?"

"She'll be fine," Sloane said, exhaling as he smiled. He nodded at Niall. "Now."

"Good." Thorolf's relief was obvious. The other *Pyr* were uncertain, but Niall knew there was no romantic interest between his mate and her most recent project.

"Because you still owe her big-time?" Niall teased, and Thorolf grinned.

"I'm going to pay you all back with interest," he said.

Erik's approval was more than clear. "And in so doing, you will honor the legacy of your father and grandfather." He offered Thorolf his hand. "Welcome to the team."

"I just gotta get me an affinity with an element," Thorolf said.

"I have an idea or two about that," Rafferty said softly, but shook his head at Thorolf's obvious interest. "Heal first, then we'll talk."

"I'm going to kick that Chen's butt," Thorolf said. "It's only fair after he nearly finished me."

Sloane fixed a stern eye on Quinn. "What happened to you?"

"Ambushed by a shadow dragon on descent," Quinn said, his words taut. "But it'll be the last time the shadow dragon made of my brother Michel will trouble me."

"You'll want to look at this," Rafferty said to Quinn, offering him the brand that Chen had used.

Quinn whistled through his teeth. "This is old metal, reforged a hundred times." He turned the brand, considering it warily. "It has a strong charge about it."

"Can you reshape it?" Erik asked.

"I wouldn't risk it," Quinn said thoughtfully. "There is a charm woven into it, likely one that will be released in an unpleasant way if anyone tries to destroy it. Whose was it?"

As Sloane tended Quinn, the *Pyr* reviewed what had happened underground. Quinn continued to examine the brand, humming periodically to it. Garrett reached for it once, but Quinn lifted it away from his son with flashing eyes. When the stories were told, Erik frowned with concern.

"Now that they're loose, when do you think the other shadow dragons will attack?" he asked Delaney.

Delaney shrugged. "It could happen at any time."

"They might want to take advantage of our injuries," Niall said.

Rafferty frowned. "It'll happen when Chen commands them to do it. We must be vigilant."

Quinn and Sara exchanged a glance, and she opened a book. "I dreamed a second prophecy as well," she said.

"Two prophecies?" Delaney teased with a low whistle. "A bit greedy, isn't it?"

Niall waved a hand, intent on what Sara would say. She read the verse with care.

> When the Dragon's Tail turns in the sky,
> When the year of tiger rises high,
> The Phoenix and the Dragon mate,
> Desire does their child create.
> But at this junction the old charm,
> Can be performed to make great harm.
> Elements four in union do conjure,
> The chance to invoke the fifth's measure.
> Master the four, command the thoughts
> of all Gaia's populace.

"Rox was right," Sloane said. "Chen wants Niall to be able to control all four elements in union." He reviewed Rox's summary of the elements Chen already controlled.

"Then he'll be able to command the thoughts of everyone?" Thorolf asked with obvious horror.

"So long as the firestorm burns, he'll want Niall," Sloane said.

"The decision to end the firestorm has to be made

by Rox," Niall said. "She has strong feelings about not having kids."

"You'll be in peril," Rafferty warned.

"Surely you're not telling me to annoy my mate," Niall responded, and the older *Pyr* smiled.

"He's going to want this back so he can gather the shadow dragons again," Quinn said, indicating the brand. "Why don't we invite him to come get it? That way, the battle occurs on our terms."

They quickly agreed upon this course, and Rafferty volunteered to send the invitation through the earth. "I will taunt him. I know he has an affinity for the earth. We shall trap him, with the prospect of both Niall and the brand."

Erik assigned a sentry rotation. Niall, Quinn, and Thorolf were excused for the short term in order to heal and the others were quickly dispatched. Sloane cleaned Niall's shoulder, Niall refusing to leave Rox's side.

Niall got his laptop as Sloane turned his attention to Sloane, knowing he couldn't sleep just yet. He had to finish the checks for his tours and dreaded the number of messages that were probably in his e-mail in-box.

Responding to them was better, however, than counting shadow dragons.

Chapter 17

It was dark when Rox awakened and she was disoriented for a minute. She looked to be back in her own bed, but her dream was vivid in her thoughts. Had the adventures she remembered even happened? Or had she dreamed them all?

Then she saw Niall sitting on the floor beside the window. His right shoulder was bandaged, proof that Rox hadn't imagined their trip into the tunnels. He wore only his jeans and had a fair five o'clock shadow.

The night sky outside the windows told her she'd slept at least a day. It was still pouring, the raindrops beating against the window in a steady drum. The clouds were flat gray and the air was damp.

Niall was as yet unaware that Rox was awake—or at least he was pretending to be oblivious. With his keen senses, Rox would never be sure.

Once again, he had his laptop braced on his knees and his back against the wall, and the light from the screen touched his features with blue. He was intent upon whatever was displayed, typing something, then checking his cell phone, which lay on the floor beside him.

There was an ache in the back of Rox's shoulder, but

the wound from Phelan's talon wasn't as painful as she would have expected. It felt as if it was healing. She was mostly aware of the tingle fed by the firestorm and the silky smoothness of the sheets against her bare skin.

Who had undressed her?

She hoped it had been Niall.

Her heart clenched with the conviction that he must have seen her dragon tattoo, and she wondered what he thought of it.

Were there *Pyr* groupies? It would be awful for Niall to believe she was just a fan girl, when her fascination with him went far deeper than that. She watched him through her lashes, pretending to be asleep, wondering how she'd find out all the things she wanted to know.

"Hey," a man said softly from the doorway. Rox saw the silhouette of another muscular man, although this one was leaner and taller than Niall. His hair was short, but auburn in color. "I talked to all the tour leaders again," he said, keeping his voice low. Presumably he didn't want to disturb her.

Niall nodded and gave him a thumbs-up. "Thanks, Delaney."

"Anything else you need covered?"

"No." Niall shook his head. "Everything's good, for the moment." He shut down his laptop and looked suddenly tired. "I'll solve the office issue later. Get some sleep."

Delaney hesitated, though. "You should hire some staff," he scolded gently, and Rox knew he was a good friend.

She remembered Niall mentioning a Delaney who was Niall's former partner and the *Pyr* who had recovered from the Elixir.

"I know, I know. I just never seem to get around to it." Niall shrugged.

"Well, get to it," Delaney said. "You push yourself too hard."

"Thanks," Niall said; then Delaney quietly closed the door.

Niall leaned his head back against the wall and closed his eyes. Rox thought he might fall asleep on the spot and jumped when he spoke. "Know of any empty live-work space at a good price?" he asked quietly, and she realized he knew she was awake. "Reliable employees who don't care or won't notice that their boss is a dragon sometimes?" Then he smiled.

Rox sat up and wrapped her arms around her knees. She kept the sheet tucked around her so that only her shoulders were bare. "I can ask around."

Rox did know one person who was good with the dragon bit, but she wanted to think about the idea a little more.

She needed to know more about how Niall felt.

Niall yawned. "Me, too, but not now." He rubbed his eyes and looked exhausted. Rox was sure he hadn't slept, that he'd been so busy taking care of his responsibilities that he hadn't worried about himself.

The man needed more than an employee.

Rox deliberately kept her tone light, half afraid of the thought that kept pushing into her mind. "Your trips okay?"

"All good."

"That's good."

He flashed a bright glance her way. "Feel better?"

Rox nodded. "Is that the Delaney who was your partner?"

Niall nodded. "Delaney was always the idea guy and I was the one who made it work. We started the company together; then he sold out to me."

"Why?"

"Well, the short version of the story is that he had his firestorm. You'll like Ginger—they run an organic farm with heritage breeds of cattle in Ohio. She calls him hot-shot and sets him straight." Niall arched a brow without opening his eyes. "He thought he was in heaven, even before Liam arrived."

Rox smiled. "I like her already."

Niall opened his eyes then and looked straight at her. "She's here, you know. They're all here."

"All?"

Niall counted off the *Pyr* and their mates on his fingers. "Erik and Eileen and their daughter, Zoë. Delaney and Ginger and Liam. You know Rafferty and Sloane already, and of course, Thorolf. Quinn and Sara and their son, Garrett. Erik said Donovan and Alex and their son, Nick, will be here by morning. It'll be a full house."

"But they want to stay close." Rox appreciated that the *Pyr* had gathered in defense of their own. They were exactly as she'd always imagined dragons would be—powerful, loyal, and protective of their own. They were also good friends to have.

"The shadow dragons are loose," Niall agreed. "Which means they'll follow Chen's command. Rafferty thinks they'll attack at any time. We're ready." He fixed a bright blue glance on her and changed the subject. "How are you really feeling?"

"A bit sore, but it's not that big a deal." Rox shivered. "I thought he'd buried a piece of ice in me."

"A piece of darkness, more like."

Rox swallowed. "You must have seen my tattoo."

His eyes glittered. "It's gorgeous."

Rox smiled in her relief. "Chynna did it. She took the outline from one of my drawings. She believes that tattoos can be talismans, that they can protect someone from harm."

"So she gave you a dragon to guard your back."

Rox nodded, liking that he understood. "His eyes are always open."

"Vigilant dragons are the best kind," Niall murmured. "And I have to admire one who defends the prize."

Rox had to look away from the intensity of his gaze.

"It's only half done. It's supposed to be a dragon and a phoenix, but I haven't drawn the phoenix part yet."

"Your tattoos all mean something important to you, as if the story of your life is on your skin. Why a dragon and a phoenix?"

Rox knew she shouldn't have been surprised by his perceptiveness. "They're a sign of good luck. In Chinese mythology, the phoenix is associated with benevolence and the dragon with material success. When seen together, they indicate a period of peace and prosperity." She shrugged and smiled. "I drew the dragon first, but it was on my skin before I realized I hadn't planned ahead."

"How so?"

"They're supposed to be looking into each other's eyes, but my dragon is looking over my shoulder, up into the sky. That's exactly how I drew it, but it was too late when I saw my mistake. Other than putting the phoenix on my chest, which I don't really want to do, I'm not sure how to solve it."

Niall looked down at his hands and Rox wondered what he was thinking. "Maybe it wasn't a mistake," he suggested, his voice low.

"What do you mean?"

"You have a dragon drawn on your back for protection," he said quietly. "Ever thought about upgrading to the real thing?"

Niall's softly uttered question hung between them as Rox stared at him. It was true that Niall was more effective than the tattoo had been. Her mouth went dry, her heart started to pound, and she found it impossible to look away from his fearless gaze.

She wondered whether it was crazy to ask him about her dream. He had a knowing look about him, though, and he seemed to be almost smiling.

As if they shared a secret.

Rox thought she might know what it was.

"You came into my dream."

He nodded; then his smile broadened. "Yes, I did."

"How did you do that?"

"I'm not sure, exactly." He frowned, as if he had been surprised, as well. "Erik said our affinities can change during the firestorm and gain in power. He said we sometimes can add to our abilities, and air is associated with dreams."

Rox liked that he tried to explain the details of his nature to her. It made her feel that he respected her intelligence, and also as if they were working together. "I was having my nightmare."

"Is it one you always have?"

Rox nodded, not wanting to think about it lest she invite it back again.

Niall spoke quickly, as if he also wanted to keep her thoughts from straying into dark memories. "Sloane said the darkness found a resonance within you, that it was feeding a shadow that haunted you. He said the firestorm might be able to light the darkness, but I didn't know what to do. Sara brought a prophecy about us, about my having the chance to become the DreamWalker." Niall's gaze danced across the floor as he sought an explanation. "I wanted to help you but didn't know how, not until Zoë grabbed my hand. Then it was easy."

"Erik's daughter?"

Niall nodded. "She's just a toddler, but she's supposed to be the new Wyvern. She seems to already have an ability to send dreams, which the old Wyvern did, too. And somehow she guided me into your dreams. When she held my hand, I just knew how to do it."

"Do you think you can do it again?"

"I'm hoping so." Niall's enthusiasm was clear, and Rox understood that he loved to learn new skills. "I need to learn how to control it, but it would be an amazing ability to have."

Rox smiled, her confidence complete. "You'll do it.

You'll keep practicing until you completely nail it." She already knew that much about Niall—he didn't give up.

He smiled at her and she felt the welcome warmth of the firestorm as it burned a little brighter. "I will. Sounds from the prophecy as if I'll need your help."

They stared at each other across the room, a pale glow illuminating the space between them. Rox felt the flames become a little stronger as her awareness of Niall grew.

She eyed the muscled strength of him, but it was more than his appearance that she found so attractive. She admired his principles, his strong sense of right and wrong. She respected his ability to think beyond himself and his own needs, to worry about others such as Thorolf and even the world at large. She appreciated how he took responsibility for both his employees and his customers, and she believed that anything Niall pledged to do would happen.

Rox thought about how he had repeatedly defended her, how he had helped her, how he was pretty much her every fantasy come true. She thought about her dream, about her conviction that she was going to die, about her realization that she had the chance to have what she wanted.

If only she had the guts to reach for it.

It was risky, caring for other people, but the reward, if that love was wisely placed, more than made up the deficit.

And if you didn't take the chance, if you didn't try, you could end up with nothing at all.

Rox had cared for a lot of people at arm's length, between her projects and some superficial romances, but it had been a long long time since she'd truly let anyone into her heart.

No one really since Suzie.

She decided it was time to change that.

"I could have died," she said quietly.

Niall caught his breath, nodded, looked away, and swallowed.

He didn't lie to her.

He eyed the window, and she knew he was thinking about Phelan. Rox didn't want him to think about his brother, about the darkness, about any of that.

"I could have died without knowing what it was like to make love to a *Pyr*," she said, her words husky.

Niall stared at her again, his eyes glowing. He seemed taut, as though holding his breath, anticipating what she was going to say but not wanting to jinx it. Rox understood how it was to want something so badly that you were afraid to lose it.

She understood that she felt that way about Niall.

And that meant she had to take a chance.

Rox sat up, pushing away the sheet. The firestorm's heat danced over her, painting her body with its golden touch, making her feel alive and invigorated. She swung her legs over the side of the bed, welcoming its promise. Niall's gaze never swerved from hers. Rox braced her hands on the side of the mattress and spoke with care.

She didn't want to jinx this, either.

"I think the world has enough babies," she whispered. "But I agree with Erik. There aren't nearly enough *Pyr*." She swallowed. "Let's satisfy the firestorm and make another one."

Niall didn't move. "Are you sure?"

"Yes." Rox smiled at him, completely confident in her choice. "I want to know what it's like."

"I want more than that from a partnership."

"I know." Rox dared to hold his gaze. "I think we can work it out." She wrinkled her nose. "Even if you do have this old-fashioned idea of marriage."

"It's not about a piece of paper, Rox."

"No." Rox held his gaze. "It's about the commitment. I'm good with that part. Finally."

Niall moved so quickly that Rox never saw him get

up. He was sitting on the floor, poised to spring; then
he was in front of her, dropping to one knee. He hesitated, his gaze sweeping over her and lingering on her
shoulder.

Rox's heart squeezed that he was so protective of her.
How could she have ever had any doubts? "I'm not the
only one who took a hit," she said. "I'm not the only one
who could have lost it all." She reached for him and it
was all the encouragement he needed.

Rox saw the flash of Niall's smile; then he locked his
hands around her waist and caught her against him. When
her breasts touched his chest, the firestorm crackled and
burned, looking to Rox like celebratory fireworks.

She was feeling pretty celebratory herself. Niall
smiled up at her as the sparks leapt with dazzling intensity. Just that contact kindled more heat, coaxing the
firestorm to a bonfire that Rox didn't want to abandon.
She twined her hands around his neck, letting her fingers slide through his hair, and touched her lips to his.

The firestorm flared bright, filling the room with orange light. Niall seduced Rox with another one of those
slow, potent kisses that dissolved her bones. Rox locked
her arms around his neck, closed her eyes, and surrendered to the moment. She kicked her feet when he deepened his kiss, loving the way his fingers spread across her
back, exploring her even as he held her close.

Rox was burning, simmering, sizzling, from her lips
to her toes.

When Niall pulled back and looked down at her, she
wanted to complain. But he was intent, his gaze fixed
upon her, his body tense. "I love you, Rox," he said, no
doubt in his tone. Her heart skipped. "I don't want just a
night. I want a lifetime."

The words put a quiver in Rox's belly. She'd ducked
permanence for a long time, or at least she'd thought she
had. But Niall was right. She committed long term to
causes and real estate, to her art, and to her career.

She could commit to him.

"Me, too," she admitted, and even saying the words made her smile. "I think I loved you even before I knew you."

"Now you sound flaky," Niall teased as he grinned back at her.

Rox touched her lips to his, feeling a new urgency in their kisses. They unleashed a power with their mutual surrender and the flames burned higher in response.

They tasted and nibbled and explored each other, the flames raging hotter with every caress. Rox framed Niall's face in her hands, her kiss more demanding than it had ever been. She wanted all of him. She wanted every bit of his lore and his body and his thoughts; she wanted it today and she wanted it through forever.

She felt the skip of his heart, felt the thunder of his pulse. She felt the heat building beneath his skin and the trickle of perspiration on her own back. She wound herself around his strength, wanting only more contact and more firestorm, more skin pressed together.

Niall broke their kiss with an obvious effort. "Hold on." He squeezed her buttocks, then dropped her on the bed. His eyes glittered like sapphires and his body was pumped. Rox admired the view as he opened the bedroom door and glared into her living room.

Then she recalled that she had an apartment full of *Pyr*.

With keen hearing.

She blushed, realizing there could be no secrets or privacy in such company.

"Don't you all have somewhere to be?" Niall demanded. There was a flutter of activity, a rumble of oldspeak, and the murmur of arrangements being made. Niall shut the door against their discussions and pivoted to face Rox as he leaned his back against the door.

He smiled.

She smiled.

"Now, where were we?" he murmured in a low voice.

Rox pointed at the mattress beside her. "You were right here, and I was just about to rip your jeans off."

"Let's keep things simple." Niall unfastened his jeans and kicked them aside, strolling nude across the floor to Rox's side. He was magnificent.

Instead of sitting on the bed, he bent and caught her nape in his hand, kissing her so thoroughly that she nearly forgot her own name.

Rox couldn't imagine that it was nearly as important as this.

In a way, Niall wanted to savor the firestorm and make its magic last. In another way, it fired his blood and made him burn with such desire that he couldn't resist it.

Or Rox.

Even better, he knew that what was developing between the two of them was going to long outlast the firestorm's sparks.

Niall tried to take it slow for the sake of Rox's injuries, but Rox showed no such inclination. Her passionate response—as always—kindled an answering desire within him. He couldn't resist her. He couldn't resist the firestorm. And he knew he would always feel this way about Rox.

The firestorm had been exactly right about his mate.

He joined her on the bed, their kiss never breaking. Her hands ran over his shoulders and down his arms, over his chest and down his ribs. He liked her curiosity about his body; he found her bold touch exciting and enticing. A line of sparks followed her hands, lit by her touch and leaving Niall simmering. The room was cast in the golden glow of firelight, the night pressed back into the sky beyond the windows.

Niall slid his hands over her, in turn, awed by the softness of her skin. He cupped her breast in his hand, easing his thumb over the taut peak. Rox gasped and he broke their kiss, bending to take her nipple in his mouth. He flicked his tongue against her, enjoying the way she writhed and gasped beneath his caress.

He let the weight of his hand slide lower, into the indent of her waist, down over her hip. She rolled her hips and purred, her fingers knotting in his hair to pull him back for another kiss.

Niall kissed her deeply, then eased his fingers between her thighs. Rox gasped when he touched her, then spread her thighs in silent invitation. Niall moved his fingers, slowly at first, then more quickly as Rox became more aroused. She moaned and her eyes sparkled as she lifted her hips against his hand. "You're teasing me," she complained.

Niall grinned. "Just wait," he said, then moved quickly down her length. He caught Rox's hips in his hands, holding her captive, then flicked his tongue against her heat.

Rox arched her back and gasped with pleasure. Niall teased her and touched her, using the firestorm's sparks to drive her wild. He held her fast, liking that she trusted him, that she wasn't afraid to show her response.

It was honest.

It was real.

He intended to make it last forever.

He felt the tension rise within her body and heard the thunder of her pulse. He aroused her with deliberate strokes, coaxing her pleasure to build until she was just shy of her release. Then he changed his gesture and rebuilt her desire all over again.

Rox moaned in complaint, but she clutched at his shoulders, demanding more and more. Niall was only too happy to comply. He felt as if they worked together for mutual satisfaction, as if each felt the other's passion as keenly as his and her own. He felt as if his body were on fire, his veins filled with molten lava, his heart pounding and fit to burst.

When Rox gasped, Niall felt as if the pleasure were his own. When Rox caught her breath, Niall felt short of air. She was slick and hot, writhing beneath his caress, sparks shooting from her fingertips. She locked her legs around his shoulders and Niall exhaled on her wet heat. Rox trembled and shook, and he flicked his tongue across her quivering softness. She gasped and he kissed her fully, lifting her from the bed as she moaned in her release. He held her tightly, giving her more pleasure when she would have moved away, coaxing her release to go on and on and on.

They fell onto the bed together; then Rox rolled over abruptly. Niall saw only the mischievous twinkle of her eyes before she pushed him to his back, her hand flat on his chest. She straddled him and took his erection into her mouth, the flick of her tongue and the answering volley of sparks making Niall clench the sheets in his fists.

She was every bit as relentless as he had been. She tormented him with her touch, first slow, then fast, first firm, then gentle. She compelled him to become harder and stronger than he had ever been, for his thoughts to be consumed with Rox, for his only imperative to be her possession. He felt his own heartbeat match time to hers; then his breath came in the same quick spurts. He could feel the heat rising between the two of them, making the boundaries of skin less relevant than they had been, blurring the division between the two of them.

When he couldn't stand it any longer, Niall seized her by the waist and turned her to face him. She stared at him in wonder as he eased himself into her tight heat, as the firestorm settled to a brilliant white light. That radiance surrounded them, blurring out all of the world except Rox and her magnificent eyes.

She smiled and Niall felt as if the world were his.

Rox pulled him deeper into her sweetness with every stroke. She locked her hands with his and rode him, slowly at first and then with greater speed. Her hips rocked against his, her gaze bored into his own, her cheeks flushed. They breathed as one. Their hearts pulsed as one. They became one. The firestorm burned brighter and hotter, becoming a conflagration that would change their worlds forever.

This was Niall's destiny.

Rox was Niall's destiny.

And he would willingly walk a thousand nightmares to keep her by his side.

He eased his fingers between them, coaxing her pleasure again. Rox moaned, rubbing herself against him as each stroke took them both closer to satisfaction. He looked into the sparkling blue of her eyes and knew that he was precisely where he needed to be. She whispered his name, and her eyes widened as the firestorm grew to greater heat, blinding in its brilliant intensity. The firestorm fused them together, its dancing flames making it unclear where one ended and the other began.

One.

Forever.

When Rox cried out and melted against him, the heat surged through Niall. It seared his skin, scorched his veins, and purified everything within him. It burned the past to ashes and tempered him into something new, someone stronger and better than he had ever been.

Niall was ready. He captured Rox's lips with his for a triumphant kiss as the firestorm rocketed through his body and claimed him completely.

Rox dozed beside Niall, unable to keep from running her hands over his body. There were no sparks lighting where she touched him, which had surprised her for a moment.

Then the reality of the satisfied firestorm made Rox smile. She felt warm and knew things were far from over between her and this *Pyr*.

She was okay with that.

The firestorm had changed her perspective. Its blaze had tempted her to reexamine her assumptions, to abandon those that weren't serving her well, to sear her wounds and move into a brighter future.

Or had it been Niall who had changed all of that? Rox didn't much care. She was happy. She was serene and sated, and it was a wonderful sensation.

She was, in fact, in love.

Rox's exploring fingertips found the bandage on Niall's shoulder and she touched it carefully. She had just recalled the scale coming off in her hands and the way Phelan had targeted the spot, when she realized Niall was watching her.

"You lost a scale," she whispered, and he nodded, proof that he had been aware of its coming away. "Does that happen a lot?"

"No." Niall got out of bed and tugged on his jeans again.

Rox had the sense that he was avoiding her gaze. Was the missing scale important? Or did it just worry him to be vulnerable? Rox would guess it was the second option. "Well, that's a good thing. Otherwise you'd have lots of holes in your armor."

Niall's expression was inscrutable, and Rox spoke quickly as she made her offer. "I was thinking about Chynna's conviction that tattoos are protective talismans." Getting out of bed herself, she pulled on a pair of jeans and a T-shirt before she dared to look at him again. "I was wondering whether you'd like me to give you a tattoo over that spot. It's not as good as having a real dragon at your back, but I could color it to match your scales so the loss was less evident."

Niall's eyes lit with pleasure and Rox knew she'd said something right. "That's a great idea."

"Even though you don't much like tattoos."

"I'm thinking I had a lack of information." His smile

broadened, the glint in his eyes becoming appreciative. "And maybe a failure to appreciate the finer details."

Rox smiled back at him, basking in the glow of his attention. Niall sobered. "Tell me about your nightmare," he said softly.

"I can't." Rox tried to turn away, but Niall caught at her hand.

"Then tell me about your sisters," he urged, touching her tattoo.

Rox exhaled, then nodded. "Okay, that's easier." She pushed up the sleeve of her shirt and touched the tattoo. "That's Chynna, my sister of choice. And that's Suzie, my sister of blood."

"What happened to her?"

"I don't know." Rox saw his concern. "It's not a memorial tattoo—at least I hope it isn't. She ran away from home when she was sixteen and I was fifteen."

"Is that why you cried in the dark?"

Rox grimaced, knowing he deserved the whole story. "No." She took a deep breath and to her surprise, it was easier to share the details once she'd started. He'd seen her nightmare, after all, and the first step to building their future was honesty about her past.

Rox sat on the edge of the bed and Niall sat beside her. "Our father died when I was six and our mom raised us alone. Then she remarried, although we never liked our stepfather. She was sure we were just being stubborn or that we'd come around in time."

Niall took her hand in his. "But?"

"But there was something slimy about him. She couldn't see it, I guess, because he always laid on the charm in her presence. We saw it." Rox sighed and frowned. "It only took him a couple of months after he moved in to go after Suzie. She said he touched her in the night. Mom called her a liar and they had a huge fight." She smiled at a very intent Niall. "You might not believe this, but Suzie was the outspoken one."

"Imagine that." Niall pulled Rox close. She put her head on his shoulder, tracing patterns on the back of his hand as she talked. It was cozy to be with him like this, listening to the rain on the window. It felt safe.

"Suzie was also the pretty one."

"She looks pretty in your tattoo."

"It's a good likeness."

His arm tightened around her shoulders. "But don't be so quick to sell yourself short."

Rox smiled against his skin, liking how he pressed a kiss into her hair. "I worked on the drawing for a long time to get it just right. Neo does great portraits, but, of course, he'd never met Suzie, and I didn't have a photograph."

Niall waited, giving Rox the time she needed. She knew he understood this wasn't an easy story to share. "Anyway, Suzie told Mom and said our stepfather thought he was getting two for one. She was a bit bold about it."

"Imagine," Niall mused.

"Mom slapped Suzie and grounded her. It was the first time either one of us had ever been struck, for anything, and we couldn't believe it. I can still hear the crack of her hand hitting Suzie's cheek." Rox shivered. "Then the silence afterward. I'm not sure my mother even believed she had done it." A lump rose in Rox's throat.

"Unhappy household," Niall mused when Rox said nothing.

"Not until he came. Not until he tried to take too much."

"I understand," Niall said softly.

"Suzie said if he did it again, she'd be gone." Rox fell silent.

"He did," Niall guessed.

"It only took two days." Rox's throat was tight. She turned the silver ring on her left hand without intending to do so.

"What is that, anyway?" Niall asked, taking her hand in his. He smiled at Rox. "Everything is filled with meaning for you. What about this ring?"

"It's a promise ring, from Suzie." There was no evading Niall's inquisitive gaze. "We bought the same ones. We promised to look after each other forever." Rox felt her tears rise.

But Suzie had left.

She couldn't even say it out loud.

Niall caught her close. "The nightmare is over, Rox. You've left the past where it belongs."

She looked into his eyes and was warmed by his conviction. She saw that he had guessed what had happened next, why she had cried in his dream, but she had to tell him.

"Turns out our stepfather thought he was getting three for one," Rox said hoarsely. "My mom called me a liar. I left, too. I thought I could find Suzie, but I guess she didn't want to be found."

"She thought the only ones coming after her would be your mother and stepfather," Niall said, "so she made sure they wouldn't find her. She must have believed you would be safe."

"She was the pretty one," Rox said with a smile.

"I told you—don't sell yourself short," Niall murmured, running a fingertip down her cheek. "And don't be fooled by what's on the surface."

Rox leaned her forehead on his chest, liking his patience and his strength. "I never found her again. I never saw her again. But I was on the street. I was young and I was naïve. I had almost no money and I was scared."

"You were only fifteen," Niall said. "Kids shouldn't live on the street then—or ever."

"Kids shouldn't be called liars by their own mothers," Rox retorted, knowing that old pain put the edge on her words.

"Did you ever go back home?"

"The only home I have is the one I've made for myself. I made myself a new life, one without those people." She tipped her head back and held his gaze, knowing he would understand her anger. "Ink is stronger than blood."

Niall nodded. "I'm sorry, Rox. I'm sorry that no one believed you or defended you."

"I had Chynna. She found me. I think at first she just felt sorry for me, but once she saw me draw, she took me as her apprentice. She talks tough, but she's a good person."

"She takes care of her own."

Rox nodded. "She gave me a chance, the only one I needed."

"She became your family of choice," Niall said, proving that he understood completely. He looked down at Rox, his smile warming his eyes. "I'm thinking it's time you met my family of choice." He winced. "Seeing as they've probably already emptied your fridge. Isn't that just like family?"

Rox appreciated that he tried to make her smile.

"Just like," she agreed.

Niall kissed her, then took her hand as he headed for the door. He reached for the bedroom doorknob, turning back to say something to Rox, and she saw his eyes widen.

A second later the window broke. The glass shattered and fell on the floor, a rock rolling across Rox's hardwood floors. The broken glass glinted dangerously as the rain and a chilly wind poured into the room. The wind smelled of death and mold, and the shadow dragon hovering outside the window had eyes that were vacant and dark. He hissed, his shadowed form blocking all view of the night.

Niall roared and shifted shape, thrusting Rox behind him. "Stay behind the smoke barrier," he instructed.

He then leapt at the shadow dragon, breathing dragonfire as he jumped through the window. The shadow dragon raged and snatched at Niall. His tail snaked around Niall's as the two of them tumbled through the window into the night, locked in a fatal embrace.

And disappeared from sight.

Rox raced to the window and looked over the sill. She saw Niall's gleaming scales and the red scab of his wound, then glimpsed the furious beating of his wings. She saw the shadow dragon lose one leg, the appendage falling to the ground as another *Pyr* burned it to cinders.

The shadow dragon soared skyward and Niall gave pursuit. Another *Pyr*, a gleaming dragon with ebony and pewter scales, raced after the pair. He and Niall latched onto the shadow dragon with savage force, but Rox didn't see the progress of the fight.

Because Phelan was standing on the sill of her window, leaning against the building, out of view from the room. He was in human form, in his black leather jacket again. One sleeve hung limply, but he terrified Rox even so.

"Hey, babe," he murmured. "Just thought I'd stop by to help."

He took a step toward her and the stone sill crumbled beneath his heel. He wavered, on the cusp of losing his balance, and Rox decided to help him fall to his death.

Rox leaned out to give him a shove. She saw his eyes flash with triumph, and realized too late that he'd tricked her. Phelan shifted shape, snatched her, and soared into the night with Rox captive in his grasp.

She screamed and kicked, even though she knew it wouldn't make any difference.

Chapter 18

Erik was sitting in the living room of Rox's apartment, listening to the sounds of the night. He heard the steady drum of the rain, distant sirens, passing cars. He heard the slow rhythm of Thorolf's breathing and that of the mates and children, the resonant ping of the dragonsmoke perimeter mark.

It wasn't an effective defense against *Slayers* who had drunk the Elixir, but it was perfectly good against shadow dragons.

As far as Erik knew.

Erik was aware of the quick watchfulness of both Delaney and Sloane on the roof. He sensed Rafferty in the basement of the building, deep in communion with the earth. He was aware of Quinn at the other end of the apartment, steadily breathing smoke.

He smiled when he heard Niall and Rox consummate the firestorm, and he lifted one hand, confirming that the spark had dimmed. Its glow would linger but by morning would have dissipated.

And another *Pyr* warrior would be in the making.

Erik felt a shimmer then, a nudge at the perimeter

of his senses. A glimmer of foresight, it warned him of impending trouble.

Erik straightened, his senses at full alert. He felt his body hover on the cusp of change and sought to identify the threat.

He went to the window, following his instincts. Trouble approached. He opened the glass door and stepped onto the balcony, his body quivering. He looked over the railing just in time to see a dozen shadow dragons explode from the sewer grates. They leapt skyward, dark talons extended, and targeted Rox's apartment.

Drawn by the last flame of the firestorm.

Erik roused the others with a cry in old-speak. He shifted shape, then leapt into the sky to intercept their attack. Quinn was right behind him, but the pair separated paths high above the building.

Donovan caught Quinn's scent before he saw the sapphire and steel splendor of his friend. He was several thousand feet above Quinn, cutting through the dense cloud cover over Manhattan. Alex shivered as they passed through the last cloud and into the rain.

"Next firestorm on a beach," she muttered. "I'm calling it now."

Donovan had no time to reply. He saw a shadow dragon draw Quinn to one side with a feint. Five more targeted Quinn once he was separated from Erik, leaping suddenly upon the Smith. The shadow dragons surrounded Quinn as he raged dragonfire at them.

"Hold on." Donovan heard Alex catch her breath but knew there was nothing he could do. He had to hold on to her and Nick as he fought, as there was no other *Pyr* to defend them.

Alex obviously realized the same thing, because she swore softly and caught Nick closer. To Donovan's relief, he saw the emerald and copper form of his brother

Delaney emerge from the building below to join the battle.

Donovan descended like a bolt of lightning. Knowing he was headed to a fight, he had worn the gloves that Quinn had made for him, the gloves that were embedded with knives that replaced his talons. He could use only one while he held his family close, but Donovan made it count.

He hauled a shadow dragon from Quinn's back, then slashed those talons across the shadow dragon's eyes. There was no blood and no scream of pain. The shadow dragon's talons left long wounds in Quinn's back, but Quinn appeared to be just as oblivious to pain.

Fury could do that.

Donovan cast the villain aside and Quinn raged dragonfire at him, the flames impressive in their volume and brilliance. Quinn burned the attacker's claws to ashes, then struck him with his tail. Alex buried her face against Donovan's chest.

Quinn's assault made the shadow dragon falter, but he immediately came after Quinn again. Before he could reach Quinn, Quinn burned the wings of a second shadow dragon with his torrent of dragonfire, compelling that one to fight from the roof.

It was a great plan. Donovan caught another and sliced the wings from his back, casting him to the roof, as well.

The first shadow dragon attacked Quinn from the back, showing the persistence typical of shadow dragons. Delaney snatched him and carried him high into the sky. Another shadow dragon gave chase. Donovan sliced his captive to ribbons, the presence of his mate and child making him more savage and decisive than ever. He then turned on the pursuer, and thrashed him easily. Quinn incinerated the pieces, the pair of them working ruthlessly together as they had before.

Delaney had pounced on another shadow dragon

from behind, dragging him away from the others. He decapitated the shadow dragon with impressive speed, making Donovan proud. He burned the pieces as they fell and the smell of charred flesh was carried on the wind.

Donovan began to chant as he descended to the roof again and he felt the elements muster. They were somewhat reluctant to answer his call, being under duress as they were. He sang more vehemently.

The two wingless shadow dragons lifted their talons in the old fighting posture, their eyes glinting hungrily as they watched Quinn and Donovan approach.

Delaney jumped one shadow dragon from behind, slitting his throat, then cutting him apart with grim determination. The last one lunged for the lip of the roof, intending to jump. Quinn leapt after him, snatching him up high.

He cut the tendons of the shadow dragon's legs, then tossed him into the air. Donovan slashed at his arms, cutting them loose at the socket. Delaney took flight and breathed dragonfire on the pieces. Quinn cut the shadow dragon's tail, and it dropped heavily. The shadow dragon spun in frustration, unable to battle all three of them at once. It would have fled, given the choice, but had none.

Donovan caught it again and tossed it high, letting Delaney take a slash at it. Its back legs fell and Quinn burned them completely. Quinn decapitated the shadow dragon, all three of them turning their dragonfire on the falling pieces. The air was full of ash, the rain driving it down to the pavement. Donovan could smell death and destruction, and he hated that Alex and Nick had been exposed to such violence.

The three *Pyr* had a chance to catch their collective breath and be proud of a job well-done before there was a cry of anguish from the apartment below.

"Zoë!" Eileen screamed, and they raced into the thicket of shadow dragons to help.

*   *   *

The shadow dragons clustered against the windows of Rox's apartment, blocking the view and filling the apartment with a malicious darkness. Their fetid scent carried through the broken window in the bedroom, making Eileen's bile rise. She held Zoë close and wished Erik would hurry back.

Sloane and Thorolf had immediately shifted to their dragon forms and nearly filled the living room. Sloane was tourmaline and gold; Thorolf was moonstone and silver. Eileen was well aware that Thorolf was at less than his best, given the injury he'd sustained.

She backed toward the interior wall. Eileen, Sara, and Ginger stood together, Liam in Ginger's arms. Garrett hung on to Sara's knees. The children were wide-awake, their *Pyr* blood ensuring that they sensed the threat. Zoë's gaze was bright, her fingers clutching at the air. Eileen held her tightly.

The brand was on the floor of the living room, before the women, where Quinn had left it. Eileen wished she'd thought to snatch it up when she retreated.

The shadow dragons hovered beyond the balcony, a horde of jeering and salivating predators. They called to the women and taunted the *Pyr*, beckoning with their yellowed talons. Their gazes flicked repeatedly to the brand.

"As if they weren't hard to resist," Ginger scoffed.

"They can't come through the smoke," Sloane said softly. "Don't be tricked. Don't go close enough to be snatched."

"Bad enough that Rox did it," Thorolf said softly.

The women caught their breath in unison and Eileen was glad for once not to have the *Pyr*'s keen hearing. Now she worried about Rox and Niall, and she understood why Erik had left so quickly. He would defend the firestorm at all costs, for the good of the *Pyr*.

This only meant that she worried about him, too.

Didn't it figure that the crafty *Slayer* split them up?

"Just be calm," Sloane said. "The others will be back and we'll take them from both sides."

"Roughly two dozen left, by my calculations"—Ginger winced—"which are admittedly incomplete."

"Looks like they're all here," Thorolf muttered.

A silhouetted dragon who seemed larger than the others joined the ranks suddenly, shoving his fellows aside. They ceded to him, these blank-eyed monsters who were usually devoid of manners, and Eileen wondered why. He landed on the balcony but didn't twitch at the dragonsmoke that must have touched him.

"Chen!" Thorolf said. "But with a new tail."

The new arrival smiled but didn't respond to this comment. He was lacquer red with gold talons. His tail did look odd to Eileen, as if the scales weren't of the same vintage as the other scales on his body. It appeared to be softer, brighter, a little less tough.

"What do you mean?" Eileen said to Thorolf, just as a shadow dragon turned on him.

"Niall hacked his off," Thorolf said.

Chen's smile broadened. "An unfortunate incident," he said.

"Newts can grow new ones," Ginger murmured. "But not that fast."

If Chen had extra powers, then Eileen was even more worried about his arrival. She held her daughter more closely.

Chen shifted shape, becoming a young Asian man in jeans and leather.

With attitude.

"So this is Chen," Eileen whispered.

"Back to get his brand, right on schedule," Ginger agreed.

"But he's too late," Sloane said. "The firestorm is sated."

Chen smiled at them all through the glass. Then he let his right index finger change to a gold talon.

So he'd drunk the Elixir and learned a few tricks from Magnus.

That wasn't exactly good news.

He cut the smoke, stepping through it with terrifying ease. He cut the hole wider, then opened the balcony door.

"Good evening," he said, the resonance of his voice echoing throughout the apartment. "I believe you have something of mine."

Then he whistled, a sharp piercing note that made Eileen want to cover her ears. The shadow dragons surged through the breach in the dragonsmoke. They couldn't cut it themselves, but they could take advantage of a gap.

"Fetch it!" he commanded, and they leapt into the apartment.

Sloane and Thorolf threw themselves against the onslaught, taking on as many shadow dragons as they could.

"They're so outnumbered," Ginger whispered.

"Aren't they?" Chen agreed amiably, then stepped over the threshold and shifted shape again. He became a woman in a tight embroidered dress, and the women gasped in unison.

"Two human forms?" Eileen asked.

"A sign of superiority," Chen answered.

One shadow dragon broke free of Thorolf and Sloane. He seized the brand and presented it to Chen with a formal bow. Chen took it, his satisfaction undisguised. He pulled a small tin from his pocket and gave the shadow dragon a pinch of some kind of powder. The shadow dragon shuddered and brightened, turning a look of avarice on the women before it attacked Sloane again.

It seemed to be more energetic and anticipated Sloane's moves better.

Eileen wondered what the powder was.

"Pulverized dragon bone," Chen said, as if he could

hear her thoughts. "So very useful in animating shadow dragons. A little initiative does wonders for their effectiveness." He twirled the brand in his hand and cast a glance toward the sky.

"And that lets you control the shadow dragons?" Eileen asked. "Having put your mark upon them?"

"It's so much more than a mark," Chen said. "But the simple answer is yes." He sauntered closer, shifting shape to an old man en route. *Three* forms? His voice became raspy then, and weaker. "The interesting question is whether they must truly be shadow dragons to become my thralls when marked. I'm looking forward to finding out tonight."

"No!" Sara said. "You're not going to mark any of the *Pyr*."

"And what do you intend to do about it?" Chen asked coldly.

"You've already failed," Eileen said. "We heard your verse, but the firestorm is satisfied. You missed your opportunity to gain a mastery of spirit."

Chen's eyes flashed with anger. "But it's never too late for vengeance, is it? I will enslave all of the *Pyr*, make them all my minions, and await the next opportunity." He held the brand high. "I have the only tool I need."

"But how will you control us?" Ginger demanded.

Chen smiled. "Easily." He shifted shape to dragon form, becoming a massive crimson dragon once more. He reared back and heated the brand so that it turned red, then orange, then yellow. "I'll begin with your children." He pointed at Garrett. "That one first. The son of the Smith."

"No!" Sara cried, catching up her son.

"Then that one," Chen said, pointing to Zöe. He paused. "Wait. A *girl*, the daughter of a *Pyr*." He smiled, showing a fearsome array of sharp teeth, and breathed dragonfire on his brand. "How *special*."

Eileen took a step back, her mouth going dry. The moment she had dreaded since the day she'd known she would have a daughter had finally arrived.

Where was Erik?

Chen's brand glowed white. "No, I'll have the new Wyvern first of all," he said, and stepped closer.

Eileen, who was not inclined to scream, screamed her baby's name with all her might. "Zoë!"

It was the only thing Erik needed to hear to know their situation.

Eileen just hoped he arrived in time.

Niall and Erik pursued the shadow dragon into the night. Another attacked them from the right and a third from the left. Erik and Niall worked together with savage force. They tore limbs and shredded wings. They chopped the shadow dragons up while they were still alive, and incinerated the pieces, creating a constant flurry of ash.

Like black snow.

Within moments, the three shadow dragons were destroyed, but Erik still had a sense of dread.

"That was too easy," Niall said grimly.

"Agreed." Erik scanned the horizon. It was difficult to see clearly, given the incessant rain and the jagged roofs of the buildings.

"It felt like a feint," Niall murmured.

Erik's heart stopped when he saw a shadow dragon flying in the opposite direction.

Quickly.

With a struggling woman in his grip.

"Phelan!" Niall muttered.

That must mean the woman was Rox.

Before Erik could speak, Eileen screamed, her single word sending a jolt through him.

"*The Wyvern!*" Niall said in old-speak, his horror clear.

Erik wanted to support Niall's firestorm but knew he

had to defend Eileen and Zoë. He spun, glancing back at a determined Niall. *"May the Great Wyvern be at your back."*

"And yours!" Niall said, then turned his gaze upon his brother. *"He's all mine."*

Erik didn't wait an instant longer. He dove over the lip of the building and shot toward Rox's apartment. He flew over the balcony and cut through the ranks of shadow dragons blocking his access, leaving shadowy limbs scattered on all sides.

He froze when he found Eileen backed into a corner, a strangely still Zoë in her grasp. The toddler was watching the *Slayer* between them, a mysterious smile reminiscent of Sophie's on her lips.

Chen's red dragon form kept Erik from his mate.

"Checkmate," Chen said with a sidelong glance. He held the tiger brand and he clearly had already heated it.

"He's going to brand the children," Eileen said quickly, her haste revealing her terror. "He's going to enslave them to his will."

"I'll start with the Wyvern," Chen said. "Unless you'd care to negotiate."

Erik settled himself slowly on the floor, taking his time as he gathered his thoughts. He couldn't make sense of his daughter's smile; he couldn't figure out what detail she knew that Chen didn't.

At least what detail could save her.

"Venice."

The single word in old-speak resonated in Erik's thoughts, echoed as if spoken by a small girl. Chen started, because he clearly had also heard the old-speak, but his confusion was clear. He looked between father and daughter with suspicion.

Erik, in contrast, knew exactly what Zoë meant. She was reminding him of Gaspar, or more accurately, of Gaspar's grandson, Lorenzo.

That told Erik exactly how this situation could be resolved.

He would never have thought of the option himself, and he wasn't at all convinced it would work, but he forced himself to believe. He flicked a look at his intent daughter, guessing that she would anticipate his need for her assistance if he was going to extend his powers.

Meanwhile, Erik smiled slowly, savoring Chen's surprise. Erik stilled his breathing and opened his eyes wide. He exhaled a long, slow breath mingled with dragonsmoke. He let the flames of beguiling light in his eyes. He felt Zoë's attention upon him and sensed her guidance in building the flames brighter.

"You have lost," Erik said softly.

Chen inhaled. He eased backward and narrowed his eyes. His pose became defensive, his back hunched and his tail curled around before himself.

"You can't beguile me," he scoffed.

But he didn't look away from Erik's gaze.

Erik coaxed the flames in his eyes to burn higher, to burn brighter, to flare vivid orange. He felt as if he were shooting sparks at his adversary, drawing him into a trap as old as time. He let Zoë guide him, show him what was possible. He believed.

And he beguiled as he had never beguiled before.

"The firestorm is sated. Your opportunity is lost."

"No! It is only a temporary setback. I'll find a way."

"You'll never find a way."

Chen glanced up at that and was snared. He tried to look away, but he failed to do so.

"The brand is flawed," Erik said, dropping his voice to the low monotone necessary for beguiling. He eased closer, coaxing the flames in his eyes to burn more brightly.

"No!" Chen said, but there was desperation in his tone. "No! I have powers beyond your comprehension. There is nothing wrong with the brand."

"No, it is flawed," Erik said soothingly. "Its song has been tainted."

Chen twitched. Chen moaned.

"Tainted," he whispered.

"It must be destroyed," Erik said soothingly.

"No!" Chen argued, though his voice had less vehemence.

"It could be used against you." Erik dropped his voice lower. "Used by an enemy to command you, or your shadow dragons."

Chen's eyes narrowed, the notion so upsetting that he managed to slip from Erik's spell for an instant. "You have no such power," he declared, his tone haughty.

"Do I not? You came to my trap, when there was nothing you could gain. The firestorm is sated. The opportunity is lost. The DreamWalker is made."

"The DreamWalker is made," Chen repeated with reluctance. His gaze fell to the brand.

"The tool is tainted," Erik said with a sad shake of his head. He kept his gaze locked on Chen. "The tool must be destroyed."

"Destroyed," Chen agreed, even shaking his head just as Erik had.

Erik opened his eyes wide and stared directly at Chen. He felt when the flames were blazing in his eyes, felt when he had completely snared the *Slayer*'s attention. He bent his will upon him, coaxing Chen to do as he desired. The wily old *Slayer* fought back, but Erik felt himself gaining ascendancy over Chen's will.

"It must be destroyed."

"Destroyed."

"So it cannot be used against you."

The idea made Chen twitch. "Against me."

"Or wielded by another."

"Or wielded by another."

"It must be broken."

"It must be broken."

"Sing the song to break it," Erik commanded. He was aware that Eileen was frozen in place, terrified to move lest she jeopardize his spell. He was aware of the *Pyr* battling shadow dragons around and behind him, of the smell of ash from burning shadow dragons, but he kept his attention focused on his prey.

"Sing!" Erik raised his voice in command.

A ripple passed through Chen's body. Erik feared he would pull out of the spell before it was completed. The women were holding their breath, the children watching, but Erik kept his attention fixed on Chen.

And he beguiled harder.

Erik lowered his voice even more. "You could be trapped with your own tool."

"Trapped," Chen agreed with agitation.

"Another could command the shadow dragons instead of you."

Chen's eyes flashed. "Never!" He reared up. "I am the last of the Dragon Kings and this brand is mine to wield!"

"*Then sing!*" Erik roared in old-speak.

And Chen sang. He sang a song of destruction and power that was horrible to hear. His voice was resonant and loud, the frame of the building rippling in response to his call. He rose to the height of the ceiling, spread his wings wide, and sang and sang.

The brand made a crackling sound.

Chen sang. Chen hummed and chanted. Chen roared.

He sang until the tiger brand shattered into seven pieces.

Chen screamed in rage when he saw what he had done; then he abruptly shifted shape.

The red salamander darted across the hardwood floor. Erik shifted to human form and leapt forward, intending to capture him. He bent to snatch him up when Chen suddenly shifted shape again. He became an elderly man, surprising Erik for a heartbeat.

It was long enough. Chen pushed Erik aside and ran with remarkable speed. Erik grabbed the old *Slayer* from behind.

Chen glittered and shifted to the form of a young woman. As astounded as he was, Erik held her tightly.

How many forms could Chen take?

The woman twisted in Erik's grip, becoming a snake that writhed in his grasp. The snake snapped and bit him, sharp fangs sinking into Erik's hand. Erik released Chen in surprise, just as the *Slayer* became a salamander again.

Chen bolted across the room, then raced ahead of Erik into the kitchen. Erik snatched at the salamander on the counter.

He had his fingers around the *Slayer* when Chen wiggled, slipped away, and leapt down the drain. Erik clung to the lip of the counter, frustrated by his inability to follow.

Then he swore.

Eileen came to Erik's side and picked up the plug, jamming it into the drain. Erik glanced up as she exhaled shakily. Then she smiled at him. "I thought *Pyr* couldn't be beguiled?"

"Chen hasn't been true *Pyr* for a long time."

"But you still did it." She leaned closer and kissed his cheek, and Erik only realized then how quickly his heart was pounding. "Thanks."

"Zoë reminded me," he said quietly, then met his partner's steady gaze. "In old-speak."

Eileen caught her breath, her astonishment echoing his own.

The scent tickled Rafferty's nose. It reminded him of Magnus, tempted him to follow it, prompted his curiosity. He was in the basement of Rox's building, where the *Pyr* had entered the labyrinth beneath the city, and he knew Chen had heard his taunts.

So, it seemed, had someone else.

Was Magnus alive? Or was his scent a trick of Chen's? Rafferty and Magnus had sworn a blood feud, one which could leave only a single survivor. When the Elixir's source had been destroyed, Rafferty had been sure that he was triumphant.

This scent fed his doubts. Had he left the job half done?

He had to know for certain.

Rafferty composed himself. He thought of Sophie's powers and begged for her help. He touched the ring that was the reminder of her and Nikolas, the ring that changed size to remain always on his left hand, and then he wished. The Wyvern had been able to move between physical spaces on a whim. Could he do the same thing? Rafferty tried, with no immediate result.

Then he tried again.

He felt a breeze in his hair, a blur of movement.

Unexpectedly Rafferty found himself in another cellar. It was empty, except for a slick calendar on the wall and a wooden table. A doorway led to an adjacent room and another opened to darkness. Rafferty could smell water and sewage, as well as herbs. There was also a sweet, heavy perfume lingering in the air, one that reminded him of the woman in the tight jeans. There was a large glass jar on the table and he moved closer with care.

A jade and gold salamander lay in the bottom of the jar. Its breath had formed condensation on the inside of the glass.

Magnus!

But was he dead or alive?

"*Our challenge is yet outstanding,*" Magnus whispered, his old-speak winding into Rafferty's thoughts with surprising clarity. "*Just release me, and let's be done with it.*"

Alive, then, despite all odds.

"Can you not release yourself?"

"Would I not have done so already if I could?" Magnus demanded.

"Then perhaps you should stay where you are. I need not kill you to see you dead."

"But we exchanged challenge coins!"

And Rafferty knew that Magnus had summoned him because he could not free himself. Was that because he had been so weakened, or because the stopper was reinforced by the will of another?

Rafferty didn't doubt that if that were the case, interfering with Magnus's incarceration would carry a heavy price.

Rafferty was disappointed to realize, though, that he had not moved through space himself—he had been moved by Magnus. Clearly that power was reserved for the Wyvern and those *Slayers* who had drunk the Elixir.

Perhaps that was the *Slayer's* plan.

"Surely you cannot be afraid of me in this weakened state?" Magnus taunted.

"Surely you cannot imagine that I will ever trust you again."

"There will be no dignity in this victory."

"I will not be tempted by pride."

Rafferty heard a scuttling on the stone and saw Magnus glance up with trepidation. Rafferty changed swiftly to a salamander and retreated to a chink between the stones. He heard Magnus inhale sharply and wished his old foe hadn't known he could do this feat.

But he had hidden himself just in time. Although it sounded like a small creature in the next room, it was a woman who strode into the room where Rafferty hid.

It was the same woman who had winked at Thorolf. Now, though, she appeared to be in a foul mood. She moved directly toward the jar and gave it a shake. Magnus rolled limply around inside, as if dead.

"You do not fool me," she said, her voice rough.

She murmured to herself as she removed the stopper from the glass. She poured Magnus out onto the table, but he didn't move.

She smiled at the jade salamander, her red lipstick glossy. It was a cold smile and one that did not bode well. She flicked at his body with her lacquered nails. "I knew better than to trust you," she hissed.

Magnus played dead.

"You told them," she whispered. "And my chance was lost. Now you will pay." She made to seize the salamander as if she would crush it with her bare hands.

Magnus lunged at her; then she became a furious dragon as red as rubies. It was Chen! Rafferty was shocked that he could become a woman.

Chen snatched at Magnus, his livid gaze proving he was the more vital of the pair. Magnus shifted to his human form, but Chen followed suit, becoming a young man bent on violence. Two human forms? Chen struck Magnus, punching him hard.

Magnus shifted to a salamander again, diving through the crack in the floor. Chen followed suit, the pair disguising their scents so surely that there remained no sign they had ever been there.

Rafferty tried to follow them without success. He was irritated and annoyed, frightened by the truth of another potent *Slayer* in the world. Then he heard the summons of his fellows and knew he had to help the *Pyr*.

The rain poured down, soaking Rox to the skin, as Phelan carried her captive into the night. It occurred to Rox that fighting him was futile and that maybe there was a better way to ensure his destruction.

She knew that Niall would give chase.

She knew that Niall had keen senses and would likely be able to hear whatever she and Phelan said.

She decided it was time that Niall knew without a doubt there was no spark of the divine left in his twin.

"It's about time you saved me," she complained. "Anybody can see that the firestorm should be with you and not with Niall."

No one would believe that except Phelan. At least she might be able to get the truth out of him.

She had pretty much nothing to lose.

"Kismet!" Phelan smiled. "You and I together, just as it was destined to be."

"Exactly," Rox agreed. "About time you solved it."

"Chen promised to give me a firestorm, but he lied." Phelan slowed his flight, preening as he looked down at Rox. His eyes shone with dark intent and his body seemed to be partly decomposed. The old wound on his chest was white and soft, as if it had been infected. He smelled like death and had a cold aura that made Rox shiver.

Rox tried to hide her revulsion.

He landed on a roof and shifted shape. He leaned closer to her in his tight jeans and leather jacket. Funny how he could look so much like Niall and yet do nothing for Rox.

Less than nothing.

"Nothing like a destined mate," he said, reaching one hand to caress her cheek. "Nothing like fate bringing lovers together forever."

"Nothing like it," Rox agreed, and held her ground.

She really hoped she didn't puke.

She saw Niall's silhouette then. He was easing closer, flying with caution as if he meant to sneak up on Phelan. She deliberately kept her attention fixed on Phelan.

She had to keep him talking.

She had to prove to Niall that his brother was a snake.

She knew exactly how to encourage this kind of loser.

Rox swallowed, then raised her hand to Phelan's chest. She traced her fingertip around his neck in a gentle caress. His skin was as cold as ice. "Why did you say Niall killed you, babe? He said it was your father."

Phelan's smile broadened. "Technically, that's true. But I could see Niall's influence in our father's choice. Anyone could." He shook his head, apparently dismayed by his twin's bad character. "He's like that. Deceptive. Charming. Focused on his own goals to the exclusion of all others." Phelan leaned closer. "Selfish."

It sounded to Rox as if Phelan was describing himself. He certainly wasn't describing the *Pyr* she'd come to know.

And love.

"I'm sorry you were deceived," Phelan whispered, and leaned closer for a kiss.

Rox turned her head so his lips touched her cheek. She saw Niall land silently on the lip of the roof. "What about your mother?"

"She knew us well. She understood the difference between us. I was always her favorite," Phelan bragged. "Our father, though, didn't have a clue, and he was ready to believe Niall's lies."

"Then why was Niall so determined to give you a second chance?"

Phelan shook his head and smiled. "Another lie, and you believed him. You are so trusting." He wound his hand into her hair, urging her closer. Rox pretended to be compliant, trying not to shudder when his breath fanned her cheek. "Don't you see that he said what he had to say to seduce you?"

Niall came closer again.

"He could have just killed you," Rox said.

"But he knew he would lose. I was always the better fighter. Always the one who practiced and had discipline. Niall never studied or worked for anything." Phelan shook his head. "He got by on charm and deceit."

Again, Rox thought Phelan was describing himself.

"So, he was afraid to fight you?" Rox thought it untimely to note that Phelan had sent a shadow dragon to take out his brother.

"And he was right to be afraid, because he knew he'd lose." Phelan smiled. "But now the firestorm is satisfied and our line will continue. I'll raise Niall's son as my own and teach him everything he needs to know."

"Yes," Rox agreed, even as the idea horrified her. "I thought shadow dragons couldn't think for themselves."

Phelan smiled. "Chen gave me ground dragon bone. It woke me up again; it gave me my own thoughts and initiative back." His fingers tightened in her hair. Rox gasped at the pain and saw him smile. "Don't worry, babe. I'll find more. Now you're mine, all mine," he murmured, then bent his head to kiss her.

Rox saw Niall leap and knew she had to get out of the way. His eyes were shining with fury and she knew the fight wouldn't be pretty.

She'd done her part—Niall's doubt was banished.

Rox slapped Phelan hard. She dragged her nails down his face, guessing he wouldn't feel the pain but hoping she surprised him. He snatched at her with a snarl, but Rox pivoted and ran.

She hoped Niall moved fast, because the lip of the roof wasn't far away.

Quinn, Donovan, and Delaney worked together, cutting through an endless stream of shadow dragons. It was disgusting work and Donovan feared they'd lose heart before it was done. It wasn't easy to fight with his mate and child in his grasp, either, but he was afraid to put Alex and Nick down. He was aware of Sloane and Thorolf battling more shadow dragons in the apartment below, of Erik's descent there, of Niall fighting his brother.

There was no relief coming to help them, so they had to work one talon at a time.

And shadow dragons didn't tire.

Rafferty appeared from the street below. He took out a shadow dragon, his presence giving Donovan the encouragement he needed.

Donovan sang with greater vigor, feeling the elements stir more than they had. The rain turned to ice pellets, slicing between their phantom opponents. The earth heaved and buckled, sending missiles of dirt and concrete into the air.

The shadow dragons fought on, as oblivious to the weapons of the earth as they were to their own injuries. Donovan feared they might not triumph against such odds.

"Look!" Alex whispered, and Donovan turned to see the Dragon's Tooth warriors descending from the sky in pairs.

It couldn't be any other *Pyr*, given the discipline of their formation. Their leader came straight to Donovan and Quinn, adding his talons to the fight. His men divided ranks without a word, some heading down to fight shadow dragons in the apartment and others pursuing strays. Within moments, the air was thick with dark ash and the smell of burned shadow dragons.

When the last one had been hacked apart and the *Pyr* paused to catch their breath, Donovan felt the cool caress of the wind. It frolicked between them, pushing aside the rain clouds, in promise of a better tomorrow.

One without shadow dragons.

Niall's decision was made.

That Rox had helped him see the truth and might pay the price for her bravery was absolutely unacceptable. He slashed at Phelan's tail, his anger giving him strength.

He breathed dragonfire, roasting Phelan's other arm to cinders right on his body. Phelan cried out in protest, pretending to feel pain, but Niall knew better than to believe his deceitful brother.

He cut that arm loose and incinerated it.

Phelan hissed and leapt at Niall, his gaze filled with hatred. Niall shredded his tail, frying it to cinders. He made short work of his brother, removing his legs with vicious force. Phelan writhed and bit, thrashing as he swore with vigor.

Niall locked his claws around his brother's neck, then bit hard into his chest. He ripped open the old wound once more, recognizing that he was making the same choice as his father for the same reason, and that his father had been right.

Then he tore Phelan's head free of his body. He stood back and raged dragonfire, destroying every last shred of Phelan's body.

When it was done and Phelan was no more than ash, he called to the wind. It swirled over the horizon and rolled toward him, churning the clouds and sending his brother's cinders scattering over the city. The wind flicked and danced, spreading the ashes far and wide at Niall's command. Then he sent the wind to aid Donovan, Quinn, and Delaney, watching it disperse the last of the shadow dragons.

His quest was complete.

His firestorm was sated.

Niall felt potent as he never had, in full grasp of his abilities.

That was when he saw Rox standing on the roof, watching him. She was smiling with pride and happiness, her hair tossing in the wind. She reached out to him, opening her arms as if she'd embrace the sky and Niall swooped down to her.

His past was gone forever.

And the future belonged to them both.

Chapter 19

Niall decided upon a yin and yang symbol to cover the place where he'd lost the scale, choosing an emblem of balance over a more aggressive design. He'd picked red and black.

Rox thought it was the perfect choice. His injury had to heal first, so it was several weeks before the skin could accept the tattoo. The *Pyr* remained in New York until the tattoo could be completed, which Rox didn't entirely understand. They were good company and good people, though, so she didn't mind having an apartment full of dragons.

Especially the one who shared her bed.

Niall bought a building close to Imagination Ink for his new office, surprising Rox with his wealth. The new building was the perfect place for some of the *Pyr* to decamp, although Rox still had a few in her apartment. Delaney helped Niall with equipment and setup, and Rox knew Niall was relieved to be establishing his routine again. Barry proved to have a talent with computers and an interest in eco-travel, so he became Niall's new employee.

Imagination Ink had been damaged in what came

to be known as the second of two freak earthquakes, but the insurance covered the repairs. By the time Niall was healed, the shop was open for business and bustling once again.

When it came time to do Niall's tattoo, the *Pyr* came along. It was a bit unnerving to have them all watching Niall get his protective tattoo. Rox wondered whom they were prepared to defend. Even Chynna made a brief appearance to see what all the fuss was about and added her goodwill to the process. Niall was a good client—he didn't flinch or complain, and Rox liked having the excuse to run her hands over his muscled back.

Not that she needed any excuse, given the balance between them.

"I've been thinking," Sloane said when Rox was finishing the last of the red. "I've been wanting a tattoo for a while but needed to find the right artist. I think you're it."

"Rox is the best," Niall said flatly.

"Especially if you need a dragon," Rafferty said with approval.

Rox smiled. She got a mirror for Niall so he could check out her work, and he stood to look. His approval was more than clear.

"I want two dragons, actually," Sloane said. "Like a caduceus but with dragons instead of snakes." He tapped his left bicep. "Right here."

"How big?" Rox asked, liking how well that could symbolize Sloane's role as Apothecary to the *Pyr*.

"As big as you think it should be," he said with a grin. "You're the expert."

"Bigger costs more," Rox warned.

"Bigger means more detail, too," Thorolf added.

"I can afford it," Sloane said, then winked at Rox. "I've been saving up for a few centuries."

Rox was about to offer to do a sketch when Niall spoke. "I think Rox is going to be a bit busy," he said lightly, and she glanced his way in surprise. His eyes glittered like sapphires and he was almost smiling. "Come here," he invited, then tugged at her collar. "Let's see your back piece."

Confused, Rox pushed her jacket off her shoulders. She was wearing a halter top underneath and now understood why Niall had suggested it that morning.

She'd just thought he'd liked the turquoise color.

He stood with his back to the big wall mirror and put his arm over her shoulders. He held the hand mirror so she could see the reflection in the big mirror. "What if your dragon isn't wrong?" he said. "What if the circle is just bigger than your own back?"

"What do you mean?" Rox asked, even though she could guess.

"What if the phoenix is on my back, curled toward the dragon in the composition you mentioned?" He lowered the mirror and looked down at her, his manner intent. "What if our respective back pieces are each half of the whole?"

Rafferty gave a low whistle. "Just as the firestorm brings mate and *Pyr* together into a whole that is greater than the sum of the parts."

Rox caught her breath, knowing the implication of his suggestion. "But ink is forever," she whispered.

Niall smiled. "That's exactly the point." He cast a quick glance at the *Pyr*, then turned his attention back to Rox. The glittering blue of his eyes mesmerized her and the warmth of his smile was evocative of the firestorm.

But it was even better, because Niall's smile would be in her life for good.

"I love you, Rox," Niall said, his words making her heart pound. "I want to commit myself to you, to our son, and to our future. I know you're not as traditional as I am, but let's find a middle ground. Let's make a union of choice and seal that pledge in ink. It doesn't have to be the ink on a marriage certificate."

It was exactly the offer Rox wanted to hear. "I never had my dragon colored," she whispered. "Even though I wanted it in color, I could never decide. Now I know he should be amethyst and silver"—she smiled—"just like the *Pyr* I love."

Niall bent and kissed her thoroughly, showing his approval with his touch. The *Pyr* hooted and laughed, but Niall ignored them, lifting Rox into his arms and sealing their promise with another kiss.

A kiss that would keep her simmering forever.

After he had lifted his head and the *Pyr* had shared their congratulations, Rox grabbed the mirror and took a more critical look. She immediately saw how the composition would work. As had his idea of the trellis on Chynna's sleeve, Niall's suggestion provided the perfect solution to the design. His back piece would be unique and beautiful, maybe Rox's masterpiece. She knew she'd draw the phoenix freehand on Niall's back to ensure that its curves flowed best across his muscles.

Their union would be a part of their skins for all of their lives.

"It'll be perfect," she said, knowing her excitement about the design showed. "But there's one more thing we have to do first," Rox said, digging into her pocket. She pulled out the single amethyst and silver scale, the one Niall had lost in the tunnels, the one that no one knew she had. Niall inhaled sharply at the sight of it. "You need armor over that new tattoo, not just mumbo jumbo to watch your back." She offered the scale to Quinn. "Isn't that your department?"

"It is." Quinn smiled and stepped forward to accept the scale. He turned it in his hands, studying its condition, then gave Rox a smile. "You have cared for it well."

"Can you do it?" she asked.

Quinn nodded, his gaze flicking to the open doorway. "Tonight."

*   *   *

Niall was amazed by Rox one more time. He hadn't realized that she had kept the scale and had assumed it lost for good in the network under the city. He was fiercely glad she had liked the idea for his tattoo, and he was even more glad they would be together for the duration. With Phelan gone, there was no obstacle to his raising his own son. With Rox's tattoo on his back, their union was permanent.

His mouth was dry that night as he stood in her apartment, surrounded by his best friends and his family of choice. Rox's hand was in his, and Quinn stood before him like a master of ceremonies. The windows were open, as well as the door to the balcony, a cool wind wafting into the apartment.

"We all have to shift," Niall explained to Rox once again, and she nodded with some impatience.

"I know. I just hope you all fit in here."

"Nothing like high ceilings," Erik said, then nodded at Quinn.

Quinn shifted shape first, becoming a muscled dragon clad in gleaming sapphire and steel scales. One scale, the replacement made of wrought iron and Sara's tears, caught Niall's attention because it gleamed.

Donovan changed next, the Warrior mailed in magnificent lapis lazuli and silver scales. The jet and garnet pin from Alex that adorned his repaired scale shone in the darkness. It was an emblem signifying that he had loved, and that love had made him stronger. He lifted his mate, Alex, in his grasp and held his son, Nick, aloft so he could see.

Erik shifted shape, becoming a dragon with ebony and pewter scales. On his forehead was his own repaired scale, its surface shining with the rune stone of his father's, returned to him by Eileen. He lifted both mate and daughter with reverence and Eileen kissed his neck.

Delaney became an emerald and copper dragon, his

scales shining like jewels now that Ginger's love and his firestorm had brought him back into the circle of the *Pyr*. Their son, Liam, was awake, his eyes wide, and Niall wondered how much the baby understood of what he witnessed.

Rafferty shifted shape, becoming an opal and gold dragon as formidable and serene as he was in human form. Sloane followed Rafferty. His gold-edged scales contained all the hues of tourmaline, shading from green to gold to purple and back again. Thorolf shifted finally, his moonstone and silver scales glinting like moonlight in the living room.

They were magical and marvelous, his powerful and loyal friends, and having them with him in this moment made Niall feel doubly blessed.

"You're up," whispered Rox, her eyes sparkling.

Niall kissed her fingertips, then summoned the change. It rolled through him like a tidal wave, sending a surge of blue electricity through every fiber of his being. The shift made his body hum, made his heart sing, and made his thoughts fly.

It was right.

Because his mate was by his side.

Quinn reared back, lifting Niall's lost scale in his talons. He breathed dragonfire on the scale, the white-hot fire of the Smith, and the scale sparkled in his grip. Niall was amused to see Garrett breathe mock fire, mimicking his father's pose even as Sara held him close.

"Fire," said Quinn, and breathed upon the scale again. Niall breathed on the scale, as well, demonstrating his own affinity for the element of fire.

Then Niall summoned the element he knew best. He felt the wind swirl around them, lifting the women's hair and caressing the scales of the *Pyr*. He felt the wind's fingers in the clouds and sensed new dimensions to his own affinity. He was aware of the tingle of Erik's foresight, the bright, perceptive gaze of the leader of the *Pyr*.

He felt the power of Zoë and her knowledge as Wyvern of the language and secrets of dreams. He was joyous that she had shared some of her wisdom with him, and was determined to master his role as DreamWalker.

"Air," said Niall, hearing triumph in his own voice.

"Earth," Rox said. She slid her hands over Niall's scales and he turned so that his shoulder was toward Quinn. He knew the tattoo she had given him was visible because the scale wasn't repaired. It was a good talisman.

Having the scale back would be even better.

Rox's small hands were on his exposed flesh and Niall could feel the accelerated beat of her heart through the warmth of her fingers. She was his earth and his water, pragmatism and tough talk of earth tempered by the compassion of water.

His own heart thundered with the power of their match. The firestorm had been right, after all.

Quinn stepped closer, breathing his dragonfire on the scale for the third time. Then he pressed it back into its rightful place. Even though Niall had been prepared for the pain, it still shocked him to his core. The touch of the hot scale seared his flesh, sending a jolt through his body. The pain made him arch his back and clench his teeth. His entire body was taut, the cleansing heat strengthening him.

As fire tempers steel, Quinn would say.

He heard Rox gasp. He felt her caress his flesh with sympathy. And he sighed in relief at the cool impact of her single tear on the repaired scale.

"Water," Quinn murmured.

The heat changed then, becoming warm instead of hot, healing and setting the injury.

"Are you all right?" she whispered, her eyes filled with concern.

"Fine," Niall murmured. "Better than ever," he added, knowing it was true. The wind swirled around them, as if it, too, would celebrate, and Niall shifted back to human form. He caught Rox close and kissed her, knowing there was one last thing he had to do for his firebird.

He was going to walk in her dream.

By the end of the summer, Rox had finished the color on Niall's tattoo. She'd shaded the phoenix's feathers in hues of red, orange, and yellow, with accents of darkest blue. When it was done and she gave Niall the mirror to look, he had assured her it was the most beautiful piece she'd ever done.

Then he admitted that he had to leave and that Thorolf would watch out for her in his absence. Niall knew Rox was curious, but he appreciated her trust in him.

She didn't ask where he was going.

Niall wasn't entirely sure himself. He had tiptoed into Rox's dreams over the intervening weeks. He had found a few pathways and followed them diligently. He had checked each one in turn until he had found the one he needed to follow.

But he had to follow its trail physically, which meant leaving Rox for the moment.

He knew it would be worth the journey.

Niall rapped on Rox's door a week and a half after his departure, the last Saturday night in August. He had a suit bag slung over his shoulder and a new optimism in his step. To his pleasure, the dragonsmoke barrier was woven deep around the apartment and it resonated with a clear ping.

Thorolf *was* learning something.

Rox opened the door, and her eyes lit with pleasure. "You're back! You don't have to knock."

"Hey, firebird. Miss me?" Niall couldn't wait to see her response to what he had done.

Although her response to his presence was pretty

good itself. He laughed as she threw herself into his arms, and he swung her around.

"Shut up and kiss me already," Rox said, then pulled his head down for an enthusiastic welcome.

Niall laughed and stepped into the apartment, knowing he didn't have a lot of time.

"Hey," Thorolf said by way of greeting, standing with one foot in the kitchen. The big *Pyr* was eating frozen burritos as if he'd scored the last dozen on the planet.

At least he'd taken care of Rox while Niall was gone.

Niall kissed Rox as if he'd been gone a year, then reluctantly pulled out of her embrace. He hung his suit bag over the door and she frowned at it.

"What do you need with a suit?"

"Turn it on, Rox," he said, spinning her around. "We've got a dinner reservation. We have to celebrate."

"Again? Where?"

He named the Japanese restaurant uptown that she'd been wanting to try and Rox's surprise showed.

Then she eyed him, curiosity making her eyes bright. "Why now?"

"Trust me."

"What're you celebrating?" Thorolf demanded, even as he threw back another burrito.

Rox regarded Niall with good-natured suspicion. "You're up to something."

Niall feigned innocence and failed. "Me?"

Rox chuckled. "I love that you can't lie," she said, then walked toward him. She let her hips swing and a provocative light gleamed in her eye. "I can work the truth out of you," she threatened.

"You probably could, but there isn't time," Niall said. "First dinner, then we're off."

"Where?"

He fished an envelope out of his pocket and handed it to her.

She frowned and turned it over, then flicked a glance at him.

"You'd better open it to find out," he advised.

Rox ripped open the envelope. "Train tickets?" He knew the moment she read the destination, because she shook her head. "I appreciate what you're trying to do, but there's no way. . . ."

Niall caught her shoulders in his hands. "There are families made by choice and families made by blood," he said softly. "Neither is better, and some families are both."

Rox inhaled and shook her head, then looked up at him. She swallowed. "But what if he's still there?"

Niall bent down so that their noses were almost touching. He let his gaze bore into hers so that she could see his determination, so that she would know how committed he was to her defense. "Do you really think I'd let anyone hurt you again?"

The tension eased out of Rox's body. Once again, her trust gained the upper hand, and Niall's heart pounded with pride. She pulled the tickets out of the envelope and counted them, then looked at him in confusion. "But there are four. That's too many tickets."

Niall smiled. "No, it's not." He leaned down and whispered to her. "Rox, I do details. Four tickets is exactly right."

Her lips parted and he knew she already had an idea what he'd planned.

The door buzzer rang at just that moment. Perfect. Niall glanced pointedly at the intercom, then back at Rox. She stared at him as he leaned against the wall and folded his arms across his chest. He let her work it out.

She did, just as quickly as he'd anticipated. Her hands rose to her mouth in shock and he saw the first glimmer of her tears.

"Where were you this week?" she whispered.

"California. Beverly Hills, actually."

"I don't know anybody in Beverly Hills."

"You sure?" Niall arched a brow. "Funny how your dream led right there, then."

Rox's mouth opened and closed. "Not that dream."

"The very one."

The buzzer rang again. Rox hurried to the intercom and pressed the button, her gaze locked on Niall. "Yes?"

"Rox?" a woman asked. "Roxie, is that you?"

Rox's eyes went round and her voice rose high. "Suzie!"

"Well, yes!" the woman said, and Niall couldn't tell whether she was laughing or crying. "Do we have to do this over a crummy intercom?"

"Come in, come in!" Rox hit the button to open the door, holding it down with her fist.

"We're in!" called the woman, and it was only then that Rox launched herself at Niall. He caught her close and kissed her. Then he wiped the tears from her cheeks, framing her face in his hands to kiss her again.

"I can't believe it. You found her," she said, her words falling fast. She was almost dancing in front of him, her excitement all the reward he needed. "You found her! You found her after all these years!"

"All part of the deal," Niall said, wiping away her tears. "She changed her name. That's why you couldn't find her."

"But you did!"

"I had a few advantages on my side," he admitted, and she eyed him with wonder.

"DreamWalker," she whispered.

"Yeah. It's pretty cool." He smiled down at her. "I thought the first time should be for you."

"You already did it the first time for me."

Niall opened his eyes wide. "Should we send Suzie home, then?"

Rox laughed, hugged him tightly, then looked down

at the tickets again. "But we can't just go. They might not even live there anymore. . . ."

"Suzie phoned. Your mom is eager to see you." Niall brushed a fingertip across Rox's nose, knowing what she wanted to ask. "And she threw *him* out a decade ago. Something about both her girls leaving made her reconsider the evidence." He let his voice drop. "She's been looking for you two."

Rox exhaled. She shook. And then a wonderful light filled her eyes. Niall was ready to enjoy her pleasure in what he'd done, but there was an untimely rap at the door.

Rox squealed as she never did, pivoted, and flung open the door. The two sisters stared at each other in astonishment for a long moment. Suzie was a beautiful woman, finely boned with long hair the same ebony hue as Rox's. Her eyes were green instead of blue, and she was—incredibly—even more outspoken and blunt than Rox. She was elegantly and expensively dressed, but Niall could see the similarities between them.

He would have argued who was the pretty one, though.

Suzie smiled and lifted her left hand. The silver promise ring shone on her pinkie. Rox caught her breath and echoed the gesture, the two rings identical. "I'm sorry," Suzie said. "I thought you'd be fine. I thought you'd be okay, but Niall told us. . . ."

"You couldn't have known," Rox said with her usual ferocity for those she loved. "You had to take care of yourself first."

Suzie shook her head. "I never imagined he would . . ."

"He didn't," Rox interrupted firmly. "He tried once, and then I was out of there."

"Just like me."

Rox wiggled her hand and smiled. "Sometimes living by example is the best you can do."

"Roxie!" Suzie's tears spilled and she opened her arms. Rox flung herself into her sister's tight embrace, and Niall knew he'd done exactly the right thing.

They were both fighters, one dressed in velvet and one in steel. They had survived and become stronger for it. He stepped back to watch their reunion, glad he had been able to give this gift to his mate.

His Phoenix.

His love.

Thorolf came to Niall's side, straightening his T-shirt and swallowing his last bite of burrito. He was staring at Suzie as if he'd never seen a woman before.

"*I could, like, come with you*," Thorolf offered in old-speak.

"*You could, like, stay home and practice*," Niall retorted, no sting in his words.

Thorolf might have argued, but Suzie's husband appeared in the doorway then. He nodded at Niall, then smiled at the two sisters. He, too, was elegantly and expensively dressed; a man at ease with money.

Thorolf made an almost undetectable growl of dissatisfaction.

Niall heard it.

"*Successful*," Niall said. "*I think he has more money than God.*"

"*The guys with the bucks snag the best babes every time*," Thorolf complained.

"*Just think—he's maybe forty-five. You're, what? Eight hundred years old, give or take?*" Niall gave Thorolf a look. "*What* have *you been doing with your time?*"

Thorolf stared at Niall and swallowed. "*You know, I'm thinking I'll practice this weekend. Cultivate a little success. Breathe some smoke.*"

"*No*," Niall said. "*You've nailed the smoke. Great boundary mark here.*" He smiled at his student, not missing how Thorolf smiled with pride.

"*What, then?*"

"Work on shifting faster. You have to hide your clothes in less than half the time it takes you now."

"Why?"

"If someone sees where they are, you're dead meat."

"I'm on it." Thorolf gave Niall a high five, then headed back to the kitchen.

Suzie's husband glanced toward the window and grimaced, sparing a glance for his Italian leather shoes. "Anyone else hear thunder?"

"No," Niall said, well aware that Rox was sparkling like a galaxy of stars. "But we should hurry so we don't miss that reservation."

It was late when Rox and Niall retired to her old room in the house she had thought she'd never see again. Her mom had redecorated, turning this room into a sewing room and Suzie's room into a guest room. There was still a sofa bed, though, and a big mirror.

Aware that it wasn't just the *Pyr* who had keen hearing, Rox beckoned silently to Niall. He'd fulfilled her every dream, and she was feeling like the luckiest woman in the world.

"Let me see how your tattoo is healing," she whispered. "Did you take care of it while you were gone?"

"Are you kidding?" Niall asked good-naturedly. "I wasn't going to sign up for the infection as a result of careless maintenance lecture."

"Prove it," Rox said, tugging at the hem of his shirt.

"You just want me naked," Niall complained, and Rox smiled.

"You got a problem with that?"

Niall grinned. "Actually, no." He peeled off his shirt and turned, glancing over his shoulder at the reflection of his tattoo in the mirror.

The yin and yang symbol was at the lower edge of his right shoulder blade, covering the place where he had lost a scale. It looked to be held in the talons of the phoenix. The phoenix looked as if it would take flight over Niall's left shoulder. The tail feathers swept over his back, spilling around his waist and over his ribs on the front. There were clouds behind the phoenix, stylized silhouettes in shades of blue and green.

The phoenix represented the elements of air and fire.

"I still think it's the best piece you've ever done," he said with an admiration that warmed Rox like the firestorm.

The tattoo had healed beautifully, but then she'd known Niall would follow her instructions. She gave it a thorough check, then took off her own shirt. She nestled at his left side, holding up a hand mirror to see their tattoos together. She knew she'd never tire of seeing the two halves make a complete whole.

"Perfect," Niall murmured, pressing a kiss into her hair.

Rox's dragon was now colored in hues of amethyst and blue, accented in white to mimic platinum. The dragon curved like a letter *C*, his tail rising high on her left shoulder and his head curving up from below. Those orange stylized flames flowed behind him, but they looked more brilliant now that he was colored.

The dragon represented earth and water.

Rox liked that they each had the two elements of their own affinity represented on their backs, along with a symbol of the other's role in their partnership. She was earth and water to Niall's air and fire, but she was his Phoenix and he was her Dragon. The yin and yang symbol on his back represented the balance of their union, while the pearl on hers indicated—to Rox's thinking—the richness of the life they were making together.

Maybe even the precious gem of their son.

When Niall drew Rox more tightly against his side, she felt the thunder of her heart. She also knew that their tattoos fit together, forming the traditional circle across both of their backs. Rox's dragon looked directly into the eyes of Niall's phoenix. It was how they were meant to be, encircled and entwined, balancing each other, the whole greater than the sum of the parts.

And their tattoos stood testimony to their bond in a way that words never would.

"Happy?" he asked softly.

Rox nodded, knowing he had no doubt. "Thank you."

Niall smiled, then bent his head as if to kiss Rox. He froze before his lips touched hers, his gaze dancing over her cheek. "Hey, what happened to that broken heart?" he murmured.

"I wondered when you'd notice." Rox grinned. "Chynna colored it in solid for me when you were away," she whispered. "I don't figure it's ever going to be broken again."

"You've got that right," Niall said with vigor, then gave Rox a kiss so hot and sweet that it made up for every minute he'd been away. She happily kissed him back.

Ink, as it turned out, wasn't the only thing that was forever.

Rox had been wrong about that, but she didn't mind finding out the truth.

Not one bit.

Author's Note

If you are intrigued by what is hidden beneath the streets of New York City, I recommend *New York Underground: The Anatomy of a City* by Julia Solis. Not only are there many eerie and wonderful photographs, but she provides a terrific history of the city's underground.

Read on for a sneak peek of the next thrilling
romance in the Dragonfire series by
Deborah Cooke,

Darkfire Kiss

Available in May 2011
from Signet Eclipse

E thics were so inconvenient.

Melissa Smith had worked with many people who either had no ethics or could easily ignore them. She'd never been that way, even in pursuit of a story.

No matter how much was at stake.

She parked her car on the street, not too close to the house she'd driven past a hundred times, and took a deep breath. It didn't help. She was still freaked-out. She closed her eyes and saw the wreckage of Daphne's body—still a vivid memory she couldn't escape—and wondered whether it was time for a change.

In a real sense, her principles were all she had left. Melissa had lost her fiancé, her house, her dream job, and her future. All that she had left was the chance of restarting her career.

And maybe those ethics were the only thing standing in her way.

Did she want success enough to bend her own rules?

Daphne, Melissa knew, would have told her to make her own luck.

Melissa frowned, unhappy with the available options.

She pulled out the note from Daphne one more time. It was terse, just as Daphne had always been, and just reading it made her feel an obligation to the girl.

It was her fault. . . .

The note had come in the mail two days before as if it were no more important than a credit card bill. Enclosed with the note had been a key—a key to a storage locker.

Melissa had spent the whole day trying to guess where that storage locker might be. She hadn't really believed that Daphne was dead. The girl was a consummate liar, albeit one with a good heart. She'd had to deceive to survive on the streets of Baghdad, which was where Melissa had first met the engaging, pretty, opportunistic girl. Daphne had had a charm about her, and she'd been reliable in unexpected moments.

Melissa had lost track of Daphne when her health had brought her home. She'd thought of the beggar girl often, worried about her even when she should have been worrying about herself.

No one had been more surprised than Melissa to encounter Daphne again three years later in the most unlikely of places—right in D.C., dressed to the nines and on the arm of an affluent older man.

Magnus Montmorency.

It couldn't have been a coincidence; Melissa had known that immediately. Montmorency had been the rumored power behind illicit arms deals in Baghdad—every trail led to his vicinity and stopped cold. Melissa had wanted to get that story more than anything, had wanted to reveal Montmorency for the villain that he was, but she'd run out of time.

In more ways than one.

Still, she would have known him anywhere. Seeing Daphne with Montmorency hadn't reassured Melissa at all. She didn't like that Daphne had become his mis-

tress, that she had used Montmorency as her ticket to
the future.

And it really didn't help that in Baghdad Melissa had
once asked Daphne to find out more about Montmorency's connections. That had been before she'd realized
how brutal he was.

She had a responsibility. . . .

The memory of Daphne's burned body flicked
through her thoughts again, as if the dead girl would
taunt Melissa with her obligation. Montmorency must
have killed Daphne. Melissa suspected it but couldn't
prove a thing. It was the past all over again—the trail led
to Montmorency's vicinity and stopped cold.

But Daphne had provided the inside intelligence that
Melissa needed.

Melissa could have taken the easy path, but she'd
done her homework. She had gone to the morgue, and
was astonished when she found Daphne there, labeled
as a Jane Doe.

She'd never forget that sight.

Melissa had found the lock that fit the key at the air-
port, Reagan International. There'd been a duffel bag in
it filled with Daphne's apparent necessities. It confirmed
that Daphne had been poised to run, that she'd known
she was taking a big risk.

The stuffed puppy Melissa had first given Daphne
in Baghdad was in the bag, now well loved. The sight
nearly stopped Melissa's heart.

Deeper in the bag, she found Daphne's diary.

It was a riveting read. The girl was a good reporter,
thorough and detailed. If she'd survived, though, her
story would have created questions. She was, after all,
a beggar girl who had been saved from the streets by
Montmorency.

But in her diary Daphne had documented where cor-
relating evidence could be found against him—in a small

leather-bound blue book, one that was always in a certain place in the top-right drawer of a desk in Montmorency's fortified D.C. residence. Everything—*everything*—was documented there, according to Daphne.

It was the evidence Melissa needed.

She was parked across the street from the house.

Daphne had also provided the security codes to the house.

But Melissa hesitated. It was a crime to break and enter. It was wrong. Even though Montmorency was suspected of being an arms dealer, even though he made sure nothing ever stuck to him and nothing could be traced to him, even though bringing him to justice would tip the balance in favor of good guys everywhere and would fulfill a personal goal of Melissa's, it was still wrong to break into his home.

Dangerous, too.

Melissa swallowed, and eyed the house. She could almost hear Daphne calling her bluff. That girl would never have worried about a relatively minor infraction, especially one in the pursuit of a greater good.

Melissa had taught Daphne to record the evidence. Maybe Daphne was teaching her to take a chance, to reach for what she wanted.

Headlights swept over Melissa's car, and she instinctively hunched down in the seat. A large, black armored Mercedes sedan pulled out of Montmorency's driveway, the engine gunning as it headed downtown. Where was it going at this hour? It had to be midnight.

Melissa checked her watch. Ten past.

Maybe the car was going to pick up Montmorency. Melissa could see only the silhouette of a driver when it passed, as the windows were tinted dark, but she was sure its departure was a sign.

If not an invitation. If the house was empty, this was her chance. Who knew how soon the car would return?

Daphne deserved justice. . . .

Melissa knew that a person couldn't always count on getting a second chance. She wouldn't damage anything, wouldn't take much, would just get that little blue book from Montmorency's desk. It wouldn't take five minutes.

It would be easy.

It wouldn't matter in the greater scheme of things.

Melissa didn't believe that for a minute, but she got out of her car anyway. It was snowing slightly, the snow melting on contact with the pavement. There would be no mark of her footsteps—another sign.

She pulled on her leather gloves and turned up her collar. She wrapped her scarf across her face as if she were cold, even though she was strangely warm. She reasoned it was adrenaline—after all, she wasn't in the habit of breaking the law. She reminded herself of the power of the greater good.

Then Melissa marched across the street toward Montmorency's house, as if she had every right to be there.

In a way, she did.

Daphne would have insisted as much.

Rafferty's pursuit of Magnus had led the *Pyr* through dark passages and hollows, deep into the earth and under the ocean. That the old *Slayer* was wounded hadn't slowed his passage that much, apparently. That Magnus had the ability to disguise his scent, at least at intervals, meant that Rafferty had taken many wrong turns.

In the end, he had followed the trail to the most obvious location of all—Magnus's home in Washington.

Rafferty hadn't expected his enemy to be so brazen. Maybe he should have known better. Maybe it was a trap. Either way, he was tired of the unfinished business that lingered between the two of them. He and Magnus had exchanged challenge coins, which meant a fight to the death—until one was dead, the challenge continued. Rafferty had thought Magnus dead several times.

This time he would be certain.

He'd guessed that Magnus had restored his own strength from Niall's firestorm—with Chen's assistance and maybe a last hidden dose of the Dragon's Blood Elixir. He'd wanted to corner his old foe before the lunar eclipse that would occur in the wee hours of the morning, but hadn't been sure of Magnus's location until this day.

Rafferty would have bet that Magnus had planned it that way.

It hadn't helped that Rafferty had been distracted by the chaos in the earth. It hadn't helped that he'd felt compelled to halt his hunt and sing to Gaia, to calm her and try to soothe her. Recent months had seen earthquakes, tsunamis, and mudslides mar the surface of the planet. There had been blizzards and droughts, monsoons and tornadoes. The weather had gone wild, and humans were suffering on every continent. Rafferty had tried to help, but he was exhausted from his efforts.

He was beginning to think that it wasn't just Gaia, but that she had been incited to violence by someone else.

Was it Magnus? The old *Slayer* could sing the songs of the earth, as well. Rafferty wouldn't have believed Magnus to be so strong, but his old adversary had secrets Rafferty hadn't begun to guess.

Rafferty had only one secret, one that had been hidden from Magnus with complete success. Each passing day made Rafferty fear that truth would be revealed.

And that Magnus would turn his eye upon the Sleeper.

It was time to finish their blood challenge, to see Magnus dead. Rafferty had come to do the deed before the eclipse, but had remained in the shadows as Balthasar left the house, started the car.

The big sedan had left, which meant that at least one of Magnus's staff was gone. Probably two. Was Jorge here? Mallory? No one had sensed their presences since Delaney's firestorm almost two years ago. Rafferty didn't like when *Slayers* were quiet—it usually meant they were scheming something.

Maybe they were terrorized by Chen.

Or controlled by him. That *Slayer* was a new variable, one impossible to predict or pursue. He was older and stronger than anyone had guessed, and he had drunk the Elixir.

Magnus first.

His was a quiet neighborhood, one with large houses and discrete entrances, beautiful landscaping, high-tech security systems. Rafferty could see the stars overhead and smell a storm coming off the ocean. Snow. It was beginning to fall already.

He felt something else, too—something nameless that resonated deep in his marrow. Was he becoming more sensitive to the eclipses as he grew older? Or was it the influence of the Dragon's Tail, the cycle of karmic retribution and the last chance for the *Pyr* to defeat the *Slayers*? Rafferty wasn't sure, but he felt tingly and agitated in a way that wasn't characteristic for him. He was the temperate member of the *Pyr*, but in this moment he felt audacious. Impulsive.

Edgy.

Maybe that was a trick of Magnus's, intended to set him off guard. Rafferty gritted his teeth and fought the quiver deep inside him. He would be as resolute as ever.

The house was dark, with windows that gleamed squares of impenetrable blackness. Rafferty smelled malice, but couldn't hear a dragonsmoke perimeter mark.

It made sense that Magnus would abandon that tradition, since he could cross it himself. Also the resonance of a dragonsmoke ring might draw the attention of *Pyr*.

Attention Magnus wouldn't want.

No, he wanted everyone to believe he wasn't at home. The absence of a dragonsmoke ring indicated that the house was unoccupied.

Rafferty wasn't persuaded. He couldn't sense or smell anything that told him Magnus was in the house, but he believed it with every fiber of his being. Tonight was the night.

Rafferty turned the black and white ring on his finger one last time. It would be a fight to the death, and he wouldn't necessarily be victorious. Right didn't always prevail, unfortunately. Rafferty prepared himself for the possibility of his own death, then stepped out of the shadows of the cedar hedge.

The woman stopped him cold.

He stared, but she was no illusion. She marched up the driveway with all the force of a hurricane hurtling toward the shore. She was slender and tall, her features hidden by her scarf, her skirt swinging as she moved. Her hair was short, but as dark as a raven's wing.

Ebony curls.

Her skin was golden, the hue of buckwheat honey. She had terrific legs, lean and muscled, and she walked with a purposeful femininity. Rafferty stared.

And her perfume, so feminine, so faint, snared him with one whiff. His body responded to her presence with such enthusiasm that he was startled—startled enough to ease back into the shadows.

Lust at first sight? That wasn't like Rafferty. Was it the influence of the moon? He didn't know; he only felt his body harden as he watched the sweet sway of her hips.

And wanted.

How long had it been?

He forced himself to think rationally. Could Magnus have a guest? At this hour? Was she a mistress? She didn't appear to be Magnus's type—he favored flashy women, while this one was dressed simply, in dark colors. She was older than the usual jailbait Magnus chose, as well.

A woman, not a girl.

And that perfume. Not sweet so much as seductive. Musk instead of honeysuckle. It was the perfume of a woman who knew her powers, knew her allure, and wasn't afraid of either.

Rafferty's mouth went dry. He was intrigued when she went directly to the back door. Was she visiting someone else in the house? Presumably Magnus had staff. Why so late at night?

It couldn't be a coincidence that she came right after the big sedan's departure. Not at this hour.

Rafferty eased closer to watch her. He narrowed his eyes, his *Pyr* vision enabling him to see the delicate line of her leather-gloved hand. She raised her hand to the pad of the security system, the movement revealing an increment of skin. Rafferty could see the bone of her wrist, fine and delicate.

When had a glimpse of a woman's skin aroused him so?

She didn't knock or ring the bell. Instead she cast a furtive glance over her shoulder, then punched a sequence of codes into the security system. Though she had the codes, her every gesture revealed her conviction that she wouldn't be welcome.

Not staff, then.

Not a mistress.

But she had the codes right. The door opened, revealing a slice of darkness. Rafferty was sure he saw her hesitate for a moment before she slipped into the shadows of the house.

Then he was horrified. He couldn't begin to imagine how Magnus would treat an intruder in his lair.

Well, he *could* imagine—that was the problem.

The woman was either brave or stupid. Either way, she was a human who would shortly be in need of his protection.

Rafferty was across the property in a heartbeat, refusing to think further than that. He moved quickly enough to catch the lip of the closing door with his fingertips. That perfume taunted him, teased him, led him on.

And he followed the woman into the house, wondering all the while at her audacity.

Instead of thinking about Magnus, Rafferty Powell wanted to see the face of the woman who dared to take such a chance.

No. He wanted more than that.

About the Author

Deborah Cooke has always been fascinated by dragons, although she has never understood why they have to be the bad guys. She has an honors degree in history with a focus on medieval studies, and is an avid reader of medieval vernacular literature, fairy tales, and fantasy novels. Since 1992, Deborah has written more than thirty romance novels under the names Claire Cross and Claire Delacroix.

Deborah makes her home in Canada with her husband. When she isn't writing, she can be found knitting, sewing, or hunting for vintage patterns. To learn more about the Dragonfire series and Deborah, please visit her Web site at www.deborahcooke.com and her blog, Alive & Knitting, at www.delacroix.net/blog.

THE FIRST NOVEL IN THE DRAGONFIRE SERIES

KISS OF FIRE
A Dragonfire Novel

by DEBORAH COOKE

For millennia, the shape-shifting dragon warriors known as the Pyr have commanded the four elements and guarded the earth's treasures. But now the final reckoning between the Pyr, who count humans among the earth's treasures, and the Slayers, who would eradicate both humans and the Pyr who protect them, is about to begin...

When Sara Keegan decides to settle down and run her quirky aunt's New Age bookstore, she's not looking for adventure. She doesn't believe in fate or the magic of the tarot—but when she's saved from a vicious attack by a man who has the ability to turn into a fire-breathing dragon, she questions whether she's losing her mind—or about to lose her heart...

Also Available
Kiss of Fury
Kiss of Fate
Winter Kiss

Available wherever books are sold or
at penguin.com

Also Available

KISS OF FURY
A Dragonfire Novel

by DEBORAH COOKE

Scientist Alexandra Madison was on the verge of releasing an
invention that could save the world—until her partner was
murdered, their lab burned, and their prototype destroyed.
When Alex learns that her recurring nightmares of dragons have
led to a transfer to a psychiatric hospital, she knows she has to
escape to rebuild her prototype in time. And that she must
return to the wreckage of the lab for one last thing...

Handsome, daring, impulsive Donovan Shea knows the
Madison project is of dire importance to the ongoing Pyr/Slayer
war, but resents being assigned to surveillance of the lab. He's
surprised by the arrival of a beautiful woman in the middle of
the night—not that she's being followed by a Slayer, not that
she won't admit her name, but that she's his destined mate. As
the sparks of the firestorm ignite and the Slayers close in on
their prey, Donovan knows he'll surrender his life to protect
Alex—even risk his heart, if that's what it takes...

Available wherever books are sold or
at penguin.com